THE LIGHTNING RULE

Also by Brett Ellen Block

THE LIGHTNING RULE

BRETT ELLEN BLOCK

WILLIAM MORROW
An Imprint of HarperCollins*Publishers*

This novel takes place in the city of Newark, New Jersey, in the year 1967. Some liberties have been taken regarding the representation of the city and its institutions, including the police department. This is a work of fiction, and while some historically accurate names and events are referred to in the novel, the actions and characters are completely fictitious. Any resemblance to actual incidents or persons, living or dead, is entirely coincidental.

HarperCollins books may be purchased for educational, business, or sales promotional use. For information please write: Special Markets Department, HarperCollins Publishers, 10 East 53rd Street, New York, NY 10022.

FIRST EDITION

Designed by Jennifer Ann Daddio

Library of Congress Cataloging-in-Publication Data

Block, Brett Ellen.
    The lightning rule : a novel / Brett Ellen Block.– 1st ed.
        p.   cm.
    ISBN-13: 978-0-06-052506-4
    ISBN-10: 0-06-052506-1
        1. Detectives—New Jersey—Newark—Fiction.
2. Newark (N.J.)—Fiction.   I. Title.
PS3602.L64L54 2006
813'.6—dc22   2005058354

06 07 08 09 10   WBC/RRD   10 9 8 7 6 5 4 3 2 1

For my mother and father,
always.

This book is dedicated in loving memory
to Joseph Kapustik.

It is also dedicated to the city of Newark
and to those who lost their lives or
lost loved ones during the riots.

Certainly there is no hunting like the hunting of man and those who have hunted armed men long enough and liked it, never really care for anything else thereafter. You will meet them doing various things with resolve, but their interest rarely holds because after the other thing, ordinary life is as flat as the taste of wine when the taste buds have been burned off the tongue.

—ERNEST HEMINGWAY,
FROM THE ARTICLE "ON BLUE WATER,"
ESQUIRE MAGAZINE, APRIL 1936

ACKNOWLEDGMENTS

I would like to express my deepest gratitude to my parents for their unwavering encouragement and continued support.

Many thanks must go to my friends as well: Ruth Foxe Blader, Grace Ray, Heather Frater, Beth Foster, Alex Parsons, Alice Dickens, Amy and Brad Miller, Ann Biddlecom, Anne Engelhardt, Caroline Zouloumian, Carrie Gross, Maureen Squillace, Sara Gegenheimer, Sue Zwick, Matthew Vaeth, Rich Natale, and Barbara Sheffer.

I would also like to acknowledge all of the efforts of my editor, Jennifer Pooley, and my agent, Jonathan Pecarsky.

The books that were invaluable to me in researching this novel were *Report for Action* by the New Jersey Governor's Select Commission on Civil Disorder and *Memoirs of a Newark, New Jersey Police Officer* by Anthony Carbo, with special credit going to Carolyn Bonastia for referring it. The book *Ours: The Making and Unmaking of a Jesuit* by F. E. Peters taught me everything I needed to know about the novitiate experience, and *The Ultimate Guide to Small Game and Varmint Hunting* by H. Lea Lawrence taught me even more than I wanted to know about small game hunting. I would have been lost without the website Old-Newark .com, and I am indebted to Glenn Geisheimer, who runs the site, as well as everyone who contributed to it. I also want to thank Charlie Cheskin for sharing his experiences during the riots with me.

ONE

Wednesday
July 12, 1967

The basement was where the dead were kept. The murder victims, accidental deaths, and suicides were on the top shelves. Next down were abductions followed by arsons, assaults, then auto thefts. Below were burglaries and robberies, filling tier after tier. Vice charges were at the bottom. Solved or unsolved, every case died with the passing of time. Their final resting place was the Records Room of Newark's Fourth Precinct.

Rows of manila files lined the labyrinth of shelves, like a library that carried thousands of copies of the same book. Due to the dampness of being underground, the folders had a tendency to rot at the edges, giving off a peculiar odor of decay. Some cops called the basement the "paper graveyard." Detective Martin Emmett called it his office.

He had a corner to himself with a metal desk, a chair, a lamp, and a telephone, not much more. There were no windows. He had gotten used to that. What Emmett couldn't get accustomed to was the silence. The basement spanned the breadth of the police station, a quarter of a city block, and the absence of noise echoed around the aisles. Emmett tried a radio, but couldn't get any reception, so he brought a windup clock from home and left it in the desk drawer. The muted ticking chipped away at the quiet, though it was almost as maddening.

The Fourth Precinct wasn't the city's largest, however it handled the heaviest caseloads and the highest volume of reports. Once a case was closed or over three months cold, it was sent to the Records Room to be cataloged. That was Detective Emmett's new job. Oddly enough, being in the basement gave him a bird's-eye view of the goings-on at the station. No doubt his lieutenant realized that would happen when he assigned him the post. Emmett wondered whether that was part of the punishment.

In the two and a half months since he had become the station's unofficial undertaker, he learned not to shelve the reports too fast. Filing them took mere minutes, and his shift was eight hours long. He would be twiddling his thumbs by lunch if he didn't give himself something to do. Each day a few folders would trickle down, dropped off by cops happy to have cleared them or disgruntled at having a file hang open and having to admit defeat. Emmett understood how they felt. Putting a case to bed was better by far. For him, the worst was knowing he might not get the chance to close one of his own again.

Three cases had arrived that day: a purse snatching, a domestic assault, and a rash of bicycle thefts where somebody had taken a bolt cutter and snipped the chain links holding the locks. Ultimately, the mugger was never identified, the woman in the domestic refused to press charges against her boyfriend, and the bikes could not be recovered. Because the files had become as futile as the chains on the bicycles, the Records Room was where they would meet their end.

Emmett had read through each of them carefully, sifting through the paperwork to pass the hours. The woman whose pocketbook was grabbed while she waited at a bus stop on Irvine Turner Boulevard listed a nickel hidden in a pillbox among the stolen items. The coin had been given to her by her grandfather. It was the first wage he ever earned. The man responsible for the assault had hit his girlfriend with the frying pan she was cooking his breakfast in. He knocked out two of her teeth. Five of the seven bicycles stolen from the area surrounding the Stella Wright Housing Projects were red, the remainder blue. The details made the day go by. Details were what Emmett had in lieu of a real crime, a poor substitute under poor circumstances.

He waited until the end of his shift to shelve the files and took his time weaving through the stacks. All Emmett had was time, yet every second, he was running short. The case that had gotten him exiled to the Records Room would go on the top shelf in ten days, a plain manila folder indistinguishable from the other murders. He didn't need the ticking of his windup clock to remind him that the minutes were steadily slipping by.

"Hello? Anybody here?"

Emmett emerged from the stacks. A young patrolman was standing at the basement door. He was a smooth-faced kid straight out of high school, his collar overstarched, his pants khaki instead of blue, the distinguishing mark of a rookie recently accepted to the force. The pin above his breast pocket said his name was Nolan. At thirty-three, Emmett wasn't that much older than the patrolman, but the shine on the kid's shoes and the eagerness in his eyes made Emmett feel twice his age.

"I got orders to bring this to the Records Room," Nolan said, fidgeting with the report. "This is it, right?"

Emmett cast an obvious glance at the multitude of shelves. "Yeah, that's right."

Most officers would flop the folders onto his desktop without a word. Some wouldn't even make eye contact. Many openly shunned him. Emmett expected as much. Filing in the Records Room was a chore normally foisted on recruits such as Nolan, though not anymore. No one had passed along the gossip about Emmett, or else the kid would have dumped the case and hurried off. The rookie would appreciate his error once his buddies had ribbed him for it.

"Guess this is an easy racket for you," Nolan remarked, "what with you being so tall. Five bucks says you don't need a step stool to reach them tippy-top shelves."

Emmett stood a full head above the majority of cops on the force. Not a single officer in the Fourth Precinct could look down on him. That didn't mean they wouldn't act like they could.

"You got lucky being in the basement, I tell ya," Nolan went on, hungry for somebody to talk to.

"Lucky, huh?" Emmett presumed that the kid had arrived early for the 4 P.M. shift change and been given an errand to occupy him until roll call, probably because he was blabbing his sergeant's ear off. Now Emmett was stuck with him.

"Yessiree. It's an oven upstairs. Everybody's roastin'."

That summer had been brutal. Mornings broke to ferocious heat and the thermometer stayed in the nineties well after sunset. The air was thinner, as if it had already been breathed. In the past day, the weather had become unbearable. A pall of humidity drifted in off Newark Bay and draped over the city. Rain refused to come. The Records Room may have been a degree or two cooler than the rest of the station, but the basement's moisture made the papers wilt and the walls sweat.

Nolan fanned himself with the file. "Be glad you're not on the third floor. Makes hell seem like Point Pleasant."

The third floor was where Emmett formerly worked. His reassignment had nothing to do with luck and wasn't something to be glad about. Last time he set foot in his old squad room, his desk had been moved and the other detectives had piled filing on it, a symbol of his demotion to Records and a less than subtle message for him to keep out.

"This is my first week of probation and so far, the weather's all there is to talk about. Between you and me," Nolan confided, "it's been pretty slow."

Emmett had come to understand the true definition of the word *slow* when he was forced out of Homicide. This kid didn't know slow, he thought. This kid didn't know much at all.

"You were hoping for firefights and bomb threats?"

"No, sir." Nolan was quick to correct himself. "I just thought there'd be more to do."

The three-month-long probation period was a test of will as much as aptitude or ability. Patrolmen were inundated with routine tasks such as reading parking meters, checking licenses, and pumping gas to refuel radio cars. At a starting salary of $6,900 per year, it was a minor miracle any of them stuck it out for a single month let alone three. Wide-eyed as he was, Nolan might not last the weekend.

Anyone who met the minimum entrance requirements of age, residence, education, and health was eligible to take the civil service examination for patrolmen. That amounted to anybody who could walk, talk, read, and write. About 30 percent of the applicants passed the exam, a test that reflected a tenth-grade achievement level. Out of the fourteen hundred men on Newark's force, twelve had associate degrees from two-year colleges and ten had received bachelor's. Emmett was one of the ten.

Those who qualified on the entrance exam were evaluated by a staff of five detectives who conducted what was called a "character investigation" of the candidates. The investigation was supposed to consist of interviews with former employers, friends, and neighbors, as well as a check of military and credit records. What really happened was the detectives shot the breeze over beer and peanuts, debating whether or not they thought the guy was up to snuff or if he had any relatives in service, making him a shoo-in. The grounds for rejection were a criminal record, numerous outstanding debts, or a history of truancy. Given the rising crime rate and the city's ratio of a single officer for every 250 citizens, applicants were rarely rejected, regardless of their pasts. The department was too desperate for new recruits.

Emmett tried to recall his own probation, and for a blinding instant, he couldn't. Buried under nine years of duty on the force, the memory had burrowed too deeply between the creases to be retrieved. He changed the subject.

"Have you ever been in the Central Ward, Nolan?"

"Yes, sir. I mean, no, sir. Not as a cop. Not until two days ago when I started here."

Brick City, the nickname Newark went by when it couldn't stand its own, was split into wards, and they were as clearly divided as the bricks in a wall. A person could step off a corner in a certain ward, cross into the next and not have to be told. The Italians lived in the North Ward, the Jews in the Weequahic section in the South. The Irish were concentrated in Vailsburg in the West and the Portuguese dominated the East, in the Ironbound and Downtown. The Fourth Precinct sat in the Central Ward, where the only white faces were the Jewish shopkeepers and the cops, most either Irish or Italian. Emmett was an anomaly. He was Polish. He had heard every joke in the book during his school days, but because his name didn't sound Polish, having been hacked to pieces and retooled when his grandfather landed on Ellis Island, he caught no flack at the station, at least on that account. He could pass for Irish and didn't correct people if it played to his advantage. Since everyone at the precinct knew who he was—everybody besides Nolan—Emmett didn't have many advantages.

"This is where all the coloreds live," Nolan said. "I'm not scared, if that's what you're getting at."

"But you didn't request the assignment. Or did you?"

The patrolman shook his head no, unsure if he should be ashamed of his answer. Nolan was too naive to comprehend what Emmett was getting at, proof that he hadn't come to the Central Ward for the same reason most cops stayed: easy payoffs. The prevailing rationale was that if crime in the ghetto couldn't be stopped, then the police should be compensated for their efforts. Some skimmed money off the lottery pickup men who worked the ward's corners. Others collected dues from dealers who gladly handed over hundred-dollar bills to forgo arrest. Opportunities for personal gain were abundant in the Central Ward, and white cops were loathe to leave, particularly high-ranking officers who could take their share from the safety of their desks. Patrolman Nolan may not have been scared. That was because he didn't know what to be scared of.

"I bet your mother begged you to put in for a transfer when she found out where you'd be stationed," Emmett said. "I bet she went to church and prayed for you. I bet you prayed a little too."

Nolan dipped his chin, stunned and embarrassed, as if Emmett had read his mind.

"Won't be slow forever," he told him, plucking the case from the kid's grasp.

The young patrolman backpedaled, then hightailed it upstairs, leaving the door to the Records Room wide open. Emmett shut and locked it.

His shift was over. The new file could wait until tomorrow. That would give him something to do. He snapped off the tracks of fluorescent lights, and darkness strode across the basement. He kept a single strand on to see by. The light was brightest at the uppermost shelves, obfuscating everything below. Except for that top shelf, the Records Room was organized alphabetically. The deaths were out of sequence. Maybe someone had decided they were a higher priority. Or perhaps they were intended to be harder to reach. The case that was costing him his career would soon number among the dead on the top shelf, and though Emmett could reach there with ease, he was helpless to stop it from happening. With that day drawing near, he was grateful to turn off the lights and abandon his windup clock to tick through the night alone.

Instead of walking out the police station's front entrance, Emmett took the back. He cut through the boiler room to get to the building's rear exit, which remained bolted for security. The key to the Records Room fit the back door too, allowing him to come and go as he pleased, unnoticed.

Emmett stepped outside into the gauzy afternoon air and relocked the door behind him. He avoided other officers as much as they avoided him. He didn't need to see them to know what they thought. He had overheard the whispers, guys saying he'd lost it, that he was a liability. Somebody left a note on his old desk that said "Quit, nigger lover. Quit." The rumors were he shouldn't be wearing a badge. He ignored them. But in the basement of his mind, Detective Emmett worried that the rumors might be true.

TWO

Evenings came later than usual that summer. The sky dimmed, buffing off the heat's edge, and dusk lingered long beyond purpose, as if the day didn't want to be forgotten. When night did fall, it dropped like stone. Emmett made sure he was home well before dark.

"It's just me," he said, tossing his keys and badge onto a side table next to the telephone, his habit upon arrival. The lamps in the living room were off, the shades drawn. A baseball game was playing on the radio.

Emmett lived in the house he grew up in, a two-story clapboard that was a cookie cutter copy of the others on his street. To distinguish their homes, owners varied the paint colors or the flower beds or the flagpoles, nothing especially radical. There was a certain safety in the similarity. His parents had moved to the Down Neck section of the East Ward for a different type of safety. The Down Neck neighborhoods were mixed with smatterings of Poles and Lithuanians, people from their part of the globe, and it didn't hurt that the butcher's shop that made the best kielbasa was only two blocks away. The name Down Neck referred to the narrow "neck" of land that ran along the lower Passaic River. On a map, it looked more like a fist, knuckling the river out of joint. The locals weren't nearly as pushy. Their worlds revolved around church and family, so much so that whenever anyone asked where in Down Neck somebody was from, they would answer with the church they attended instead of the street. In the diocese of Newark, boundaries existed for each parish. The church a person named was shorthand not only for their religion and location, but also for their ethnicity and class. A single answer could tell a life story.

Saint Casimir's Roman Catholic Church was Emmett's answer. It said more about him than he cared to recount. Casimir had been a fifteenth-century Polish prince who lived a severe, disciplined life, remaining celibate, spending his nights in prayer and sleeping on the ground rather than in a bed. When Hungarian nobles begged Casimir's father to send his zealous, fifteen-year-old son to be their king, Casimir obeyed, taking the crown yet refusing to exercise power because it went against his principles. An ineffectual ruler, Casimir returned home to take up his true calling: dedicating himself to supporting the sick and all those who suffered. Canonized forty years after his death as the patron saint of the helpless and the poor, Saint Casimir was the embodiment of selflessness, a trait that was extolled to Emmett on a daily basis while attending parochial school and serving as an altar boy. He got an extra dose of virtue every Sunday at the 9 A.M. mass, which was said in Polish, as if to make the message more potent. A large chunk of Emmett's childhood had been spent mastering the Decades of the Rosary in English and in Polish. He remembered the Polish version best. Over time, he had gotten rusty at the language, but to that day, he could pray as fluently as a native.

Newark was a city of immigrants, banded together block by block, tight as rosary beads, each clinging to their traditions and mother tongues. Emmett's parents were no exception. They preferred pierogi to baked potatoes, swore in Polish, not English, and never ate meat on Fridays, even though the pope, an Italian, had sanctioned it. To them, holding on to the past was a matter of pride. For Emmett, it occurred by default.

His house hadn't changed since his youth. The flocked wallpaper and reproduction furniture that aspired to give the impression of middle class were exactly the same, and getting further from middle class every year. His father's lounge chair, now threadbare on the arms, still hunkered in the spot it had been in when he was alive. After a stroke took his mother, Emmett inherited the place, its contents, and more memories than he had room to store.

The *thwack* of a baseball resounded from the radio, followed by cheers. Apart from the play-by-play, the house was conspicuously quiet. He lowered the volume on the game.

"Edward. Edward? *Edziu?*" Emmett's voice rose half a note when he called his brother's Polish nickname.

"I can hear you, Marty. You don't have to holler. It's not as if I ran away from home." Edward rolled out of the kitchen in his wheelchair, a beer can wedged between his useless legs. "You sound like Ma when you do that."

Edward took a swig of beer, then mimicked him, calling his own name, a perfect impersonation of their mother shouting at him to stop playing stickball in the street and come in for supper. His tone was too bouncy to be sober. Every day Emmett gave thanks that his parents weren't alive to see what had become of his younger brother. That would have been too much for them to bear. It was almost too much for him.

"Who's playing?" he asked, loosening his tie.

"It's the Mayor's Trophy. Mets are up one over the Yanks," Edward said sullenly. "A cryin' shame."

"Have you eaten?"

His brother shrugged and coasted closer to the radio to listen.

"I'll consider that a no."

Emmett took two TV dinners from the icebox and dropped them into the oven. Edward groaned from the other room at the familiar noise.

"Why bother with the stove? Put 'em on the front stoop. They'll cook in five minutes flat."

"Ain't that the truth." Emmett forced a laugh. Whenever Edward was drunk, Emmett did his best to humor him. Alcohol brought out the fight in his brother. Edward couldn't hurt him. But he could hurt himself. He would throw books, break dishes, and make a general mess of whatever he could get his hands on. Once he had tried to knock over the television and nearly tumbled out of his wheelchair in the process.

"Sure was a hot one today, huh? I hope tomorrow's not another scorcher."

The small talk was camouflage so Emmett could open the squeaky cupboard above the sink where he hid a bottle of Jim Beam, placed purposefully out of Edward's range. The bottle was exactly where he had left it. Next, he checked the refrigerator. The twelve-pack purchased a day ago, also to humor his brother, was gone. Emmett regretted buying the booze, but hated to deny Edward his sole pleasure. The thing that made his brother's life tolerable made Emmett's more burdensome sip by sip.

"Say, when are you gonna take a day off and keep me company? I'm sick of playing solitaire, and I sure as hell can't play gin rummy alone."

Edward's question was timed with the closing of the refrigerator door, guilt to distract from the missing beer. Each had guessed the other's game.

"Soon," Emmett replied. "Soon."

He had already used most of his vacation days when Edward first came home and was saving the remainder in case of an emergency. The ploy aside, his brother was genuinely lonely. Edward refused to let his friends visit and wouldn't take calls from the women he had dated. He was too ashamed to see them. Though his seclusion was self-imposed, the confines of the house were grating on him. Emmett had built a plywood ramp up the steep pitch to the front door, seven feet above street level, however the slope was too precarious for Edward to manage. Stranded, he whiled away the hours sitting on the back porch in the shade under a tin awning, overlooking their small scrap of a yard. That was as far as he would or could go unaccompanied.

"Soon ain't soon enough, Marty, because lemme tell you, it's a real ball of laughs being trapped here by myself when it's a million degrees. I'm bored outta my skull. This isn't *Rear*-friggin'-*Window*, my friend," Edward ranted, slurring. "There's no Grace Kelly and there's nobody murdering anybody across the alley. The murdering part, that's your bag, man. Hell, I don't even get the lousy little dog." He hung his head, as though he had actually been deprived of a dog of his own. "This is abuse, man. Cruel and unusual punishment. Hey, you know what I should do? I should call the cops."

Emmett watched from the kitchen as his brother cracked up. Tipsy and giggling, a stray lock of hair fell onto his cheek. After leaving the VA hospital, Edward had let his beard grow in and his hair grow out. It skimmed his chin where a scraggly goatee struggled to gain ground. Emmett kept his hair cropped close in a flattop and shaved every morning, department regulations. He was four years older than Edward, yet they were the same height. Were it not for the wheelchair, they still would be. In their younger years, they had often been mistaken for twins. Now it was a stretch to see how they were related.

Once the TV dinners were ready, they ate dinner off trays in front of the television, Edward's balanced across the arms of his wheelchair. Emmett silently said grace over his food. He didn't invite Edward to join him in prayer. That would have gotten another laugh or started a fight. Saying grace was something they had done every evening as a family when their parents were alive. Their mother had died a little over a year ago, their father the year before that. Emmett had boxed up his grief along with his parents' possessions, which he carted off to Saint Casimir's to be donated as per their wishes. Edward had no such closure, and Emmett believed the quick succession of their deaths was what had driven him to the army and to his eventual fate, confined to the wheelchair he despised more and more each day. Suggesting they say grace together would have rubbed salt in a wound that had yet to heal for his brother, so Emmett prayed by himself.

As usual, he sat in his father's old lounger, not the couch. That way Edward could pull next to him and they could sit side by side. The couch went untouched, a constant reminder of his brother's new limitations. Their father's chair had once been off limits as well. No one was allowed on it besides him, including their mother. A meager throne, the fabric was worn soft, the cushions molded to their father's form. As comfortable as the chair was, Emmett couldn't get comfortable in it.

"This is a great show. I love this show," Edward said, clapping in drunken encouragement when an episode of *Gunsmoke* climaxed with a barroom brawl. He lit a cigarette, finished the dregs of his beer, and lazily set the empty can beside his half-eaten meal. The beer can toppled to the floor. "Oops."

Emmett picked it up. "Are you finished with your food? You barely ate."

"I'm watching my figure. All this beer goes right to my hips."

Edward would goad him into an argument if he could. Emmett wouldn't let him. "Your hips or your bladder? Do you need to . . . you know?"

"Naw," Edward waved him off. "I'm getting the hang of it."

His wheelchair was tough to maneuver through the house's narrow doorways, especially the bathroom. If Edward didn't align the chair accurately, he would smash his fingers between the wheels and the jamb. He had special gloves to prevent his palms from getting blistered, which he never wore, and a special seat that went over the toilet, which he was training himself to use. He had been home for a month. It seemed like more since Emmett cleared the dining room and moved Edward's bed and dresser down from the room they shared as kids. Edward couldn't get in or out of bed without help and he couldn't feel if he wet the sheets. Emmett had to change them every morning.

The nightly news came on, reporting troop movements and knitting in old footage from the anti-Vietnam march in Central Park. Hippies burnt draft cards in the foreground while police in riot gear stood in a rigid phalanx behind them. Edward let out an exaggerated sigh, as if the news was a rerun he had already seen. He had enlisted following his lay-off from Westinghouse nine months earlier. Their father also worked at the plant and had the good fortune to die of a heart attack well in advance of the factory shutting its doors and moving to the suburbs, led away by tax cuts and lower wages. Had he been around, the closing would surely have killed him. A machinist, he cut parts for toasters and dryers for two decades, coming home with flat feet, a bad back, and a paycheck that couldn't cover college tuition for one son, let alone both.

"What else is on?"

That was Emmett's cue to get up and change the channel. He spun the TV dial until Edward said stop at an episode of *The Andy Griffith Show*. The warbling whistle of the theme song was inappropriately cheerful considering the heat.

"Beggars can't be choosers," Edward said.

It was a sentiment, one of a scarce few, upon which Emmett and his brother could agree. In a city that had seen its share of prosperity dwindle with each company that fled for cheaper pastures, with every ounce of water the breweries siphoned from the polluted Passaic—water the tanneries had poisoned to begin with—and with every tenement that crumbled under the weight of its owner's disinterest, there were more beggars and fewer choices in Newark than ever. Emmett hadn't been to mass in ages, but he was confident they still passed the collection plate. Begging wasn't a sin. Wanting choices might as well have been. Becoming a cop was Emmett's second choice. The decision to relinquish his first was a splinter in his conscience, forced deeper each time he looked at his brother.

Edward eventually fell asleep in his wheelchair, and Emmett dozed off too. He later woke to the telephone ringing. Light from the television was flickering across Edward's face. His cigarette smoldered in the aluminum TV dinner tray. Emmett snubbed it out and picked up the phone.

"Detective Emmett?"

The desk sergeant's raspy voice was unmistakable. As a rookie, a drunk rousted from an American Legion bar had come at him with a screwdriver and nicked his larynx. The battle scar earned him respect that stuck through the ranks. On the force, reputations spoke louder than words or actions, and often outlived their owners. Emmett worried that his reputation wasn't being permanently cemented in the Records Room like the mortar between the basement's cinder block walls.

"What can I do for you, Sarge?"

"We've got a, um, problem here. Brass said to call everyone in. S'pose that means you too," he said, unsure.

Bursts of shouting and the pounding of feet bled through on the phone line. The normally stiff-lipped sergeant sounded tense. Emmett grabbed his keys and badge from the side table in one swipe.

"I'm out the door. I'll be there as fast as I can."

"Better make it faster than that."

THREE

Emmett smelled the fire before he saw it. Smoke was billowing out of a burning abandoned car on Livingston Avenue, opposite the Fourth Precinct, a common sight in the Central Ward. The city wouldn't pay to tow abandoned cars, rendering them fair game to be stripped for parts. Their skeletal hulls were left on the curb and often set alight, as this one was. Silhouetted in the glow of the flames, figures darted across the road. From somewhere far off, a fire truck was wailing. Close by, glass was breaking. None of it was uncommon for the neighborhood. What Emmett witnessed next was. As he drove closer, he saw packs of people hurling bottles, stones, and debris at the police station. Officers outside were dodging the onslaught, scrambling for the safety of the precinct.

Adrenaline and disbelief churned in Emmett's head. He had to get into the station house. The precinct's lot would be prime pickings for vandals, so he circled and parked at a distance. His Dodge Coronet was almost ten years old and it blended in with the other automobiles on the streets. The sole benefit of his low civil service salary was that he couldn't afford the kind of car that would catch a criminal's eye.

Since running might attract attention, Emmett moved in quick, measured steps toward the station. While he was safer dressed as a civilian, many in the ward would recognize him as a cop nonetheless. In the dark, in the confusion, Emmett would be a target either way.

His key let him duck in the station's rear door, and he hurried to the entrance hall, where it was pandemonium. With its high ceiling and massive staircase, the hall was a grand space in an otherwise unremarkable building, and it was filled to the corners with jostling bodies, a blur of blue uniforms and black faces. Patrolmen were hustling men two at a time toward the holding cells, towing them by their handcuffed wrists. The din of voices and shuffling feet reverberated through the hall. Some of the station's front windows were cracked, some broken, paper hastily taped over the missing panes. Emmett spotted Nolan rushing past and caught him by the shoulder.

"What happened?"

"It's crazy. This is crazy." The kid was panting, rambling, eyes frantic. "They all just showed up and starting shouting that they wanted to see him, that we had to let him go."

"Officer," Emmett said sharply, snapping Nolan from a tailspin. "Who's 'him'?"

"Ben White. The cabdriver. I thought it was a phony name. I thought this was some kinda joke, some kinda initiation. But I saw Tillet and Donolfo bring him in. Said they were double-parked on Fifteenth Street and this guy in a Safety Company cab cut around 'em. Said he was resisting arrest. Took four guys to carry him in here. One on each arm and leg. They brought him to a cell and they um. . . ." Nolan couldn't put what he had seen into words or didn't want to. "The cabbie, he didn't look too hot when they were finished. Get me?"

Emmett didn't recognize the arresting officers' names, however he was acquainted with what they had done. It was referred to as "handling" an arrest, an activity that took place with the troubling regularity of a hacking cough that comes back again and again, portending some more serious illness. In the last year, two suspects had been shot by officers from the Fourth Precinct, the first during a routine traffic stop, the other after a search for contraband. Both incidents were labeled as "accidental weapons discharges." A third suspect had died in custody under what the newspapers called "mysterious circumstances." The real mystery was how the higher-ups kept the press from learning about the man's crushed skull, care of a nightstick. Those were the reports that never made it to the Records Room: no file, no way to press charges.

The abuse was needless, reprehensible, but Emmett's hands were tied. His father used to say, "Keep your hands away from the moving parts or you won't keep your hands." That was the rule at the Westinghouse plant. Men lost fingers to the saws, wrenched their spines operating machinery, had arms crushed in presses. If they put themselves in harm's way, they would get hurt. The same was true of the department. Emmett was being ostracized as it was, and making a stink would only worsen his situation. He had to keep his hands to himself.

"They must've hurt Smith bad. The floor of the cell was covered with blood." The memory made Nolan visibly queasy.

Most local residents were too afraid to lodge complaints against the police for fear of harassment or retaliation, fretful of meeting a similar fate as the cabdriver. If someone did venture to make a formal statement, the investigation would be forwarded along the chain of command to the police director, Wallace Sloakes, who would determine if the case merited a departmental trial. Such trials were unique unto themselves because Sloakes alone sat as judge. A born salesman who happened to wear a badge, he was as dirty as he was undiplomatic, and of the seventy complaints of brutality received that year, Sloakes permitted three to be taken to trial. Only one officer was deemed guilty. The punishment was a reprimand and a three-day suspension. Even the chief magistrate of the municipal court had ceased hearing civil cases dealing with charges against policemen, claiming they needlessly clogged the courts. Anybody brave enough to file a complaint faced an impenetrable bulwark of policemen and city officials. The system favored the force, and that was as strong a deterrent as a billy club. Normally, there would be no recourse for a cabdriver carried in by his arms and legs and beaten in a holding cell. That night, there was.

"I don't know how they found out," Nolan said. "I guess somebody saw Tillet and Donolfo wailin' on the guy."

"They?"

"Them. The people outside. They came pouring outta Hayes. You'd a thought it was a goddamn parade."

The Hayes Home Housing Projects was a sprawling, ten-building complex situated catty-corner from the Fourth Precinct. Cops were called there on a daily basis, and those reports constituted a sizable share of the station's cases. Thirteen stories tall, the brick behemoths loomed over the neighborhood, a ramshackle stronghold punched through by windows set apart like arrow slots in a castle. Hayes had seen its share of battles—battles about the landlord's lack of repairs, rampant burglaries, and drug pushers prowling the halls. Apparently, the tenants had brought the fight out into the streets.

"Then that guy, that preacher guy, he came and demanded to see the cabbie."

"Who? Mose Odett?"

"Yeah, that's him. The one who's always getting himself in the news."

Mose Odett was a self-fashioned activist from Hayes who wore secondhand three-piece suits and spoke to everyone as though he was on a podium. More a radical than a militant, he organized rent strikes and sit-ins to push for enforcement of housing codes in the tenement. Slumlords and councilmen alike cringed at the mere mention of Odett's name, which was in the paper as much as the mayor's, where he made a point of punctuating every interview with the phrase "police brutality," whether it applied to the topic or not. Emmett respected Odett's convictions, if not his showboating, and admired his antiviolence stance. He wondered if that stance had changed.

"Did Odett get in?"

"We got the word to let him through. Then the inspector gave Odett a bull horn and fifteen minutes to make everybody beat it."

Inspector Herbert Plout ran the Fourth Precinct. Twenty years on the force and a yielding personality had garnered him the position. A reed-thin man who moved his hands too much when he talked, Plout was as good as gum on the heel of a shoe when it came to a crisis. Emmett didn't see him in the crowd. The inspector was presumably holed up in his office, having reports ferried to him from the front lines.

"What happened when Odett—"

A barrage of stones pummeled the station, interrupting Emmett midsentence. The hail of rocks and garbage thundered against the exterior walls. The precinct was under siege. Squeals of shattering glass made Nolan jump. The young patrolman's eyes glazed, unable to regain his train of thought. Emmett grabbed Nolan's sleeve to force him to focus. "Keep talking, Officer."

"Odett was preaching to everyone to go home. But they wouldn't go. They shouted him down. They won't go away. Why won't they go away?" The kid was pleading for an answer Emmett didn't have.

A hush came over the room, and the bodies packed into the entrance hall parted. Police Director Sloakes was hacking a path through the melee, ordering officers aside. Someone had smuggled him in the back door, an indignity the image-conscious director would have resented if it weren't for his own personal security.

Nolan was staring along with everyone else. "Who's that?"

"A man whose acquaintance you're better off not making."

Emmett had met Sloakes twice, two occasions too many. His fourth year on the force, Emmett had taken the civil service exam to become a detective and passed with only one error. In spite of his score, he needed Sloakes's approval to advance. As director, Sloakes had the discretion to assign patrolmen to the Detective Division, and his inaugural act upon entering office was to shuffle the squads, inserting his cronies into the plainclothes and gambling details that raked in the most profit from their precincts. During Emmett's first meeting with him, Sloakes paged through his personnel file with a sly grin, vaguely amused, then slotted him into the Robbery Division with nothing more than a handshake and a cryptic suggestion to do his best. Recently, Emmett had had his second meeting with the director. Sloakes called him in unexpectedly. He was advancing Emmett yet again. This time, inexplicably, up to Homicide. Emmett hadn't requested the assignment. Robbery was simple, safe, and, in the Central Ward, there was a constant supply of cases. He would never have requested to be in the Homicide

Division, however he couldn't refuse the promotion. That seemed somehow fitting to Emmett. His Catholic morality made him feel as if he deserved the position for that exact reason—because he didn't want it. Emmett had spent three weeks on the squad before bottoming out in the basement. He couldn't blame Sloakes for that. Nevertheless, he preferred to stay off the director's radar. Emmett eased toward the staircase and out of view.

"What in the name of all that's holy is going on here?" Sloakes bellowed. He had a bland face and worked hard to fake charisma that didn't come naturally to him.

Inspector Plout finally appeared, fawning over the director and trying to usher him to his office. "I went out and explained that the cabdriver was gone, that he'd been taken to the hospital. It didn't help."

Plout whispered a postscript in Sloakes's ear, to which the director shook his head adamantly and said, "No, damn it. These men should be outside. Around the building."

Suddenly, a Molotov cocktail exploded against the station's facade. Emmett yanked Nolan behind him, and everyone hit the floor. A spray of orange flames licked the broken windows.

"Get these men in helmets. I want a nightstick in every hand," Sloakes barked while Plout did his best to disappear into the wall. "Give me a perimeter. Where's the fire department? Where are the damn fire trucks?"

A band of officers brushed by Emmett and Nolan, going toward the supply room for the helmets and nightsticks, which they passed out bucket-brigade style. Contrary to an actual bucket brigade, neither would help quell the fires outside.

"You coming?" Nolan asked, being swept into the receiving line.

Emmett was about to reply when he was jerked by the arm and pulled up the stairs.

"What do you think you're doing here, Detective?"

Lieutenant Declan Ahern couldn't meet Emmett eye to eye even with an extra step between them, but he made up for the height difference in sheer presence. At fifty, he had a full head of bristled silver hair and a boxer's flat-bridged nose. Born and bred in the city's West Ward, where the Irish gangs and the police were one and the same, Ahern had to choose at a young age between being a criminal proper and being a cop. Emmett pictured him flipping a coin.

"The desk sergeant called me."

"He shouldn't have. You're on restricted duty for striking an officer, remember?"

The lieutenant took a dark delight in reminding him. During an argument, Emmett had punched another detective in his division, though that infraction was not the real grounds for his reassignment. The truth behind his demotion struck harder than any right hook and hit below the belt. Emmett knew it, and so did Ahern.

"You ready to get out of the basement and back on a regular shift? Say the word. You've kept me waiting a long time, Martin, and I'm not one for waiting."

Men shouldered past them on the stairwell, forcing the lieutenant chest to chest with him.

"How long can you wait? Huh, Emmett?"

Being in the basement was like holding his breath. To come up for air, all he had to do was tell Ahern what he wanted to hear. On principle, Emmett couldn't do it. He hemmed his mouth, holding on to the words to prevent them from prying out.

"Fine," the lieutenant said. "You started this. Until you have an answer for me, I'm gonna forget you're alive."

Entombment in the Records Room with his career on hold indefinitely was no idle threat. Ahern didn't make idle threats, only real ones. He let go his grip on Emmett's arm, yet Emmett continued to feel it.

"Go home, Detective. You're no good to me here."

Emmett bit down on his anger and said nothing. Disobeying a direct order wouldn't do him any good either. At that moment, he wasn't much use anywhere or to anyone, especially himself.

Sloakes was furiously motioning Ahern over and shouting to nobody in particular, "Put the windows in tomorrow morning and get this place cleaned up. Return to normal and don't treat this as a situation. Because once you start treating problems as problems they become problems."

The main door to the station swung open, wafting in the scent of seared metal and the dying whine of sirens. Reinforcements had arrived. Patrolmen in yellow helmets wielding their newly acquired nightsticks went pouring outside, clubbing anyone within reach. Emmett was sucked into the swirling throng of men clamoring to get at the action, and for the first time in months, he left through the Fourth Precinct's front entrance. The lieutenant had made it clear that this was not his problem. Emmett had problems of his own.

Fire trucks were blocking off the end of Livingston Avenue. Lines of hoses crisscrossed the asphalt and hydrants gushed on both sides of the street. The abandoned car was shrouded in flames, its tires fuming. Several trash cans had been lit too. Emmett was pinned between the precinct and the snarl of cops flailing nightsticks to thresh back the crowd. People fled into the Hayes projects and scattered along Springfield Avenue, hurling stones at the fire trucks as they ran. A teenage boy threw a brick through the plate glass window of a nearby liquor store, then another picked up a pipe and swept aside the jagged shards that framed the hole. Three more climbed in the window, raiding the shelves. Soon others were following suit, smashing windows and flooding into stores. Some of the patrolmen spotted the looters and took off after them, creating a gap for Emmett to slide through.

He cut around the side of the station, glass crunching under his shoes as he hugged the walls, sticking to the shadows. He was afraid of being mistaken for a looter. The tendency would be to attack first. Questions would come later, if at all.

Rounding the street corner, Emmett knocked into a woman cradling stolen fifths of liquor in her arms. "Sorry," she mumbled, her politeness a stark contrast to the chaos. With the alcohol held tight, she sped away, glass bottles clinking, and vanished into a plume of smoke.

From his car, Emmett watched firemen battling to douse the blazing abandoned car. Water collected in the potholes in the road where the old cobblestones showed through, reflecting the flames in a mirror image, and making it seem as if the fire was burning in every direction. Emmett feared it soon would.

FOUR

The house was dark when he got home. The television hissed static. It was late, and the stations had gone off the air. Even with the windows open, the heat inside was intense, almost audible, like the sizzle emanating from the TV screen.

Emmett went into the dining room. Edward's bed was empty, undisturbed since Emmett made it that morning. His initial impulse was to call to Edward, then he remembered his brother's mocking imitation earlier that evening. He headed into the kitchen to look for him instead.

The cupboard above the sink hung open. The bourbon was gone. Two wire hangers had been unwound and twisted together into a contraption to reach the cabinet handle and hook the bottle. The device sat, discarded, on the counter.

The screen door was ajar. Outside, Edward was splayed across the porch next to his overturned wheelchair. The empty bottle of Jim Beam lay beside him in a puddle of vomit.

"Christ, no."

Emmett rushed to him and checked for a pulse in Edward's neck. The skin was warm to the touch. Beneath it pumped the rhythm of his brother's heart, steady as the breathing Emmett finally heard over the drumming in his ears. He would have cursed Edward, except Emmett didn't swear. He didn't smoke or drink either. He had purchased the bourbon prior to his expulsion to the Records Room, thinking it might aid in his debate regarding whether to give in to Ahern, but he couldn't bring himself to taste it, not a drop. The rules and rigors of his Jesuit seminary training were reflex, irrepressible. Taking the Lord's name in vain was Emmett's one, occasional slip.

Fear and fury deflated into exhaustion. He righted Edward's wheelchair, got a dishrag from the kitchen, and wiped the vomit from his brother's face. Edward didn't stir even as Emmett lifted him from under the armpits and hauled him to bed. As his brother's heels dragged limply across the floor, lines from Saint Ignatius's Prayer for Generosity droned in Emmett's mind. *To give and not to count the cost. To fight and not to heed the wounds. To toil and not to seek for rest. To labor and not to ask for reward.*

A scholarship to Saint Peter's College in Jersey City had been Emmett's ticket out of Newark. Entering the priesthood after graduation was a pardon from a thirty-year sentence of cutting parts at Westinghouse like his father or working the bottling line at Anheuser-Busch. At the time, a life of servitude was a small price for escape. His parents had been beyond proud that he had chosen to become a priest, especially his mother, who believed her years of devotion had at last paid off. That pride shriveled when Emmett left the monastery and turned his back on the church. For that, he felt he paid his own price. He was still paying.

Edward was heavy, though he was getting lighter. The muscles in his legs were wasting, the knees growing knobby, the calves thin. He wouldn't eat. He would only drink. He could forget about the wheelchair was when he was drunk and when he slept. So Emmett would let him sleep.

He settled Edward into bed, making sure his legs were uncrossed to maintain circulation, and pulled a sheet over him. In that weather, the sheet was unnecessary, yet putting his brother to bed uncovered seemed wrong somehow. Emmett shut off the television and felt his way to the staircase in the dark, running his hand across his father's lounge chair to get his bearings. As he climbed the stairs, he was careful to forgo the steps that creaked in spite of the fact that, in his present state, nothing would wake Edward.

Emmett's bedroom had originally been his parents'. For weeks after he inherited the house, he slept in his childhood bedroom in his old bed, a tiny twin, with his feet hanging off the end. He couldn't sleep where they had slept. It wasn't until he moved their mattress into the garage and brought over the queen-size bed from his old apartment that he could finally change rooms.

He undressed in the dark, peeling his sweat-dampened shirt from his body, and folded it for the laundry, then he knelt on the floor to pray as he did each night, hands clasped atop the bed. When he was a novice at the monastery of Saint Andrew's on the Hudson, his mattress had been filled with straw and propped on a steel frame cot. Beneath his pillow lay a foot-long whip made of braided white cords and thin chains. That was where all the members of the novitiate kept their whips. There was no whip under Emmett's pillow anymore, only a memory that stung.

Every Monday and Wednesday, a bell would ring at bedtime, a call to the novitiate class to remove their shirts, take up their whips, and flagellate. Flogging one's self for the duration of an Our Father was mandatory. The pain was marginal compared to that inflicted on Tuesday and Thursday mornings, when the inch-and-a-half width of the whip's chain was to be tied around the thigh, its wire prongs driven into the skin for a span of three hours. If wrapped too loosely, the chain would drop to the floor with a telltale thud. Numbness set in if it was strapped too tight. All the while the prongs dug into the flesh, restricting the wearer's gait to an awkward hobble and turning sitting into a torture akin to a tourniquet. The chain was a constant reminder that obedience equaled pain. The red welts it imparted were evidence that a true Jesuit never forgot Jesus' pain, that a true Jesuit ignored his own.

At Saint Peter's College, Emmett had been educated in the sect's fierce intellectual style, where everything hinged on obedience and evidence. Their teaching emphasized a nimble brain. Logic was lightning fast or it was lax. The brothers would grill pupils constantly, relentlessly. *Why do you say that* and *Give me a reason* were common refrains. They had taught Emmett discipline, that the quality of his thinking and his arguments was as important as the quality of the result. When he graduated from college and left for the monastery in Hyde Park, New York, intent on taking his vows, he believed it was logic leading him there. Except logic didn't live in his heart.

Feeling the grain of the floorboards grinding into his knees, Emmett prayed from rote. That night, his prayers sparked a memory. It was about one of the priests from the abbey who had been sent to do missionary work in the Pacific islands. The main territory of the New York Province had long been the Philippines, a highly civilized region seeded with a healthy amount of Catholic converts, thus not a hardship post. At the end of World War II, the pope broadened the province's scope to include the South Pacific, a less cushy and less predictable destination. The picturesque locale of thatched huts and palm trees bore the threat of mosquitoes, malaria, and the absence of modern medical care. During his mission, the young priest contracted a case of tuberculosis so serious it sunk to the bone. Every couple of months, he would return to the States to recuperate at Saint Andrew's. Once well enough, he would travel back to some remote island to resume his work. Emmett had watched him grow paler and more frail with each passing visit. In time, he ceased to see him altogether. The tuberculosis had killed the young priest. Emmett couldn't recall a funeral, however the other novices whispered about his sacrifice with reverence. His story was as much heroic myth as a cautionary tale. That was the Jesuit way. To toil and not seek rest. To labor and not ask for a reward. To give and not count the cost.

Jesuits called themselves "Ours." Everyone else was an Extern, an outsider. The teenage boys Emmett encountered at Saint Andrew's hungered to be members of Ours, to be a part of something bigger than themselves, whereas Emmett found himself constantly tabulating the price of what being one of Ours would cost him.

Cost was a concept Emmett had ample time to contemplate from the Records Room. Newark was a world away from the South Pacific, but like the dying priest, Emmett kept going back to the Fourth Precinct, day in and day out. Penance for past sins, the compulsion had seeped into his bones, and every second he spent in the basement, an Extern from the force, was a second spent not fulfilling his duty. Though he had renounced a life of service to the church, he had taken on a life of service to the city, an act that would have made Saint Casimir proud, yet no sacrifice Emmett made or could ever make would cancel out his wrongdoing from his conscience. The ever-present tug of an invisible chain around his leg was getting tighter and tighter even as he got into bed and uttered another silent prayer that sleep would find him as it had Edward, then Emmett could forget too.

FIVE

The night's events had made the front page of the Thursday morning *Star Ledger*, though not the headline. Sandwiched between news from Vietnam and a piece about the clash between Israelis and Arabs, the article started off with the caption, "Cops and firemen attacked, stores looted." The name of the cabdriver, Ben White, was never mentioned. Neither were the names of the officers who had beaten him. The story centered on the dozens of arrests and quoted figures estimating the losses at approximately two thousand dollars, substantial but not irreparable. The police were portrayed as heroes for suppressing the scuffle as quickly as they did, and Director Sloakes was lauded for his command. The word *riot* was printed only once.

Edward sat across from Emmett as he read the paper, his wheelchair pulled up to the kitchen table. He poked at the toast Emmett had made for him, uninterested in food. The rustling of the newsprint roused him from his stupor.

"Was it as bad as they're making it out to be?" he asked, more to have something to say than because he was curious. Edward hadn't brought up the bottle of Jim Beam. His bloodshot eyes and the bruise on his forehead from the fall said everything short of an apology. The realization that all of the alcohol in the house was gone had yet to set in.

"Worse," Emmett said.

Whether the papers were willing to acknowledge it or not, the beating of the cabdriver was a wick in the growing powder keg that was the Central Ward. That April, police had gone after picketers peacefully protesting at the Clinton Hill Meat Market. In June came the scandal regarding the potential appointment of James Callaghan to the Board of Education over the better-qualified candidate, Wilber Parker. Callaghan hadn't gone to college while Parker was the first black man to become a certified public accountant in the state of New Jersey. The residents of the Central Ward were starting to keep score of the city's blatant indiscretions, the most egregious of which was the proposed demolition of countless homes in the ward to make room for a 150-acre medical school and hospital complex that would bisect the black community. While the city council praised the projects as urban renewal, opponents such as Mose Odett decried it as "negro removal." Whispers of dissention were turning into war cries. Newark was balanced on a knife's blade. No matter which side the situation fell, somebody would get cut.

"Hey. You see that?" Edward pointed at a photo of Elvis Presley and his pregnant wife, Priscilla, on the opposite page. "Elvis is gonna have a baby."

Presley's impending fatherhood was more exciting to him than the riot. The violent clash was yesterday's news, literally. For Emmett, the shock was still fresh, still vivid.

"You believe that? Congrats to the King, man." In his enthusiasm, Edward had spoken too loudly. He winced in pain.

Emmett cleared his brother's dish and retrieved a bottle of aspirin from the medicine cabinet in the bathroom. "There's ice in the freezer if your head hurts. I'll do my best to get home early."

"Cool. I'll be here," Edward replied, his sarcasm undulled by the hangover, then he picked up the *Ledger* and flipped to the sports section.

The newspaper article hadn't done the damage outside the Fourth Precinct justice. The brick front was scorched from the Molotov cocktail, and the broken windows were boarded up. Along Springfield Avenue, storefronts were replaced by gaping voids. Wet trash littered the sidewalks. The charred remains of the abandoned car hulked on the curb, the sweltering morning air preserving the stench of burnt rubber.

Patrolmen were posted on the streets to prevent further looting, temporary security for storekeepers who were dredging through what was left of their stock and starting repairs. One man was hammering plywood to replace a broken door. Another was sweeping glass chips into the gutter. The uneasy peace between the neighborhood and the Jewish store owners had been replaced by a palpable anguish and disgust. Decades earlier, the Central Ward had been home to a sizable concentration of immigrant and second-generation Jews, many of whom had recently been decamping to the suburbs of West Orange and Livingston at a head-spinning pace. They weren't the only ones. Property taxes, the city's chief source of revenue, had reached an all-time high, driving employers and homeowners into the hills. Newark's population was over 400,000 and another 500,000 commuted in every day to work at the manufacturing plants, banks, or business conglomerates like Prudential, however, the exodus was beginning to rival the influx. At the current rate, the city would be a ghost town in a matter of years. The local motto had become: Newark was open eight hours a day. That was the duration of Emmett's shift. For a city, eight hours was the blink of an eye. For Emmett, it might as well have been an eternity.

The Records Room was uncomfortably quiet that morning. It was as if he were in a bomb shelter and the bomb had already gone off. The file Nolan delivered was lying on his desk. Emmett had no interest in reading it. He paced the aisles, running his hands across the folders as he went. The hushed flicking of paper lulled him to distraction, then the telephone rang, tugging him into reality. For as long as he had been in the basement, Emmett had never heard the phone ring. He wasn't sure how to answer.

"Records."

"Can you come up?" Lieutenant Ahern's voice was hoarse, the strain of a sleepless night. He hadn't forgotten that Emmett was alive as pledged. Ahern forgot nothing.

"Your office?"

"The roof. I'll meet you."

That would be another first for Emmett. He had never been up to the station's rooftop and had to resist the urge to cross himself as he opened the trap door into the scalding sun. The lieutenant had arrived ahead of him. He was leaning against the waist-high ledge, gazing into the distance and smoking a cigarette with the vigor of a man trying to exhale his problems.

Emmett joined him at the ledge. From that height, they had an unobstructed view clear to the river. The city was twenty-three miles square—a quarter of which was taken up by the airport, the seaport, and uninhabitable marshland—giving Newark the highest population density of any major city in the country. The statistics paled in comparison to the panorama of the New York City skyline ten miles to the east. By contrast, Newark seemed stunted, an undernourished sibling.

"Are we sightseeing?" Emmett asked.

"Figured you could stand some sun. You're getting too white being in that basement."

For a full minute, Ahern said nothing else. He wasn't the type who had conversations. He talked. Others listened. The lieutenant had built his reputation on what he didn't do, not on what he did. Once, a detective had made the mistake of getting into a shouting match with him in the third-floor hallway in front of an audience of a dozen officers, intentionally making the argument public. Lieutenant Ahern calmly lectured the detective while backing him toward the stairwell. When the detective went to storm off, he fell down the steps and broke his leg. Ahern never touched him.

The lieutenant peered at the destruction on the street below. "Thank Christ this shit is over, right?"

"Right," Emmett repeated, uncertain if he was agreeing to something else. That concerned him as much as what he was waiting to hear.

"Yesterday I told you I couldn't use you. Today's a different story. This morning a transit worker found the body of a colored kid at the Warren Street subway station."

To call the boy "Negro" would have been too progressive for Ahern. "Colored" was an insult, and the lieutenant preferred insults, no matter who they were aimed at.

"You've got four detectives under you. Why recruit from the Records Room?"

That was as far as Emmett could push. Around Ahern, he had to tread lightly. The lieutenant hadn't warmed to him when Director Sloakes moved Emmett into the division. Although commanding officers had little say in the composition of their squads, Sloakes had forced Emmett down Ahern's throat. The lieutenant resented that, and he resented Emmett. In a rare show of benevolence, Ahern had stifled the department inquest into Emmett's squad room brawl and cut him a break by relegating him to the Records Room instead of requisitioning Sloakes to have him formally reassigned. Afterward, Emmett realized that Ahern hadn't acted out of charity. He had his own motives for sparing him stiffer measures. By banishing him to the basement, the lieutenant could keep Emmett under his thumb.

"Haven't got another set of eyes to spare," Ahern explained, casually tapping cigarette ash over the ledge. Standing three stories up didn't bother him. The lieutenant was accustomed to being on top. However, when the division was spread thin, that put him in the pinch, an infrequent position for Ahern. Emmett also had a sneaking suspicion it was the lieutenant who had convinced the feckless Inspector Plout to grant Mose Odett access to the cabdriver, assuming Odett could persuade the crowd to disband. That way the police wouldn't need to get involved. The strategy had backfired. If Lieutenant Ahern was taking heat for his maneuver, the body of a murdered black boy would fan the flames.

"This sort of situation requires a gentle touch," he told Emmett, savoring his delivery, "and you've been known for your . . . discretion."

The first and only homicide Emmett ever worked was the shooting of Vernon Young, a twenty-two-year-old from the Scudder Homes projects, who ironed laundry at night for a dry cleaner. Young had been dumping the store's trash in the alley behind the cleaner's when he was shot in the back. Obviously, he had been running from somebody. Emmett was assigned to figure out who. The odd man out in the division, he had no partner, no one to show him the ropes, and murder cases didn't come with training wheels. Emmett was on his own. Once the crime scene photographer had gotten his shots and the coroner had taken the body,

Emmett studied the vacant scene to see what Vernon saw: overflowing garbage cans, empty crates from the restaurant next door, and a chain-link fence with dead leaves enmeshed in it, nothing out of the ordinary. It was a discouraging start. Then Emmett noticed a light on inside the dry cleaner's, so he rapped on the front door.

The man who appeared at the window was Otis Fossum, and Emmett could instantly tell that he had witnessed Vernon Young's murder. Fossum was terrified. He was in his forties, thin and lanky, and looked as if he had lived every day twice. At first, he was too rattled to speak. He was steaming collared shirts in a press, mumbling answers to Emmett's queries, unable to meet his eyes. Emmett tried to earn his trust by telling Fossum about leaving the seminary, making himself vulnerable, careful not to say exactly why he left. He had used the story before. Much as he felt guilty for it, the feeling couldn't hold a candle to the guilt of actually leaving. His tale convinced Otis to confide what had him frightened.

Fossum had heard the shot. Through a back window, he had seen two men in the alley. Experience told him one was a cop. His gut said the other was a mobster, giving him double the reason to be scared. Otis guessed that Vernon had stumbled into something he wasn't supposed to see, and the men had killed him for it. His instincts were correct.

When Emmett interviewed the patrons and staff from the restaurant next door, one of the diners turned out to be Sal Lucaro, second in command to Ruggiero Caligrassi, a mob boss who ran the entire East Ward and commanded a huge cut of every piece of cargo that came through Port Newark, which alone was a king's ransom. It was no coincidence that another diner was Frank Giancone, a detective from the Fourth Precinct's Vice Squad. Their tables were at the opposite ends of the restaurant, however a waitress said she saw the two of them go to the bathroom at about the same time.

Both men had stuck around the scene, assuming a friendly face from the force would arrive to escort them away, tell them not to worry, and to have a nice night. Emmett wasn't quite that hospitable. Giancone got anxious and kept fishing for who they knew in common. Emmett simply took his statement, then advised him that he might have to provide his service revolver for comparison if the bullet in the body was identified as a .38. That sent Giancone scurrying for the nearest pay phone. Lucaro was harder to shake. His suit and his fingernails bore the same high sheen, and he had a dimple in his chin that seemed as though it was carved in by an awl. When Emmett asked him if he carried a weapon, Lucaro said, "Good Catholics don't need to carry guns."

"Neither do bad ones," Emmett had responded, convinced to his core that Sal Lucaro was responsible for killing Vernon Young.

Vernon's wallet hadn't been taken, so robbery wasn't a motive, and there were no signs of an altercation that would have led to violence. Vernon was simply in the wrong place at the wrong time as Otis Fossum had inferred. It turned out Emmett was too.

What the newspapers ultimately printed about Vernon Young's death was a single paragraph about him being shot by an unknown assailant and left for dead. Due to an artful smudge of the details, Emmett's report echoed the article. For him, the irony of being a cop was that it wasn't that different from being a machinist, like his father. The rewards were for productivity and speed. During his years in Robbery, he stamped out cases, closing them as fast as he could. Most of it was penny-ante stuff, nothing that involved the mob, so he had never been told to look the other way, not until he arrived in Homicide. On the Vernon Young case, Ahern ordered him to do exactly that.

Because Fossum valued his life too much to volunteer to view a lineup of Giancone and Lucaro, Emmett was stuck with a case he couldn't close, a bad precedent for a new Homicide detective to set. Emmett didn't blame him, but Fossum wasn't out of the woods. He was a witness. Listing him in the report as such would have signed his death warrant. If the mob didn't hit him, a cop in Caligrassi's pocket would. To protect him, Emmett had omitted Otis's name from the file, referring to him only as "a Negro bystander." Emmett didn't want to wind up with another unsolvable case, this one with Otis Fossum's name on it.

Emmett had been forced to fudge the Vernon Young report, and that got under his skin. A common practice at the precinct, it ran counter to his Jesuit training and counter to who he was. Beneath his moral protocol, however, pulsed the allegiance Emmett's father had pounded into him. A union man through and through, his father never sided against his own kind. When the union said "Strike," his father took to the picket lines, regardless that the family would have to survive on bologna sandwiches and stewed cabbage for weeks at a stretch. Emmett's father detested the scabs who crossed the picket lines and raised his sons to respect the union as if it were its own religion and never to fight the flow. Boats made waves. People paddled. That was his father's favorite phrase, and he repeated it so often that Emmett couldn't help but take it to heart. Fortunately, Emmett didn't have to cross any line to keep Fossum alive. At least, he thought he didn't.

Word of his selective editing circulated in the division. Giancone must have dropped a hint. That was when the pressure started. Ahern had called Emmett into his office, an alcove at the rear of the squad room, and implied that the report was incomplete. He suggested that Emmett redo it. Ahern wouldn't say explicitly what was missing. He didn't need to.

There were no secrets in the police station. Everyone was aware of who was on the take and who wasn't. Emmett had no loyalty to the Irish gangsters or the East Ward's mob. Being Polish made him a minority in more ways than one. When Emmett was on probation as a patrolman, a few of his fellow rookies had peaked at the personnel files and found out where he had been prior to the academy. From then on, nobody would walk a beat with him. As a detective, no one would partner with Emmett. Though he hadn't actually become a priest, the stigma persisted. Nobody was keen to be in the company of a man that they felt the impulse to confess to. They knew better than to confess anything to a cop.

The night after his meeting with Ahern, Emmett had bought the bottle of Jim Beam and sat up all evening deciding what he was going to do, unable to open the bourbon. To the Jesuits, obedience entailed following the direct commands of the superior *perinde a cadaver*. The translation: "much like a corpse." A Jesuit followed orders without hesitation. Blind faith in the superior's wisdom was all the faith required. If Emmett gave Ahern what he was asking for, he had complete faith that Otis Fossum would be dead within a week.

The next morning, Emmett resubmitted the same report, uncorrected, and the lieutenant was clear where he stood. Retribution was swift. Emmett caught fellow Homicide detective Nic Serletto digging through his drawers that afternoon, searching for the missing name of the witness. Serletto and his partner, Larry Hochwald, had graduated to Homicide via Vice. Giancone was a friend of theirs, and they made no effort to hide their affiliation with him and with Ruggiero Caligrassi. They were garden variety thugs, the sort who would steal tips off restaurant tables when the waitress wasn't looking, then use their badges to get free coffee. With his hand in Emmett's top drawer, Serletto had the nerve to claim he was borrowing a pen.

"Maybe you should've enlisted with your brother," Serletto had whispered to him. "Maybe you woulda come back in a bag instead."

Emmett decked him. He had never hit another man in anger in his entire life. The second his fist connected with Serletto's jaw, Emmett realized that it was a trap, Serletto the bait. Emmett blamed himself for falling for it.

Rather than suspending him for striking Serletto, the lieutenant ousted Emmett to the Records Room. So began the slow squeeze. Whoever Ahern truly took orders from—because it certainly wasn't Inspector Plout—had demanded Fossum's name, and the lieutenant was going to get it by whatever means necessary.

"When I heard about this case with the colored kid in the train tunnel, I knew you were the right man for it, Martin."

Lieutenant Ahern took a soulful drag off his cigarette for emphasis. Two months earlier, he had put Emmett in his hip pocket until the day came when he could use him. That day had arrived.

To investigate the crime, Emmett would likely have to go into the projects to interview the family. After last night's skirmish, that would be a challenge. He was white and he was a cop. Without a partner, he had no backup. If instead Emmett let the case drop and did nothing, he would take the hit in the press and at the precinct, proving the rumors true, that he was unfit for duty. The lieutenant was offering a lose-lose proposition. Or so Ahern must have assumed.

Emmett still had his badge and he still carried a weapon, however his demotion to the basement told everyone that Lieutenant Ahern didn't trust him. Getting an investigation of his own would change that. It would also give Emmett the chance he had been hoping for on the Vernon Young case.

"You want the body or not?"

Emmett didn't answer. Ahern stabbed out his cigarette on the stone ledge. He wasn't about to push Emmett down the proverbial stairs. He was going to let him fall.

"Yeah. I'll take it."

The lieutenant wouldn't allow his satisfaction to show. "Then you should get a move on. Transit's stopped service on the subway line on my orders. They're telling the public it's for maintenance. Won't be able to hold the trains for more than an hour."

The Warren Street stop was on the city's main subway artery. The fact that Ahern could get it shut down for any length of time attested to his power, a strong warning to Emmett. If the lieutenant could stop a train, there was no telling what else he was capable of.

"Listen, Martin, I don't want to see this niggerboy's body on the front page of tomorrow's newspaper. Whole city'd go up in smoke. Watts would look like a backyard barbecue. You hearing me?"

Emmett had heard exactly what he needed to hear, but before he went to see the body, he had a call to make.

SIX

Two patrolmen were there to meet Emmett at the subway station. They huddled in a sliver of shade under an overhang, acting like they had better things to do. When a woman in a minidress strolled by, the younger of the two swiveled his head after her. He would have whistled if Emmett hadn't walked up.

"Hot enough for you, Detective?" the officer with the wandering eye asked, grinning as if they were old friends.

"Where's the body?"

"Over here, sir," the older patrolman replied, flashing his partner a stifling glare.

Repair signs and traffic cones cordoned off the doors, preventing people from entering. Inside, the station was steamy. The tiled walls retained the heat. Decorative mosaics depicting the old Morris Canal seemed molten in the humidity and ready to drip.

Newark's Seven City subway system had been constructed in the 1930s in the dry bed of the canal, which had been drained and filled forty years prior because the stagnant waters were a health hazard. Subway lines had run above and below ground, using cars that were similar to street trolleys. At its height, the system covered seven lines, operating from Newark to Bloomfield, Caldwell, East Orange, Jersey City,

Montclair, and Orange, hence the name "Seven Cities." Emmett had vague memories of the trolleys from his childhood. For a nickel fare, they were as close to an amusement park ride as he and his brother could get. Sadly, service on the streetcar routes was short-lived. They were eventually discontinued and converted to buses, all save one—the Number Seven, which looped through Newark. Most residents had been sorry to see the trolleys go, Emmett included. The cars brought a certain charm to the city, and they were a symbol of what Newark could have been. Their departure marked a kind of demise, a step in the wrong direction. It wouldn't be the last.

"You'll need this," the older officer said. He handed Emmett a flashlight.

"Wait. The body's inside the tunnel?"

"Yes, sir. Conductor noticed it this morning."

The patrolmen hopped off the platform onto the tracks. Emmett followed tentatively. He hated tunnels. His phobia was born when he was a boy, when being afraid was something he thought he would outgrow. This was a fear he hadn't shed.

"Watch your step, Detective," warned the younger officer, boldly leading. "Once we get into the tunnel, you can barely see your hand in front of your face even with the flashlights."

As they passed from the lighted section of the station into the mouth of the tunnel, the wall tiles transitioned into concrete. The deeper they went, the dimmer it got. Soon the darkness swallowed them. They snapped on their flashlights, casting wide arcs of light that glinted along the iron tracks. The sound of their footsteps bounced off the vaulted walls. Panic was swelling in Emmett's chest. He gripped the flashlight so it wouldn't betray his shaking hands.

"Least it's cooler in here," the older patrolman commented.

"Yeah, there's a little breeze." The other mopped his neck with a handkerchief.

A thin wind blew through the tunnel, swirling wisps of dust. It was no relief to Emmett, nor was the chitchat. "How much farther?"

"Right up ahead, sir. See?"

Their flashlights illuminated the outline of an immense figure lying faceup on the ground, straddling one side of the tracks. When Emmett got closer, he saw that the leg between the rails had been severed and rolled away from the torso. At its center, a white pearl of denuded bone glowed in the dark. The sight of the mangled body diverted his anxiety and helped him hold it under wraps.

"I was told the victim was a boy. This looks like a grown man."

"He had a student movie pass in his pocket," the older patrolman explained. "Name's Ambrose Webster. This address was paper clipped to the pass." He rattled off an apartment number in the Hayes Home projects.

"Did you call it in and confirm that was his address and not somebody else's?"

"Sir?"

"You assumed the address was his."

"I get it," the younger patrolman said, proud of himself. "Why would the guy have his own address in his pocket?"

The body lying on the tracks was either that of the real Ambrose Webster or of a John Doe who stole the movie pass from him. Emmett hoped for the latter. Only the infirm or the mentally ill would keep their own addresses on their person, and this victim didn't appear to fall into the first category.

"So you didn't confirm it?"

They shook their heads. "No, sir."

Emmett traced the length of the victim's massive, muscled body with his flashlight. He was about Emmett's height, but a hundred pounds heavier. Even in death, he was menacing. It would have taken tremendous courage or coercion to get the upper hand on someone that large.

"Ten to one this kid played high school football," the older officer mused.

"Five to one he was a linebacker. He's the size of a frickin' house."

Emmett deflected the beam of his light from the body onto the officers. Despite his rank, he no longer had the status to threaten. A glower would have to suffice.

"Sorry," they muttered in unison.

At the abbey, speaking ill to or of the brethren had been frowned upon. In Jesuit terms, that translated to forbidden. The other novices were four years younger than Emmett, and they had come straight from posh Jesuit prep school such as Regis, Fordham, and Xavier in New York. To them, his alma mater, Saint Peter's, was a backwater, third-rate barn, and the fact that Emmett had arrived at the monastery at the old age of twenty-two made him ripe for recrimination, if not outright, then in furtive stares. Although communication at Saint Andrew's had been conducted entirely in Latin, most of it clumsy and poorly conjugated, the subtlest insults were trumpeted like curse words. Emmett got them loud and clear, and they became louder in his own mind when he left. That taught him to think before he spoke and not to speak at all without cause.

"Did you find anything besides the movie pass on him?"

"A dollar and change and a house key. That was it."

The rattle of a distant train welled into the tunnel. The three of them turned. Emmett scouted for an approaching light and the darkness gaped back at him.

"This route's shut down, isn't it?"

Worry swept across the older patrolman's face. "They said it was."

The margin between the tracks and the wall was negligible. If a train did come through, there was no room for them to step aside. Emmett was fast on his feet, but he doubted he could outrun a subway car.

"You'd better cross your fingers *they* were right."

He knelt to study the victim. Aside from the bodies of his own parents, this was the second corpse Emmett had ever seen up close. Vernon Young had been lying facedown. That made him easier to look at. Nothing was easy about this body except that the victim's eyes were closed. Emmett considered that a blessing, for him and the deceased. Tiny brown ants clustered around the victim's eyelashes and at the edges of his lips. Emmett wanted to dust them away. He didn't.

"Where's all the blood?" the younger patrolman asked. "Shouldn't there be more blood?"

Emmett had also noticed the absence of blood. He hadn't planned to bring it up. He wasn't there to give a lesson. This being his second homicide, he was in no position to teach the officers anything. "The leg was probably sheared off by a passing train postmortem and the dead don't bleed." He left it at that.

"Oh, okay," the patrolman said. "That's some cut on his neck though, ain't it?"

Cut was an understatement. The injury to the leg was clearly the result of a train car. The slash across the victim's throat most certainly was not. Knives usually produced scratches or lines on a body depending on depth. This wound was on a par with the mark an ax would leave in a tree trunk. The position of the body was all that kept the head from unhinging altogether.

Rivulets of dried blood streamed from the gash, and the front of the victim's T-shirt was stained brown from a geyser of arterial spray. The T-shirt was a size too small, and the pants, shredded by the train, were thin at the knees, earmarks of hand-me-down clothes. Emmett had gotten his share as a novice. When he received his cassock, it had been donned by countless others. The elbows and sleeves were frayed, and the stains of a million meals were embedded in the fabric even though it had been washed so often that the black cloth had turned an off-putting greenish gray. Novices were issued four pairs of shirts, shorts, and socks each week, purchased from army surplus for little more than a prayer by one of the lay brothers. The victim's clothes had presumably been bought at the Goodwill for a slightly higher price and were worse for the wear. Mud was streaked across his chest. More was caked on his shoes and flecked along the pant leg to the shin. Emmett panned his light across the tunnel floor. All he saw was gravel and dry dirt.

"We checked for footprints," the younger patrolman told him. "There were none."

"Guy could've walked on the wood slats in the center of the tracks."

"Or on the rail."

"On the rail? That'd be like walking a tightrope. What is he? One of the Flying Wallendas?"

Emmett allowed the officers to carry on with their conjecture to occupy them. Normally, he would have told them to wait outside. Since he couldn't tolerate being in the tunnel alone, he would have to tolerate them. He touched the mud on Ambrose Webster's shoe. It was fresh.

That summer's heat wave had brought on a drought. The city was under water restriction. People were barred from washing their cars or running their sprinklers. Water was being rationed the way it would in a desert. Emmett thought of the previous night's upheaval, the fires and the hoses spraying gallons upon gallons of water into the streets. The victim could have been at the riot. Emmett was more interested in where he went afterward.

The lack of blood meant that the body had been dumped in the subway tunnel. There were no drag marks leading in from the station. Someone had gone to a lot of trouble to bring a victim that large to that exact spot. How they did it, Emmett couldn't begin to imagine. Why they left him on a train track where his body was bound to be discovered was equally baffling. The mud crusted in the palm and nail beds of the victim's right hand didn't make sense either. His being in the vicinity of the Fourth Precinct and the fires might account for his muddy shoes, but the crowd that had surrounded the police station was slinging mud figuratively, not literally.

The victim's left hand was tucked under his hip, indicating that he had been dropped without care or that the train that ripped his leg off had dragged him, twisting the body, impossible to tell which. As Emmett bent down to get a better view, a pigeon flew out of the darkness, wings flapping loud as applause. The noise startled him as well as the patrolmen.

"Stupid bird," the younger officer said.

Emmett felt dizzy. His heart was racing. If he didn't rein in his nerves, he might faint. He put his hand on the ground to steady himself.

"Before you got here, dispatch radioed to say the photographer's running late. You wanna hang around, Detective?"

Newark employed one forensic photographer for all five wards. His name was Albert Rafshoon, and he would have shown up late even if he didn't have such a broad area to cover. Rafshoon had rolled onto the Vernon Young crime scene an hour and a half behind schedule, waddling under the weight of his equipment, his thinning hair combed over his scalp in the expert swirls of an iced cake. What he lacked in punctuality, he compensated for in thoroughness, getting pictures from every conceivable angle. Rafshoon's shots of Vernon Young were burned into Emmett's brain more indelibly than the original crime scene. The lagoon of blood surrounding the body reflected the camera's flash in every image. Had he been anywhere else, Emmett would have held out for the photographer, but the tunnel was breaking him.

"No, tell Rafshoon to get the pictures to me as quickly as he can."

"Will do. Wagon's here to take this guy to the coroner. Can we bring 'em in?"

The body no longer interested the patrolmen. The thrill of the location and the severed leg had faded. They'd had enough.

"Yeah. They can't touch him until the photographer's finished. Got that?"

They answered "Yes, sir" in tandem.

Heading back, Emmett's pulse peaked when he saw light shining from the subway station ahead. He was leaning forward as he walked, like a runner nearing a finish line. The younger patrolman climbed onto the platform to confer with the coroner's men, who were wheeling in a gurney, while the other helped lower it onto the tracks. The fluorescent lamps were a comfort compared to the dark, yet Emmett couldn't catch his breath. His knees were about to give.

"You okay, sir?" From the platform, the younger officer held out his hand to him.

Emmett ignored the gesture and hoisted himself up unaided. "I'm fine. It's the heat."

Red-faced, the patrolman went to the entrance to await Rafshoon while the older one accompanied the coroner's crew to the body, the gurney clattering over the train tracks. Alone on the platform, tension eased its stranglehold on Emmett. He uncurled his stiffened fingers from the flashlight, picturing the victim's muddy nails as he shook the powdery dirt from the tunnel floor off his own hands. It didn't make sense. Nothing about murder made sense to Emmett. In the past, he had been able to disconnect himself from compassion or anger because he was dealing with robberies and thefts, not death. With a murder, compassion and anger could overtake him as the tunnel had. Emmett had to ignore his feelings. Feelings wouldn't help him. Logic could. He wondered how the body had gotten in that far and who would have wanted to put it there. Then he wondered if he really wanted to know. If he did, it was going to cost him.

He had two choices: let the file on the boy's murder sink or allow himself to drown. The victim was beyond saving. Emmett had to decide whether he was too.

SEVEN

Daylight felt like a beating. The sun was a jab to the face, the heat an uppercut that knocked the wind from Emmett's lungs. He would take that kind of abuse over a tunnel any time.

The coroner's wagon had drawn a clump of people who gathered outside the subway station, trying to peek in past the signs. The patrolman would wave them away, and they would move off a bit, then inch in again, similar to shooing pigeons. As Emmett cut through the throng, someone shouted to him, "What's going on in there?"

"Why's the cops here?" another asked.

"Sign says repairs," Emmett told them.

"Cops don't do repairs."

"That's exactly what we do," he said.

At his car, he realized that he had accidentally walked off with the flashlight the officer loaned him. He was clutching it as though he didn't trust the blaring noon sun to stay bright. Returning the flashlight to the patrolmen would have been the right thing to do, but Emmett couldn't bring himself to go back into the tunnel. He would replace the flashlight in the storage closet at the station instead, just not yet.

A flyer was stuffed under the windshield wiper of his car. In bold print, it read: "Stop Police Brutality. Come and join us at the mass rally tonight at the Fourth Precinct at 7:30."

If anything, the rally would be an invitation for more brutality and an encore of last night's disorder. Whether that was the organizers' goal was open for debate. Emmett folded the flyer into his pocket. To be safe, he got his spare radio from under the front seat of his car and propped it on the passenger seat, close at hand. Edward had rigged it to the police band frequency for him. The department didn't have the budget for walkie-talkies, and only the patrol cars were equipped with radios. Assuming another riot broke out during the rally, Emmett wanted to know where not to be.

When he switched on the radio, dispatch was summoning the Traffic Division for any available assistance. Teams of reporters with television cameras were assembling around the Fourth Precinct and attracting a crowd. By normal standards, it was hardly an emergency. After the riot, normal standards no longer applied.

Factoring in Albert Rafshoon's usual delays, the coroner wouldn't get to the victim's autopsy for hours. Emmett had calculated for that when he phoned to make his appointment earlier that morning. He stowed the borrowed flashlight in his glove compartment and drove home, unsure what was in store for him.

The house was painfully hot, the air stale. Edward was napping in his wheelchair, head nestled into his shoulder, and the television was turned down to a whisper. Emmett closed the door gently. At the click of the latch, Edward snapped awake. Groggy, he asked, "What're you doing home?"

A wet hand towel lay across his lap. It had been a compress for his head, and the ice in it had melted, soaking through to his pants and staining them embarrassingly at the crotch. Edward couldn't feel it. He followed Emmett's gaze to the spot.

"It's okay. Let me get another towel."

"It's the ice," Edward said defensively.

"I know. It's okay."

A knock came at the front door, interrupting them.

"You expecting someone?"

"Sort of."

"Sort of?"

Emmett gave his brother a chance to cover the stain with the towel before he answered the door.

A black woman stood on the stoop, clutching her purse in one hand, a note in the other. White hair feathered from her temples, and she wore a floral cotton dress over broad hips as well as stockings despite the heat.

"Is this the Emmett residence?" She read the name off the note in a drummed-down southern drawl.

"It is. Can I help you?"

"I'm Mavis Poole. The hospital sent me. Somebody phoned about hiring a nurse's aide." She smiled hesitantly.

Emmett had been expecting someone white. He was embarrassed by his assumption. The oversight was a far cry from the overt racism that spurred the riots, yet he realized that it grew from a common root. He considered apologizing to her, but there was too much to apologize for.

The call to the hospital was the one Emmett had made after speaking to the lieutenant on the rooftop. Edward's fall had convinced him that he couldn't care for his brother on his own. It hurt him to admit it, and it hurt him to see Edward's expression slide from stunned to hostile, his jaw working under the cheek.

"Come in, Mrs. Poole. I'm Martin Emmett, and this is my brother, Edward."

She shook Emmett's hand, a soft, polite grip. When she offered the same hand to Edward, he wheeled away. The back door slammed, resounding through the house.

"Would I be right to assume you didn't mention my coming ahead of time, Mr. Emmett?"

"You would." He regretted springing the poor woman on Edward.

"No harm done, dear. I can be on my way if you think that's best. If not," she added, hopeful, "I'd ask if I might not sit a spell. Took me two buses to get here."

"Please. Make yourself at home."

She opted for a spot on the unused couch and perched on the edge of the cushions daintily. Emmett noticed that Mrs. Poole had a slight limp that she tried to conceal by her posture and the style in which she carried her purse. His guess, her lower back bothered her. He couldn't understand why she didn't pick a firmer chair.

"I don't move as fast as some, but I'm strong," she said. "I've taken care of men as big as you, Mr. Emmett, and bigger. My late husband weighed over two hundred pounds. He lost both legs in Korea, and I learned to flip him like a pancake, so don't mistake me for weak. I'm no stranger to hard work. I can do the job. That is, if you want me to."

Emmett saw in Mrs. Poole a quiet need, for a paying position or to be working, to have something to fill her days. She wouldn't let on which. It wasn't desperation, though it wasn't that different. He could relate.

"I imagine you're no stranger to hard work either." Mrs. Poole gestured at the badge hanging from his belt.

"Your accent's too nice to be from Newark," he said, dodging a response with a compliment. "Where are you from?"

"Swainsboro, Georgia. You heard of it?"

"I'm afraid I haven't."

"Not many folks have. When the farming dried up, my daddy moved us here, me and my ten brothers and sisters. Lordy, that practically cut the population of Swainsboro in half. For as many years as I've lived in Newark, I shouldn't have any accent left. Some things just stay with you, I suppose."

There were things that stayed with Emmett too, things he couldn't let go of, like an accent he couldn't drop.

"Let me see if I can talk to Edward," he told her, turning to go.

"Must be tough, caring for your brother on your own," Mrs. Poole said in a tone tender and low to ensure Edward wouldn't overhear. "You're a grown man. You have a career, a life to lead."

She was giving him permission not to feel guilty for asking for help. Emmett had confessed nothing, yet she saw through him to his heart as clearly as she had seen his badge.

"Give me a minute with him," he said.

Edward was at the far end of the porch, staring at the backyard, hands knitted tight. Emmett stepped outside, the screen door creaking and announcing his arrival. Edward wouldn't acknowledge his presence. Emmett went and stood beside him. He had to let his brother speak first.

"That crabgrass is going to ruin the lawn. You see it? By the garage," Edward said. A patch of scrubby, yellow blades was encroaching on the property. "You'll have to pull it up or else the grass'll die."

"Okay. I'll pull it up."

"And you'd better put some of that weed killer Pop used on it too."

"Okay."

Edward shook a cigarette out of his pack. He didn't light it. "You coulda warned me, Marty."

"I know. I should have."

"I don't have to like her."

"No, you don't have to like her. But you might."

"And if I don't?"

"Then you don't."

"You'll get somebody else, won't you?"

"It can't be me, Ed. I can't quit to be here with you."

"I know that," he said, a hitch in his voice. "I wish . . ."

"What?"

Edward was wavering, wary of loosening some emotional valve. Being in the wheelchair, it was easier for him not to meet Emmett's eyes, to act as if they were on the telephone talking long-distance rather than person to person. The moment passed. He dammed up whatever it was he was going to say, sealing it inside him again. "Nothing. Never mind."

Emmett held the screen door, and Edward wheeled himself inside. Mrs. Poole was roosted on the edge of the couch, smoothing her dress over her knees.

"Have you ever worked with somebody like me?" Edward asked her, getting right to the point. An awkward silence bloated the room.

"I don't know, dear. I just met you. What're you like?"

Mrs. Poole was looking Edward squarely in the face as though the wheelchair didn't exist. She looked at him the way Emmett couldn't.

Rarely at a loss, Edward's bravado dissolved. Emmett realized that Mrs. Poole had picked the couch because it was the lowest seat in the living room and it put her right on Edward's level. It would hurt her to stand up again. She had sat there nonetheless.

"I have references if you need to see them." Mrs. Poole unsnapped her purse, prepared to present them in case Edward was on the fence.

He deferred to Emmett. "Do we need to see her references?"

The woman was tougher than Emmett initially thought, and it would take more than Edward to fluster her. That spoke louder than any reference could.

"Do we?" He bounced the question back, leaving the final say to his brother, who deliberated for a beat.

"No, that's all right."

With that, the deal was sealed. Emmett gave Mrs. Poole a tour of the house, told her that she was welcome to whatever food was in the refrigerator, then wrote her a check for a week's pay in advance.

"You don't have to give this to me now, Mr. Emmett."

"Really, I do."

Mrs. Poole tucked the check into her purse, taking the hint. "Is this a bribe so I'll stick out the week?"

"If I'd known you were that easy to bribe, I would have paid you for a month," Emmett said with a wink. He jotted the phone number to the police station on a pad. "Here's where I can be reached. It's the Fourth Precinct."

"Ain't that something. I live on Charlton Street. We're practically neighbors." Her inflection telegraphed the message that she was aware of what went on at the precinct, but this was business. Any differences would be left at the door.

"I usually try to get home by five. If I'm late, you don't have to stay."

"If you're late, you're late, Mr. Emmett. It's okay. Life isn't always predictable."

Life wasn't predictable. All he could be certain of was that the victim from the subway tunnel was lying in the morgue with his throat slit. Nothing and no one could change that, including Emmett. He hadn't settled on what he was going to do about the case. It was a decision even he couldn't predict.

EIGHT

The entrance to Newark City Hospital was as inviting as a vise grip. The stoic, redbrick building had been designed in a horseshoe shape, creating a cul-du-sac with the main door at the center. Throughout different eras, the original structure had been expanded upon, so additions protruded from the roofline like growths gone unchecked. The hospital seemed less like a refuge than a last resort.

Established to serve the city's indigent and needy, City Hospital was as poorly funded as its patients. Its equipment was outmoded, its staff a skeleton crew, and its security nonexistent. Bedside curtains and toilet seats were considered luxuries, and mice could be seen scampering along the corridors' baseboards. A diarrhea epidemic had broken out two years earlier, resulting in the death of eighteen infants and branding the hospital with a reputation as a place where people had a higher chance of dying than getting better. It was appropriate then that the Essex County coroner's office was situated in the hospital's basement. Knowing the elevators carried cadavers, lice-infested linens, and infectious patients as well as the visitors, Emmett took the stairs down.

In order to reach the morgue, he had to navigate an intricate network of hallways, each virtually identical in their blandness, all of the doors closed save for the occasional supply closet. Emmett had gotten lost on his first trip there to see the body of Vernon Young. No signage marked the path. The morgue was the sort of place that seemed intentionally difficult to find.

When Emmett finally did find it, he almost wished he hadn't. Heavy double doors opened into the examination area, which bore an uncanny resemblance to a mechanic's shop. Spray nozzles dangled from the ceiling, and metal tables split the basement into bays. Because of the coolers, the air was chilly, congealing the oily odor of innards with the tartness of chemicals and cleaning fluid. Tiled floors and walls created the faint echo of an empty pool. A bald man in a rubber apron was standing at the sink, the water running high. His back was to the door and to the corpse of an elderly black man lying on a slab, the chest cavity exposed, the skin peeled open.

Emmett wasn't squeamish. Life at the abbey had prepared him to be dispassionately passionate. Denied worldly possessions and frequent contact with family, he had mastered the art of detachment. Beliefs were to be intense, fervent. Emotions were not.

"Didn't hear you come in," the man in the apron said amiably, cranking off the faucet as soon as he noticed Emmett. He was so trim that he had to loop the apron strings around his waist repeatedly to keep it tied on.

"Is this a bad time?"

"I'm sure this gentleman won't mind. He's not in a rush."

"Is Doctor Aberbrook around?" Emmett shifted his jacket to show his badge.

"Nope. He retired. Moved to Florida."

That was news to Emmett. Working in the Records Room had the same effect on him as living at the seminary, where television, books, papers, and all links to the outside were prohibited. Emmett was utterly ignorant of change. Again, the world hadn't waited for him and he was sprinting to catch up.

"Retired? When?"

"Two months ago."

"Are you the new coroner?"

"New is a relative term." He motioned to his balding pate. "How about you? You new to the department?"

"Like you said, it's a relative term. I'm Detective Emmett."

"Well, Detective, I'm Doctor Ufland. We'll have to skip the handshake." He was holding a length of entrail that he had been examining over the sink. He slopped the organ onto a scale. "Who're you here for?"

"The deceased's name is Ambrose Webster."

Before leaving his house, Emmett had checked the phonebook listings. The address clipped to the movie pass in the victim's pocket matched. That alone didn't confirm that the body in the tunnel had been that of Ambrose Webster. Emmett had a strong suspicion that it was, though. While he should have been grateful for the lead, that the victim wasn't a John Doe, he couldn't deny the twinge of disappointment. Something about this murder was off.

"Is he the one with the severed leg?"

"That's him. He was only delivered a couple of hours ago. I was going to ask if you had any idea what time you'd be—"

"He's done. I just finished him. It's been slow today. The kid would still be on the table if it weren't for this heat. If it doesn't break soon, my coolers are going to conk out. Trust me, that would be unpleasant."

"I'll take your word for it."

Ufland rolled a drawer out from a wall of individual coolers. Ambrose Webster's naked body lay on a metal tray, his dark skin gleaming. His torso was thickly roped with muscle and unmarred apart from the stitches in the Y incision left from the autopsy and the slash across his neck that arced like a smile. His amputated leg lay beside its mate, the foot facing away, the knee turned out. Vernon Young's body was completely different in shape and scale, but standing over Webster's body brought Emmett right back to that day.

The bullet the former coroner, Dr. Aberbrook, had pulled from Young's body was a .22, not a .38, a fact that did little to further the case. All it established was that Detective Giancone hadn't shot Vernon with his service revolver. He very well might have had a second piece. Like many a cop, Emmett himself also carried a .22 in a calf holster.

Giancone could have had one too and discarded it. Lucaro was the likelier suspect. While he claimed not to have a weapon, Emmett didn't believe that a mobster of his distinction went anywhere without one. Emmett had searched the crime scene thoroughly, sifting through crates of rotten food and garbage cans, dirty work that yielded nothing. He never found a gun. Without the murder weapon or Otis Fossum's cooperation, the case stalled. His reassignment to the Records Room had convinced Emmett that he wouldn't get another opportunity to jump-start it. Ambrose Webster had changed that. As Emmett stood beside Webster's corpse, he had to remind himself that the dead boy wasn't a means to an end.

"Autopsy was pretty cut-and-dried if you'll pardon the pun," the doctor began. "I'd put his age at sixteen, maybe seventeen. He was in perfect health. Strong as an ox. Didn't need me to tell you that. The laceration to the throat was what killed him, obviously. It was deep, down to the vertebrae. Could've taken his head clean off if the neck muscles weren't so dense."

Dr. Ufland wasn't saying anything Emmett hadn't intuited. On the ride from his house to the hospital, he had been going over the scant information he had, hashing through various scenarios. Webster could have gotten into a fight that went bad, pissed off the wrong person, or owed somebody money. Emmett didn't know enough yet to point him in any specific direction.

"Time of death?"

"Last night. Between midnight and three."

"The riot had already started."

"Read about that in the paper," Ufland said with a shudder. "Were you there?"

Emmett preferred not to go into it. "It was my night off. Listen, Doc, I'm flying blind here. This kid was dumped on the train tracks. I don't have the original crime scene."

"I'm not sure how much help I can be. Prior to death, he took a heck of a beating. He had bruises everywhere, a sprained ankle, a chipped tooth. What I thought was interesting was that he had about three pounds of steak in his stomach. Chunks of it. Partially chewed. The good stuff. We're not talking ground chuck. That's a lot of meat. Even for a guy his size. Maybe he won a supermarket raffle or something."

Webster's address was in the Hayes Home projects across from the Fourth Precinct, where welfare families lived cheek to jowl, often sharing cramped apartments with a second family to cover the cost of rent. In Hayes, a freezer was a status symbol. Women cooked on antiquated coal- or wood-burning stoves because the landlords refused to upgrade, and tenants ate their meals with a can of insect spray within reach. Rats and roaches added to the number of mouths to feed. Emmett doubted that Ambrose Webster would ever have tasted steak, let alone eaten three whole pounds of it.

"Almost forgot. The leg wasn't all he was missing."

Ufland raised Webster's left arm, holding the hand aloft. The pointer finger was gone, cleanly cut at the base of the knuckle. The incident in the tunnel with the pigeon had prevented Emmett from noticing. Suddenly, a memory fluttered at the back of his brain, like a note being slid under a door. Before he could grab onto it, the doctor was talking again.

"It was removed postmortem. Different knife from the throat."

Despite the gruesome manner of the murder, the fact that the boy's finger hadn't been cut off while he was alive was a small comfort to Emmett.

"I heard that the guys who kidnapped Sinatra's son were going to lop off one of his fingers to send it in as proof that they had him," Ufland said. "Scare Old Blue Eyes into coughing up the cash."

"I have a feeling this kid's family doesn't fall into Frank Sinatra's tax bracket. Any chance the finger was sheered off by a train?"

"This is what train wheels do to tissue." The doctor twisted the root of Webster's severed leg toward Emmett. The flesh was mangled, ragged. "The knives that were used on the finger and the neck were sharp, not serrated. And the one that caused the neck wound had to be a big blade. See? There's a single line all the way around. No switchblade could do this amount of damage in one fell swoop." He demonstrated, drawing his own finger across his throat. It was too short to bridge the circumference.

"The angle of the wound is upward. A nifty trick, given how big this kid is. That would suggest one of two things. The first would be that the boy's attacker was bigger than him. You'd be looking for a guy pushing seven feet. If that's the case, I'm glad I'm not in your shoes, Detective."

It was a sobering speculation. It was also far-fetched. Other possibilities spun through Emmett's head. He doubted that Webster would obligingly bend over and allow someone to slit his throat or stand idly by as they stood on a stool in order to kill him.

"And the second choice?"

"Door number two: he was leaning forward or backward, affecting the angle of the wound. The degree would depend on where the killer was in relation to the victim."

An unwelcome image sprang into Emmett's mind. "What if he was kneeling and someone came at him from behind? Would that be consistent with this wound."

A similar picture must have appeared to the doctor. He grimaced. "Yeah, that would work."

Webster's huge stature belied his actual age. He was just a teenager. The idea of someone so young on the ground with a knife at his throat was deeply unsettling. Emmett's shins were calloused from all the time he had spent in prayer, and he tried to think of what could have brought Ambrose Webster to his knees.

"This body was in a subway tunnel, right?" Ufland asked. "Must've been dark. The finger may still be at the scene. It'd be easy to miss, especially if it rolled away from the body when the train took off his leg. You could go and check."

That wasn't an option Emmett was eager to entertain.

"If I found the finger, would that tell us anything?"

"Maybe. Maybe not. Would be nice to give the boy back to his family with all the pieces."

Emmett was ashamed to admit that he hadn't stopped to consider Ambrose Webster's family. They might not have even realized he was missing.

"Are you going to take his personal effects, Detective? Or should I save them for the next of kin?"

Leaving the effects for the family to collect would get Emmett off the hook, if that was what he wanted. He could avoid any calls or make excuses, claim there were no leads, no evidence to connect anyone to the crime, which at present wasn't a lie. He could let the Webster file wither and go cold, then investigate Vernon Young's murder full-time. If he took the boy's belongings, Emmett would have to deliver them to the family himself. He would have to face them with the news that Ambrose was dead. It would mean he was on the case.

Dr. Ufland set a brown paper bag containing Ambrose Webster's personal property on an empty surgical table, as if to remain impartial. "I have to finish this gentleman so I can get to my next customer," he said. "Glad to have met you, Detective."

"Likewise. Thanks, Doc."

"You know your way out, right? It can be kind of confusing. An orderly once told me that the builders did that on purpose, so visitors wouldn't stumble into the morgue by accident. Strange, huh? The things people think of."

Emmett knew the way out, his way out. But he couldn't take it. Because Ambrose Webster hadn't ended up in the morgue by accident.

He picked up the paper bag and left.

NINE

The dispatcher on the police band frequency sounded bored. Since leaving the hospital, Emmett had been listening to his radio for signs of trouble and heard only the average chatter. The television crews that set up camp on various corners surrounding the Fourth Precinct hadn't caused quite the commotion originally anticipated, so the responding officers from the Traffic Division were redeployed. Cleanup at the Fourth Precinct had commenced, and extra sanitation workers were called in for assistance. Otherwise, nothing out of the ordinary was going on. That was as foreboding to Emmett as the calm that preceded a storm.

He parked on Boyd Street, a block between the Hayes Home Housing Projects and the police station. He had the ominous sense that this case was anything but cut-and-dried as the coroner had suggested, and he was intent on talking to Ambrose Webster's relatives before the rally that evening, before any more trouble could start. Webster's address was in the building closest to where Emmett parked. He headed, instead, to the apartment building farthest away.

The Hayes Home Housing Projects was a small city unto itself. Spread over a five-and-a-half-acre hunk of land, its towering tenements and signature smokestack figured prominently into the city's skyline. Up close, the compound was imposing. His years in the Robbery

Division had brought Emmett to Hayes on too many occasions to count, and he had chased and lost his fair share of suspects until he memorized the project's layout, its blind spots, pass-throughs, and exits. There was no cover and no place to hide. Anything other than trash that wasn't nailed down disappeared. The basketball backboards were stripped of their hoops and nets, the benches were missing slats, and even the trees seemed to be short on leaves.

Because the grounds had more square footage of cement than grass, every noise was magnified. The rhythmic *whap whap* of a handball game throbbed through the brick ravines that ran between the apartment buildings. It was a familiar sound from Emmett's past. Handball was a game he had mastered during his stay at Saint Andrew's on the Hudson. On Thursday afternoons, the regular work assignments were suspended, and novices were given the run of hundreds of wooded acres as well as the softball field and the handball court. Playing had been an escape for him, an opportunity to sweat out the stuffiness of constant prayer and piety. He missed the game. That was all he missed about the monastery.

Rounding a corner, Emmett came upon a group of teenage boys cheering on two friends pitted against each other in a handball match. They were whipping the rubber ball back and forth at lightning speed. The wall acting as their backboard was part of the building where Emmett needed to go. For them, handball was probably an escape too. Maybe not from prayer or piety, but from everything else. He would have liked to watch them for a while. He thought better of it.

Emmett walked toward them at an unhurried pace, carrying the paper bag that held Ambrose Webster's effects. He was practicing a Jesuit exercise known as "custody of the senses," keeping the body, bearing, and voice under strict control. The dictum had dual purposes. The first was to cultivate a modest composure befitting a priest, the second to prevent the adolescent novitiate from barreling through the abbey hallways shouting their lungs out. The objective was not to exude confidence but rather to emit an air of placidity and self-possession, which would render a person practically invisible. At the moment, custody of the senses came in handy. It had been less than twenty-four hours since the riot, and Emmett preferred that the teenage boys not notice him. He glided smoothly past the teens, undetected, and went directly to a fire door on the side of the building, not the main entrance. When he was there last, the lock had been knocked out. It still wasn't fixed.

The fire door opened into a stairwell. From the bottom, the view up the staircase was dizzying. Emmett needed to go to the ninth floor, and the elevator wasn't an option. When they weren't out of service, the elevators ran in slow motion and were puddled with urine. The lightbulbs were busted or stolen, forcing passengers to ride in the dark at their own peril. Between nine flights of stairs and the elevator, Emmett chose the stairs.

The climb should have winded him. He was too preoccupied about being spotted as a cop to pay attention to the burning in his legs or the reek of broken sewage pipes. Health inspectors in charge of enforcing sanitation codes were paid off by the landlords to overlook citations, so the pipes were never fixed, and litter accumulated in every nook and crevice, the trash facilities inadequate for the high number of tenants. The garbage continued to pile up, a testament to perseverance—the landlords' as well as the tenants'.

When Emmett got to the ninth floor, two women were chatting in the hallway. They passed the stairwell, then went into separate apartments. Once they were gone, he sped along the graffiti-covered corridor and knocked on the door to an apartment at the end of the hall. Nobody answered. Emmett knocked again, harder. Voices were echoing from the bottom of the stairs, hooting and shouting, toes bounding up the steps. Emmett assumed it was the kids who had been playing handball. He wasn't afraid of them. He had the badge and the gun. What gave him pause was the possibility of a scuffle breaking out between a policeman and a bunch of black teenagers in the wake of last night's fireworks.

At the opposite end of the hallway was another set of stairs. The elevator Emmett had been avoiding was in the middle. If he was going to make a dash for either, he would have to move fast.

He knocked one last time. The door inched open. Behind it was the forlorn face of Otis Fossum. Emmett had banked on him working nights and sleeping days, as he did when Emmett visited to try and persuade him to come flip through mug shots to see if he recognized Vernon Young's assailant. Fossum had refused him flat out. Emmett was counting on Otis not to refuse him again.

"Mr. Emmett," he said with a drowsy sigh. He was dressed in a cotton robe. A hole dotted the sleeve. "Knew I'd be seeing you sooner or later. I's just hopin' it'd be later."

"Are you going to invite me inside, Otis?"

Fossum heard the voices. They were getting closer. Emmett could feel them like wind on his neck.

"I'm thinkin' it might not be too good fo' me if'n I do. Might be worse fo' you if'n I don't." He let Emmett through and shut the door behind him as the teens crested the staircase.

Otis was thinner than when they first met. His robe hung from his shoulders the way it would from a hanger, the fabric rippling at gusts from an electric fan circulating the hot air. The heat was packed into the tiny apartment as tightly as the furnishings—a pair of armchairs, a sagging sofa, and a kitchen table with a visibly uneven leg that was propped with matchbooks. Tenants paid thirty dollars extra per month on top of their rent for junk furniture that the landlords wouldn't remove. If the renters got rid of anything, they were billed.

"I know my manners and I know I should ask you to sid' down, but part 'a me's wishin' you won't be stayin' long."

"I'm not here about Vernon."

"You're not?" That made Otis more leery.

"I need a favor."

Fossum chewed the inside of his cheek, ruminating. "You did me one, Mr. Emmett. S'pose I owe you for it."

Emmett wasn't insulted that Otis didn't refer to him as "Detective" or even "Officer." Coming from him, dropping the title was a sign of respect.

"I have a new case. It's a boy from here, from Hayes. His name is Ambrose Webster. Do you know him?"

"Project's a big place, and I work nights. Don't see many folks real regular."

Fossum led an inverse existence. He slept when the world was awake and worked while it slept, preferring the privacy that provided. His voice was gravelly from lack of use, his eyes unaccustomed to sunlight. Regular life didn't suit him. Emmett thought that was why Otis looked so much older than he was. Fighting nature had taken a toll.

"This boy, he was kil't?"

"He was, and it's important I speak with his family and get some information from them. They may not open the door for a policeman though, especially after what happened yesterday. I wanted to see if you would come with me."

"What's the catch?"

"There is no catch."

"I go with you and that's all?"

"That's all."

It was and it wasn't. Emmett never had to notify the next of kin before. Vernon Young had no living relatives outside of a sister, who Emmett had tracked to her last forwarding address in St. Louis. When he called, the phone had been disconnected. He sent a letter and received no word back. Ambrose Webster would be his first. Having Otis along wouldn't guarantee that the family would talk to Emmett, but at least it saved him from having to go alone.

"I quit that place, the dry cleaner's," Fossum told him. "Couldn't go there after what happened to Vernon. I work fo' a floor waxing company now. We go into the buildings at night when no one's 'round. The work's not hard and you can't mess up. Sometimes at the dry cleaner's I'd burn the collars on the shirts. I hated havin' to tell my boss. That's what's nice about this job. Don't have to give nobody no bad news."

Emmett was about to deliver the worst kind of bad news. In all the classes he took at the monastery and the academy, nobody had ever taught him the right way to tell somebody that their loved one was dead. There was no right way.

TEN

Otis Fossum didn't utter a single syllable until they reached Ambrose Webster's apartment. He was too nervous to talk.

"I ain't done nothing like this befo'."

Neither have I, Emmett thought. Saying as much would have sent Fossum running for home.

"What do I gotta do?"

"You knock and say you have a policeman with you, that he came to the wrong apartment and that he's looking for Ambrose Webster. You've got to act like nothing's wrong so they'll open the door. Understand?"

Otis nodded solemnly, collecting himself. He took a deep breath and knocked.

"Who is it?" a female voice demanded.

Fossum recited his line. "I live, uh, downstairs. This here policeman came to my door by mistake, asking 'bout Ambrose Webster. I told him he lived here."

His delivery was rocky, but it did the trick. The locks clanked and the door opened, three chains jangling between the jamb. An elderly black woman stared out at them. Only one eye, half her face, and a slice of her chest were visible between the door and the frame.

"Where is he? Where's Ambrose?" All of her toughness had sloughed off.

"I'm Detective Martin Emmett. Are you his mother, ma'am?"

"I'm his grandmother. What's happened?"

"Would it be all right if I came inside and spoke with you?"

She hesitated, then undid the chains.

"Thank you, sir. For your help," Emmett said to Otis, pretending they weren't acquainted.

"That be all, Officer?" Fossum was reluctant to leave.

"Yes. That'll be all."

Emmett had wanted Otis there for his own selfish reasons. Fossum had played his part. Emmett had to let him go. Mrs. Webster closed the door and relatched the chains.

The apartment was as small as Fossum's, though tidier. A framed picture of Jesus hung on the wall, staring benevolently down onto a sofa with a lace doily laid over the back. The plumbing from the floor above had leaked through the ceiling in a brown stain, ensconcing the empty light fixture in a dark halo. In its place, a bare bulb hung from an extension cord. Faulty wiring was rampant in the entire complex. Fuses blew continually. Every month the fire department was called out because of overloaded circuits, one of a multitude of daily hazards faced by the occupants of Hayes Home.

"Tell me your name again, Detective?" Mrs. Webster was clutching the neckline of her housedress as if she had been caught disrobed. Without the door between them, Emmett saw that her other eye was cast milky white by a cataract. She couldn't see out of it. Before he could repeat his name, her good eye meandered to the bag in his hands. She pursed her lips and her chin quivered. She knew.

Mrs. Webster went weak and faltered onto the sofa. She drew in a sharp, pained breath but wouldn't cry, not in front of him. Emmett couldn't tell if it was because he was a cop or a white man or a stranger or because he was all of those things.

"When?" she asked.

"Last night."

She was holding herself together so tightly that she began to shake.

"When Ambrose didn't come home, I thought he was with Freddie, that maybe he slept at his place. Freddie's his friend. He stuck by Ambrose when the kids would make fun, call him names. Ambrose is simple, you see," Mrs. Webster explained, confirming Emmett's suspicion. "His mama was a junkie. She was on the stuff when she had him. Doctor's said his brain didn't grow right because of it. She couldn't take care of him. So I did."

"Where's his mother now?"

"Downtown somewhere. South Broad or Washington."

South Broad and Washington streets were known prostitution drags. Mrs. Webster referred to them as though they were on another planet. She wouldn't admit whether Ambrose's mother was her daughter. Emmett assumed she was. Unwed mothers were banned from the projects, and if a child was born out of wedlock while a woman was a resident, she was subject to summary eviction. The irony was that public assistance was intended to be exclusively available to families where one parent, usually the father, was absent and the children depended on the mother for care. The system was as defective as Hayes Home's wiring.

"Did she visit Ambrose?"

"Not in months."

"What about his father?"

"Ambrose never knew his daddy. Neither did his mama for that matter. Made me grateful Ambrose was too slow to know better." Old anger flared, then faded as fast as it had come, overtaken by memory. "Ambrose was always big for his age, and he walked on his toes. He would wear out the tips of his shoes. Feet that size, it was a miracle to get sneakers that fit 'im. Sometimes I'd wonder if his daddy did that too, walked on his toes, or if it was on account of Ambrose being how he was. Kids would tease him for it and he'd take it. He wouldn't fight back. He didn't understand what they were doing. But Freddie wouldn't let anybody talk down to Ambrose. He was small, got picked on too. 'Cept when he and Ambrose was together, nobody'd say boo to 'em." Mrs. Webster smiled at that small triumph.

Emmett hated to take the smile from her. "When did you last see your grandson?"

"Yesterday morning when he was leaving for summer school. Teacher's told me Ambrose couldn't learn like normal kids. They kept him, though. He was quiet in class, no trouble to them. He could read some. Not much. Same as most kids these days. I thought if he got a diploma, he could get a job at a factory maybe. If you showed Ambrose how to do something, he could repeat it real well. He enjoyed going to school, being around people, watching and listening to them talk. Mostly, he wanted to be wherever Freddie was. When Ambrose didn't come home, I didn't think much of it. Freddie's mama don't got no phone. I couldn't call to check on him. I just figured Ambrose would come back once he got hungry for supper."

A stillness settled over Mrs. Webster. She had taken custody of her senses with such exquisiteness that she ceased to tremble. "How did he die?"

The impassive face of Jesus was gazing at Emmett from above the sofa, awaiting his answer along with Mrs. Webster.

"That's what I'm trying to find out."

If Emmett could spare Mrs. Webster the details of her grandson's death, he would. He hoped she wouldn't press for them. When she didn't, he realized she was sparing herself.

"Can you give me Freddie's address? I'd like to speak to him."

Emmett handed her his pad and pen, and she wrote out the information. He put his phone number on a separate sheet. "This is my home number, Mrs. Webster. You can call me whenever. Day or night. Okay?"

She took the paper. He doubted he would hear from her.

"These are some of Ambrose's things." Emmett held out the brown paper bag to her. The bloody clothes and shoes had been retained as evidence, leaving the movie pass, the house key, and some pocket change, a life distilled to so little. Mrs. Webster gazed at the bag, unable to touch it. Emmett set it on the sofa beside her.

"I'm half blind, Detective, but I see plenty. I know what Ambrose did and didn't do. He was no thief and no junkie. Whatever happened, believe me, he didn't bring it on his'self."

Emmett did believe her. That was what bothered him.

ELEVEN

Emmett found Otis Fossum pacing the lobby like an expectant father. He reminded Emmett of himself when his mother had her stroke. He and Edward had been stationed outside her hospital room, wearing down the linoleum in the hall, counting the minutes until the doctor came to tell them their mother was going to be okay, that she would make it. She wasn't and she didn't. Every hope and dream that Emmett had longed to fulfill for his mother soon died along with her. Neither he nor Edward cried when the doctor told them. Not for lack of sorrow, but for fear of it and the floodgates it might open. Edward had held off to see if Emmett would tear up, to see if it would be okay to cry. That was how it had been when they were younger, Edward always cautious, yielding to his lead. It was the first time in years his brother had done that and the last since then.

"I was waiting on ya, Mr. Emmett. To see if you needed anything else."

Kindness didn't come easy to Fossum, and he quickly became self-conscious.

"You didn't have to, Otis."

"That's why they call 'em favors, right?" Hundreds of mailboxes lined the empty lobby, as safe-deposit boxes would a bank vault, amplifying what Otis said and adding to his discomfort. "So what's next?" he in-quired in a softer voice.

Emmett would have liked to ask someone that himself. This was his second homicide investigation and he was making it up as he went along, treating the murder as he would a robbery because that was what he knew how to do. He had busted shoplifters in dime stores stuffing their pockets, worked with pawnbrokers to track burglars who made off with housewares and holiday silver, and caught kids fencing whole pal-ettes of uncut leather that had literally fallen off the back of a truck. Emmett was an expert at hunting down thieves, not killers. To compen-sate, he imagined Ambrose Webster as stolen property—a boy stolen from his grandmother, from his friend, from life—and Emmett had to find the thief. Only this thief was more dangerous than any Emmett had ever encountered, and he was still out there.

"What's next?" Emmett echoed Fossum, stalling. "I have to inter-view a kid named Freddie." He read what Mrs. Webster had written. "Freddie Guthrie. He was a friend of the deceased."

"Want me to come with you? I can."

It was Fossum who wanted to come, and Emmett couldn't de-code why.

"This is police business, Otis. And more to the point, it's against department policy for me to bring you."

"You listening to yo'self, Mr. Emmett? You brought me here. Wasn't that against the rules?"

Emmett felt as though he was the only one giving the rules a second thought. Lieutenant Ahern should have assigned him a partner. Out of spite, he hadn't. Now Emmett was on his own, and that definitely went against department policy.

"It's not smart for you to be seen with me, Otis."

Ahern was itching for Fossum's name and could have put others on the lookout. Foot patrolmen avoided Hayes as much as possible, so he and Otis were safe in the projects. The streets were a different story.

Once an hour, officers on foot patrol had to make a pull at one of the call boxes spread five to ten blocks apart throughout the city. With-out walkie-talkies, that was how the brass kept tabs. Patrolmen had to make their pulls by the appointed time or a car was sent to search for them. Two pulls in a row was the signal for help. As soon as a pull was placed, the routine was to hang around the call box for a few minutes in case the precinct had additional assignments or information to relay. There was a box on Bergen Street. They would have to pass it to get to Freddie Guthrie's house.

"I can follow you," Fossum said.

"Then you're either very stubborn or very stupid."

"Or both."

"Suit yourself."

"Where we headed?"

"Rose Street."

Otis grinned smugly. "Good. My legs could stand a stretch."

They were midway through the Hayes complex, moving in and out of the vast shadows cast by the tenements, when the group of teenage boys who had been playing handball began trailing them. Emmett noticed first. When Otis caught on, he panicked and picked up his pace.

"Hey," one of the boys shouted.

"Keep walking," Emmett whispered to Fossum.

"I'm talkin' to you," the same kid yelled.

"We keep walkin' and they keep followin'."

The group was closing in fast. This was exactly what Emmett had been trying to avoid. They would have to stop and face them.

Emmett gave Fossum strict orders. "Don't say anything, don't do anything, and don't run."

"Ain't that what Marlin Perkins on *Mutual of Omaha's Wild Kingdom* always says?"

"This isn't the zoo, Otis."

"'At's for damn sure. If'n it was, there'd be a fence between us and them."

Emmett slowed and turned, putting himself a pace in front of Fossum to partially block him. He didn't say a word, just looked at each of the boys one at a time.

"What chu starin' at? Huh, honky?"

The kid doing the talking was bouncing a rubber handball against the concrete. Five others filed up alongside him, each of them seventeen or eighteen years old, about Ambrose Webster's age. They were shorter than Emmett, though two had the benefit of growth spurts that had replaced skinny limbs with serious muscle.

"He asked you a question," one said.

"Yeah, he asked you a question," another repeated.

None had the nerve to invent their own insult. Emmett remained silent, eyes latched on the kid bouncing the ball. He was lithe, all leg, and could have gotten in Emmett's face in a single stride.

"You deaf?" the kid with the ball sneered.

Emmett wouldn't answer. In his peripheral vision, he could see Fossum creeping farther behind him.

"I said, are you deaf?"

The kid stopped bouncing the handball and folded his arms as a final warning. Emmett thought this was their form of practice, roving in packs and learning to intimidate whomever they could. Ambrose Webster would have made an easy mark for bullies like these. They had mastered how to strut and swagger but hadn't graduated to violence—yet.

"Ain't this rude, not speakin' when you spoken to. Somebody needs to teach this cracker a lesson," the kid with the ball said. He shifted his weight, preparing to take a step over the invisible line he and his friends were poised upon. The others muttered in agreement, psyching themselves up for action.

Beneath Emmett's jacket, on his right hip, hung his badge. Above his left was his gun holster. Emmett had to choose.

"I'm not deaf," he told them. Then he opened the left side of his jacket, revealing the Smith & Wesson strapped to his shoulder. "There's nothing to hear when you're listening to a bunch of punks full of hot air. Now get out of here."

The line of teenagers wavered, waiting for the kid with the handball to respond. He didn't, a tacit surrender. Emmett ushered Otis on ahead, and they started to walk away. Fossum was obviously fighting the urge to look back.

"Don't," Emmett instructed.

"What if they sneakin' up behind us?"

"They aren't."

"Then what harm'd it do if I looked?"

"They would see that you're scared."

"I am scared."

"There's nothing wrong with being scared. It's acting scared that gets you in trouble."

"That's how Vernon died," Otis grumbled. "Putting his back to them men."

Emmett came to a dead halt. "Those men would have killed him whether he ran or stared them straight in the eye, and that's the truth."

Fossum's expression hardened with clarity. "You know who it was, don't you, Mr. Emmett? And you can't do nothin' about it."

Frustration was a stopper in Emmett's throat. He was positive Sal Lucaro had killed Vernon Young. Giancone wouldn't have run the risk of shooting Vernon. Lucaro wouldn't have run the risk of letting him live. Young's murder weighed heavily on Emmett's conscience, and he was desperate for another crack at Lucaro. Only he wasn't sure how to get it.

Neither he nor Fossum exchanged another word until they were safely out of the Hayes complex and had reached Bergen Street. People filled the sidewalks, going through the motions of their day mired in the heat. The air was laden with the odor of melting tar from the asphalt. Emmett was on watch for foot patrolmen and radio cars when he realized that Otis had fallen a few steps behind.

"What is it?"

"I was just thinkin'. Why didn't you show them kids your badge?"

"Because we wouldn't have walked away without a fight."

Disheartened, Fossum said, "That's what I figured."

Emmett's badge meant different things to different people. To some, it earned him automatic respect. To others, it made him the enemy. He wasn't sure what it meant to him anymore.

"I told you, Otis. You don't have to come. This isn't your job. It's mine."

"Some job." A truck rolled by, the squeal of its loose axle acting as an exclamation point to his comment. Fossum lingered on the curb where they would cross from Bergen Street onto Rose. "I remember what you said to me, Mr. Emmett, about you deciding not to be a priest. That's why I trusted you. You wanted me to look at them pictures, see if I saw the men who shot Vernon. I'm sorry I didn't."

Emmett had misread Otis's intentions. By accompanying him, Fossum was attempting to work off his mistake in what small manner he could. Emmett knew the feeling.

"It's all right, Otis. I understood why you did it."

"Thanks. For saying so."

The road was clear, no traffic in either direction. Otis kept checking anyhow, as if a car might appear out of nowhere. Finally, he stepped off the curb.

"I know this ain't my job, Mr. Emmett. I'm comin' anyway."

TWELVE

Rose Street wasn't that different from any other street in the Central Ward except for the fact that it bracketed one side of Woodland Cemetery. The graveyard was the largest span of grass in the entire the neighborhood. People treated it more like a park, disregarding its true function. Come nightfall, dealers sold dope behind headstones and junkies shot up among the dead.

The houses on Rose were mainly four-floor walk-ups. They leaned against one another as a row of drunken sailors would, listing at the slightest breeze. The porches were over ten feet off the ground, the incline a test of fortitude. If you could handle the climb, you might have the stamina to live there.

According to Mrs. Webster, Freddie Guthrie shared an apartment with his mother on the top floor of a tenement in the middle of the second block. The dilapidated building distinguished itself from the others with a BEWARE OF DOG sign hanging from a rusty nail out front.

"Terrific. More animals," Otis said. He eyed the rickety steps. "Don't ask. I'm still comin'."

Inside, they were greeted by the musk of cooking grease and an entry hall full of uncollected mail.

"What do I do this time, Mr. Emmett?"

As if in response, a shower of plaster dust rained down on them from the ceiling, syncopated with footfalls from the floor above.

"I hadn't made up my mind." Emmett brushed the grit from his suit.

Otis patted his shirt and coughed. "Don't much care as long as I don't have to stand here getting dirty."

He trudged up the stairs behind Emmett to the fourth floor. An argument was throbbing behind the door marked EIGHT. It was the Guthrie residence.

"This it?"

"Unfortunately."

"Made up your mind yet?"

"Yeah. I'll do the talking. You keep quiet."

"I won't move or run neither. Just in case."

When Emmett knocked, the door flew open as if spring-loaded. A runty black man dressed in nothing but boxer shorts stood at the threshold, ready to rip into whoever had the gall to darken his door. Emmett was holding his badge at eye level. It was the first thing the man in his underwear saw.

"I'm looking for Freddie Guthrie. Is he here?"

"No," the man grunted. His skin was covered in an angry sheen of sweat, his fists balled.

"Are you Mr. Guthrie?"

"Hell no."

"Who is it, Cyril?" asked a woozy female voice.

"Shut the hell up, Lossie," Cyril shouted back. "It's the police. They here for that damn boy 'a yours."

Emmett stepped into the doorway, crowding the man and forcing him inside the apartment. Otis followed. He floated behind Emmett as his shadow. "This joint could make you seasick," he mumbled.

All of the windows and walls were tilted, and the floors pitched unevenly. The building's foundation had gone soft on the right side. Someday soon, the structure would collapse. Emmett said a prayer that "someday" wasn't that day.

"Who's this?" Cyril demanded, getting in Fossum's face. "Where's your badge, nigga?"

A cautionary glance from Emmett silenced him, though he continued to hover close to Otis, straining like a dog at the end of its tether. Across the room, a woman was lying on a love seat, legs swung across the armrest, eyelids drooping. Cigarette burns stippled the seat cushions. The argument Emmett had heard through the door must have been one-sided. The woman was too strung out to stay awake.

"Are you Freddie Guthrie's mother, ma'am?"

"Who wants to know?" she singsonged, a bottle of beer held loosely in her hand.

"Act right, Lossie. I told you, this is the cops."

"I have to speak to your son, Mrs. Guthrie."

She hummed to herself and was on the verge of dozing off when Cyril slapped her shin. "Wake up. Tell him what he needs so he can leave."

Lossie Guthrie was thin, her eyes sunken and hollow. The silhouette of her ribs pressed through her chest. She had slept in her clothes. "Come again, Officer?" she said.

"Your son, Freddie. Can you tell me where he is?"

"You should know."

Emmett didn't understand.

"Don't you cops know everything?" She said that as though the answer was a given. "He's in jail. Got picked up yesterday. He had one phone call. And he called me, his mama," Lossie boasted, then the beer bottle slipped from her grasp and spilled everywhere. She watched the beer seep across the floor, puzzled. Cyril was about to boil over. He hadn't thought to get dressed.

"Did you post his bail, ma'am?"

"Not on your life," Cyril growled.

"Didn't have the money," Otis said under his breath.

That snapped the tether. Cyril lunged at him and grabbed Fossum by the collar. Plaster dust puffed from his shirt. As Cyril cocked his right hand, Emmett kicked him in the back of the knee, dropping him to the floor in a heap. Pain made Cyril curl into a ball. The spilled beer soaked into his boxers.

Emmett hustled Fossum toward the door. "What happened to you keeping quiet?"

"I got the not runnin' part right."

"You're going home now, Otis. And don't argue with me."

"Wouldn't dream of it, Mr. Emmett."

This time, Fossum wasn't tempted to glance over his shoulder. Emmett was, though. He stole a final look at Lossie Guthrie. Contrary to what she believed, the police didn't know everything, not even close. Ambrose Webster had been dead for less than a day and Emmett had no clues, no witnesses, and no leads, and the only person who might have an idea of Webster's whereabouts was in jail.

Lossie was humming a lullaby and watching Cyril writhe. Emmett couldn't tell if the lullaby was for him or for herself. He was positive it wasn't for her son, Freddie.

THIRTEEN

The Fourth Precinct could have passed for a condemned building. With plywood boards covering the ground-floor windows, burn marks on the brick, and last night's spent ammunition of trash and broken bottles strewn across the sidewalks, the only sign that it was an operating police station were the cops out front.

Patrolmen stood watch at the entrance, more for effect than any real function. They milled around the steps, smoking, talking, and baking under the vicious sun, their faces and forearms burnt red. A television crew had staked a plot directly across from the precinct, and the cameraman was killing time, tinkering with a tripod while a reporter in a wrinkled summer-weight suit was testing out the best angles. The crew had been on the block for so long that they ceased to interest passersby. Although the protest rally was hours away, the sense that something big was about to take place had diminished, the previous night's uproar a fading thought.

Emmett hadn't intended to return to the station that day, however he needed to get the scoop on Freddie Guthrie's charges, and something was tapping at his conscience, begging to be remembered, a detail from a case that had recently come through the Records Room. He bypassed the front door and its fence of patrolmen and used his key to the rear.

The light he usually left on in the Records Room was off, which immediately put him on guard. Somebody had been there. Emmett lurched through the pitch-black basement, brushing against shelves that appeared in his path like phantoms. The darkness was disarming. Blind, he groped the walls for the light switch, then the fluorescent bulbs buzzed to life, stinging his eyes until they could adjust.

Three new cases were stacked on his desk, ready to be filed. Whoever had delivered them might have shut off the lights, force of habit when exiting a room. Nevertheless, Emmett checked the desk to see if anything had been disturbed. The drawers didn't appear to have been rifled through. He wrote off the lights to happenstance, hung his jacket, rolled up his sleeves, and started in on the top shelf where he had filed the most recent cases.

The folder Emmett was hunting for was one of the first he had read after his demotion. It had been sent down from Homicide, unsolved. What had welded it into his memory was the fact that the investigating officers were Detectives Larry Hochwald and Nic Serletto, the guy who baited him. Petty as it was, Emmett got a certain satisfaction from the seasoned detectives' inability to close the case. Their failure put him on equal footing with them, though Serletto and Hochwald weren't men Emmett would ever consider equals.

He ceased to feel quite so superior once he had read the report. The details were grim, and guilt over his gloating had Emmett wishing for the culpa beads he wore inside his cassock as a novice. Twice daily at the seminary, before lunch and in the evening, Emmett would stand beside his desk, bend and kiss the floor, then for fifteen minutes he had to recollect his actions and examine his conscience. He and his novitiate cohorts were given tiny notebooks in which to catalog the number and types of transgressions they made, and they were provided a string of culpa beads to be hung vertically on a safety pin by the heart. If a novice indulged in a particular vice, they were to reach into the cassock and move a bead from the top down, tallying their moral conduct. Emmett's culpa beads were gone, yet he continued to keep a mental count.

Although he had filed Serletto and Hochwald's case himself, Emmett couldn't recall the victim's name. He had to skim through dozens of others to find it. Most were fraught with unintelligible scrawl or words slanting across the page because someone had fed the paper into the typewriter crookedly. Typing class was compulsory at the academy, but the two-finger method prevailed, and the sound of men pecking at the station's typewriters could be heard at any hour of the day. The staccato metal clicking of keys, interspersed with the odd swear, had become the precinct's de facto background music. Sometimes it sifted to the basement through the vents. Not that day.

A pile was growing at Emmett's ankles. Displaced folders began sliding across the shelf, pushing the next right into his hands. He instantly recognized the name on the tab: Julius Dekes.

Clipped to the top sheet of the report was a school photo of a black teenage boy in a striped shirt, his hair grown into an Afro. He was smiling, showcasing the wide gap between his two front teeth. His shoulders were so broad there wasn't enough room for them in the camera frame.

Whoever had been in charge of managing the file—be it Serletto or Hochwald—hadn't typed their portion of the report. It was practically illegible. Deciphering it would take effort. Luckily, the coroner had better handwriting.

Sixteen-year-old Julius Dekes was discovered in an overgrown empty lot on Sayre Street by a vagrant scrounging for something to pawn. The boy's body was badly decomposed and showing signs of predation. The autopsy attributed numerous injuries on the teen's arms and legs to rats. It also blamed them for Dekes's missing ring finger. When he first read that, Emmett had trouble believing a rat would gnaw off an entire digit and ignore the rest. That was the detail that had been thumping in his mind since Dr. Ufland told him about Webster's severed finger.

Emmett paged ahead to the line diagram of the human body that was included in every autopsy. On Julius Dekes's, the ring finger on his left hand had been scribbled out with a pen to indicate that it was gone. Seeing that in black and white gave Emmett a disorienting jolt, similar to when the fluorescent lights had snapped on. He didn't believe in coincidences. Coincidences weren't logical, and this coincidence was more than just illogical—it was disturbing. Emmett read on.

Numerous other slashes and circles dotted the human diagram, displaying a broken wrist, sizable abrasions, and untold rat bites. Cause of death was listed as loss of blood from a stab wound to the liver. The location was marked on the lower abdomen with an X like a treasure map. The weapon was listed as a large knife. Dekes's height and weight put him over six feet and two hundred pounds, not as large as Ambrose Webster, but close, too close to be coincidence.

The signature on the coroner's report was that of Dr. Conrad Aberbrook. Emmett had only met the old man once, standing across a surgical table from him with Vernon Young's body between them. Aberbrook had retired shortly after that, meaning Julius Dekes's was one of the final autopsies he performed. The procedure might be fresher in the doctor's mind or muddled in the haste to ditch the daily grind for the blue skies and golden beaches of Florida. The odds of Aberbrook recollecting Dekes's autopsy with any clarity were an even split.

Emmett could get a hold of Aberbrook by telephone if need be. What he would have preferred was to review the case notes. Hitting up Serletto and Hochwald for them promised to be an exercise in futility. Cops guarded their cases as their own private domains. Those two would have made Emmett grovel for the notes and never relinquished them. They would demand to know why he was interested in Dekes and would undoubtedly tell Lieutenant Ahern. Emmett couldn't allow that. It was too soon. There wasn't sufficient evidence to link Ambrose Webster's death to Julius Dekes's. Their deaths were similar—a missing finger, their age, build, and race. Emmett couldn't go to the lieutenant with mere similarities, not if he wanted to hold on to the case. The second Ahern sniffed a connection between the murders, he would yank them from Emmett and toss them to Serletto and Hochwald. Emmett couldn't allow that either.

Logic told him the cases were connected. The idea appalled and intrigued him, like a riddle he wasn't certain he wanted the answer to. Earlier that year, the media had been abuzz about the conviction of Henry De Salvo as the Boston Strangler, murderer of thirteen women from 1962 to 1964, and that April, Richard Speck had been sentenced to life in prison for killing eight nurses in Chicago. Those were big city investigations that had terrified the nation, multiple premeditated murders that hinted at a unique, new breed of killer. But Speck and De Salvo targeted women, catching them when they were unaware and helpless. Ambrose Webster and Julius Dekes were anything but helpless. That didn't weaken Emmett's logic, however it didn't provide him with any leads.

In Robbery Division, Emmett had come across repeat offenders, burglars who stole for a living. Tracking them was often harder than finding the kid who broke into his neighbor's apartment or the woman who swiped bottles of perfume off store counters. The pros worked at random, and Emmett would be forced to wait until they struck again to pick up their trails. He didn't want to wait for whoever murdered Ambrose Webster and Julius Dekes to kill again, so he would have to work backward, piecing together what he could from the file he had, which was relatively thin, just the necessary paperwork, along with the crime scene photographs. In the pictures, Dekes's body lay among trash and thriving weeds, a miserable end to an all too brief existence. Emmett couldn't permit the sadness of it all to sink in or it would derail him and his logic. He removed the report and stored the empty folder in his desk drawer with the other files that had been delivered so it would seem as if he shelved them, then he rolled the documents regarding Julius Dekes's murder into his inner breast pocket where his culpa beads would have been.

Ideally, Emmett would have taken his time to read the report thoroughly, but finding Freddie Guthrie took precedence. The desk sergeant would have the details of Guthrie's arrest on the police blotter. A trip upstairs, beyond the seclusion of the basement, carried the risk of a run-in with Ahern, albeit remote. The lieutenant rarely deigned to come down from his office unless it was for his lunch break, when he would make a beeline for a cop bar on Belmont Avenue to have a gin and tonic and a sandwich, or when he cut out early to go to the house on Gold Street that had been set up as a gentlemen's club for off-duty brass, no patrolmen allowed. Liquor and gambling as well as white and black prostitutes were available noon and night. Rumor had it that Ahern would play poker until the wee hours of the morning, and he was a notoriously bad loser, at cards and everything else. It was Emmett who was about to take the biggest gamble. He had two murders now. He had to chance it.

The precinct's front desk stood five feet high, a promontory of shellacked wood that was the focal point of the main hall. Presiding from atop it was the desk sergeant. A cigarette poked from the corner of his mouth. The threads of rising smoke caused him to squint his left eye. With his right, he perused that day's newspaper.

He acknowledged Emmett by way of a question. "You read this article about last night?" he asked in his distinctively husky voice. "Says, 'Hundreds of teenagers began forming roaming bands. The youths were rampaging in the blocks surrounding the police station.' 'Roaming' and 'rampaging.' Sounds like a movie, like *Spartacus* or somethin', doesn't it? Wonder who they'd get to play me if it was. Humphrey Bogart'd be good."

"Humphrey Bogart's dead," Emmett told him.

"I'm just sayin' he'd be good. So what can I do for you, Detective?"

"I'm looking for a kid who was booked last night. Name's Freddie Guthrie. Can you tell me why he was brought in?"

The sergeant set his cigarette in a full ashtray, dragged over the blotter, and turned the page to the previous day's arrests. "Says here, 'Loitering.'"

"Loitering? When was the last time someone was booked for loitering?"

A shrug was the sergeant's best guess. "I'm supposta keep track 'a that?"

"Who arrested him?"

"Ionello and Vass. They're in Auto."

"And they made a collar for loitering?"

"Like I said, I don't keep track. What I can tell you is that this Guthrie fella ain't at Central. He's at Newark Street."

"What? Why?"

The Central Cellblock was a way station for defendants due in court, ten cells for men and six for women, no lights, no toilet seats, and no mattresses, only concrete shelves that served as a bed or a bench. Few people spent longer than a night in Central, and it was designed so that one night would discourage a repeat visit. Compared to Newark Street, which housed four hundred male prisoners, most en route to state penitentiaries, the Central Cellblock was a deluxe hotel. Freddie Guthrie was a minor and shouldn't have been detained at either facility. His being transferred to Newark Street didn't bode well.

"Why was he sent there?"

"I couldn't say." The desk sergeant knew more than he was letting on.

"Have you ever heard of that happening or don't you keep track?"

"Other people's business. Not mine. You don't see me asking you why you're interested in this guy Guthrie, do ya?"

That was a warning, a shot fired across the bow. The desk sergeant plugged his cigarette back into his mouth and resumed reading his newspaper. His position made him privy to the inner workings of the precinct, like a view inside a clock at the moving parts, however, seeing too much could get a man, even a cop, in trouble. Staying out of other people's business was sound advice, advice Emmett might be sorry he didn't take.

FOURTEEN

The name "Newark Street" was department slang for the Essex County Jail, a boxy building that had the look of a lead safe. At the front of the prison compound was a small, stately house that acted as the entry gate. It was the city's original jail and had been erected in 1837, a year after Newark incorporated, confirmation that crime was a motivating concern from the earliest days. The house's brownstone facade and gracious front door gave off an air of affluence and civility, but in the jail beyond, the occupants weren't affluent, and nothing about the place was civil.

A mesh cage encased the receiving desk. The heavyset prison guard sitting inside had an electric fan positioned a foot from his face. His uniform pulled across the chest, puckering at the buttons with every breath he took. "Visiting hours is on Monday and Wednesday," he said flatly.

Emmett proffered his badge. "I'm here to see Freddie Guthrie."

"That kid must be a star. You're his third visitor today." The guard retrieved the visitor's log from a drawer, exasperated at having to move out of the direct path of the fan for even a second. "Sign in please." Saying "please" was as close to polite as he would venture.

The last signatures in the log were those of Detectives Ionello and Vass. They had been there an hour ago. Emmett couldn't ask for details. The guard might get suspicious.

"I missed the fan club. I was running late. Couldn't tag along with my buddies. They told you to keep this quiet, right?"

"I figured it wasn't a friggin' conjugal visit. What do I care about some stool pigeon who hot-wired a car or whatever. Let him rot. I'd put him on the third tier with the nut jobs if it was up to me, 'cept your pals said to segregate him 'cause of his age. Said to watch his hands too. He's a pickpocket, got fast fingers. Came in packing a water pistol, if you can believe it. Pretty dangerous character, huh?"

Emmett had been hoping for more from the guard. Ionello and Vass must not have shared much because whatever Freddie Guthrie was into involved them too. They had pulled strings to get him locked up in Newark Street. If their aim was to frighten Freddie that badly, they must have been frightened of him.

"Kid's on the first tier. I'll have somebody take you. Mind yourself, Detective. Most of the inmates know they'll get hosed if they throw piss at 'cha, but they'll spit if they think they'll get away with it."

"I'll keep that in mind."

Another guard came to escort Emmett from the reception area through a set of iron sliding doors into the jail. The pungent odor of four hundred sweaty men was a slap to the senses. A cacophony of shouting, talking, and off-key singing crowded Emmett's ears. The cells were stacked three stories high, connected by narrow gangways and surrounded by warehouse-size windows embedded with chicken wire. Sunlight struggled to penetrate the dingy glass.

"Best stick close," warned the guard. "If they try an' touch you, lemme handle it, okay?" He was skinny, his shoulders stooped, the opposite of intimidating.

"Okay," Emmett said.

The guard led him up a metal staircase. Paint was molting off the railings and walls in scabby flakes. Since the gangway wouldn't accommodate two astride, Emmett held a tight pace behind him. The noise level dropped at the sound of their footsteps. The men in the cells were waiting to see who would go by. Some lay on their bunks while others were right at the bars, arms hanging through. Many pulled their hands inside as the guard approached. One, however, timed it so he could snag Emmett's sleeve. Emmett kept walking, yet the prisoner held on, reeling him backward. The instant the guard noticed, he spun on his heel and smashed his baton across the prisoner's outstretched wrist. The man recoiled with a yelp.

"See," the guard said, holstering the baton. "They're sneaky."

Afterward, the prisoners pushed to the rear of their cells when Emmett and the guard passed.

"Your guy's on the end. Can't let you inside with him, but I'll give you some privacy. Wave when you're done." The guard ambled to the other end of the gangway, lightly strumming his baton as he went.

In the last cell on the tier sat a black boy. He was perched on the bottom bunk, his feet hanging over the edge of the bed, too short to reach the ground. He could have passed for twelve. The collar of his T-shirt was torn. Somebody had grabbed him and pulled too hard to make a point. Emmett could guess who.

"Freddie Guthrie?"

"Who's askin'?"

"Are you all right?"

"What's it to you?" Freddie fired back. His sarcasm and perfected scowl confirmed him to be a teenager. He had the come-out-swinging attitude of a kid who had been picked on because of his size, just as Mrs. Webster described.

"You a cop. I can smell your kind comin' a mile away."

"If that were true, you wouldn't be in jail, would you?"

"Whatever, man."

"Look, I'm not with those other detectives who arrested you, Freddie."

"You all the same to me."

"I'm here about your friend, Ambrose Webster."

Freddie's eyes flashed, a moment of weakness, then his defenses rearmed. "What about him?"

"When was the last time you saw Ambrose?"

"Dunno."

"Was it last night?"

"Can't remember."

"Yesterday afternoon?"

"Not sure."

"That morning?"

"Maybe. My memory's real fuzzy," he said dryly, covering for Ambrose in case he was in trouble. "I ain't talking to you, cop. So beat it."

"He's dead, Freddie. Ambrose is dead."

Confusion softened Freddie's face. He finally looked his age. "Nut-uh. This is some kinda trick. You lyin' to get me to say stuff."

"I'm not lying. And I'm not here about stolen cars. My name's Martin Emmett. I'm a Homicide detective. I need you to tell me where Ambrose was from yesterday morning on."

The reality of his friend's death descended on Freddie as a hammer would an anvil, stunning him into a daze. He pushed himself in the corner of the cell farthest from Emmett and began to cry.

Emmett was at a loss. He had been unable to bestow any comfort on his own brother that day outside their mother's hospital room, and he had nothing to offer the boy before him now. Emmett didn't know how to console Freddie or his brother or even himself. That was one of his reasons for abandoning the priesthood, and it was why he stayed in Robbery and never sought out a slot in Homicide. People rarely shed tears over stolen property. Their possessions were inanimate, usually replaceable. Murder was all about the irreplaceable.

"Tell me how," Freddie said, regaining his composure. Emmett hesitated, but the kid was persistent, playing brave. "Tell me."

"His throat was cut. His body was found in the Warren Street subway tunnel this morning."

The facts dissolved Freddie's courage. He wiped new tears

from his cheeks. "'Brose wasn't smart like regular folks. I had to protect him. He woulda protected me too, if he knew how." Freddie had succumbed to the sadness. He sounded grown up beyond his years.

"You can help him, Freddie, by helping me."

"No, I can't, Mister. I can't help nobody. Your cop friends, they said that when I get back from court I won't be in this cell alone, not no more."

Freddie was smart enough to comprehend the implication. By rights, he should have been in Juvenile Hall, not jail. Emmett couldn't get him transferred without tipping his hand, but the kid wouldn't stand a chance fending off another prisoner.

"You're what? Sixteen? What could you have done that has two police detectives breathing down your neck?"

All the fight had washed out of Freddie. Resigned, he told his story as if he was giving away his own ransom. "I was ditchin' summer school, hanging around this junkyard on South Orange Avenue. I'd bring 'Brose with me sometimes. Show him the cars. He liked that. Some'd be smashed up, missing windshields and wheels and crap. But some still had good parts, so I took 'em and sold 'em to this guy who's got a body shop on Springfield."

The location rang an alarm to Emmett. "This guy wouldn't happen to be Luther Reed, would it?"

Freddie nodded regretfully that it was. "You know him?"

Every cop at the Fourth Precinct did. Luther Reed was to the Central Ward what Ruggiero Caligrassi was to the Mafia's crime syndicate. Reed ran his entire operation out of a body shop in the heart of the ward, however, he didn't deal in hubcaps and dented fenders. He was the first to bring raw heroin in from New York City. Once he got it to Newark, he would cut it with quinine and sell it in glassine packets called "decks" for five dollars a pop. Reed was careful to steer clear of the mob's numbers traffic and pimped solely black prostitutes. There was no love lost between his crew and Caligrassi's, but they got along by sidestepping each other's turf.

"Freddie, Luther Reed would knock your teeth out as soon as talk to you. Why on earth would you go to him?"

"The parts were stolen. I couldn't sell 'em to just anybody. Luther started giving me lists. I'd bring him what he asked for, and he'd pay me. After a while, I got this idea about switchin' the deeds from the wrecked cars for ones he boosted. Luther told me where all the identification numbers were on the locks and chassis, and I'd file them off. He'd buy the junkers, get the pink slips, and sell 'em so the stolen cars looked legit, then we'd split the money."

"Luther Reed gave you half?" Emmett didn't believe that for a second.

"Didn't say it was a fifty-fifty split. More like a hundred bucks for every car."

"That's far from half. But it's a hell of a lot of money and a pretty impressive scam. I bet Luther loved it."

"Your cop pals did too. The day they came to the body shop to shake Luther down I was in the garage sanding a serial number off the door to a Plymouth. They dragged me out. Luther said I was nobody, that I swept up the place, and they was gonna let me go, but. . . ." Embarrassment sapped Freddie's momentum.

"But?"

"Those cops were saying how smart Luther was to think up the scheme with the cars, givin' him compliments. I spoke up, said it was my idea. I wasn't gonna let him take the credit. Not for my idea." As clever as Freddie was, he was only a kid. His mistake had adult consequences.

"The cops said me and Luther'd go to jail if we didn't give them some of the money we was making. Every two weeks, the one named Vass would come and collect, act nice, talk about which model cars we was pickin', how we did it. That made me get another idea. I took my mama's boyfriend's tape recorder and put it under a car in the body shop. When that guy came back, makin' like he was our friend, I hit record."

Suddenly Emmett understood why Freddie was incarcerated. "You told the detectives you had them on tape."

"You bet your ass I did. I said I was gonna get them fired. I thought that'd make them leave me and Luther alone."

"Cops can't get fired, Freddie. It's more complicated than that. The detectives would have to be brought up on formal charges, and there would have to be a hearing to determine if they should be relieved of duty."

"Hold up. You're saying that if a waitress spits in your food, she gets canned, but a cop is allowed to do all kinda bad stuff and he won't lose his job?"

"To put a fine point on it, yes. Except the tape you recorded could be used as evidence at trial."

"Then I got 'um, right?"

Emmett gestured to the cell bars. "No, they've got you."

"Man, I wasn't doin' nothing. I was mindin' my business, walkin' out my house, and they roll up in a cop car, tell me I'm loitering, and throw me in the backseat. They took me to the station, then to court, and when the judge guy asked me if I was guilty, I said, 'Hell no.' I been here since."

"They want the tape."

"Well, they ain't getting' it. It's hidden. Somewhere safe."

"Tell me you didn't give it to Luther."

"I said it was somewhere safe. I mighta run my mouth, but I ain't that stupid."

"Listen to me, Freddie. You and I can make a deal. An even split. Fifty-fifty. You help me. I help you."

"You mean I help you, I help Ambrose."

"Exactly. Now tell me where he was yesterday morning."

"No way. Not until you get me outta here."

"You don't understand. I won't be able to protect you until you've been released."

"Then get me released."

"If you haven't noticed, you're in jail. I can't just open the door and let you go."

"Yes, you can. You're the police. You can do anything."

To Freddie, that must have seemed true. Ionello and Vass had unfairly locked him up for a bogus arrest, a flagrant abuse of power. In his eyes, the police could do anything, right or wrong, and they could get away with it.

"Your mother can't cover your bail?"

"It's not that she can't. Her boyfriend won't let her 'cause he's mad at me for takin' his tape player."

"I met him. He's a real charmer."

"If that's cop lingo for he's an asshole, then yeah, he's a real charmer. He beats on her, and me, and I'm the one who goes in front of a judge."

The comment tripped a wire in Emmett's memory. "When you went before the magistrate, that was your preliminary hearing. You should have another court date set. Did anybody tell you when?"

"Nope." Freddie shook his head as though it was a lost cause.

"I think I know how I can get you out of here. Don't talk to anyone. Not the prisoners or the guards. Not until you see me again."

"When'll that be?"

Emmett glanced at his watch. "In the courtroom in an hour."

Freddie mimed zipping his mouth shut, and Emmett saw the child in him, a child alone in a men's prison. Emmett signaled for the guard. Arms darted inside the cells domino-style as they went back down to reception.

"When is Guthrie's hearing scheduled?"

The guard in the mesh cage was rocking in his chair, tottering on its hind legs. "I'd have to check."

"Do that."

The chair legs fell to the floor with a thud, giving voice to the guard's aggravation. He grudgingly flicked through the pages of a clipboard. "Little prick's on the list for today's two-o'clock bus. But your buddies told me to lose the paperwork and put him on tomorrow's bus instead."

"Change of plans. I need Guthrie in court this afternoon."

"Suit yourself. I was just tryin' to give you guys a hand." He scratched out the correction on the clipboard. "You're damned if you do and damned if you don't," the guard grumbled.

That was precisely what Emmett was thinking. He had twenty-four hours until Ionello and Vass would come looking for Freddie and for him.

FIFTEEN

In Newark, justice had a face and a name—it was Abraham Lincoln. A bronze statue of the former president was mounted outside the county courthouse, seated on a bench in an informal pose, like an innocent man awaiting an innocent verdict. Few who would pass him on their way up the cascade of limestone steps and through the chamfered columns into court wore expressions as placid or confident as Lincoln's, including Emmett.

The pomp of the post and lintel stonework on the courthouse facade faded as soon as he stepped inside. The building's interior had the ambiance of a run-down music hall. Mold had enveloped the hand-painted wall murals, and grime blotted the color from the trio of Louis Comfort Tiffany stained-glass ceiling domes, the consequence of years of delayed and shoddy repairs as well as neglect. Plasterwork rotted by rain damage blistered the walls while naked cords for electrical wiring snaked along carved moldings and over swooping archways, nesting in the decorative filigree. The sixty-year-old courthouse, which served as the model for the U.S. Supreme Court in Washington, had resoundingly lost its trial against the ages.

Misdemeanors and disorderly conduct cases, such as Freddie's trumped-up charge for loitering, fell under Part I of the municipal court system, and those hearings were held on the second floor. Court was in session when Emmett arrived. A handful of family members were in attendance. Otherwise, the benches were empty. Freddie and a string of defendants were biding time on the front row until it was their turn. Freddie was a head shorter than the rest, all of whom were black but two. There were no lawyers, only the magistrate and the court clerk, and they were whipping through the proceedings at a breakneck speed, clocking five minutes per case. In assembly-line fashion, one man after another rose to listen to the clerk read the charges against him.

Emmett slid in behind Freddie and put a hand on his shoulder. The kid flinched.

"Oh, it's you." He tried not to act too relieved. "What now?" he whispered. "I already told this guy I wasn't guilty."

"If you'd said you were, you might be free."

"Huh?"

"When you plead 'not guilty' they remand you to jail until your case comes up again. A plea of 'guilty' can get your case disposed on the spot."

"How was I supposed to know that?"

"You weren't. That's what Ionello and Vass were counting on."

"I shoulda stuck to lyin'. I'm better at it."

The clerk called the name of the guy sitting beside Freddie, who stood to hear his charges. He wore a red T-shirt with a picture of a Coca-Cola bottle on it and was visibly battling a hangover. He had been arrested for urinating by a tree in Military Park.

"Do you have counsel present?" the magistrate asked. Framed by a hefty desk and pitted wood paneling as dark as his robes, the judge looked pale and diminutive and indifferent.

"Do I what?"

The magistrate may as well have been speaking a foreign language.

"Do you have an attorney, a lawyer?"

"No." The guy's response fell somewhere between a statement and an apology.

"If you wish to proceed without counsel you must sign a formal waiver indicating that you, the defendant, have been informed of your right to counsel and that you, the defendant, have declined."

The clerk thrust the papers at the guy in the T-shirt before he had a chance to make sense of what the magistrate had spouted at him. The guy signed the documents without reading them.

"Freddie, when the judge asks if you have an attorney, say yes."

"But I don't. Unless you is one of them too on top 'a being a cop."

"You won't really need a lawyer. We're just getting your bail back on the table. If the judge asks you anything else, say that your attorney was called into another trial and that he advised you of your right to remain silent. Tell the judge you are exercising that right. And don't forget to call him 'sir.'"

"He's gonna believe all that?"

"You said you were good at lying."

Three minutes had ticked by and the clerk was wrapping up the hearing. In a monotone, he pronounced, "The defendant is released on his own recognizance and scheduled to appear for trial on the date set forthwith."

The guy in the T-shirt simply stood there, not knowing what to do, as if he had accidentally bid at an auction.

"You're free to go," the clerk explained. Pleasantly surprised, the guy hot-footed it out of the courtroom, afraid the judge would change his mind.

"How'd that guy get outta here?" Freddie demanded. "I coulda got drunk off his breath and he's free to go. He didn't even say nothin'."

"People released without bail have a higher rate of showing up for their trials."

"Take my word for it, that guy won't."

"Maybe not, but he definitely wouldn't if he had to pay bail through a bondsman. The bond fee is nonrefundable regardless of whether the guy goes to court, so there's no incentive."

"Incentive?" Freddie was unfamiliar with the term.

"It's like motivation or encouragement, something to force the guy to come back."

"What's my incentive gonna be?"

Before Emmett could reply, the clerk was announcing the next name: "Fredrick R. Guthrie."

"Stand up," Emmett whispered.

Freddie rose and straighted his ripped shirt.

"Do you have counsel present?" the magistrate asked, repeating the query without a glance at the individual case file in front of him.

"Not yet, sir. My lawyer, he, um, had to go to this other trial."

The magistrate peered over the top rim of his glasses. "So you have counsel?" This was clearly the first occasion he had heard that all day.

"Yes, sir. And he told me that I shouldn't talk until he gets here."

"When will that be?"

"Could be awhile. This other client 'a his, he ran somebody over with a truck. Sir."

Freddie glanced at Emmett to see if his improvisation had done any irrevocable damage. Emmett rolled his eyes.

"Bail stands. You can pay it or return to jail until you and your otherwise occupied attorney can get your acts together."

Emmett motioned for him to take the bail, but Freddie mouthed that he didn't have the money.

"Is there a problem, Mr. Guthrie?" Freddie's hesitation was decelerating the magistrate's turnover time, and he didn't appreciate that.

"He'll pay the bail, Your Honor," Emmett said, jumping to his feet.

"Thank you for the vote of confidence, sir, however unless you're his attorney, the defendant has to tell me that himself. Well, Mr. Guthrie?"

"Yeah, I'll pay it," Freddie said unhappily.

"Then consider yourself free to leave."

The clerk gave him the documents with his new court date, and Freddie brought them to Emmett. "What do I do with these?"

"Mark that date on your calendar. That's when you have to come back. Maybe your attorney will be finished with that hit-and-run case by then."

"Very funny."

They were exiting the courtroom as the clerk called the next defendant, the wheels of justice rolling onward without a speed limit.

"Now we've got to find a bondsman to pay your bail."

Freddie stopped in the center of the second-floor rotunda, his sneakers squeaking on the stone floor. "I told you I didn't have the money. And I gotta feeling whoever this bond man is, he ain't gonna wanna play Santa."

"What you told me was that Luther Reed gave you a hundred bucks for every car you brought him. So where's this big bankroll of yours?"

"It's gone," Freddie exploded. "It's all gone. Luther made me pay him for snitching to the cops about it being my idea. Said I owed him for getting us both in trouble." The kid sunk into himself, hating to admit what had happened. "Guess that means I did this for nothing, huh? You gonna send me back to Newark Street, right?"

Emmett wasn't about to let his sole lead return to jail. "No, Freddie. Fifty-fifty, remember?"

"But I told you I'm broke. Fifty percent 'a nothin' is still nothin'."

"Ten percent of your bond should only be a few bucks. You can pay me back."

"You take spark plugs or distributor caps? 'Cause I ain't got no cash."

"We'll worry about that later."

Emmett had far bigger worries, not the least of which was what would happen once Ionello and Vass tracked Freddie down. In lockup or out on bail, Freddie was a walking bull's eye.

A block from the courthouse on Market Street, they found a bail bonds company located above a pet shop. The sign said FAST CASH FOR BONDS. The minute Emmett laid eyes on the guy behind the desk he said a prayer that the sign was right, that this would go fast, because he could tell that the bondsman was a former cop.

"Don't you hold me to that, you bastard," the bondsman joked loudly into the telephone, then he cupped his hand over the receiver. "Be with you in a jiff."

His meaty forearms, auburn hair, and ruddy drinker's complexion weren't what had given him away as an ex-cop. It was the slapjack on the edge of his desk. Preferred by some to a nightstick, the seven-inch piece of pipe bound in thick leather was a tiny yet formidable weapon, and anybody who got hit with one wouldn't soon forget it.

Most policemen earned extra money moonlighting. The plumbers' and electricians' unions were full of officers, spanning every rank. A paltry pension kept many in their second trades past retirement. Private investigations and bail bonds—jobs that required similar skills as police work and familiarity with the criminal element—were also favored professions of men who had left the force. Emmett was angry at himself for not having foreseen this.

"That guy's a cop," Freddie said out of the corner of his mouth.

"Was."

"Close enough. I told you. I can smell 'em."

The office was a converted studio apartment with a miniature fridge and a sink. Glossy posters of tropical islands were tacked to the walls, likely ferreted out of a travel agency's trash bin. Emmett wished he had made Freddie wait downstairs. He hadn't been willing to let him out of his sight. Now it was too late.

"This'll go more smoothly if you're not here. That way he can't ask you anything. When the guy gets off the phone, I'll say something about going to the pet store. Pretend you're excited."

"Puppies and kittens. Yay," Freddie deadpanned.

"Oh, and if you run off on me, I'll call Ionello and Vass myself."

"Wouldn't we both be in hot water then?" Freddie was raising Emmett's call.

"Who do you think they'd come after first?"

The kid gave him a sarcastic salute, assenting to play along.

"Sorry," the bondsman said as he hung up the telephone. "Was an old friend."

Another cop, Emmett thought. He had to make this quick. He put his hand on Freddie's shoulder. "Why don't you go and look at the dogs in the window while I take care of this," he suggested.

"Goodie," Freddie replied, a little too enthusiastically.

After Emmett heard him go down the steps and out the door, he said, "I'm watching my cousin's boy. The rest of the family won't talk to her anymore. You can see why."

That goosed a grin out of the bondsman. "Naw, he's got your eyes."

"I need to spring a buddy of mine and your sign says you're fast."

"Fastest there is."

Emmett passed him Freddie's paperwork. The guy whistled with dismay. "Awful generous of you. Bail's a thousand. Makes the fee one Franklin. That's steep."

The number caught Emmett between the eyes. The charge was loitering, and Emmett had assumed the bail would be set at the low end of the range, a hundred tops. This was ten times the average, another sign that the detectives from the Auto Squad weren't messing around. Emmett would be lucky if he had that much cash on him.

"Must be some friend."

Emmett counted out the last of his money and handed it over. "Yeah, we go way back."

"He skips, it's on you, ya know."

"He won't skip. You've got my word on that."

"No offense, pal, but your word ain't worth a dime. Nobody's is. If every man, woman, and child was an honest, upstanding citizen, I'd be out of a job. As you can see, I ain't."

When Emmett exited the bond office, Freddie was crouched in the stairwell, listening distance from the door. He had feigned going to the pet shop, footsteps and all, and was eavesdropping on everything that was said. Emmett opened his mouth, about to give the kid an earful, but Freddie hushed him, signaling that they should take the stairs in sync so it would sound as if one person was walking out, not two.

"If I'd 'a known you had a hundred bucks on you, man, I'd 'a copped your wallet myself," Freddie said once they were outside.

"That's reassuring." For every step Emmett took, Freddie jogged three to match his stride.

"What? You don't believe I can do it. I'm a legend when it comes to wallets. Watch this."

Freddie bumped Emmett's hip hard, distracting him. In a flash, he had Emmett's wallet. Emmett hadn't even felt Freddie's fingers slip into his pocket.

Emmett held out his palm. Freddie gave him the wallet. "Come on. My car's at the courthouse."

"You bought it, didn't you? That I left."

"When you're good you're good," he answered blandly.

"I'm not good. I'm great."

"If you're so great, why didn't you Houdini yourself out of jail."

"I did," he said, strutting, pleased with himself. "And you was my talented assistant." He waved his hand with a magician's flourish.

Emmett halted midstride and spun Freddie by the arm. "You think you played me? Is that it? Well, the only person you're playing is yourself. Let me tell you what I know about Fredrick R. Guthrie. That water pistol they took off you at Newark Street, you push into the ribs of little old ladies when you stick them up for their purses. It's an old trick. You're no big shot gangster. You're a pickpocket. That's the bottom of the totem pole. I've arrested punks just like you, and you know what happens to them at the end of the story? They wind up in Bordentown Reformatory or Yardville or Trenton State. You might be smart, but you're too dumb to see where you're going."

Humiliation made Freddie seem smaller than he was.

"As of today, you owe me one hundred dollars. That might be chump change to a master criminal such as yourself. It's a week's pay to me. So unless you can pull that money out of a hat, you don't leave my side until I get paid or you go back to jail."

Emmett's word might not have been worth much, but he would keep it.

SIXTEEN

The sun was glaring off a sea of car chrome in the courthouse parking lot, heat roiling off rows of hoods. Emmett chaperoned Freddie to the passenger side of his car and opened the door. The handle burned to the touch.

"Get in."

Freddie was busy appraising the car's tail fins. "A Dodge Coronet. Didn't picture you drivin' something with so much style. What is it? A '58? '59? This was the base model for the Royal and the Custom Royal. Doesn't have as much dress work and no teeth in the grille. Identical turret to the De Soto's 'cept this baby's got a Getaway L-head Flat 6 engine. That's one mighty engine. Original paint?"

"Yeah and it'd better not go missing."

"Man, how'm I gonna steal paint off a car?"

"I said get in." Emmett pushed him onto the passenger seat and got behind the wheel.

Freddie lowered his window. "Where we goin'?"

"Nowhere. Not until you tell me everything about Ambrose and what he did yesterday. Down to the last minute."

"We gonna sit here in this hot ass parking lot? You crazy? You tryin' to cook me?"

"Do you think this is a game, Freddie? Your best friend was murdered."

"You don't have to say that." He pouted.

"Start from the beginning."

"Fine. Ambrose came 'round my house that morning. Same as every morning. We was 'posed to be in summer school, but we'd been ditchin' to go to the junkyard and look for parts to pay off Luther. 'Brose tagged along, and we sneaked in under the fence. He was always quiet. He'd just follow me through the junk heaps, helpin' me pick up the heavy stuff. We searched for hours. All I could find were a couple carburetors. Nothin' special. Weren't no new cars to buy for switchin'. I knew Luther'd be sore, so I took Ambrose to the body shop with me. I shouldn't've. But I thought if Luther saw me with somebody big and tough-lookin' like Ambrose, he might go easy."

Freddie picked at the leather piping on the seat cushion, remorse making him humble.

"There's this room in back of the body shop where Luther and his guys sit around drinkin' and playin' dominoes. It's got an air conditioner. A huge one. Makes it so cold you can see your breath same as winter. Two guys stand outside, guarding the door. At first, they wouldn't let Ambrose in with me. Then Luther musta said it was okay. We went into the back room and I tried to give him the parts. He didn't care much. He was more interested in Ambrose. Luther got in his face, showing him who's boss. 'Brose didn't get it. He wasn't saying nothing, and that got Luther steamed."

The story slowed, as though the ending might be different if Freddie delayed it.

"He punched Ambrose right in his gut. Then the other guys were trying to hold him down. 'Brose was swinging his arms, swatting 'em off like they was flies. Not to fight 'em but because he was scared. They kept hitting him. I told Luther I'd pay him double what I owed if they'd stop beatin' on Ambrose. When Luther heard that, he made 'em stop. Told his guys to take 'Brose outside. I'll never forget his face when they was draggin' him out. He had blood runnin' from his lip. He was so confused. That was the last time I ever saw him."

Freddie's eyes welled. He blinked to clear them.

" 'You got some balls bringing muscle to my place.' That was what Luther said. Then he told me I owed him two thousand dollars. Double the grand he'd paid to the cops. I said it was impossible. I'd need a million junkyards to dig up that much money. He laughed. Said it was my problem now. I went home, hoping Ambrose would come there. I waited and waited. I was going to his grandma's place to look for him when the cops arrested me."

He sniffled and wiped his cheek on his shoulder, collecting himself. "When you came to the jail and told me Ambrose was dead, I figured it was Luther. I wish I didn't take 'Brose with me. If I didn't. . . ." Grief got him by the throat, strangling off the end of the sentence.

Luther Reed was a drug dealer, a pimp, and a thief. Violence wasn't beneath him, but Emmett hadn't heard of any murders in connection with the man. Outside of the mob, Reed had no direct competition in the Central Ward, no rivals that required bumping off. Emmett wouldn't put murder past him or his goons, however the circumstances of Webster's death—the slashed throat, the missing finger, the location of the dump—were too contrived for the likes of Reed.

"Luther didn't kill Ambrose, Freddie."

An instant of relief twisted into confusion. "If it wasn't him, who was it?"

That was the same question tumbling around Emmett's mind. "Maybe Luther can tell us that."

"You mean you're going to see him?"

Emmett started the car.

"Nuh-uh. I ain't comin'."

Frantic, Freddie grabbed the door handle, then Emmett grabbed him. "Where I go, you go."

"You get me outta jail just to deliver me to the guy who wants my head on a plate? Hell, take me back. Jail couldn't be as bad as this."

"Yeah, Freddie, it could."

From the courthouse, it was a short drive to Reed's auto body shop on Springfield Avenue, a street that originated faraway in the suburbs and wended through the tony enclaves of Short Hills, Milburn, and

Maplewood, to dead-end in the center of Newark in an area called the Strip, a procession of bars, liquor stores, and barbecue shops with filmy windows. Traffic was creeping along as though the heat made cars' tires suction to the road.

"Where's your partner at?" Freddie asked. "Don't cops always have partners?"

"Some do. I don't."

"Why?"

"Ask my lieutenant."

"Maybe nobody would ride with you 'cause 'a your attitude."

"I'm sure that's the reason."

They parked down the block, giving Emmett a clear view of the body shop. A station wagon was jacked up on a lift in the garage, which was filled with the requisite tools and parts to pass the place off as operational. Nobody entered or exited for fifteen minutes.

"Ain't we goin' in?"

"A half hour ago you refused to go anywhere near Luther Reed and now you can't wait to see him?"

"No, I wanna get this over with 'cause I'm hungry," Freddie whined. "At least in jail, they have to feed you."

Emmett popped the glove compartment, dug out a candy bar and gave it to him.

"It's melted."

"If you won't eat, I will."

As Freddie gobbled the candy bar, Emmett took a pair of handcuffs from the glove compartment.

"What're those for? You gonna lock Luther up?"

"Not exactly."

Freddie stopped chewing. "Why you lookin' at me?"

"Put out your hands."

"You kiddin', right?"

"Reed's only met Ionello and Vass. Auto's a big division, and a badge is a badge."

"Then you don't need me."

"Think about it: when you push a plastic squirt gun into somebody's back, they don't know it's not real. They give over their money so they won't get shot, even though they can't. I walk in with you, Reed doesn't know I'm trying to find out who killed Ambrose. He talks so I won't come down on him any harder for the auto fraud, even though I can't."

"Being in this hot car musta boiled your brains. There's usually six or seven of them in that back room with Luther. Sometimes more. And they got guns. I seen 'em stuck in their belts."

"And those are the ones they let you see." Emmett opened the cuffs.

Freddie finished the last of the candy bar. "I shoulda stayed in jail."

Emmett led him into the garage by the handcuffs. The station wagon on the lift was missing a wheel. There was no replacement tire in sight. Wrenches and loose washers were strewn about, yet the smell of motor oil was faint, the floor dry, no spots. The body shop was as fake as a cardboard set for a puppet show.

"Act as if I just arrested you and you don't want to be here."

"I won't be actin'."

Behind the garage was an office. Two large men sat on either side of the door, their heads leaned against the wall, languishing in the heat like sleeping giants. But they weren't really asleep. Through heavy lids, they assayed Emmett, deciding whether he was worth standing up for.

"I've come to see Luther Reed. Some mutual friends sent me." Emmett flashed his shield.

One man lumbered into the back room. The other positioned himself squarely in front of the door, filling its frame. A minute later, the door reopened, sending an icy gust into the hall, then Emmett and Freddie were let through.

The back room was dim and frigid. An industrial air conditioner was chugging in the corner, beer bottles chilling on top. Six men were seated around a folding table playing cards. A pile of cash sat in the center. All of them had guns in their waistbands. Presumably an extra was strapped under the table as well. They continued playing without a word, flicking down cards.

Emmett said nothing. Freddie was twitching at his side, unable to stand still. Finally, the player at the head of the table showed his hand. The others folded, and he swept the money toward his lap.

"You a patient man. Most cops ain't," the winner remarked. He had a slight build and empathetic eyes that gave him the appearance of being gentle. It was Luther Reed and he was anything but.

"I'm in no hurry," Emmett told him. "It's nice and cool in here. I could stay all day."

Reed contemplated that. "Quite a pet you got. He housebroken?"

"Yeah, except he bites."

Luther laughed softly. "I met a lot 'a cops in my day. I don't think you and me's had the pleasure."

"No, I don't think we have." Emmett couldn't play coy for long. He wouldn't give his name unless he absolutely had to.

"I already made my contribution to the Policemen's Benevolent Association, if that's what you're here about." Reed eyed Freddie, intimating that he was the contribution.

"I didn't come for a donation, however you are in the position to make a generous one I see."

The game's winnings were mounded at Reed's elbows. He grouped the bills into a neat stack. It was his turn to be coy. He appeared to be debating whether he should tolerate a second round of police shakedowns.

"Keep it. I bet your electric bill's a doozy."

Surprised, Reed passed the cash to the man beside him. It went into his pocket, under his gun.

"I won't take up too much of your time," Emmett said. "I just need you to tell me where the other one is?"

"The other what?"

Reed was at a loss, and he didn't like it. Emmett let him squirm for a minute, then he pinched Freddie's neck until the kid squirmed. "Your friend here doesn't work alone. It's a two-man gig. I believe you've met the second half of the act."

"A couple days ago. Ain't seen him since."

"That's funny, because this is the last place anybody saw him. You can imagine how that might come off to those impatient sorts of cops."

It took a second for Reed to weigh his alternatives. "Tell him," he ordered.

"All's we did was rough him up some," one of the men at the table began.

Another finished. "We let 'im go. I saw him walk out onto the Strip. Swear to God."

"Cross your heart and hope to die?" Emmett asked.

The back room fell silent aside from the hum of the air conditioner. The man closest to Reed who had taken the money moved his hand to his gun. Emmett could feel Freddie go tense.

"Put 'cho goddamn hands on the table," Reed hissed. The man did as he was told.

"Well, you all seem very sincere. I'll be sure and pass that along so nobody else comes by to barge in on your card game."

The chill had gone out of the room. It wasn't cold anymore.

"Whatcha gonna do with that new pet 'a yours?" Ever the businessman, Reed was probing for his own interests. Freddie owed him money.

Emmett squeezed the kid's neck again. "I think I'll put him on a short leash."

"You do that," Reed said. "'Cause anybody can take a stray off the street and say its theirs."

He wouldn't dare mention the debt, yet his disappointment was obvious. Emmett's wasn't, though it affected him as keenly. After Luther Reed's men had finished beating Ambrose Webster, the teen had disappeared without a trace, a stray somebody else had claimed.

SEVENTEEN

The day was escaping, leaving Emmett empty-handed with nothing to show for his efforts besides Freddie, who was rubbing his neck theatrically and saying, "I thought we was gonna be acting."

"I had to make it look real."

"Felt pretty damn real to me."

They got into the car and Emmett uncuffed him. Freddie massaged his wrists. "What now?"

Emmett was wondering that himself.

"Hey. Don't you know it's rude not to answer when somebody's talkin' to you?"

"Yup. I've heard that before." He went for the glove compartment. Freddie withdrew from him skittishly. "Relax. We're done acting."

He had put the Julius Dekes file he took from the Records Room in the glove compartment.

"I'd take another candy bar if you got one."

"Sorry. That was it." Hunger had hit Emmett as well. It would have to hold. "Do you recognize this kid?" He showed Freddie the school photo of Dekes.

"No. Why? He dead too?"

"Actually, he is."

"Jeez, I was just kidding."

"You've never seen him?"

"I said no."

The address for the next of kin, Dekes's mother, Dorothea, wasn't far from Freddie's house. "He was your age and he was from your neighborhood. Are you sure you don't know him?"

"Because we both brothas we got to know each other? Is that what you sayin'?"

"No. But it would help."

"Help how?"

Emmett hadn't intended on telling Freddie about Julius Dekes, but Webster's trail had run cold. He would have to forge a new path.

"They had something in common, Ambrose and this kid."

"They was Negroes. We covered that."

"Someone cut off one of Ambrose's fingers. The kid in the picture was killed two months ago. He was also missing a finger." Emmett flipped to the autopsy diagram displaying where the ring finger had been scratched out.

"Don't be showing me that stuff, man." Freddie wrinkled his nose.

"You see the connection?"

"Yeah? And?" He was only half-heartedly convinced. It was the same response Emmett could expect from Lieutenant Ahern.

"Never mind."

They drove in silence until they reached Freddie's neighborhood.

"Are you taking me home?"

"No."

"We ain't done?"

"Done? Didn't you hear what Reed said? He's not going to be satisfied until he gets his two grand from you. Assuming you don't have that saved in your piggy bank, don't you think you might be safer with me?"

"With you? You cuff me, bring me to Luther, almost get me shot, and I'm gonna be safer with you?"

Emmett parked the car as Freddie continued to mutter bitterly.

"This'll be safer for both of us." He slipped the handcuffs on Freddie again, shackling him to the steering wheel. "You're in debt to me and to Luther. I won't hurt you to get my money. He will."

Freddie was contorted across the front seat, seething. He was about to start swearing a blue streak.

"Now don't scream and try to attract attention. You wouldn't want anybody calling the cops, would you?"

The address in Julius Dekes's file was a tenement on Treacy Avenue. Three elderly black women were sitting on the stoop. They were fanning themselves with folded newspapers while a toddler maneuvered a slot car around their feet.

"I'm here to see Dorothea Dekes. Can you ladies tell me if she's home?"

One nodded warily, and they watched Emmett go inside.

Dorothea Dekes answered her door while wiping water from her hands with a rag. She had been washing dishes. Two young girls clung to her legs. "Yes?"

"Mrs. Dekes?" He let her see his badge.

"Yes?" she repeated.

Emmett introduced himself. "May I talk to you about your son, Julius, ma'am?"

Her expression saddened. "Go on in your room," she told the girls, then she invited him in.

A pot was boiling on the stove. Though Emmett was starving, the smell told him what she was cooking wasn't anything he would care to eat. Simmering lye in water was a home remedy for warding off rats and roaches.

"I have to admit I don't recall you," Mrs. Dekes said, offering him a seat at the kitchen dinette. Her hair was combed into a bouffant, and her dress had been ironed into sharp angles. "Were you one of the detectives who came here after they found him?"

"No, ma'am. That wasn't me."

"I only saw them that one time. I went to the police station and the man at the desk said they were out. I went twice more. He said the same thing."

"I'm sorry about that." Serletto and Hochwald had discarded the case. They were the last people Emmett would make excuses for. There was no excuse.

"Did you find who killed him? Is that why you're here?" Her voice held cautious hope.

"Not yet."

"But you're still looking?"

Emmett couldn't close Vernon Young's case, and he'd had misgivings about taking Ambrose Webster's. Here he was signing on for another. He held as cautious a hope as Dorothea Dekes that this wasn't an error in judgment.

"Yes, ma'am. I'm still looking."

She reached out and rubbed his hand, grateful. "I knew it. I knew those officers couldn't see me because they were busy searching for who did this to Julius. Everybody told me I was wrong, that the police had gave up on him. But I knew they hadn't. In my heart, I believed."

Emmett didn't have it in his heart to tell her otherwise.

"Could you go over some things with me, Mrs. Dekes? I was, um, recently assigned to help the detectives with Julius's case," he lied, "and I wanted to get the background from you in person."

"Of course. Of course." She was eager to help. "I was at the nursing home where I work. I have the dinner shift. I don't get home until midnight. I would always leave food for supper, and Julius would heat it up for his sisters and him. When I got back that night, the girls were awake. They were crying, saying Julius never came. That wasn't like him. He was a good student, a good boy. He was going to be a schoolteacher," she said, his aspirations evidence of his virtue. "I waited up all night. When I telephoned the police, they said he must have run away. They called me a week later to come to the morgue."

"Would Julius have been heading here straight from school?"

"No, he played basketball with some friends. I talked to them boys myself. I asked them if they saw where Julius went. Everybody said they saw him walk home same as usual." The pot of lye was bubbling on the burner, filling in the silence and adding to the heat. Her son had vanished, just as Ambrose Webster had.

"I couldn't afford the funeral on my own. The casket had to be made special because of how big Julius was. Our church had a collection. It was a beautiful service, so many flowers." Her mind seemed to wander, then she was back. "Are you a churchgoing man, Detective Emmett?"

"Not as much as I used to be."

"I'll put you in my prayers tonight. I'll pray you'll get who did this to my baby."

Mrs. Dekes rubbed Emmett's hand again, as if it was he who needed consoling. When he stood to go, the two young girls were at the door to their bedroom, staring up at him. The smallest was sucking her thumb. Emmett wasn't even in his own prayers. Being in someone else's couldn't hurt.

The women on the stoop stopped their talking when Emmett stepped outside, all except for the one who had the toddler on her knee. She was teaching him how to count, folding down his fingers one at a time. The boy was mesmerized. He stared at her mouth as she said the words aloud: "One. Two. Three. Four. Five."

Emmett was overcome by the skidding feeling of a sudden realization. Julius Dekes was missing his ring finger, Ambrose Webster his pointer. They were out of sequence.

He hurried to the car. Freddie had commandeered the driver's seat. "Move," Emmett ordered.

Freddie scooted across to the passenger side as far as he could with the cuffs on. He had Julius Dekes's autopsy report in his lap. He had been reading it.

"I thought you didn't want to see that stuff." Emmett unlocked the cuffs.

"Wasn't anything else to do. What's the rush?"

"I have a problem."

"I coulda told you that."

Emmett leaned over to get his radio out from under the passenger seat.

"What's that thing?"

"A radio."

"Don't look like no radio I ever seen."

"My brother built it. It was a gift."

"Maybe you oughta ask for somethin' else next year."

The radio was a clunky amalgam of parts Edward had patchworked together, topped off with a big dial from an old Packard Bell. He had a knack for taking things apart and reassembling them and could breeze through issues of *Popular Mechanics* as effortlessly as reading the comics, a talent their father shared, which Emmett hadn't inherited. Edward had given him the radio his third year on the force, tuned specially to pick up the police band. It was too cumbersome to carry on foot patrol, but Edward had made it for him to have in case of an emergency. Emmett's current situation qualified.

A joggle of the tuner and the frequency came in clear. Dispatch was announcing that, citywide, officers were being put on mandatory emergency duty, twelve-hour shifts on and twelve off. All vacation days were suspended until further notice.

"Sucks for you," Freddie said.

Emmett shushed him, listening. It was almost seven, and the rally was about to get under way. The dispatcher ordered those in patrol cars to stay by their radios because a dozen picketers had planted themselves outside the Fourth Precinct. No other commands were issued.

"Now you gonna take me home?" Freddie groaned. "I'm hot. I'm tired. I'm hungry. And I'm sicka being in this damn car."

Sunset hadn't put a dent in the weather. The humidity curdled the air. Emmett was hot and tired and hungry too, and he had a sickening sense that with nightfall would come more violence.

EIGHTEEN

When Emmett pulled into his driveway, all of the lights were on inside the house, glowing through the curtains in the open windows. He hadn't seen the place that lit up since his mother was alive. The heat had been a convenient excuse to leave the lights off. Somehow that made it easier for him and Edward to avoid interacting with each other. It took a stranger, a woman, to turn the lights on again.

"When I said I wanted to go home, I meant my house. Not yours."

Emmett prodded Freddie up the front steps. "It's this or the handcuffs."

"Is that a slide?" Freddie was gawking at the wheelchair ramp.

"Yeah, this is Coney Island. The first ride's free."

Mrs. Poole came into the living room at the sound of the front door opening. A dish towel was tucked into the elastic waist of her skirt as a makeshift apron. The aroma of cooking food met Emmett and Freddie like a welcome breeze.

"I know that ain't your mama," Freddie mumbled.

Emmett fastened a hand on the kid's collarbone, forcing him forward into an introduction. "Mrs. Poole, this is Freddie Guthrie. He's going to be spending a few hours here."

"I am not—"

A hard squeeze and Freddie clammed up. "If you can spare an extra hour, I'll tack a whole day's pay onto your next check."

"Of course I can stay, Mr. Emmett."

The money didn't seem to matter to her. He had a feeling she would have stayed simply at his request. "I appreciate that."

"You mind him, young man, hear?" Mrs. Poole sidled toward Freddie, who cowered, more frightened of her than of Luther Reed. "Don't make me say it twice."

"Yes, ma'am," Freddie answered, his manners materializing out of nowhere.

"I fixed some supper. Best I could do with what was here. Thought you might be tired 'a those frozen dinners. You can help me set the table," she told Freddie, guiding him into the kitchen. "Silverware's in the top drawer. Forks go on the left."

Freddie didn't attempt his usual back talk and went willingly to work.

"My hat's off to you. He's been giving me lip from the get-go."

"Having ten brothers and sisters will teach you a thing or two."

"And I thought having one brother was an education. Speaking of which, where is Edward?"

"Out on the back porch. He's been there awhile."

"How was he?"

"Not too chatty. He's the kind 'a horse you can't even lead to water. Forget about making him drink. Just got to let him be."

The evening sky hung low, as if it skimmed the awning over the porch. A cigarette was smoldering between Edward's fingers. He was watching the neighbors pass lit windows in the houses across the yard. The screen door squawked when Emmett opened it and when it banged closed.

"You could put some oil on that door hinge, you know."

"Then you wouldn't hear me coming."

"I'll always hear you comin', Marty." He took a drag of his cigarette. "You're late."

"Something came up."

Edward didn't inquire as to what because then it would have seemed like he cared.

Mosquitoes were out in droves, buzzing by Emmett's ear and bobbing around the porch lamp. "Aren't you getting eaten alive out here?"

"Nope. Bugs aren't interested in me. Was a godsend when I was in over in Nam. The other guys in my battalion would be covered in bites. But I didn't get a single one. My blood must taste bad."

He rarely talked about the war and stopped himself abruptly, as though he had let something slip.

"So? How did it go today?"

"It was fine, Marty," Edward answered, his tone remote. "She was fine."

"You want me to get someone else?"

"I said she was fine."

Acknowledging that he needed help had been tough for Emmett. It would be tougher for Edward.

"She's a good cook," he conceded. "She made sandwiches and she cut the bread the way Ma used to. They were good. For sandwiches."

A light popped on in a nearby apartment window and the silhouette of a woman appeared. She was in a rush, combing her hair and primping in a mirror they couldn't see. Then she shut off the lights to go. Edward crushed his cigarette into an ashtray on the porch railing. "Show's over."

Emmett opened the door for him to wheel inside. Freddie looked up from setting the table. He and Edward regarded each other for a moment.

"Is he the something that came up?"

"This is Freddie Guthrie. He'll be, uh, joining us for the evening. Freddie, this is my brother, Edward."

"You're grown. You can shake the man's hand," Mrs. Poole instructed.

Hesitant, Freddie walked over and stuck out his hand. Edward shook it hard, taking measure of him. "Department must really be hurtin' for new recruits. Ain't he young for a rookie, Marty?"

"You could say he has . . . an interest in the law."

"I bet."

Mrs. Poole broke the tension. "I hope you boys are hungry. Weather like this, the food can't get cold. Doesn't mean we shouldn't eat it when it's ready. Y'all come on to the table."

She had laid out place mats and their mother's linen tablecloth, which Emmett never did. Between the smell of the food and the perfectly set table, Emmett forgot about the heat and everything else that had been weighing on his mind. He and Edward hadn't had a home-cooked meal since the women from Saint Casimir's stopped bringing over casseroles following his mother's death. Emmett didn't realize how much he missed real food and eating at the table instead of in front of the television.

Mrs. Poole served a plate to each of them, then proceeded to say grace. Freddie bowed his head, afraid of crossing the woman, and murmured along with her. Edward lowered his head as well. Emmett spoke the prayer in time, sneaking a glance at his brother, who he hadn't said grace in years. Emmett had missed that too.

"Amen," Mrs. Poole intoned. They all repeated after her. Emmett and Freddie dug into the food, too famished to talk. They finished their meals in minutes.

"Either it was awful tasty or you two were awful hungry," she marveled

Emmett dabbed his mouth with a napkin. "Dinner was excellent. Wasn't it?"

"Yeah. Yeah, it was," Edward said, moving his food around with his fork. He was eyeing Freddie while Freddie was eyeing the leftovers.

"Mrs. Poole, will you fix him another plate?" Emmett said. "I have to go out for a bit. When I get back, I'll drive you two home."

"For real this time?" Freddie was skeptical.

"Eat your food," Mrs. Poole told him, refilling his plate.

When Emmett got up from the table, Edward trailed him into the living room. "I know trouble when I see it, Marty. That boy's trouble. And you're gonna leave me and an old lady to babysit him?"

Edward had a unique ability for reading people. He could hear a lie before it sprang from a person's lips and pick out a phony from across a room. Emmett had always thought his brother would have made the better cop.

"He's harmless. But the guy he owes money to isn't. It's just for a couple hours. He'll be safe here."

"Will we?"

Emmett lifted his right pant leg, exposing the .22 caliber gun strapped to his calf. "You want it? For babysitting?"

Offended, Edward rolled toward the kitchen. "Don't take too long. You'll keep the kid up past his bedtime."

The line of picketers outside the Fourth Precinct had grown from the ten reported earlier on the police band to a crowd of three hundred that clogged the street. There wasn't a single patrolman on the scene. From where Emmett was parked at the far end of Livingston Avenue, he could see Mose Odett wielding a bullhorn and wearing one of his trademark suits in a pale blue hue the color of pool water.

Odett's evangelizing bubbled through the horn. "We are not here to talk about the cab driver, Ben White. We are here to talk about what we see happening in this neighborhood every day. We are here to talk about Newark. Newark is a black city. The white folks leave at five o'clock. And what do they leave us with? Falling-down buildings and rats and garbage. In exchange, they give us liquor and heroin and hair straighteners, then they want to know why we're mad. We're mad because all we want is a fair trade. Nothing's fair in Newark anymore."

What Odett was saying wasn't wrong. But Emmett felt the timing wasn't right. Yesterday, Inspector Plout had given him a bullhorn to try and pacify the crowd. Now he had his own and he was inciting it. The congregation was cheering him on.

"We've prayed and we've preached and we've protested and it ain't done no difference. What are we supposed to do? Tell me, what are we supposed to do?"

Emmett had a feeling he knew what the crowd's answer would be.

He had left the lights in the Records Room off on purpose. They were still off when he got there. They would have to stay that way. Like the window that he and Edward had seen the woman in, turning on the basement lights might draw attention.

With only the flashlight borrowed from the patrolman to see by, Emmett sieved through the cases that predated Julius Dekes's murder.

The reports transformed people into paper, their wounds splotched in pen across a two-dimensional body, then crammed inside a manila folder, where they would exist in suspended animation until somebody opened that folder and reintroduced them to life. Emmett went straight to the autopsies, looking for fingers that the coroner had scratched out. His clock was ticking softly from the desk drawer. As a novice, Emmett had been denied a wristwatch or a calendar. Time was a material object outside his possession, dispensed by chapel bells that parsed the day into doses of work, play, prayer, and sleep. The term of Emmett's novitiate was twenty-four months, exactly 730 days, the preordained number set by the Society of Jesus. On the date of July 31, the Feast of Saint Ingatius of Loyola, he was to have taken his vows. It was July, ten years later, and he had to face yet another monumental decision: whether to tell the lieutenant about his suspicions, then potentially lose the cases and, perhaps, his career, or try and solve the murders himself. What Emmett found next made his choice all the more crucial.

An autopsy report dated in April showed an eighteen-year-old with an X across his heart and ink-slashed pinkie finger. His name was Evander Hammond. Reading the file, Emmett got a sensation in his stomach that teetered between nausea and exhilaration. Hammond, an athlete who lived on Bruce Street in the Central Ward, had been missing for four days. His body was discovered by a construction crew in an alley. The murder weapon was a knife, identical to the other boys. Knives were the most commonly used weapon in the ward, but the sites of the victim's wounds were all different, a cunning pattern that wouldn't pique the coroner's curiosity. In a morgue as busy as Newark's, the missing fingers would be written off as oddities or accidents. But to Emmett, these were no random irregularities. They were the strongest link he had.

The line drawing of Hammond's hand was encircled in the flashlight's beam. He was missing a pinkie, Dekes a ring finger, Webster his pointer. No case matched the middle finger. The irony wasn't lost on Emmett. He had gone through every murder on file for that year and was about to start over when a volley of breaking glass rattled the precinct. Shouting echoed through the air ducts. Feet were pounding above his head, a kind of morse code that prompted him where the file would be: it was on somebody's desk in Homicide.

A monstrous logic was clicking into place. This murderer was targeting strong black teens, stabbing them and snipping off their fingers, then leaving their bodies in various corners of the Central Ward like so much trash. Horrifying as the riot was, this killer put an unfamiliar fear in Emmett. He knew what this person was capable of, and he still had no way to identify him.

The bombardment wasn't letting up. All of the debris left on the street from the night before provided a bounty of munitions. From the basement, it sounded like a hard rain. Emmett wished that was what it was. With the station under attack again, patrolmen would be the precinct's infantry, sent out as the first line of defense until officers from other wards could arrive. Any detectives on shift would remain in their squad rooms awaiting orders. Emmett couldn't chance going up to the third floor, not in the middle of the blitz. He would have to come back.

If there was a Fourth Precinct to come back to.

NINETEEN

The summer heat had a way of making the nights seem especially dark. But no night was ever dark enough for Lazlo Meers. Somewhere a streetlamp or a parked car or a neon sign was always leaking ruinous light. Meers preferred complete darkness.

The light didn't hurt his eyes, however he didn't need it. He had extremely acute vision, which he considered a gift in exchange for his infirmity. At the age of twelve, Meers had contracted polio. He had awoken one morning suffering symptoms of the flu, a fever and sore throat. His father forced him to go to school regardless. A stern man, Meers's father did not abide illness. Only the weak got sick. He had never missed a day of work at the zinc mines, and his temperament was as strong as the raw ore he oversaw being excavated from the earth. Lazlo had the misfortune of inheriting his mother's tender constitution. She had died giving birth to him, and her delicate nature was a legacy his father loathed in him. Meers stuck it out at school while his legs steadily went limp, too afraid to go home early and face his father. When he attempted to get out of bed the next day, he fell to the floor, his limbs incapable of holding him. He spent the ten months that followed in an iron lung, his chest muscles too debilitated to pump and keep him alive. The bellows motor of the massive respirator would push air in and out of the tank, squeezing Lazlo's small chest to expand and contract his rib cage. A distinctive *whooshing* noise replaced every breath. Decades later, Meers could still hear that *whoosh*. He heard it at work when a door would swing shut or when a truck would pass on the road or when he would roll down the windows in his car and the breeze would gush through, ever-present reminders of what he was.

It was in his car though that Meers could forget too, cruising the streets until something sparked his fancy. The humid weather brought the teenage boys out into the night to cool off. So many boys in the Central Ward, right there for the picking, but Meers had discriminating tastes. Only a certain type would do.

Once he made his choice, he had to catch the boy's eye. He had purchased a brand-new Cadillac Eldorado for just that purpose. It was a two-door hardtop coupe in vampish red with oxblood leather interior to match. Meers had gone to great expense to outfit it with reclining bucket seats, an AM/FM stereo, white sidewall tires, and most importantly, power door locks including a remote control to the trunk. With its angular body and hidden headlights, the Eldorado was arrogant, an attention grabber. It cost him a year's salary and then some, but it was worth every penny.

Meers stayed off the main thoroughfares where the Cadillac would get too much scrutiny as well as certain side streets where too many people were on the stoops. That particular evening, he was cruising the long blocks of Peshine and Jelliff and Badger avenues. He trolled until he saw a lone teenager crossing on Bigelow. He wasn't as tall or strapping as Ambrose Webster, the boy from a few days ago whose name Meers had taken off a student movie pass, yet he had appeal.

Webster had been a disappointment, not the prize Meers presumed. When he first spied the teen loping along Springfield Avenue looking lost and bruised, Meers thought he was too damaged to be of use. Webster was such an impressive specimen that Meers simply couldn't resist, even after he realized that Ambrose was impaired. What would that matter, Meers contended at the time. Instinct was instinct. That was a miscalculation. Webster couldn't follow the rules. He didn't understand them. Such a waste.

This new prospect had promise. Snug dungarees and a T-shirt thinned from too many launderings showed off the kid's physique. He was lanky with whipcord muscles and a runner's legs, built for speed. Meers liked that. He coasted alongside him and lowered the window.

"Pardon me, young man," Meers called. "Would you mind giving me a hand?"

The kid would have kept walking if it weren't for the Cadillac. He actually did a double take and stared longingly at the car's curves as if it were a woman. Meers relished the glint in his eye.

"My tire's going flat. You see it?" Earlier, Meers had let some air out of the rear tire, enough to be convincing, though not too much. He still had to be able to drive on it. "This is my boss's car and I was only supposed to take it to get washed. If he finds out I went joyriding, he'll fire me."

"Can't, man. I'm in a hurry."

"If you could just help me get the spare tire out of the trunk," Meers pleaded, amping his voice into a high, whiny range so he would come off as helpless.

"There's a filling station up the road."

"I doubt I can make it. I could pay you. Twenty bucks."

That much money was difficult to pass on. The kid hesitated, vacillating.

"I'll pull into the alley, okay?"

"Yeah, all right. But we gotta do this quick, man, 'cause I gotta go see a girl."

"Don't worry. It'll be quick."

Meers pulled into a deserted alley. When he climbed out of the driver's seat, he let the kid get a full view of him. In the iron lung, Meers's muscles had atrophied from inactivity, stunting his growth. He was small-boned and had the gaunt countenance of a sickly man. Except Meers wasn't sick anymore.

He pressed a button to pop the trunk and hobbled to the rear of the car, accentuating a mild limp caused by the disease. His breath was labored, asthmatic, an affect to add to the impression. Meers had plenty of practice with labored breathing. The Christmas after the polio struck, he and the other children in the iron lung ward tried singing Christmas carols. They couldn't finish the choruses until the bellows would exhale for them, so they sang each bar of the song, then had to wait for the *whoosh* to continue singing. Standing there in the alley watching the kid silently appraise him reminded Meers of those pregnant pauses between the holiday carols.

"Gosh, I really appreciate this," he panted. "My boss would kill me if he ever found out I borrowed his car. He treats it like it's his baby."

The manufactured backstory didn't interest the kid. "Gimme the money first."

"Oh, of course. Silly me. Where are my manners?"

Meers peeled a twenty from his wallet, opening it wide to display the wad of bills inside. Ambrose Webster was the only one who hadn't fallen for the temptation to rob him or at the very least attempt to steal the car. The notion hadn't even occurred to him. This kid was already two steps ahead. Meers could practically see the cogs in his head spinning. The Cadillac and all of that cash were irresistible.

A satire was being set in motion whether the kid was aware of it or not. The car he was lusting after had gotten its title from the mythical kingdom of El Dorado, renown for its unsurpassing wealth. For hundreds of years, men had searched without luck for the legendary city, and the name itself had become synonymous with the vain pursuit of riches. The pursuit to take the car and the money from Meers would also be in vain.

He held out the twenty-dollar bill, and the kid stuffed it in his pocket. "Let's get that tire, shall we?" Meers said.

The Eldorado came with a full-size spare, and it had the largest trunk available in the Cadillac line. Meers had selected it expressly for that amenity.

"You got a jack?"

Something to hit me with, Meers was thinking. This one was smart. That pleased him.

"Hmm. Let me look."

Meers pretended to poke through the trunk's contents, demonstrating that he didn't have full use of his left arm. Crippled by polio, it hung at his side, underdeveloped and idle. He forearm had limited strength, but his fingers worked well, and he could easily extract the tiny bottle of ether in his pocket to anesthetize the boy if necessary. To do that, Meers would have to get up close, which was why he kept an electrified cattle prod on his person. He had modified the cattle prod so it was small enough to smuggle under his pant leg, secured by a sock garter. Such contingencies were essential in case things got out of hand.

"Here we go." Meers caught the kid eyeing the heavy tire jack.

"Gimme it."

"Shouldn't we get the tire out first?"

It was a wrinkle in the kid's plan. He tried to act unfazed. "Oh, yeah. The tire."

"Careful. The tire's heavy," Meers cautioned.

"Relax. I got it."

As the kid leaned in to retrieve the tire, his wrist brushed a concealed wire that ran from a truck battery in the backseat through the trunk to the wheel well. The instant the wire made contact with his skin, he closed the circuit. The shock jerked his body and his eyelids fluttered, the voltage knocking him unconscious. His knees buckled, sending his body slumping into the trunk. That did most of the work for Meers. He simply had to lift the kid's legs over the lip of the trunk and he was done.

"I'm much more relaxed now, thank you."

Meers dug through the kid's pockets and pulled out a wallet. Inside were a couple of quarters and a rubber. The wallet had come with a personal identification card for the owner to fill in their name and address. On it, the kid had written, "If you stole my wallet and you find this, I'll find you. You dead." He had signed his name at the bottom: "Calvin Timmons."

"Why hello, Calvin," Meers said genteelly. "It's a pleasure to meet you. I think we're going to have a lot of fun together."

Then he shut the trunk.

TWENTY

The Fourth Precinct had not been built to withstand the heavy combat that came to its doors. The brick and brownstone structure shuddered with each new wave of assault. Emmett's rational side told him to get out of there, to get home and make sure Edward, Freddie, and Mrs. Poole were all right, but his reflexes were screaming for him to stay and help. His body and mind pulled in opposite directions. Evander Hammond's file was hidden under his jacket in the waistband of his pants, stuck in the small of his spine like a gun, splitting him down the middle.

Reason beat out reflex, and Emmett bolted for the station's rear door. When he stepped outside, the ground was shaking beneath his feet. People were stampeding toward the precinct. Others spilled along side streets, charging at the stores that hadn't been looted and battering down doors and windows. The din crescendoed into a roar.

Emmett ran to his car and sped away with the dispatch frequency on full blast. Frenzied calls began flooding in. Robberies were being reported by the dozens. The dispatchers couldn't get a word in edgewise. At any given time, day or night, over fifty police cars patrolled the city's streets. Each of the five precincts had twelve cars apiece, and the force was bolstered by forty motorcycles as well as the horses of the Mounted Division in the Second Precinct. From the sound of it, every single car was radioing in offering aide. Some Fifth Precinct cars said they could come immediately, but the dispatcher forbade them from doing so.

"All cars, by orders of the command post, you are confined to your precincts."

No sooner had dispatch completed the transmission when one of the Fourth Precinct cars called in an SOS. "We've been hit by a firebomb. The car's on fire. The goddamn car's on fire."

The police band was mute. After conferring with superiors, the dispatcher returned with instructions. "Abandon the car. Get to the Fourth on foot."

Then a second radio car went down.

"They're throwing cinder blocks at us. They're tossing 'em from the windows. Two hit the car. The first nearly came through the roof. The other hit the hood and knocked out the engine. The car won't run. Whadda we do? What the hell do we do?"

"I repeat, by order of Police Director Sloakes, all cars are to remain in their districts."

Emmett imagined a communal curse of Sloakes's name coming from the mouths of cops listening throughout the city. At every intersection and stoplight, he had to wrestle away the impulse to turn around. The neighborhood he was cutting through was a quiet contrast to where he had come from. Residents were hunched on their stoops, oblivious to what was happening just blocks from their homes.

"Officer needs assistance," a voice shouted over the frequency. "We got a brick through our windshield. It hit my partner. He's cut and he's bleeding something fierce. We're at Camden and Fifteenth. We can't make it to the Fourth. We can't make it in. We—" The officer was interrupted by a blast. "Jesus Christ. They're firebombing us. We need help. The car's burning. We need—"

The transmission broke off right as Emmett arrived at his house. He sat in the car, deliberating whether to go back. Cars from the Traffic Division immediately began patching in, volunteering assistance to the trapped patrolmen.

"We're off Routes One and Nine. We can get there faster than the bus."

A "bus" was code for an ambulance, and the traffic cars undoubtedly could have beaten any emergency crew to the scene. Unlike regular radio cars, theirs were souped-up Chryslers that had lighter bodies built for high-speed chases. With the sirens rolling, they could get anywhere on the double.

"Stay on the highway," was the response from dispatch. "Repeat. Stay on the highway."

Powerless, Emmett put the car in park and cut the motor. Most of the lights in his house were off by then, only the bluish glow of the television showed through the blinds. He knew everyone inside was waiting for him.

When he walked in, Mrs. Poole was seated in a straight-backed chair she had taken from the kitchen, while Freddie slouched across the couch's armrest, chin propped on his elbow. Edward was in his regular spot beside their father's old lounger. Concern washed across his face the instant he saw Emmett.

"What's wrong?" Mrs. Poole asked, her reaction mirroring Edward's.

"A lot."

Emmett hit the power on the television and put Edward's homemade radio on top of it. A fretful voice was saying, "We've got stores on fire all up and down Belmont. Send the fire department now. Now, damn it."

"I need trucks on Clinton Avenue," someone shouted next. "We got fires burning in four stores I counted. Four of 'em. And the ones that ain't on fire are getting robbed. Niggers are going in and out like they're shopping. We need backup. It's just the two of us and they're throwing stuff at the car."

Mrs. Poole's hand went to her heart. Freddie sat up, alert.

"Raise the volume," Edward insisted.

Dispatch reiterated its infuriating refrain. "By order of the command post, all cars are to remain in their districts."

"The hell with the command post," someone blurted. The air went dead for a second, then the flurry of reports resumed.

"I don't understand," Mrs. Poole said. "What's going on?"

"It's the same as yesterday," Emmett said. "Only worse."

He hadn't seen exactly what set off the mayhem. The specifics were immaterial. The rally to protest police brutality had spiraled into exactly that—police brutality—and reprisals were sweeping like a tidal wave. Every radio car in the city was demanding that the dispatcher take them off their assigned routes so they could come to the Fourth Precinct.

"Breaking and entering reported at a gun shop on South Orange and Beacon. Repeat. South Orange and Beacon. They're stealing shotguns. I can see 'em. Those bastards got three under each arm."

"This is real? I mean, really real?" Freddie couldn't believe his ears.

In a panic, Mrs. Poole stood up and glanced around for her purse. "I need my pocketbook. Where's my pocketbook? I need to get home. Please, Mr. Emmett, take me home."

"I can't do that. You won't be safe there. Not tonight." He gingerly sat her back down.

"But my house? My things?"

"Unless you live in a store, lady, nobody's gonna care about your things."

"Freddie's right. Anyway, it's too dangerous for you to be there. You'll have to spend the night here. Both of you."

Neither of them was thrilled at the prospect, and Edward was giving Emmett a dirty look.

"I guess staying here's gotta be better than being in the middle of all that," Freddie said as the police band became garbled with more requests.

The next was from an officer begging for fire trucks. "There's a structure fire on the corner of Springfield and Morris. One building and spreading. Get the hoses here pronto."

Upon hearing the location, Freddie hopped off the couch. "Take me home. I need to go home."

"What about not being in the middle of things?" Emmett said.

"I said take me home."

"Freddie, no. It's too—"

"Let offa me. Lemme outta here. I said I need to go." He was imploring Emmett with his eyes.

"The fire. It's by Luther Reed's body shop. That's what you're worried about."

Freddie stopped wriggling. "Not the shop. What's inside."

"The tape?"

He nodded gravely.

"You told me you didn't give it to Luther. You said you weren't that stupid."

"I didn't. And I'm not. Figured it'd be the last place Luther'd think of."

"What tape? What are you two talking about?" Mrs. Poole was up out of her chair again.

Freddie and Emmett traded glances. There was no time for an explanation. Ionello and Vass would never believe that the tape had been lost in a fire. They would dedicate their lives to making Freddie's miserable until they were satisfied that he wouldn't turn them in.

Emmett hated to say it. "We have to go get that tape."

"Don't, Marty." Edward wheeled in close. "Not for him. It's not your problem."

"Screw this," Freddie yelled, reaching for the door. "I'll get the damn thing myself. And screw you, you damn cripple."

Emmett slammed him against the living room wall. Freddie floundered under his weight. "The next word out of your mouth is going to be an apology."

"I don't wanna hear him say he's sorry," Edward sneered. "I knew he was sorry the minute I met him. He's a good-for-nothing lowlife and he'll never be anything more."

Mrs. Poole touched Emmett's arm lightly. "Please. You might hurt the boy. He'll apologize."

Emmett released him. He didn't want to be responsible for Freddie getting hurt. That was why he couldn't allow him to go to Luther's body shop alone.

"Let him chase after his precious tape. Whatever it takes to get his worthless ass out of my house." Edward rolled into the kitchen. The screen door hinges cawed, then the door bashed shut.

Freddie pulled away from Emmett to nurse his bruised shoulders as well as his bruised ego.

"I'm sorry, Freddie. I shouldn't have done that. I'm sorry to you too, Mrs. Poole. I realize this isn't what you signed on for."

Diving into the middle of a riot wasn't what Emmett signed on for when he bailed Freddie out of jail, but that cassette tape was Freddie's future. They had to get it before the flames did.

"Take my bed. It's the big room upstairs."

"I couldn't, Mr. Emmett. The couch is fine."

"The couch might be fine for you. It won't be for your back. You brought that chair in from the kitchen because none of these would give you any support."

Mrs. Poole shook her head, amazed. "I should've known I couldn't put nothin' past you."

Very little got past Emmett. Though too much got to him. Except he wouldn't let it show.

"You'll have to get Edward into his bed. If he'll go."

"He'll go. Once he gets tired."

Edward was already tired—tired of being trapped in the wheelchair and tired of being angry. While he may have wanted Freddie out of the house, Edward wanted out of his wheelchair more.

"Shots fired," a distraught voice shouted over the police band. "Repeat. Shots fired at South Orange and Rankin."

It was the first gunfire of the night. Emmett was certain it wouldn't be the last.

"Do you have to go right this second, Mr. Emmett? Can't you wait? At least a little while?"

"The fire won't." He took the radio from off the television. "You ready?"

Feeling slighted from the fight, Freddie wouldn't respond.

"Your mouth ain't broke, young man. Speak up or you're staying here. Tape or no tape."

Freddie crossed his arms, sulking. "Yeah, I'm ready."

As they were preparing to go, the police dispatcher changed his tune. "By order of the command post, all available units are to report to the rear of the Fourth Precinct to assist in guarding the remaining cars. All available units in the area report to the Fourth."

The upbeat bulletin was undercut by the dire phrase "remaining cars."

"That means the rest of the police are coming to help, doesn't it? They'll make it stop, won't they?" Mrs. Poole seemed to need an answer, any kind of answer. "Won't they?"

Emmett's answer was: "Lock the door behind us."

TWENTY-ONE

All of the bulbs in the streetlamps on Springfield Avenue had been smashed, leaving the moonlight to illuminate the devastation. The city's main drag, which Emmett and Freddie had traversed just hours earlier, was now a four-lane obstacle course. A delivery truck was abandoned in the middle of the street, its contents spilled on the asphalt, and refuse littered the sidewalks, exhaled in the looters' maelstrom.

Emmett switched off his headlights and drove slow, weaving around the wreckage. Freddie was gazing out the passenger-side window in astonished silence. "Where are the cops?"

"They said on the radio they were outnumbered."

"So they left?"

"Wouldn't you?"

Flocks of people were roving in and out of store windows, arms loaded with anything they could carry, from toaster ovens to groceries. The Foodtown Supermarket had been decimated. Even the cash registers were gone. A car with a towline was backed up to a furniture store, having ripped free the iron security grating. Three men were stepping over the fallen grate, hoisting a chair with floral upholstery into the car's trunk.

"Forget layaway plans," Freddie said.

A woman hurried by pushing a baby carriage. Singed cartons of Peach Schnapps were stacked in the stroller. She had a pile of dresses slung over her arm too. The hangers bobbed to the rhythm of her footsteps.

"Folks be thinkin' it's Christmas."

"Christmas is about giving and receiving. This . . . this is about robbing and stealing. Whoever owns those stores isn't going to see it as a holiday."

"Whoever owns those stores ain't Negro."

"That's beside the point."

"No, that's right on top 'a it."

A curtain of smoke was moving downwind. Embers were swirling on the breeze. That didn't stop the shopping. Looters fanned cinders from their eyes, a minor inconvenience. On one side of the street, a couple was carting an elaborate chandelier on a child's red wagon. On the other, a man in suspenders was ambling off with a vacuum cleaner and holding his shirt to his mouth so he could breath.

Emmett started coughing. He raised his window. "That fire we heard about on the radio must have spread."

"Then drive faster," Freddie told him.

Black smoke billowed from the appliance store next to Luther Reed's auto body shop. Flames on the rooftop were lapping at the sky.

"Where'd you hide the tape?"

"It's in the garage. In the station wagon on the lift. Under the front seat."

"You're right. Luther definitely would not have looked there."

"It's the first car we got from the junkyard, first car we swapped the title on," Freddie revealed, wistful. His clever idea was about to go up in the blaze.

"We've got to do this fast. I'll cover you. You get the tape."

"Like pickin' one big pocket."

The body shop had been conspicuously spared the destruction faced by other businesses on the avenue. Valuable tools prime for stealing lay in plain view behind an unmarred window. Even in the midst of a riot, nobody dared damage Luther Reed's property.

Freddie jogged up to the garage and raised the rolling door. "Luther don't lock it. People too scared to break in and steal from him."

"Most people."

They slid under and closed the garage door behind them. Emmett had his borrowed flashlight at the ready. The station wagon was suspended high in the air, the mammoth body floating improbably. Its bumper hovered above Emmett's eye level.

"You know how to lower the lift?"

"Lever's over here." Freddie flipped it repeatedly. Nothing happened. "Damn. It's busted. Help me up."

Outside, a car rode by honking its horn victoriously. A dining table was lashed to the roof. Emmett snuffed the flashlight beam until the car passed, then pushed Freddie into the open driver's-side window.

"Lucky for us you're tall."

"It's got its advantages. I never thought this would be one of them."

"I always wished I was tall," Freddie said, slithering into the driver's seat. "I prayed every night that I'd grow and every morning I'd wake up the same height. Short."

"You're still a kid. Who's to say you won't wind up taller than me."

Freddie looked down at him from the car window, encouraged. "Really? You think?"

"Anything's possible."

"Anything's possible, huh?" Freddie repeated the phrase. "I like that. Gotta ring to it."

Possibilities were what the stolen dining tables and chandeliers and vacuum cleaners represented, a second shot for people who hadn't been given a first. Emmett had spent the last six years of his life chasing down and arresting robbers, burglars, and thieves. He didn't condone stealing. But he could see how someone who had been robbed of their own possibilities would feel justified in evening the score.

"Found it." Freddie held up the cassette.

"Good. Because we need to leave."

The odor of smoke was getting stronger. It scraped at Emmett's throat and nostrils, painful to inhale. Muffled through the garage windows, the crackle of flames sounded oddly similar to rushing water.

Freddie crawled out the window, saying, "I wish I could see Luther's face when his body shop—"

"Quiet." Emmett heard a noise. The front door was unlatching. "Someone's coming."

He shoved Freddie's dangling legs into the station wagon, extinguished the flashlight, and pasted himself to a wall in between two shelving units. The looters had gotten gusty and were robbing Reed, or it was Luther and his men.

"Hurry up. Fire's getting close." That was Reed's voice.

"How we supposta carry it?"

"With your hands, fool."

"But it's heavy."

"That's why I brought your dumb asses with me."

In the hazy light, Emmett could see Freddie peeking over the station wagon's dashboard. He signaled for him to stay out of sight. Reed and his men were shuffling from the storefront to the back room.

"What about the rest 'a the stuff?"

"I don't give a damn if this whole place burns to the ground," Luther said. "That's what I got the house for. And you gonna get fried up with this place if you don't get my air conditioner."

The fire radiated light into the garage, outlining the figures of the two burly guys who had been guarding the back room that afternoon. They were lugging Luther's beloved industrial air conditioner through the hall to the pickup truck idling at the curb.

"Don't drop it," Reed cautioned. He was supervising as they loaded the air conditioner onto the flatbed. Afterward, he made the two of them sit in back with it while he road in the truck's cab.

Once the truck pulled away, Emmett came out of hiding. "Okay, Freddie, you can get down now."

The kid scaled the side of the wagon and dropped to the ground, hacking to clear his throat. "I figured out why this car was at the junkyard."

"Why?"

"Smells like a cat died in there."

"Well, all I smell is smoke and it's getting a lot hotter in here."

"Don't have to ask me twice."

Shrill shrieks of bursting glass sent Emmett and Freddie sprinting from the body shop. Flames had engulfed the exterior walls. The intensity of the fire was blowing out the windows. From across the street, they stood watching the garage's demise, then came a distant *pop, pop, pop.*

"Was that the fire?"

"No," Emmett said. "That was gunshots."

More followed in rapid succession, far away yet distinct.

Freddie put the tape in his pocket. "So what're we standing around here for?"

In the car, they caught the tail end of a transmission on the police band. The speaker wasn't a dispatcher. It was Director Sloakes. "Fire-arms may be used when your own or another's life is in danger and no other measures are available to defend yourself or apprehend an offender. Only fire if fired upon." He enunciated with the clinical detachment of someone reading from a manual.

"Think those were cops we heard shooting?" Freddie asked.

"If it was, they missed the message."

"Or they got it crystal clear."

A bulletin came over the frequency that Spruce Street, east of the Fourth Precinct, was completely looted. Every single store had been scavenged to empty husks. Emmett lowered the volume.

"What did Luther mean about 'the house'?"

"Ain't no regular house. It's a warehouse. Takes up most 'a Boyden Street. Luther's always braggin' about how it's some fortress and how nobody could ever get in 'cause he's got it booby-trapped."

"What's inside that would need that much protection?"

"Luther wouldn't say. Just talked about how Fort Knox had nothin' on his place."

"What would you guess was in there?"

"Bunch 'a big old air conditioners."

"No, really."

"Dope. Cash. Guns. Whatever it is, it's somethin' special."

Since the body shop was a front, Reed had to have a hub for his operations. An unassuming warehouse would be the ideal place to cut his drugs, stash his weapons, and squirrel his money. Whether the elaborate booby traps were fact or fiction, Luther Reed would have gone to great lengths to protect his investments.

"Speaking of something special, what are you going to do with that tape?"

"Don't get any funny ideas. I ain't givin' it to you. A cop is a cop."

"And a thief is a thief. I don't want your tape, Freddie. I want you to find a smarter place to hide it is all. Maybe somewhere less flammable."

The orange aura of several nearby fires was bulging into the night sky.

"And where would that be?" Freddie asked sarcastically.

"Anyplace except your mother's apartment. They'll search there first. If they haven't already."

"I wonder what they're doing."

"Who? Ionello and Vass?"

"No, my mama and Cyril. Maybe they're at home. Or maybe they're out doin' what everybody else is."

"I can go and see if they're okay. But I can't take you with me. They'll have your house staked out."

"You don't have to go. I was just wondering. That's not the same as caring."

His mother's refusal to post bail pared away much of the sympathy Freddie had for her. He was too hurt to say he cared. Emmett could tell he did, though.

"What does the R stand for?"

"Huh?"

"At court, when the clerk read your name, he said, 'Fredrick R. Guthrie.'"

"The R's for Rodney. It's my dad's name."

"Did he get you interested in cars?"

"Taught me all about 'em before he left."

"Left for where?"

"Wherever." Freddie stepped over the issue like a crack on a side-walk. He would say no more. "Cyril don't know nothin' about cars. He don't even got one. What kinda man are you if you don't even got no ride? Someday I'm gonna get me a car. It'll be real slick too. A Corvette maybe. Or a sweet Mustang. I'll drive by and everybody'll be like, 'Hey, that's Freddie's car.'" The fantasy put a grin on his face that lasted until they returned to Emmett's house.

"Your brother still gonna be mad at me?"

"Probably."

"What am I supposta do?"

"You could try saying you're sorry."

"And that'll work?"

"Hasn't worked for me. But he doesn't know you that well. Maybe it'll work for you."

"Thanks. That's some advice."

When Emmett unlocked the front door to his house, it wouldn't open fully. An overturned chair was barring the way. The living room had been ransacked. He drew his service revolver.

"Freddie, wait here."

Emmett shouldered in the door. The TV was still there, the re-cord player too. Nothing of value was missing. The place had been tossed.

"Edward? Mrs. Poole?"

A whimper came from the kitchen. Gun raised, Emmett flipped on the lights with his elbow. Mrs. Poole was crumpled on the kitchen floor, crying.

"Are you all right?" He knelt and examined her for injuries.

"I'm okay. But I can't get up."

Emmett lifted Mrs. Poole to her feet, her bad back crimping her every move.

"She okay?" Freddie had disregarded Emmett's orders and trailed him into the house.

"Didn't I say to wait outside?"

Short on excuses, Freddie just shrugged.

"What happened?" Emmett wanted to know too.

"These men, they broke into the house. Said not to call the police because they were too busy with the riot. Then they, they . . ." She stammered into tears.

"Mrs. Poole, where's Edward?"

She motioned to the porch.

"Freddie, get a chair for her. Get her something to drink."

He passed Mrs. Poole into Freddie's arms and burst through the screen door. His brother was in his wheelchair facing the yard. "Edward, what—"

"You shoulda left me your gun." Blood was dried around his nose and lips. His right eye was swollen shut. "They said they wanted the nigger's name. Said you'd know why."

Caligrassi had sent his men to terrorize an answer out of Emmett. Rage mingled with the misery of bringing his troubles onto his brother and Mrs. Poole.

"I told you not to help that kid, Marty."

"It's not him. He's not the one they were after."

Emmett leaned heavily on the porch rail and told Edward the story of Vernon Young's murder as well as what had transpired with Lieutenant Ahern.

"Why didn't you say anything?" The secret seemed to hurt Edward more than his eye.

"In case of something like this."

"Marty. I gave 'em the kid's name," Edward admitted. "I'm sorry. I didn't realize."

Emmett's heart sank. He looked through the screen door into the kitchen. Freddie had gotten Mrs. Poole a glass of water and was sitting with her at the table, comforting her. He was sixteen years old, skinny and puny, and the most powerful men in the entire city of Newark— the cops, Luther Reed, and Ruggiero Caligrassi—were all on the hunt for him.

Emmett was torn. He hated to leave Edward and Mrs. Poole again, however he knew what was heading for Lossie Guthrie.

"They'll go to his mother's house."

Edward understood. He put out his cigarette and held open his palm. Emmett gave him the pistol from his leg holster.

"Don't worry," Edward said. "I'll wait up."

TWENTY-TWO

Midnight had come and gone, yet the Central Ward was as busy and noisy as if it were midday. Rose Street, where Lossie Guthrie lived, was at the epicenter of the riot, and every road Emmett tried to turn on was blocked by hordes of looters or fire trucks. The closest Emmett could get was Tenth Street. He would have to cross through Woodland Cemetery to get to Freddie's house.

The fencing didn't go all the way around the fifty-five-acre graveyard, so people traipsed through as they pleased, mainly kids taking shortcuts and junkies rushing to their favorite spots to get a fix. By flashlight, Emmett could follow a beaten footpath between the thicket of tombstones. He wasn't afraid to be there. Woodland was safer than most places at that hour. What he would face once he left did worry him. Sirens and distant gunshots fractured the cemetery's signature silence.

Emmett could tell that he was nearing the main gate. He had come to a section devoid of headstones, a flat tract of graves for infants and children. Were it not for the divots in the ground, that part of the graveyard could have been mistaken for a meadow.

Ahead was a small Gothic church enshrouded in trees. Its turreted spire dissolved into the night sky. The church marked the cemetery's entrance, and its gate let out onto Brenner Street, which intersected with Rose. Emmett snapped off the flashlight. From here on, he would have to do without it.

While the main roads surrounding the area were jammed, Rose Street was deserted. The residents were nowhere to be seen. They could have been barricaded inside their apartments or out indulging in the free-for-all. For their own sakes, Emmett hoped Lossie Guthrie, and her boyfriend, Cyril, hadn't stayed home.

Caligrassi's thugs would be driving a nice car, so Emmett took note of the vehicles on the street. Most were older than his with rust eating away at the edges and broken windows replaced by garbage bags. The mobsters would take no pains to conceal their car by parking elsewhere. Their goal was to make their presence known. Since there was no sign, Emmett thought he might have gotten to Lossie's first. He took the stairs two at a time up to the fourth floor and pressed his ear to the door, hand on his sidearm. He heard a pained mewling and tried the knob.

The apartment had been wrecked. The furniture was demolished. Amid the mess, Lossie's arm was protruding from under the capsized love seat. Emmett rolled it off of her. She had been sheltering beneath the cushions.

"Mrs. Guthrie? It's Detective Emmett."

Traumatized, she clenched her eyes closed. A huge welt had risen on her cheek. She was clutching a rag rug that had been kicked aside in the fracas as if it was a security blanket.

"You're okay. They're gone. You're safe now."

Lossie opened her eyes timidly. She blinked as though Emmett might be a mirage. "Where is he? Where's Cyril?"

"Is that who did this to you?" Emmett was so focused on Caligrassi's thugs that he had forgotten what type of guy Lossie's boyfriend was.

"No, it was them men. They hurt him. I saw it. They hurt him bad."

Blood droplets led from the living room down the hall, confirming what type of guys Caligrassi's thugs were. Emmett took out his revolver. Lossie huddled into herself, sobbing.

The trail ended at the bathroom. Cyril was on the floor, unconscious. His head lay at the base of the toilet in a troth of blood. The mirror was spattered, and the corner of the sink was smeared where Cyril's forehead had been bashed against it. Emmett got a pulse in his wrist but couldn't rouse him. Ambrose Webster's grandmother had mentioned that the Guthries didn't have a telephone. Emmett would have to find one.

"Mrs. Guthrie, listen to me. Listen." He had to shake Lossie to get her to reopen her eyes. "Cyril has to go to the hospital. I need a phone to call for an ambulance."

She grabbed his arm. "Don't go. Don't. Please."

"If you don't let me go, Cyril could die."

For a brief instant, she became lucid. "Okay," she said, releasing him. "Okay."

Emmett pounded on the door to the apartment below. "This is the police. There are injured people upstairs. I have to use your telephone."

Nobody answered. He did the same on the second floor, then the first. No one was home, or they wouldn't answer the door. Emmett went back to Lossie's. She was coiled on the rug, cradling herself in her own arms and humming.

"Mrs. Guthrie, I have to go get help. I need you to sit with Cyril and make sure he keeps breathing. Can you do that?"

Lossie buried her face in the carpet and hummed louder. It was useless. He had to leave.

Emmett planned to flag the firemen from the trucks that had been obstructing the main roads and have them radio in for him. To his dismay, the fire trucks were gone. Bergen Street was abandoned, already plundered. Water dripped from burnt storefronts and washed into the gutters. The marauders and the firemen had moved on.

With the streetlamps in smithereens, all Emmett had to see by was a dwindling fire in a trash can. He spotted a pay phone outside a ravaged pharmacy. Neighborhood junkies had cleaned the shelves bare. Emmett was amazed he hadn't run into any of them in the cemetery, reveling in their spoils. He picked up the pay phone's receiver. There was no dial tone. The cord had been cut. Emmett was running out of options. Earlier that afternoon, he and Otis Fossum had been standing on that very curb. He thought of Otis lamenting how he hadn't helped with Vernon Young's case, then Emmett remembered the call box.

The Bergen Street box was set up outside a bar named Woody's. Boxes were often placed in close proximity to reputed trouble spots. Most bars in the neighborhood qualified, but Woody's was notorious for its drunken brawls and for the twelve-gauge shotgun the bartender would brandish if a fight broke out. Foot patrolmen were actually prohibited from pulling at that box between the hours of one A.M. and three. Since it took five to ten minutes for a radio car to arrive at the location after a double pull, the sign for distress, it was considered too dangerous for an officer to be there on his own past one for even that short a time.

Emmett's watch read two in the morning. He pulled the lever on the call box twice and waited.

Minutes ticked by with no response. He imagined that the Central Complaints Division was inundated with calls. Still, a double from the Bergen Street box should have been a priority. Central Complaints should have rung back as per protocol. That night, Emmett's double pull didn't even warrant a response.

He looked around for any lights on in apartment windows. Every single one was dark, all except the front window of Woody's. Between the slits in the blinds, there was movement. It was the last place Emmett wanted to go or would be welcomed, but Cyril had to get to the hospital. He crossed himself and went in.

Woody's was packed as if it was a Saturday night. There wasn't a single white face in the crowd. Men were crowded at the bar, arm's length from the taps, while women clustered in the jade green Naugahyde booths, sipping drinks. A haze of cigarette smoke mellowed the lights. Heads turned as the door swung closed behind Emmett.

"I need to use the phone," Emmett announced, holding his badge in the air. "It's an emergency. A man and woman living on Rose Street were beaten up badly and I have to call an ambulance."

The address was a giveaway. Nobody white lived on Rose Street. The patrons would know that.

"Maybe you the one who beat 'em up," someone mumbled.

"I need to use the phone," Emmett repeated, unwavering. He felt someone coming up behind him.

"You all by your lonesome, Officer?" the guy said into his ear intimidatingly.

Any second Emmet expected to feel a knife or a gun press into his ribs. "All I want is to use the telephone."

"You move on off 'a him, Billy," said the bartender, an older man whose hair receded into a high arch. He was reaching under the counter with the practiced calm of someone who defused violence on a nightly basis. "Don't force me to get out this here shotgun. It's too damn hot for a ruckus."

Billy backed away a step. "You no fun," he told the bartender, who set a rotary dial telephone on the counter.

"Just don't make no long-distance calls."

Everyone stared as Emmett dialed the Complaints Division number direct. It rang and rang. Finally, somebody answered.

"Dispatch."

"This is Detective Emmett. I need a bus at—"

"No buses available."

"None?"

"Too many calls. First come, first served. You can tell me the location, Detective, but you're at the end of the line. And it's a helluva long line."

Emmett gave Lossie's address and hung up.

"Maybe you should 'a told 'em they was white folks," the bartender suggested. "Then maybe they woulda come."

"Thanks anyway."

As Emmett headed for the door, someone muttered, "You know thing's bad when even a cop can't bring the cops."

"I'll drink to that," another toasted.

Outside, the night air was dense with the acrid chemical odor of melted plastic. The fire in the trash can was almost out. The ambulance wouldn't arrive for hours, if at all. Emmett did the only thing he could think to do. He went and got his car and double-parked in front of Lossie Guthrie's building. Lossie was exactly where he left her, now asleep on the floor. Emmett woke her, saying, "We have to bring Cyril to the hospital."

"Okay." She cooperated like a sleepy child, holding open the front door as Emmett slid Cyril out of the bathroom, through the apartment, and into the hall. Unconscious, the man's muscle became ungainly dead weight.

"You're going to have to grab his legs, Mrs. Guthrie. I can't carry him down the stairs alone."

She ran her hand over Cyril's bloody brow. "Okay."

Together they got him out of the tenement and into Emmett's car. Because there was no backseat, Lossie had to squeeze in front, hunched on Cyril's lap. Emmett was spent from the effort and paused to catch his breath before he could drive.

"You okay?" It was a slight variation on the single word she had been repeating. Her cheek was so badly swollen, Emmett should have been asking her that.

"Yeah, I'm okay," he replied, though the term had ceased to signify much of anything.

An orderly helped him load Cyril onto a stretcher at City Hospital, then the orderly wheeled Cyril into the emergency room. From outside, Emmett could see that the waiting room was packed. The wounded overflowed into the hallways. Dozens were holding bloody towels to their heads and extremities. Those with leg injuries and worse lay on the floor. These were the people who had made it to the hospital. Emmett wondered how many were still waiting for ambulances.

"You go with Cyril, Mrs. Guthrie. Freddie can sleep at my house tonight."

Her expression became quizzical, as if her son's name was foreign to her. Freddie's welfare hadn't entered her mind. That made Emmett even more tired.

"Go on," he told her. "Cyril needs you."

Weary, Emmett went home. He rattled the key in the lock, a signal to Edward that it was him. "It's me," he added when he opened the door.

Edward was sitting in the dark, the pistol at his side. He clicked on the safety. "Was the kid's mom all right?"

Emmett let his brother see the blood on his clothes. "I took her and her boyfriend to the hospital. I'd take you too, except the emergency room was jammed. We'd be there 'til morning. Might as well go then."

"For a shiner? Please. I've seen worse." Edward gestured at his legs.

"You go on to bed. I'll stay up." Emmett removed his jacket, grateful to finally have it off. His muscles were stiff. Hauling Cyril to the hospital had done him in.

"You're the one who should get some sleep." Edward handed him the glass of water he had been drinking.

Emmett guzzled it. "And you're the one who got slugged."

"You shoulda seen 'em, Marty. They were a pair 'a pansy hoodlums who'd watched too many Edward G. Robinson movies. What a joke. If I wasn't. . . ." He bridled himself and abandoned the thought. Emmett knew what he was about to say. Hearing it aloud would have been uncomfortable for both of them.

"Tell me what they looked like. Do you remember?"

"'Course I remember. How could I forget? The first guy was short, stocky. His collar was squeezing his fat neck into rolls. The other was taller, nicer suit, had a dimple in his chin so deep you could eat soup outta it."

The second description fit Sal Lucaro to a T. Emmett sighed and dropped heavily onto the couch.

"What? You know them?"

"Only the one with the dimple."

"Is he that big cheese mobster? The guy you liked for the murder?"

"Yup."

"What're you gonna do, Marty?"

"For now, I'm going to make sure they don't come back and you're going to get some rest."

"I rest all day."

"Always have to argue, don't you?"

"We'll take turns. One of us sleeps while the other stays awake. How 'bout that?"

"Fine."

"You first," they both said at once.

"You win," Edward relented, tired. "I'll go first."

Emmett assisted him into bed and laid a sheet over him.

"Wake me in an hour."

"Deal."

"Promise?"

"I promise."

Emmett took the .22 from him and sat watch from the couch. He had no intention of waking his brother. Edward had been through enough. Though Lucaro and his accomplice probably wouldn't put in another appearance that evening, part of Emmett wished they would.

A true Jesuit should have prayed for them and their sins. A true Jesuit should have prayed away any feelings of revenge. Emmett wasn't a Jesuit anymore. The payback he prayed for kept him awake the rest of the night.

TWENTY-THREE

The watery dawn light woke Emmett, that and the voice of Director Sloakes. He had tucked the police band radio next to his pillow, the volume low. Sloakes was making an announcement.

"As of this Friday, the fourteenth of July, 1967, the mayor has officially declared a state of emergency. The National Guard and state police have been called in to aid our department in this time of crisis. Troopers and Guardsmen are presently arriving at the Roseville armory and will continue to arrive throughout the day. Your orders are to patrol in radio cars in groups of four. One patrolman will be assigned to guide two troopers and one Guardsman around the city. Continuing updates will be broadcast throughout the day."

"Better late than never," Emmett said with a yawn.

"You awake." Mrs. Poole was tiptoeing down the stairs.

He stood up and rubbed his face. His wristwatch said it was quarter to six. Emmett hadn't gotten up that early since he was a novice. Even then, it felt unnatural.

"At this hour, I'm as close to awake as I can be."

They were speaking in the hushed tones parents would use around a slumbering baby so as not to disturb Edward, who was asleep in the dining room. His eye was a deeper shade of a purple than last night, making the bruise on his forehead from his fall seem minor.

"I put Freddie in the other bedroom upstairs. I hope that's okay."

It was Emmett's childhood room that he had shared with his brother. Of the two twin mattresses, Edward's was now downstairs. Freddie was sleeping in Emmett's old bed.

"Of course. Did he give you any flak?"

"Nothing I couldn't handle."

"No doubt. How are you feeling?"

"Not too bad. I was more shaken up than anything."

He could tell that Mrs. Poole wanted to hear about where he had been but wouldn't ask. "I'm truly sorry about what happened."

"Don't be sorry for me, Mr. Emmett. Be sorry for him." She motioned at Edward. "If he could've, your brother would have jumped up out 'a his wheelchair and clobbered those men senseless. Not being able to, that had nothing on the beatin' he took."

Edward was breathing heavily in his sleep, his chest rising and falling tranquilly. Emmett wondered if his brother could walk in his dreams or if he was in the wheelchair then too.

"I'm gonna put on a pot of coffee," Mrs. Poole said.

She went into the kitchen, and he trailed her. "Do you mind if I ask you something?"

"Depends on the something." She poured water into the coffeepot.

"What was it like having your husband in a wheelchair?"

"It was no picnic," she admitted, ladling in the coffee grounds. "But I'd rather have had him alive and in the chair than not have him at all."

She plugged in the pot and took a pair of mugs from the cupboard. "Percy stepped on a land mine. Lost both legs from the knees down. Should've killed him. When he got out of the hospital, he couldn't look me in the eye. I'd been married to him for going on fifteen years and he couldn't look at me. Said he was ashamed to be half a man. I told him I was thankful to have half and I'd have gladly taken less. Easy for me to say 'cause it was true. Wasn't easy for him to believe. That's the rough part. Believing that life isn't over. That it hasn't been cut in half and is still worth living."

The coffee began to perk. "Try explaining that to Edward," Emmett said.

"Have you? Tried, I mean."

"He won't tell you this, so I will," Emmett confided. "Edward wasn't supposed to be there when it happened. The troops had driven the Vietcong out of the Iron Triangle and captured their supplies, crates of M-16s and medical kits and rations they'd stolen from American bases. He was fresh off the plane from Fort Dix, been in Vietnam for less than a month, and his job was to repair the radios and radars on the howitzers. That day, they had him driving a six-by-six truck to cart off all the contraband. When Edward got out of the truck to load in the crates, a sniper shot him from a concealed tunnel, hit him in the base of the spine. Do you want to know what was in those crates? Tin cans of peas. My brother will never walk again. And for what? For a crate of peas."

The coffeepot stopped bubbling and fell quiet.

Emmett hadn't been in favor of the war. Every day, he went to work in a war zone, and he had seen firsthand that there were never any winners. He hadn't been able to talk Edward out of enlisting, so he held himself partially responsible for the accident, an older brother who had failed his younger brother. It was one of many in a long list of failures.

"You can be angry, Mr. Emmett. You got every right. But don't you think Edward's angry enough for the both of you? Somebody's got to show him how not to be."

"I'm not sure I'm the person to do that, Mrs. Poole."

She poured him a mug of coffee and pushed it along the counter, as if passing him a note. "You're his brother. You're all he's got. You don't do it, nobody will."

Emmett brought the mug to his lips and blew on it. The coffee was too hot to drink. He put the mug aside. "I have to get ready. I have to go."

"Again?"

"It'll be okay. Gangsters don't get out of bed this early in the morning."

"I'll have to remember that," she said.

"There's a file I need from the station house. As soon as I get it, I'll come straight home."

"You promise, Mr. Emmett?"

He had broken his promise to Edward last night. This time, he wouldn't. "Yes, I promise."

Emmett showered, shaved, and changed into a clean suit, then tucked an extra box of bullets into his jacket pocket. He went by his old bedroom on the way downstairs. The door was half open.

Baseball pennants hung on the walls. Atop the dresser, Edward's basketball trophies mingled with Emmett's from track and field. The rising sun glinted off the medals and brass figurines. Freddie lay curled on the bed. He had kicked off the covers and was hugging the pillow tightly to him, anxious even in his sleep.

In the burgeoning daylight, the living room looked like a crime scene. Chairs were flung over, and books and lamps were scattered across the floor, chaos for the sake of chaos. It was as if the riot had spilled into Emmett's house.

"They did a real number on the place, didn't they?"

Mrs. Poole was putting away yesterday's dishes from the drying rack. "I'll clean up, Mr. Emmett. I don't believe they broke anything."

Nothing tangible, Emmett thought.

"I should be back before Freddie or Edward are up. If I'm not, you can't let Freddie leave. Not for a second. He listens to you, Mrs. Poole. He'll do what you say."

"The boy's in real trouble, isn't he?"

Telling her how much would frighten her. "Just don't let him go anywhere."

Emmett's mug of coffee had cooled. He finished it in three gulps, then went and hid his .22 under the bedsheet, right beside Edward's hand.

TWENTY-FOUR

Getting into the Fourth Precinct was more difficult that morning than it had been yesterday with a mob of protesters outside. Out front, state troopers in full garb—light blue shirtsleeves and dark blue pants with yellow stripes on the sides—were lined up awaiting radio cars to patrol in. In the rear, a formation of officers was guarding the cruisers as they fueled up. Emmett elected for the front door because the troopers wouldn't recognize him.

The station's entrance hall was carpeted with glass. The boards on the windows made the hall dusky despite the lights. No one was around, not even the desk sergeant.

Emergency twelve-hour shifts went from eight A.M. to eight P.M. and eight P.M. to eight A.M., splitting the day. They were long hours, especially for detectives. Patrolmen usually worked five days on, two days off. Detectives often worked a day less. The end of the second shift was approaching, and Emmett was relying on those long hours to have emptied out the Homicide squad room.

"Hey, Detective." Patrolman Nolan was bounding down the staircase as he was going up, happy for a familiar face. "You get a load 'a those state troopers outside? Talk about calling in the cavalry? I wish I had a camera. Wasn't it nuts last night? We had ourselves a genuine riot. Everybody—"

Emmett cut him off. "Officer, is your shift over?"

"No, sir."

"Where were you assigned?"

"Back of the building, sir. To pump gas. I had to go to the john."

"If you were assigned there, why are you standing here talking to me?"

"Understood, sir." Browbeaten, Nolan ambled off.

Emmett had to be blunt. The narrow wedge of time when the station was deserted was his best shot at getting in and out unobserved. He would apologize to Nolan later.

Though the sun had only recently risen, the third floor was already agonizingly hot. Split by the stairs, the top floor was chopped into two cramped squad rooms, one for Vice, one for Homicide. Emmett slunk past his division's door, prepared to dart into the men's room if anyone was inside. All of the desks were empty, including his old desk, which was now home to the coffeemaker. He hadn't been welcome when he was transferred to Homicide and he still wasn't, so Emmett had no qualms about sneaking in when the squad room was unguarded.

Any of the four detectives could have been sitting on the murder case he was after. He had to start with somebody. He chose Serletto.

His desk was in the corner, facing the door. That way he could see who was coming and going. In a room full of cops, Serletto was too suspicious to put his back to an entry. His desktop was covered with paper coffee cups and unfinished reports. Emmett picked through the dog-eared piles, then dug into the drawers. Racing spreads and candy wrappers were mashed in among the cases. Shoved at the bottom in an envelope was Serletto's diploma from the academy, stashed like an incriminating secret. Nowhere among the clutter did Emmett see any mention of a missing finger.

Hochwald's desk was pristine compared to his partner's and virtually empty. In the top drawer sat a single pencil and a string of paper clips linked together, the sort of thing someone assembled out of boredom.

Of the two of them, Hochwald was the brawn. Serletto did the talking and, apparently, all the paperwork. Emmett didn't trouble with the rest of Hochwald's desk. If the guy didn't have a single notepad, he wouldn't have held on to a file.

The other detectives' desks were relatively clean, which gave Emmett an idea. Overflow of active and pending cases was stored in the squad's standing filing cabinet until due to go to the Records Room. He rolled open the cabinet's top drawer and paged through the folders, skipping any with female names. Evander Hammond's body was discovered in April, Julius Dekes's in May, and Ambrose Webster's in July. If the killer was staying true to form, the report Emmett was searching for would have been posted in June. The files weren't packed together as tightly as they were in the basement, yet the number of murders was greater than Emmett had foreseen. That was bad for him, though not nearly as bad as it was for the victims and their families.

From outside the squad room came muffled voices, getting louder. People were coming up the steps. Emmett shut the drawer and positioned himself in the middle of the room so he wasn't near any desk in particular. The voices passed, going across the hall to Vice. Emmett realized he had been holding his breath. He exhaled and embarked on the next drawer.

The room was stuffy and he was sweating. His fingertips were sticking to the folders. He would have removed his jacket, but the seconds that would have taken were too precious. Diagrams speckled with wounds flicked by, a gruesome comic strip of the same man murdered by various methods. Some were shot, some strangled, and many stabbed. None were absent a finger. Emmett began to doubt his theory. Then, from the back of the drawer, came the autopsy of Tyrone Cambell, a seventeen-year-old whose body was spotted by a sanitation crew. The teenager had been rolled behind a row of garbage cans on a dead-end street, and he had a stab wound to his right inner thigh. On his autopsy report, the middle finger on his left hand was circled in pen.

Cambell's file restored Emmett's faith in his theory and shook it simultaneously. He had been so busy trying to prove his hypothesis correct that he hadn't given much thought to the killer or why these boys had been killed. In his haste, Emmett had forgotten about the quality of his thinking. *Give me a reason.* That was what the Jesuit priests from college would have demanded from him. He was new to the logic of murder, but in his experience with robberies, some thieves had predilections for certain items such as vintage records, teddy bears, or picture frames with the owner's photos still in them, a quirk that made them easier to pursue. Perhaps this killer had his own predilection for a type of victim and for hacking off their fingers. Beyond that supposition, there was little quality to Emmett's thinking. He had no evidence as to who the killer might be. Maybe Cambell's file would change that. After Ambrose Webster, Tyrone Cambell was the most recent victim. His case was a month old, not recent by Homicide's standards, but it was all Emmett had to go on.

He removed Cambell's report from the folder, closed the cabinet, and made for the door, shoving the file under his jacket. The pages got stuck on his gun holster. He was disentangling them when someone said, "Got an itch you can't scratch, Emmett?"

Detective Nic Serletto was standing at the threshold to the squad room, smiling under his thick mustache. The top button of his dress shirt was open. His tie was knotted loosely. Behind him stood Detective Larry Hochwald. He had fifty pounds on Serletto, though only a few inches, and his prominent brow branded him with a perpetual glower. Emmett hadn't heard them coming. They had walked up with the others who went into Vice.

"Look who it is, Larry," Serletto chimed.

"I'm lookin'."

"Haven't seen you since Jesus was a boy, Marty. You been hiding down in Records through this whole riot?"

"Not quite."

"You back from the boonies for good? We'll have to move the coffeepot."

"No, I was hoping to catch the lieutenant."

"Catch 'im at what?" Serletto smirked at his own lame joke. "Seems like you was on your way out."

"I've been here for fifteen minutes. He didn't show."

"I coulda sworn I seen Ahern around here somewhere. Oh well. He's a busy guy."

Serletto was gabbing away amiably as a distraction while Hochwald scanned the room for anything amiss. It was a well-rehearsed routine. Cops lied for a living. Coercion was their stock and trade. Except Serletto and Hochwald couldn't come on as strong with Emmett as they would a suspect. Serletto watered down his approach, swapping the typical bluster and bravado for buddy-buddy cordiality that couldn't have been further from kind.

"We miss ya, Marty. No hard feelings, right? We should have a drink. Catch up."

"Yeah, we'll have to do that some time." Emmett accepted the invitation as he crossed between the men and out of the squad room toward the stairway.

"Thought you were waiting on the lieutenant?" Hochwald said.

"Just tell him I stopped by."

"Ay, what are we?" Serletto hollered. "Ahern's secretaries?"

Emmett clamped the Tyrone Cambell file under his arm so it wouldn't slide out from beneath his jacket, and said with a smile, "You don't have the legs for it."

TWENTY-FIVE

The station's front door was in Emmett's sights. He was almost in the clear. Then the desk sergeant stopped him.

"Hey, Detective. You got a delivery yesterday." The sergeant had just come on shift. He was lighting a cigarette.

"A delivery?"

"I had a patrolman put it on your desk in Records."

"Thanks."

"You ever get a hold of that guy you were after?" he asked offhand-edly, waving out the match. "What's-his-name? Guthrie?"

The desk sergeant was going against his own advice. He was snoop-ing. With everybody outside gearing up for patrols, they were alone, and he was exploiting the privacy. Something was up. Either Ionello and Vass had learned that Emmett sprung Freddie or the sergeant was doing some digging on their behalf.

"It was the wrong guy. My mistake."

Trusting that the sergeant wouldn't mention his interest in Freddie to the arresting officers was Emmett's real mistake. Given the havoc of the riot, he thought such a minor detail would have escaped inquiry. He was wrong.

Emmett went down to the basement to see what the delivery was.

Sitting on his desk was a wide manila envelope. Sitting at his desk was Lieutenant Ahern.

"I ran into your new pal, Nolan. He said he bumped into you, so I came down to check on how your case was going, and low and behold, you weren't here."

"Funny. I was upstairs looking for you, Lieutenant."

"I see you got your crime scene pictures from the subway tunnel." He drummed the manila envelope with his fingers. "What's the deal on your dead body?"

Folded under Emmett's jacket was verification of the connection between Ambrose Webster's murder and three others. As he was contemplating the right words to explain, Emmett noticed that the desk drawer where he kept his clock was ajar. That was not how he left it.

"I've got a name and an address. Things are going fine." He tried to brush off the topic.

"Any suspects?"

"Not yet."

"Any witnesses?"

"None."

"What about the kid's friends? You talked to them?"

"The victim was a bit of a loner," he lied.

"That's not the definition of 'going fine.'" Ahern leaned back in Emmett's chair, making himself at home.

"The body was dumped on the train tracks and the victim's guardian hadn't seen him since the previous evening. There's not much to work with."

"It's a damn shame how these kids are running wild nowadays."

This was no simple platitude. Emmett could sense where Ahern was headed. It made his pulse race.

"Say you want to get a hold of a particular kid," the lieutenant said, "but you can't find 'em. The mother doesn't know where he's at. What do you do?"

Ahern was talking about Freddie. Sal Lucaro must have contacted him, furthering the misunderstanding that Freddie was the witness in

Vernon Young's murder. Emmett heaved the lieutenant out of his seat by his lapels.

"Do you have any idea what they did to my brother? Do you?"

Lieutenant Ahern leveled a blasé gaze on Emmett. "This temper of yours keeps getting you in hot water, Detective."

"Did you send them to my house?"

The addresses of policemen were confidential. The only way Lucaro could have gotten his was from someone in the department.

"Did you?"

Ahern lowered his eyes to his lapels, indicating that he would talk once Emmett released him, which he did.

"No, I wouldn't send them to your home, Martin. That wasn't me. But they were getting impatient. You can put me off. Not them." The lieutenant smoothed his jacket and strode toward the door. "You give me that name, I make a phone call and this all ends."

Emmett wouldn't budge or blink or even breathe.

"No? Well, it can't be Julius Dekes." Ahern glanced at the desk. "'Cause that nigger's dead. Your filing's getting sloppy. There was no report in the folder."

The lieutenant had been spying on him. He was probably the one who had turned off the lights the other night. Emmett couldn't feel betrayed because he had never trusted the lieutenant, but he was surprised by how low Ahern had stooped.

"Maybe you should help me look for it," Emmett proposed. "You seem to have a knack for finding things."

That got a rise out of the lieutenant and he retaliated. "Do you wanna know why Director Sloakes moved you into Homicide? He pegged you for a patsy. College degree. Dropped out of the priesthood. He figured you for a head case if you couldn't hack it in the church or at some regular job. Sloakes said you'd flip, get on the payroll, or you'd wash out, the perfect candidate to take the fall in the papers if he ever needed that someday."

Emmett was reeling. Ahern's spite stung, though not as badly as the truth.

"I believe that day's coming real soon, Detective," the lieutenant said, then he left.

The basement was silent. Emmett's clock was no longer ticking. He hadn't been around to wind it and the clock had stopped. He opened the drawer and turned the key until it wouldn't turn anymore. That was all he could do to put time between him and the inevitable.

TWENTY-SIX

The sun was up, but Meers would not have known it if it weren't for his watch. There were no windows in the pen and only one door. Immense industrial pipes protruded from the ceiling of the subterranean room, and the floor was made of dirt, so the scent of earth was strong, laced with a whiff of sulfur and the reek of sewage. A ten-foot-square iron cage of Meers's own construction abutted the pen's far wall. In the glare of the room's lone light, a bare high-wattage bulb, he was examining Calvin Timmons, asleep in the cage.

Pacing its perimeter, Meers surveyed his new pet. Calvin bore no open wounds or abrasions that required tending, which was a relief. Meers had taken the utmost care in conveying the boy so as not to cause him harm. He had used a set of harnesses to get Calvin from the trunk of the Cadillac onto a padded rolling dolly and into the cage. Meers fashioned the twin harnesses himself, his being the smaller of the two. The thick leather straps would thread over his shoulders, across his chest, and behind his back where he connected his harness with a carabiner clamp and sturdy rope to its mate, worn by the unconscious Calvin. As slight of build as Meers was, the harnesses allowed him to pull great loads. He could haul his pets with relative ease as long as he had the dolly to reduce friction.

The dolly was ideal on flat surfaces, inferior on rugged terrains. That was where a sled's rails prevailed. Meers had gotten his from a toy store. Crafted to be fast on slopes and take bumps, the sled was light. He could easily carry it with him for when it was time to clean up. He had made mistakes in the past, left messes that sullied his game. Over the last weeks, Meers had honed his skills, perfecting the routine with the harnesses and the sled. He had the technique down pat.

Then Ambrose Webster spoiled everything. Meers had wrenched his shoulder freighting him into the subway tunnel. The injury continued to ache. That aggravated him. And that was why Meers treated himself to another pet. This time, the boy was quick. The extra effort would earn out.

Meers usually rationed one per month, careful not to arouse suspicion. Patience was fundamental, as was planning, yet he felt shortchanged. Webster was a disaster. He was too scared to leave the cage when Meers raised the pulley, sliding the rear wall up like a tiger trap and providing him an exit. The rear wall of the cage was positioned to open onto an access hatch. Meers had removed the hatch door, exposing a gaping hole that connected to the city's sewer system. The warren of tunnels that lay beyond the door was his hunting ground.

He had discovered the secret door as a teenager, thanks in part to his father. After years of overseeing the zinc mines in Franklin, the company Eli Meers worked for, New Jersey Zinc and Iron, transferred him to be a foreman at the refinery in Newark. The refining plant operated out of a behemoth warehouse the size of a hollowed-out mountain, spanning acres of land bounded by Brill and Chapel streets and the Passaic River, making it an island unto itself. Raw ore was transported to the refinery from the mines on trains or barges by the tons. Three hundred men labored around the clock seven days a week smelting the virgin zinc into metals and oxides, and reducing iron ore to pig iron for making castings. It was dirty, strenuous work that kicked black soot into the air and created a stench that got embedded into clothes, hair, and skin. Workers would finish each day at the refinery with their coveralls as filthy as if they'd been in the mines themselves.

Although the transfer entailed better pay, Meers's father had taken it grudgingly. He abhorred big cities, Newark in particular, and hated having to leave rural Sussex County where they lived. Eli Meers preferred the wide open spaces of the country and taught his son to appreciate the bounty nature had to offer. The day Lazlo turned seven, his father put a .22 rimfire rifle in his hands and took him out to learn how to hunt squirrel.

"If you can hunt a squirrel, you can hunt anything," he had told Lazlo as they crossed a marsh into a hardwood stand in the predawn light. "Squirrels got the sharpest eyes, and they hear everything. Can't even sneak up on a dead 'un unless you know how to move just so."

From that day forward, his father trained him. Lazlo was taught how to walk Indian-style, to pass through a forest without making a sound and to traverse tinder-dry leaves as deftly as balancing on a tightrope. He practiced focusing his eyes without fixing on any individual spot in order to take advantage of his peripheral vision. That gave him the ability to sense every twitch of motion in a full 180-degree field of view. His father disapproved of sights and scopes for rifles. They cost too much, and a skilled hunter wouldn't have to rely on them. Skill was the very thing that separated the hunter from his prey.

Before they moved, Lazlo and his father would hunt every morning. He improved at a rapid pace, to the point where he could distinguish the clatter of acorn hulls falling from the forest's leaf canopy and the *whooshing* the squirrels made when jumping from tree to tree, a sound he would later come to hear as regularly as his own heartbeat. Lazlo got so good that he could pick off a gray squirrel on a beech branch from fifty yards, put a bullet through its head with a solid cartridge and not destroy any of the meat. Some of his fondest memories were of he and his father going home as the sun rose with rings of squirrels swinging from their belts like coattails.

Mastering how to clean the kill was almost as important as hunting. With squirrels, it was as simple as slipping off a sock, and his father had shown Lazlo the best methods for paring off the pockets of fat that would taint the taste. A two-inch slice from a folding blade across the squirrel's hips and the skin stripped right off. The head, feet, and tail were severed, the body cut into pieces, rinsed in cold water, and set in the icebox to chill. His father canned, pickled, dried, or smoked whatever they caught, and he had a special recipe for cooking squirrel with vinegar, salt, and cracker crumbs. It was Lazlo's favorite meal.

There were squirrels in Newark too, traipsing over telephone wires and scaling windowsills, yet Lazlo and his father certainly couldn't hunt them in the city. Lazlo was eleven when they moved, and every day, he missed the vastness of the countryside. When he contracted polio, his father blamed the infection on the city, the congestion, all of the different races that crowded it. He blamed Newark for making his son lame and fragile. And he blamed Lazlo for being weak enough to fall ill. His company paid Lazlo's medical bills, but after ten months in the iron lung, Eli Meers took his son out of the hospital despite the doctor's protests.

"If you're meant to live, boy, then you will" was what he said.

Lazlo did live. However, he couldn't gain weight no matter what his father fed him, and his left arm was permanently maimed from the elbow down. The hand had limited feeling, a feeble grip. Because two hands were necessary to hold a rifle, Lazlo couldn't hunt with a gun anymore. Of all the side effects from polio, that was the worst. His father would leave him in their rented apartment a few blocks from the refinery and return to Franklin on his days off to hunt alone, abandoning Lazlo to his own devices.

With little money, Lazlo had only one place he could go: the public library. It was warm in the winters, cool in the summers, and he could linger there for hours in the silence, reading whichever books he pleased, far from his father's indifference and the torment of his classmates, who teased him mercilessly about his ailments. Better still, he could take books home for free, as many as he could carry. He read rapaciously, devouring novels and history texts on a gamut of topics. His favorites were guides on hunting, especially those about big game. Lazlo imagined himself alongside the men in the books, stalking Kodiac bears in Alaska or rhinos in the Africa bush. He could practically feel the snow crunching underfoot or the sun shimmering on the plains. In his mind, Lazlo could still hunt.

His father left him to his books. He ignored him and barely acknowledged his existence even when, as a teen, Lazlo would limp to the plant on foot to deliver food to the men working the late shift. Collecting pails from the neighborhood wives and bringing them to the zinc works earned Lazlo two cents per pail. He had devised a method of stringing the handles on twine and slinging them around his neck, enabling him to cart a dozen at a time. The garland of pails full of sandwiches, hard-boiled eggs, and thermoses of coffee clanged like cans tied to a car bumper, which embarrassed his father so badly that he would retreat to the foreman's office to avoid seeing his son doling out the food. For Lazlo, that was a slight improvement over being ignored, and the money he received slowly amassed into an ample trust, funds he would eventually put toward his new hobby.

One day, after his deliveries, Lazlo's father ordered him to go into the storeroom behind the foreman's office to retrieve a ream of paper, mainly to get him out of sight. Lazlo had never been in the storeroom before. Boxes teetered in towers taller than him, and the shelves wobbled as though the dankness and lack of light had forcible weight. It was no place for someone his size. While struggling to heave the ream off a rickety shelf into his good arm, something in the dim light caught Lazlo's eye: a set of stairs leading below ground level. He put aside the paper and followed the stairway down to an anteroom carved into the earth, an unfinished afterthought built to allow access to the massive pipes that fed in from the refinery floor to the sewer system. Between the blast furnaces, the slime catches, and the electrolytic baths for heap leaching, wastewater accumulated from the zinc works by the hundreds of gallons per hour and was siphoned into the sewers to run off into the Passaic River. The pipes plugged directly into a main sewer hatch the size of a door, and Lazlo could hear the water frothing and seething and racing through the tunnel behind the hatch. Because the pipes were active, he never entered the door, but he dreamed of what lay behind it, an underground world all his own.

Underground was where Lazlo Meers felt most at home. In his youth, before the polio, his father had frequently taken him into the zinc mines. They would traverse the tunnels, inspecting the miners' progress, the bright light of their carbide lamps blazing into an ocean of blackness. Lazlo didn't fear the tight, dark quarters, quite the opposite. He found solace in the narrow mine shafts, where his small frame was perfectly in scale. There in the womb of the earth, he was safe.

When, years later in the early 1960s, New Jersey Zinc and Iron finally went out of business, as had many industries in the city, Meers read about its closure in the newspaper and visited the lot. The gigantic refinery sat vacant. The vats and furnaces and dross kettles were gone, sold for scrap, their parts melted down in similar blast furnaces and kettles somewhere else. The plant was empty apart from the echo of birds nesting in the crossbeams and the abrasive odor of sulfur dioxide that remained, intractable as the building's girders.

Vandals had broken some of the vent windows at the roofline, letting in rays of light. Otherwise, devoid of electricity, the refinery was dark. Just the way Meers liked it. He went directly to the room under the old foreman's office and found that the pipes leading to the sewer had been capped. The entrance to the tunnel was open wide. His secret maze was waiting for him. That was how it started.

Darkness yawned from the entrance now, spliced by the cage bars. The pulley door was trussed, well out of reach from Calvin Timmons, who lay sleeping on the mattress in the middle of the cage, beneath which Meers had installed a plush shag carpet cut to fit the bounds. Beside the mattress was a quart carton of whole milk as well as a paper plate covered in aluminum foil holding a half-dozen scrambled eggs and a pound of bacon. Meers didn't supply utensils. They could be used against him. When he become more proficient, he would consider providing them to add to the challenge, though not yet. He needed more practice.

That was what Calvin was for.

TWENTY-SEVEN

By the time Emmett returned home, Mrs. Poole had tidied the living room and swept the floor. Everything was back where it belonged. Clean as it was, he couldn't scrub the mess Caligrassi's men had left from his memory. It was as if the curtain had closed on a play and re-opened to a set change. The stage was the same, and the anger was still there.

"Check this out, Marty." Edward was awake and holding a compress to his injured eye. He pointed at the TV with a lit cigarette. "The riot's all over the news."

On the screen, footage depicting masses of people outside the Fourth Precinct hurling bottles and stones was intercut with figures streaking past pillaged stores. Whirling police lights created a strobe effect on the film. Mrs. Poole came in from the kitchen during the reel of a flower shop being consumed by flames.

"Mercy me. I been to that store. They had such pretty flowers. Now look at the place."

"The state police and National Guard have been called in," Emmett informed them. "I saw troopers at the station."

"Staties and the Guard, huh?" Like Emmett, Edward was dubious that the military presence was a move in the right direction. "Well, it'll take awhile for the Guard to get to full capacity. Reservists'll have to be called up from throughout the state."

"Puts me at ease to hear they're coming."

Edward didn't share Mrs. Poole's optimism, and Emmett hadn't been at ease since leaving the precinct, far from it.

"Is Freddie still in bed?"

"Uh-huh." Edward peeled off the compress. His eyelid was mottled in colors flesh shouldn't be.

Mrs. Poole took the washcloth from him. "I'll run this under cold water again. Should help the swelling."

While she was gone, Edward said, "I'd be asleep myself, no thanks to you, Marty."

"You needed the rest for today."

"What's today?"

"I don't know yet. That's the problem."

Emmett put on the police band radio to get an update. The transmissions mainly concerned burglaries and vandalism and requests for officers to take dispositions. The cops calling in weren't wracked with panic as they had been the night before. By then, they were tired and tense. Outrage had displaced fright.

"The shopkeepers must be arriving at their stores."

"They're in for a hell of a shock," Edward scoffed.

Mrs. Poole reappeared with a fresh compress and a cup of coffee for Emmett. "Feels like it's gonna be hotter today than yesterday, don't it?"

As she spoke, the police frequency unexpectedly went mute.

"Something I said?"

"Did the radio break?" Emmett twisted the volume knob and played with the tuner.

"Let me see that." Edward waved for Emmett to bring his creation to him. He inspected the moving parts. "There's nothing wrong with it."

The dispatcher came back on the air, clearing his throat as a preamble to the announcement. "The governor has issued an emergency proclamation under the National Defense Act of New Jersey. According to the regulations of the proclamation, all vehicular traffic in Newark will be prohibited between the hours of ten P.M. and six A.M., excluding authorized vehicles and traffic using the major highways. The proclamation also imposes a curfew from eleven P.M. to six A.M., during which the sale of alcohol is banned. The ban extends to the possession of alcohol as well as narcotics, firearms, or explosives. This emergency proclamation will be in effect until further notice."

The dispatcher's mechanical cadence made the message more surreal. His disembodied voice stopped as abruptly as it had started, followed by dead air that was filled by the reporter on the television relaying details of a bombing in Vietnam.

Edward exhaled a stream of smoke through his nose. "They're turning the city into a demilitarized zone."

"That sort of thing doesn't happen here in America," Mrs. Poole said. "Not here."

"As of today, apparently it does," Edward railed. "They're locking down Newark. None of us are going anywhere. Or should I say almost none of us." He glared at Emmett.

"Mrs. Poole, would you be so kind as to get me a refill?"

She got the hint, took his cup, and retreated to the kitchen.

"Gonna leave a cripple to keep the home fires burning and 'stand guard'?" Edward slapped his feelingless knees to underscore the pun.

"What choice do I have?"

"Marty, you have choices. But you can't stand the idea of making a decision and having it come out wrong. You can't always be right. Not always."

"I'm not." A nod at his brother's bruises was Emmett's proof.

Their argument ended in a draw. Edward ceremoniously squashed out his cigarette while Emmett went and got the telephone directory. He needed to talk to Tyrone Cambell's family. Their residence was listed on the police report as Prince Street, putting it in the Stella Wright projects. Emmett wanted to hedge his bets and call ahead. He dialed the number. It rang and rang.

"Whoever it is, Marty, they ain't home. Hell, I wish I wasn't home."

Emmett hung up. He considered the fact that his own phone number and address were unlisted. The lieutenant claimed not to have given the information to Sal Lucaro. For a change, Emmett had believed

Ahern. As he closed the phone book, Emmett realized how Lucaro had found him.

"I have your coffee, Mr. Emmett." Mrs. Poole was peeking into the living room to see if the skirmish was settled.

He ignored her, hurrying from window to window, lowering the shades to the sills.

"What's the fuss?"

"Those men from yesterday were watching the house. They probably tailed me from the precinct. Last night, they couldn't find Freddie at his mother's place."

Edward finished the thought. "So they'll come here again, hoping you'll lead them to him."

Mrs. Poole was unconsciously backing away from the windows. "They're outside? Now?"

"Only one way to be sure."

"Mr. Emmett, don't," she begged.

Edward agreed. "You can't just go take a stroll, Marty. They'll figure you're onto them. Today's newspaper should be on the stoop. When you get it, you can check."

"That's an idea," Emmett conceded.

"I'm full of 'em."

"You're full of something."

"Do you hear the mouth on him Mrs. Poole? Would you believe he was gonna be a priest?"

She registered the remark but said nothing. She seemed to be biting her tongue, which Emmett appreciated. This was hardly the ideal occasion for him to unfurl the indiscretions of his past. Emmett opened the front door.

"Act natural," Edward coached.

"Thanks. That's real helpful."

The early morning mugginess had clotted into a solid wall of heat. He bent to retrieve the paper from the top step. The headline was facing skyward: "New Violence in Newark." A picture displayed a trash can embedded in the window of a police car. Below it was a larger photograph of Lyndon Johnson sitting on a sofa beside General Westmoreland, looking chummy. The words "LBJ to Ask for Tax Hike" hovered above the president like a banner. The war was halfway around the world and it got better coverage than the riot brewing right under the city's feet.

Pretending to read the front page, Emmett surreptitiously surveyed the cars parked on his street. A crystal blue Oldsmobile Delta 88 was snuggled into the curb midway down the block. The model and color stood out among the family sedans. The coupe was too showy to be Lucaro's. It was likely the property of his stubby sidekick. Glare from the sun prevented Emmett from seeing if anyone was behind the wheel.

"Well?" Mrs. Poole asked, when he came back inside.

"Were they there?" Edward's voice took on an edge.

Emmett tossed him the newspaper. "I'm not positive, but I'm pretty sure it's them."

"I thought you said gangsters didn't wake up this early, Mr. Emmett."

"I guess I was wrong about that." He directed the admission to her and to Edward, who met his eyes for an instant, then dug into the newspaper. "I understand you're frightened, Mrs. Poole. I'll take you home."

She nodded, relieved, and went upstairs to collect her purse.

"So you know, I have to go check on something after I drop her off."

"You gonna be gone for long?"

"As long as it takes."

"Great. More babysitting. What do I do when the kid wakes up? Play Parcheesi with him?"

"Whatever. Just keep him here."

"He could waltz right out the front door. What would I do? Chase him?"

"You're the one with the gun."

"I'm not going to point a loaded weapon at a sixteen-year-old."

"Take the bullets out. He won't know the difference. But if you do, remember to put them back in."

"Get this," Edward said and began to read aloud, holding the newsprint to his good eye. "'Negro looters smashed into the heart of Newark's shopping district early today. They turned an entire mile of Springfield Avenue into a shambles and laid siege to the same police station that was attacked Wednesday. The gangs of Negroes—mostly teenagers—looted stores, beat elderly whites, pelted police cars with stones, and ran amok in a wide area.' Sheesh. Why can't those mob hoods go after some of these teenagers?"

"I'll bring them the paper. Ask if they'll put them next on the list."

"They'll follow you to Mrs. Poole's house, you know. Might think she's involved."

"The thought had crossed my mind."

"Gonna try and shake 'em?"

"If I can."

"If not?"

Emmett shrugged.

"That's reassuring. Maybe I should give you the twenty-two back."

Mrs. Poole came down the stairs.

"Ready?" Emmett asked. "Where's your pocketbook?"

"I'll have to take a rain check on that ride home."

"Really? Why?"

"If I leave, he's alone." She put her hand on Edward's shoulder. "I go home, I'm alone. Seems silly. Anyhow, I never missed a day's work in my life and I am most certainly not going to start today."

Emmett admired her conviction. Maybe some of it would rub off on him. Because he was the one who was going to be alone.

TWENTY-EIGHT

Barricades had been erected at every major intersection, funneling streams of cars to a standstill on Broad Street, including Emmett's. Cones and sawhorses marked the roadblock, which was being regulated by a pair of state troopers. One would question drivers while the second stood guard with a Reising Model 50 submachine gun at the ready. Emmett was in the middle of the line. The blue Oldsmobile was three cars behind him. In his rearview mirror, the figure of a lone driver was outlined by the sunlight.

Emmett slid the police band radio under the seat and waited. The traffic light ticked through green, amber, and red countless times, but the line barely moved. When an army green personnel truck pulled up, the trooper motioned for the cars to hold their positions so it could pass the blockade. Through the truck's rear flap, Emmett saw a dozen National Guardsman in fatigues, M-1 rifles sandwiched between their knees. The truck drove on and the line resumed.

"Unless you have real important business in this section of town, sir, you oughta go home," the trooper recommended when it came Emmett's turn. He was in his midtwenties and his accent said he was from southern Jersey. Sweat was purling down his sideburns.

"It's pretty important." Emmett produced his badge.

"Oh, sorry, Detective. You're the first person to come by who ain't been colored. You going to the Fourth?"

His answer was noncommittal. "I'm headed in that direction."

"Sure could use as many hands as we can get. You see that Guard truck go by? Driver told me there's already six personnel carriers at the armory and nine battalions en route. Plus there's five hundred of us troopers. Sounds like a lot. Sure doesn't feel like it."

Nine battalions tallied out to be about four thousand Guardsmen. Added to that were the hundreds of troopers and the city's fourteen hundred cops. It was a formidable force on paper and a drop in the bucket against the Central Ward.

"You and your pal had any trouble?" Emmett pointed at the trooper with the machine gun.

"Not so far. We're taking turns. I do the work. He gets to stand in the shade."

The other state trooper donned mirrored sunglasses and was holding the Reising on his hip, aloof.

"You'll get your turn in the shade," Emmett said.

"From your mouth to God's ears." The trooper patted the hood of Emmett's car. "Gook luck, Detective. You're gonna need it."

If Emmett was the first white face the trooper had seen, whoever was driving the Delta would have to concoct a decent cover story to get through the barricade. Saying he lived in the neighborhood wasn't going to fly. That would buy Emmett a little time.

By taking side streets, he managed to avoid any more roadblocks. He had lost the Olds but didn't doubt that the driver would comb the area for his car. It was what he would have done.

Emmett dug through the glove compartment, his ersatz file drawer, and confirmed Tyrone Cambell's address, then parked on Prince Street, a short distance from the Fourth Precinct. Considering the location, whoever was tailing him might hesitate to make a scene.

Cambell's last known residence was in the Stella Wright Housing Projects, a minimetropolis of seven thirteen-story tenements, identical as a daisy chain. The address was an apartment on the fourth floor of a building that overlooked the street. Emmett had been there before when he busted a guy for selling stolen stereos off the roof. If a stereo was too heavy for the buyer, the guy would put the equipment in a laundry basket and lower it with a rope over the side to the ground. Emmett hadn't been back to Stella Wright since then. He imagined that the guy had taken his business elsewhere and was hawking stereos off some other rooftop.

As he walked the tenement's halls, Emmett experienced the same uneasiness he had when he was at Hayes Home, suspecting trouble around every corner. He knocked on the Cambell's apartment door repeatedly. Like the call he had placed earlier, nobody answered.

"They gone," a teenage girl said from a neighboring doorway. She had curlers in her hair and an infant cradled in the crook of her arm. The baby was clothed only in a diaper.

"The Cambells? Where did they go?"

"Dunno. South, maybe. Where they kin from."

"Do you happen to have any idea how I could get in contact with the family?"

"Nope. You could talk to they uncle, though. He hangs at that bar Franklin's on Howard."

Franklin's Lounge was infamous for being a gay bar. Foot patrolmen dreaded being assigned to that beat during the evening shift. Fights were as common at Franklin's as they were at Woody's. Only these brawls usually involved women, big ones who would belt an officer for acting as referee, and the scuffles drew a cavalcade of onlookers from inside the bar who would cheer and clap, rooting the women on. Many a patrolman had earned the ridicule of their fellow shift mates for making the blunder of getting in between some of "Franklin's girls."

"What's this uncle's name?"

"Uncle Papa. 'At's all I heard him called by." The girl cuddled the baby to her. "Come on, darlin'," she cooed. "Mama's got to feed you. Yes, yes, she does."

"Thanks," Emmett said. The girl had shut the door.

He left his car for the guy in the Oldsmobile Delta to hunt for and walked to Franklin's, two blocks away. The neighborhood was uncommonly quiet, yet people were perched at their windows, monitoring every occurrence. Emmett sensed eyes on him as he went into the lounge.

A jukebox was blaring and colored Christmas lights blinked over the bar. Paper lanterns were swagged from the ceiling. At Franklin's, it was a party every day of the year. Liquor sloshed on the bar as patrons clamored for drinks, getting their fill before the ban on selling alcohol set in at six that evening. It was as though Prohibition was about to be reinstated.

Emmett had to wade through the crowd to get to the bar. "You want a drink, suga, you gon' have to wait," the bartender informed him. The man's pale brown skin was rouged, his shoulder-length hair twirled into ringlets.

"I'm not here for a drink. I'm looking for Uncle Papa." Emmett felt awkward uttering the name.

"Business or pleasure?" the bartender inquired, putting a feminine arch in his spine.

"Business."

"Figures. That old queen is holding court in her favorite booth. Be a doll and tell her to pay her tab, will ya?" The bartender wiggled his fingers in the general direction of the booth and continued pouring drinks.

"Hey. Watch it," a black woman with closely shorn hair growled. Emmett had accidentally stepped on her foot while weaving through the bodies jammed at the bar.

"Sorry," he mumbled.

"You should be." She popped a tin of Dixie Peach pomade from her pocket and smoothed her coif, as if the incident had considerably mussed her style.

Emmett was out of his element, and the farther back in the bar he went, the more he felt like a gate-crasher. There in the last booth, an older black man in a silky indigo tunic was presiding over a small audience of fey men. Bracelets jangled from both of his wrists as he spoke. He was telling a story and gesticulating with his slender hands as though conducting an imaginary orchestra.

"Pardon me," Emmett said. "I hate to interrupt, but are you, um, Uncle Papa?"

"Why, yes I am, and you, my dear, could interrupt me any day." Uncle Papa's southern lilt spun the sentence into a purr. His companions giggled at the innuendo.

"I need to talk to you, sir. Privately, if possible. It's important."

"I prefer privacy myself." He shooed the men from the booth, and Emmett sat opposite him. "To what do I owe the honor, Mister. . . ." Uncle Papa held out his hand limply, anticipating a handshake and a name.

"Detective. Emmett."

"Quite a grip you've got, Detective. Can I interest you in a cocktail?"

"No, no thanks. By the way, the bartender wants you to close your tab."

"Oh please. She says that every single day, the whiny cow. Works my last nerve," he moaned, chewing the olive from his martini. "So, pray tell, what brings an officer of the law into an establishment such as this?"

"I'm here to discuss Tyrone Cambell. I understand you're a relative."

That sapped the flirty glimmer from Uncle Papa's eyes. "I'm Tyrone's uncle."

"His real uncle?"

"Yes, his real uncle. People been callin' me 'Uncle Papa' since before my sisters had their kids."

"Why?" Emmett was curious.

" 'Cause I be kind, like the uncle you wished you had, and take care 'a folks better than they daddy did." Seconds earlier, he would have played up the veiled sexuality. Now he was defending the origin of his nickname.

"How close were you to Tyrone?"

"Ain't right to say you got a favorite when you have as many nieces and nephews as me. Sixteen," he said, fanning himself, as if the sheer number raised the temperature in the room. "Some 'a them be bad too. Uncle Papa is not much for whoopins—had too many myself and see what it done—but I'd take a switch to most of 'em faster than you could say 'Hallelujah.' Not Tyrone, though. That boy had sense. Didn't cuss. Minded his mama. And he didn't shy away from me for what I was neither. He was grown. He understood. Didn't matter to him. He even gave me a birthday present once. A wooden plaque with hooks for hanging keys. Ty made it in shop class. Me, I don't have but one key. I didn't care. I hung that key rack on my wall like it was the *Mona Lisa.*" Uncle Papa had stopped conducting with his hands and folded them on the table. There was no music in his story, only sadness.

"Can you account for Tyrone's whereabouts the day he went missing."

"All's I heard tell was that Ty had gone to the corner store for a soda pop on a Friday night and never did come back. Simple as that."

Emmett's expectations deflated. The deeper he dug, the further down the hole he wound up. Tyrone Cambell had evaporated from the face of the earth like the others.

"I say something wrong, Detective?"

"No, no, you've been very helpful."

"Why you asking about Tyrone anyhow?"

"His murder is unsolved."

"You solvin' it?"

"I'm doing what I can."

"Shouldn't you be out beatin' on brothers with the rest 'a the police?" Uncle Papa quipped, batting his eyes coquettishly. "Or are you playin' hooky?"

"Yeah, I thought it'd be safe to hide in here."

"You feel safe with a bunch 'a queers?"

By the standards of the Catholic faith, everyone in Franklin's Lounge was a patent sinner, irrevocably damned if they did not repent. Emmett had spent the better part of his life repenting, and he wasn't convinced God was listening. *Be grateful for your sins, they are carriers of grace.* The Jesuit prayer was a fateful reminder that from ill deeds sprang goodness. If that was true, then after the riot, there would be plenty of grace to go around.

"I'm not in the habit of casting stones," Emmett replied.

Uncle Papa sipped his drink, bangles clanking. "No? Isn't that part of your job, deciding who the bad guys are?"

"The manual I read said 'protect and serve.'"

"You been outside lately, Detective?" All of the wit and cheer had been wrung from his face. Uncle Papa was speaking to Emmett man to man. "By the looks of it, you're the only one who read that."

TWENTY-NINE

A fleet of open-top, military jeeps was parading down Irvine Turner Boulevard, four National Guardsmen in combat helmets per vehicle. People on the sidewalks stopped to witness the procession. Emmett did too. The hot breeze kicked up by the passing jeeps gusted against his skin and ruffled his jacket. It seemed like an invasion rather than a rescue.

Doubt was hammering in his mind as he walked back to his car from Franklin's. The missing fingers were the strongest pieces of evidence he had. They shimmed his theory about the murders into plumb. Everything else—the wounds, the timing, the locations of the bodies— was off kilter. He couldn't reconcile logic with fact. That made the murders all the more confounding.

Parked conspicuously on the corner across the street from Emmett's car was the blue Oldsmobile. Either his pursuer was intentionally being obvious in order to intimidate him or the thug was new to the racket. Chances were he was inexperienced. Emmett would play on that if he could. Somehow, he had to con the Delta's driver into believing that Freddie wasn't at his house anymore, even though that was exactly where he was.

Emmett needed time to think. He took a circuitous route through the Central Ward, willingly letting the trail continue. In the rearview mirror, he caught a glimpse of the guy behind the wheel. He wore a Borsalino hat with the brim tipped, which cast his features in shadow except for a round jaw and double chin. He was a ringer for Edward's description of Lucaro's right-hand man from the previous night. Emmett was tempted to stop the car and have a fair fight out in the open, but that wouldn't be in his best interest or Freddie's. He led the Olds to his house and pretended not to notice when the car sailed past his driveway.

"The king returns," Edward crowed as Emmett came through the front door. Mrs. Poole was sitting vigil with him in the living room.

"I'm not the only one." Emmett spied between the shades and saw the coupe circling for a parking spot. "Say, which of those guys socked you?"

"The short one. Little bastard."

"And he's the one who pushed me," Mrs. Poole added.

"Well, that's who's keeping us company."

"Couldn't lose 'im?"

"Didn't want to."

Thrown, Edward furrowed his brow. Before he could ask why, Freddie came in from the kitchen gulping a glass of milk.

"Didn't wanna what?"

"Didn't want to wake you," Emmett told him, covering. "I thought you were asleep."

"I woulda been 'cept somebody's so deaf they got to have the TV volume on full blast."

"His majesty has delicate ears," Edward griped.

"How was it out there, Mr. Emmett? Those troopers you were talking about, they taking care 'a things?"

"So far they've set up roadblocks and they're garrisoning the Guard at the armory."

"They're not bringing in tanks are they, Marty?"

"Tanks? Man, that'd be cool," Freddie said. All of them stared. "What? Tanks are cool."

"I'm 'bout to show you cool," Mrs. Poole cautioned.

"Anything worth reading in there?" Emmett asked. Edward had the newspaper on his lap.

"Every article's the same. Says some cabdriver started everything."

Emmett recalled Patrolman Nolan's understated description of the pummeled taxi driver, Ben White, that he "didn't look so good." Now the papers were blaming him for the entire riot. The real blame belonged to almost everyone except White.

"Was there any mention of what happened to him after his arrest?"

"Released on bail. Got his license revoked. Claimed the cops were lying about him driving on a one-way street or something."

Mrs. Poole sighed. "Hard to know what's what."

"No it ain't," Freddie countered.

Both of them were right, Emmett thought.

"Then I'd settle for knowin' what's coming next," she said.

Edward tamped his pack of Carltons. "What is coming next, Marty?"

"We're going to be doing some moving."

"Where you movin'?"

"It's not where I'm moving, it's what. Are those old cardboard boxes Pop got from Westinghouse still in the garage?"

"Should be. For as many as he had, you'd 'a thunk he was planning on packin' up the whole house one piece at a time."

The lone perk of their father's job on the production line was dibs on the leftover boxes the appliances were shipped in, appliances too expensive for most employees to purchase brand-new. Their father took the boxes because he couldn't pass up something free, regardless of how unimportant or purposeless it was. For every box he brought home, Emmett imagined his father must have felt he had gotten over on the company that had been getting over on him for eight hours a day, five days a week for the lion's share of his life.

Sunlight was radiating around the rims of the window shades that blocked the view of the street. Emmett peeked under one of the blinds. The Oldsmobile had scored a spot on the opposite side of the road, a few doors down.

"From where he's parked, the guy won't be able to see me go into the garage."

Freddie folded his arms. "What guy?"

"I'll get to that in a minute. First, I've got to get the boxes."

"What the hell's going on?"

"Watch that mouth," Mrs. Poole said sternly.

"Fine, what the *heck* is going on?"

Edward had figured it out. He grinned at Freddie "Looks like you're going for a ride."

When Emmett raised the garage door, the hinges yowled so loudly that the noise seemed to take up physical space. The whole neighborhood could hear it. Emmett didn't care what the Delta's driver heard. It was what he saw that counted. From a pile of dozens, Emmett grabbed four flattened medium boxes. His father's frugality finally had value.

"Jesus, Mary, and Joseph, Marty. Those hinges could've woken the dead. You oughta oil them too when you do the screen door."

"That's not exactly at the top of my to-do list at the moment."

Mrs. Poole helped Emmett put together the boxes. "What are we going to fill them with?"

"Nothing." He folded the flaps, and the boxes closed into perfect squares. "They just have to appear to be full."

Freddie was pacing. "You gonna tell me who the guy is or not?"

"I'll tell you in the car."

"Then let's go."

"It's not that simple."

"He could sneak out the back door," Edward suggested, "and crawl on his hands and knees to—"

"Hold it. You can stop right there 'cause I ain't crawlin' no place."

"Freddie, if you don't do this, you're going to wind up with one of those." Emmett pointed to his brother's black eye. "Or worse."

"Man, you think you can hit me?"

"It wouldn't be me doing the hitting."

"I could," Edward volunteered.

Emmett rubbed his temple. "You're not helping."

"It's that cop, Vass, ain't it?"

"I wish it was," Emmett told him.

"Is it Luther?"

"It's not Luther."

"It's somebody badder than Luther?"

"Badder than Luther," Emmett said.

Freddie's expression turned dour. "Can I get somethin' to eat before we go?" he asked, a last request.

"Sure."

After Mrs. Poole fixed Freddie a sandwich, she pulled Emmett aside. "We're running low on food. Thought I should tell you. I could go to the market, but . . . ."

"No, don't. Write me a list. I'll bring home groceries."

"Should we get enough for three people or for four?" She was worried about Freddie. Emmett was too.

"If I can't lose that guy outside, we might have to get enough for five."

While Freddie ate the sandwich that heralded the end of their food, Emmett described his game plan.

"Oh, jeez. All right," Freddie reluctantly agreed. "Let's get this over with."

Emmett kept watch from the back porch as Freddie slithered along the side of the house to the middle of the driveway, where he crouched to wait for the signal, then Emmett began carting the boxes out the front door, struggling down the steps as though they were heavy. He put three of them in the trunk, filling it to capacity.

Emmett had the last box in his arms when Edward said, "Gonna shake him this time?"

"Even better. He's going to think he's found Freddie. That way he won't come back here."

"Some feat. That'd make you a magician."

"No," Emmett said, recollecting the comment Freddie had made about Houdini outside the bail bonds office. "Just the talented assistant."

He lugged the final box outside and pretended it wouldn't fit in the trunk. The passenger seat was the only space left. He opened the door, the sign for Freddie to slink over, screened by the car, and acted as if he was orienting the box on the seat as Freddie climbed into the foot well.

"See. Being short can be an asset sometimes."

"Yeah, yeah. Stop talkin' and start drivin'."

Emmett reversed out of the driveway and the Olds pursued, the outline of the driver's Borsalino visible above the wheel.

"He took the bait."

"Congratulations. I feel like a pretzel." Freddie was worming around to reposition himself.

"You'd feel worse if you were with the guy who's following us."

"What's that stuff?" He pointed at the passenger-side headrest. A prominent smudge of dried blood striped the leather.

"It's not motor oil."

"Is it blood? Whose blood is it?"

"It's Cyril's."

"You beat him up?"

"I didn't. He did." Emmett thumbed backward.

As the Delta coupe fell in behind them, Emmett recounted the sad tale of Vernon Young's death, including the dilemmas that resulted in its wake and the mix-up that now involved Freddie. When he was through, Emmett told him what had happened to Cyril and to his mother and tried to reassure him.

"I took them to the hospital. You don't have to worry."

"I'm not. Not about Cyril."

"Your mom's going to be okay, Freddie."

He nodded blankly, taking it all in. "So this guy in the car, he thinks I'm that Otis cat, and what? He wants to rough me up?" Huddled beneath the dashboard, he looked young and vulnerable, like a stowaway on a sinking ship.

The truth wasn't kind, but Freddie was entitled to it. "No," Emmett said soberly. "He wants to kill you."

THIRTY

The beauty of a cage was its simplicity. Light and air could come in and out freely. Whatever or whoever was inside could not.

Through a hole in the ceiling above the pen, Meers was peering down at Calvin Timmons, who remained unconscious, sleeping fitfully in the cage. Meers entered the pen only when delivering the food. Otherwise, he spent his free hours clandestinely watching his captives, face pressed to the hole in the floor of the old storeroom, his private version of a peep show.

The cage was one of Meers's finest accomplishments. Perfect in concept and execution, it gave him almost as much satisfaction as the hunts. Designed to specific dimensions with certain features that would have appeared questionable had he hired somebody to fabricate it for him, Meers had set about building the cage himself. The abandoned zinc refinery gave him space to work. He had purchased an acetylene torch and tanks, a welder's mask, and all the raw materials necessary for assembly, then studied up on the welding process by reading instructional manuals. Meers burned his fingers badly and often practicing the skill. Eventually, the burns healed and his masterpiece came to life, iron bar by iron bar.

He also cobbled together a pulley system, enabling him to open the cage's trapdoor from the floor above with a winch. That prevented his prey from seeing him while granting them a head start. If Meers didn't give them a five-minute lead, the game finished too quickly. Such was the complication with Ambrose Webster. He had been as bad as the women.

Twice Meers had tried using females, two separate times with the same disastrous results. Both were prostitutes, easy to entice into his car, however they disintegrated into hysterics as soon as they regained consciousness and realized where they were. They had begged and pleaded and promised him their bodies. But Meers didn't want their bodies. He wanted them to run. Moronic as mules, they stood at the entrance hatch, petrified and trembling, frustrating him. Each ran screaming through the tunnels without getting far before falling. The deafening echo irritated Meers so much that he dispatched each of them shortly after the games had begun. He dumped their bodies in the desolate reaches of Newark Bay under cover of night, food for the fish.

Ambrose Webster was almost as pathetic. Meers had been forced to fire at him with his pistol the way one would startle a horse into racing. The shot sent Webster lumbering off, though he repeatedly dropped the flashlight Meers had generously furnished him. Meers always left a flashlight in the cage along with copious amounts of food to maintain his pets' energy and endurance. Like his standard five-minute head start, the flashlight was a practical measure. Without any sort of defense against the absolute darkness of the sewer tunnels, his prey would be incapacitated, and there would be no sport in the hunt. To keep things relatively fair, Meers purchased cheap plastic flashlights, too flimsy to be implemented as weapons. Strength and speed were his prey's God-given weapons, gifts nature had not bestowed upon him. Meers was simply leveling the playing field.

Greed had gotten the better of him during that particular game. Ambrose Webster was a colossus, an unfit match for Meers, the ultimate challenge. However, his size turned out to be the ultimate disadvantage.

The sewer system was nearly a hundred years old, and while the newer lines could be considered cavernous at twenty-five feet high and half as wide, the original egg-shaped, brick-lined sewers by the zinc refinery measured under six feet tall and two across. Huge as he was, Webster was unable to maneuver through the older tunnels. Because they tapered at the bottom, he couldn't maintain his footing. He would hit his head and stumble and cry. What a pity, Meers had thought when he caught up to him. The giant was blundering through the dark on his knees, pawing for the fallen flashlight. He was too frightened to run, even when he saw Meers coming.

As a boy, Meers had watched his father put down a horse with a fractured ankle from a neighbor's farm. His father nuzzled a revolver to the bony nub beneath the mare's ear and pulled the trigger. The horse didn't drop instantaneously. It wavered, then its knees folded and the mass of its body pitched to the ground. When Meers slit Ambrose Webster's throat, he was reminded of the horse.

Meers would only hunt with a knife. His gun was purely an instrument of motivation and a safety precaution. The Linder Crown Stag bowie he carried had been the star of his father's collection. With its seven-inch blade, authentic antler handle, and solid brass guard and pommel, it was a handsome knife, efficient. For the scale of what Meers was hunting, the long blade was necessary to ensure a fatal blow versus a shallow cut. He always brought his father's old Case XX folding pocketknife along too. The deep red bone handle and nickel silver inlaid shield made it a collector's item. Meers cherished it more than the bowie. The pocketknife was tiny and artful and perfect, and it held fond memories. His father had let him use it to skin his first woodchuck.

Neighbors had often hired his father to clear the varmints from their farms. With their sons off fighting the Great War, there was nobody to cull the woodchucks into check, and they would annihilate the crops, eating and burrowing to the point that the tractors collapsed through the thinned earth. The horse that Lazlo's father shot had broken its ankle by stepping into the entrance to a den. Never one to turn down the opportunity to be paid to do what he loved, his father would go out to the farms weekly, balance a rifle on a fence post, and snipe the woodchucks from seventy yards when they stood on their hind legs to sniff the wind. The farmers let him keep the carcasses as part of his pay. When he got them home, he would pare the fur with the barbed, gut hook tip of a cocobolo knife and soak the meat in salt water for days. Afterward, it was still as tough as shoe leather and about as appetizing. Once his father began allowing Lazlo to skin his own woodchucks, the taste grew on him.

Because his mother was dead, Lazlo's father was his sole guardian. That precluded him from enlisting or being drafted into the service to fight in World War II, a depravation Eli Meers resented bitterly. Occasionally, Lazlo would look up from his schoolbooks in their old, two-room country home and his father would be staring at him as if he were a stain on the floor, a nuisance he had been stepping over all day and didn't want to deal with.

Barred from enlisting, Eli Meers took up a different cause. Wartime propaganda had labeled crows as "black bandits." The birds were robbing the nation's farms of vital grain needed for food production for the troops. A hunter's patriotic duty was to destroy as many as possible, thus they were allotted priority in purchasing the limited supply of available .22 cartridges and shotgun shells. Eli Meers's contribution to the war effort was killing three hundred crows single-handedly. Lazlo himself had shot at least a hundred. The numbers were a source of glory for his father, who normally wouldn't have wasted the ammunition on something he couldn't cook. Crows were not for eating. They fed on carrion, fouling their own flesh, so Lazlo and his father would leave the coal black carcasses in heaps under trees, a lure for other crows to consume.

They hunted in the early morning hours, dressed in dark clothes, hats, and gloves with bandanas covering their faces, disguised as thoroughly as thieves. The sight of human skin in the murky dawn was the equivalent of light striking a mirror and could spook the birds from as much as a half mile away. Knowing that crows were wary creatures, they would find a ridge or mound of earth to act as a blind, then his father would mimic the crows' two distinct caws. One was the fighting call of an angry crow coming upon an enemy, to which every bird in the area would hurry to its rescue. The second was a summons to birds that had strayed from the flock. Both would dust the crows from the trees or fields up into the sky where Lazlo and his father could blast them with their shotguns. The twelve-gauges put out a larger shot pattern, especially with a set of choke tubes, ensuring multiple kills. Lazlo loved to watch the crows drop from midair, pirouetting like falling bombs, then count how many they had killed. Paper decoys attached to trees or barbed wire fences with clothespins also brought them some success, but it was the birdcalls that were more reliable. To hear his father do them terrified and transfixed Lazlo. The sounds that emanated from his mouth were inhuman, haunting. Lazlo would often dream that an actual crow was poking its head from his father's mouth, flapping to escape his lips. It was the only dream he ever had of him.

Meers wondered what Calvin Timmons was dreaming about. He hoped the shock from the battery hadn't hurt him too severely. He had tested the voltage repeatedly on his first pet, a black vagrant Meers had lured with a ten-dollar bill and kept in the cage for weeks, running tests. Despite being a drunk and living on the streets, the vagrant had a hefty build, making him a suitable subject. Dry runs with a regular car battery proved to be too mild, the sedation too brief. The truck battery had just enough kick to knock out Meers's pet without impairing him, a crucial feature. He couldn't allow his prey to be damaged or depleted or else he would have to nurse them extensively, and that would create a delay. The conflict was that the longer they stayed in the cage, the sooner they cracked. He had to pace things perfectly or they would get overripe. Frazzled nerves would render them careless.

That was the fate that befell his first pet, the vagrant, who Meers had named John, for no other reason than it was common. Even sober, John was an unimpressive opponent, though he had his utilities. Meers performed various trials on him. He determined how much food was needed to sustain the man, how much to fortify him. He clocked how many minutes John could run in the tunnels before tiring and what, if any, injuries he sustained, such as cuts and twisted ankles. John would constantly try and talk to Meers, ask him his name, where he was from, why he was doing this, why him. When that didn't work, John resorted to insults. He would call him a faggot or a sissy, desperate for any sort of response. Meers never answered. Not until the day he hunted John for real.

"Thank you," he said as he raised the trapdoor to the cage that opened into the sewer tunnel and let the man free one final time. "You've been very helpful."

John must have sensed that the rehearsals were over. That day, he ran fast. He ran for his life.

Meers had spent months memorizing the tunnel system. He knew the layout by heart, where the tunnels widened and which got the heaviest runoff flows. He didn't expect to keep up with his prey. His passion was tracking them and predicting their moves. If he lost the trail, he could return to a main tunnel to regain ground. Despite his maladies, Meers could travel swiftly through the constricted quarters. He wore a miner's hat with a carbine lamp to free up his hands. The added benefit was that the light burned so brightly it blinded whoever looked directly at him. He didn't see that as unsportsmanlike because he didn't need the light. He could have hunted without it. If anything, he was helping his prey. They would know when he had caught up to them.

When Meers finally caught up to him that night in the tunnels, John submitted to him willingly, panting, glad for it to end.

"Do it," he shouted. "Do it already."

So Meers did. He walked right up to John and stuck the bowie knife through his stomach, aiming for a kidney, a wound that would cause him to expire rapidly. Meers felt the blade's tip hit a vertebra, and John slid down the brick tunnel wall. He died within minutes, his blood draining into the sewer water. Meers stared at the body and waited to feel what he had the day he turned seven and his father took him squirrel hunting. He didn't. He felt much more. He felt healthy, whole, increasingly alive with every breath that coursed through his wizened lungs.

Meers cut off John's head below the Adam's apple and took it back to the zinc works. He dried the head in a cool, dark corner of the refinery the way his father dried opossum to prepare the meat. He wanted to preserve John as a game-head mount, like a buck or an elk. On the average mount, the only actual parts of the animal were the antlers and the skin. All of the organs and tissues were re-created with man-made materials. The eyelids were sculpted from clay, the soft tissues of the nose and mouth formed from wax, and the armature of the skull and neck were crafted from hard foam. Meers couldn't remove John's skull without damaging the skin, so he improvised.

He doused the dried head in formaldehyde—submerging it in a container would ruin the effect—and mounted it on an iron stand that he welded himself. For the first few weeks, the face held its shape. The hair was lifelike, however the pallor grew gray. Soon the features began to slip. The ears shrank and crinkled as would dried leaves. The lips receded, teeth bared in a pained grin. Because the lower eyelids sagged and pulled away from the eyeballs, which had gone milky in the formaldehyde, John appeared to be staring with pupil-less eyes. The head was ghoulish, monstrous. Nevertheless, Meers could not bear to part with his memento.

His oversight was that he had left John's body in the tunnel. Due to the heat and the dampness, it promptly rotted, ratcheting up the stink in the sewers. By the time Meers thought to dispose of it elsewhere, it was too putrid to move. That was when he devised the harnesses. The notion of his hunting grounds being littered with human remains was repugnant to him, so he began dumping the bodies in areas close to where he had captured his pets to make the murders appear local. He also started keeping fingers as souvenirs instead of heads. Using his father's cherished pocketknife, he sawed them from the hands of his prey. That was the true glory of the hunt: collecting his trophies.

Taking the fingers was a safeguard too. Had the bodies been discovered decapitated, surely the police would have gone on the alert. Thus far, Meers hadn't seen any of his pets' names in the newspaper, not a single one.

Calvin Timmons would likely fall into obscurity as well. Meers gave the sleeping teenager a final glance before leaving. He would allot Calvin the day to recuperate and regain his faculties. Tomorrow they would play.

THIRTY-ONE

The lines at the roadblocks were longer than they had been that morning. Cars were honking, and people were hanging out their windows to see what was causing the congestion. Emmett had taken that particular route intentionally in the hope that the same state trooper he spoke to earlier would still be there. Fortunately for Emmett, he was. Sunburned and worn out, the trooper waved the vehicles through the checkpoint one at a time.

"Why we goin' so slow?" Freddie asked from the floor, his shoulders crammed against the passenger seat.

"Because of the barricades."

"Are there any tanks?"

"No tanks. Sorry."

Some stores along the street had put up signs reading NEGRO OWNED to dissuade looters. On the sidewalk, a black minister in a pinstriped suit was handing out leaflets. "Peace, brothers and sisters," he preached. "Peace in the name of true Christian charity. Put down your guns and pray. The police don't aim to hurt us. Stop your provocatin' and pray."

Freddie spied over the dash. "Is he crazy?"

Those on the sidewalks seemed to share Freddie's sentiment. They steered wide of the reverend, as though he was begging for alms to feed the rich.

"He certainly doesn't have any takers."

"That guy still chasin' us?"

In his side mirror, Emmett had a clear view of the Oldsmobile coupe. One car stood between them. The driver was smoking, his Borsalino tipped over his brow.

"Yup."

"So? You gotta another plan? 'Cause I can't be squeezed in here all day, and I damn sure won't fit in that cardboard box."

"I've got to gain us some ground."

"How?"

"For starters, you're going to have to put that box over your head."

"Nuh-uh. No way."

"State troopers are guarding this checkpoint. We can't let them see you."

"Why not? Tell 'em to help my ass. Tell 'em to lock that guy up."

"What he's doing isn't illegal. They can't help us, Freddie."

"Ain't nothing illegal these days?" he huffed and hid under the box.

The young trooper remembered Emmett. "Back again, Detective?"

"I see you haven't made it into the shade."

"I did. For a little while." The other trooper had his Reising submachine gun on his shoulder and was sipping a paper cup of coffee under a store awning. "Not long enough."

"Can you do something for me?"

"Sure thing, Detective."

"Don't look, but there's a guy in a blue Olds right behind me. You might recognize him. He came through this roadblock a couple of hours ago."

"Nasty fella. He cussed me for not letting him through quicker."

"Well, he's a reporter. He's been following me all day. I need to get this box to the Fourth and I'd prefer not to have him pestering me about what's inside."

"What is inside?"

"Hand guns. My private stash. Couldn't hurt, right?"

"No, sir," the trooper concurred. "If you got 'em, use 'em. That's what I say."

"Can you stall him? Give me a chance to get to the precinct without him on my tail?"

"No problem, Detective. That's the best part about having a badge, right? You can do whatever you want."

The statement nicked Emmett's conscience. Like a paper cut, the reminder of frailty was more unpleasant than the pain. It was disconcerting how cavalierly the power they were entrusted with could be abused. That was how the riot had started.

"Thanks," Emmett told the trooper and drove on.

"Can I take this off now?" Freddie said. "Well, can I?"

"I'm thinking," Emmett teased.

"You a real barrel 'a laughs, you know that?" Freddie shoved the cardboard box off his head onto the seat. "We finally getting rid of that guy?"

From his rearview mirror, Emmett watched the trooper flag his partner. The one with the Reising swaggered up to the passenger door of the Delta and rested the machine gun's stock on the car's hood menacingly.

"Yeah, we'll get a decent lead on him."

They zigzagged around the Central Ward to bypass the other barricades and parked on Boyd Street, close to the Hayes Home Housing Projects, where Emmett's car could readily be spotted. It was the first place the guy in the coupe would look, so they had to move fast.

"We have to hurry. Can you run?"

Freddie stood and stretched. "I can always run."

They took off for the farthest building. Emmett led him through the fire door with the busted lock and into the stairwell. Both were winded. The humidity turned air into slush in the lungs.

"What floor we goin' to?"

"Ninth."

Freddie gazed up at the looming staircase. "Can't we take the elevator?"

The risk of getting trapped in the elevator remained, but after the run, climbing nine flights was as unappealing to Emmett as it was to Freddie. "Depends on whether it's working."

They went to the lobby. The elevator doors were open and the car reeked of liquor. Curse words were etched on the walls. At knee height, a smiley face had been drawn in crayon.

"Are you sure about this?"

"Can't be as bad as the stairs." Freddie pinched his nose and stepped in.

Emmett pushed the button for the ninth floor, then the doors rolled shut. The cables started to creak ominously, raising the elevator car.

"Somebody doin' this by hand?" Freddie asked in a nasal twang.

The pulley tugged the elevator along at a steady, stuttering rate. "Feels like it."

At the fifth floor, the elevator stopped. The doors parted to reveal an elderly black woman with a cane waiting at the threshold. "Going down?"

"Feels like it," Freddie said, repeating Emmett.

"We're actually going up, ma'am."

"Damn," she muttered, and the doors slid closed.

"Damn is right. Stinks so bad in here it's makin' my eyes water."

The elevator reopened at the ninth floor. They hurried out. A baby was squalling somewhere down the hall, and glass from a broken wine bottle was scattered across the floor in front of an apartment as though someone had christened the door with it. Emmett and Freddie skirted the shards.

"Nice place. Where we goin'?"

"To see a friend."

"A cop?"

"Definitely not a cop."

After the third knock, Otis Fossum unlocked his door. He was in his robe again, half asleep. He regarded Freddie with dreamy detachment. "Need another favor, Mr. Emmett?"

"Believe me, it'll be one you won't regret."

Fossum let them in. "Worked a double shift last night Downtown. Had no idea what was happenin' here. Saw all the burnt-up shops this morning. Was glad I missed it."

The riot touched everybody in Newark, even someone like Otis, whose world ran counterclockwise. Emmett made the introductions and pulled up some chairs. "Have a seat, Freddie. You too, Otis. This might take awhile to explain."

He filled them in on what Sal Lucaro and his sidekick had done and informed Fossum of the mix-up between him and Freddie, then Emmett proposed his scheme to fool the guy driving the Delta.

"So all him and me gotta do is stay put?" As usual, Otis was awaiting a hitch.

"I'll take care of the rest."

"Wait. I'm stuck here now?" Freddie was livid.

"Only for a few hours."

"A few hours?" Freddie sank back in his seat, moping.

Fossum walked Emmett to the door. "I'm not too good with kids. Don't got nothing 'cept beer in the icebox."

"No beer, Otis. Just water for him."

"I heard that. Might as well be back in jail."

"The boy was in jail?"

"He's harmless. Really," Emmett assured him.

"I ain't worried fo' me. You the one pulling the fasty on a gangster."

"It'll be worth it if it works, right?"

"Right," Otis said evenly.

It was the "if" part Emmett had to worry about. Enough time had passed that the guy driving the Delta would have scouted his car. "Don't open the door for anybody. Okay?"

"Shouldn't've opened it for you," Fossum joked. Then he latched the dead bolt.

From the lobby, Emmett could see the Oldsmobile idling at the curb. He went out the fire door on the opposite end of the building and listened. The characteristic *whap, whap, whap* of a handball game was coming from the rear of the tenement.

The same kids who had acted tough with Emmett and Otis two days ago were circled around the building's back wall. A black handball was ricocheting off the bricks. The leader, the one who had threatened Emmett, was pitted against a bigger boy and was trouncing him. He wore cutoff dungarees and a loose tank top that swung from side to side as he dove for the ball. Six others were cheering and refereeing the match.

"Hey you. Remember me?" Emmett strode up to the kid and called him out of the game.

"Come on, Kenny. We playin'."

"Shut up," Kenny ordered. He caught the handball, putting the competition on hold. "No, I don't remember you," he said, though obviously he did. "What chu' want, honky?"

"See, you do remember. It's me. Mr. Honky." The boys had a laugh. Kenny didn't. "Let's you and I take a walk and get reacquainted."

Instead of flashing his revolver, Emmett pulled aside his jacket to showcase his badge. He thought of what the state trooper had said, that it entitled the wearer to do anything they saw fit. Emmett considered what he was about to do supremely fitting.

"Aw, man." Kenny bounced the ball to a friend and let Emmett lead him apart from the group toward the street. Emmett put his arm around the kid's neck in a fatherly manner in full view of the Delta coupe. Kenny tensed, as though Emmett's touch was freezing cold.

"Kenny, my friend, you and I didn't get off on the right foot. So let's start over." Emmett stopped and put both hands on the kid's shoulders. To the guy in the Olds, it would read as a heart-to-heart chat. "If I ever catch you pulling that stunt you tried on me with anybody else, I'll arrest you."

"You came here just to tell me that?" Kenny said, annoyed.

"It's a big world." Emmett gestured toward the street where the Delta was so it would seem as if he was warning the kid. "Next person you come on strong to might not be as forgiving as me."

"Whatever. Honky." Kenny shrugged off Emmett's hands and stalked away.

Like a silent movie without subtitles, the pantomime was self-explanatory. Emmett returned to his car and drove off. This time, the Oldsmobile Delta didn't follow.

THIRTY-TWO

Miscommunication was that morning's running theme. The police band had been beset by calls about failed transmissions between cops, state troopers, and the National Guard. All three were on different frequencies. Neither the troopers nor the Guardsmen could get any information on patrol movements or citizens' calls for assistance because those went directly to the Central Complaints Division, and policemen were radioing in, asking why the aid they were promised hadn't arrived. Blockades had gone up at 137 intersections, cordoning off a fourteen-square-mile radius of the city, but none of the patrols could contact one another. Every order or request had to be filtered through the Roseville Armory and rereleased over the airways. Emmett was eavesdropping on the crisis when an officer hailed for backup on a breaking and entering at the Sears Roebuck on Elizabeth Avenue.

"Manager says they stole twenty-four rifles. That's more than the whole department's got."

It was true. The rioters were becoming better armed than the police, and Emmett didn't want to dwell on what was liable to occur come nightfall if the frequencies didn't get in sync. He was sitting in his car outside Evander Hammond's house, paging through the boy's file, hoping for some divine inspiration. Hammond's body had been found in

April, making his case the oldest of the bunch. His left pinkie finger had been severed. Assuming the killer was going from left to right, that made Evander the first victim. It was a big assumption, one of many. Emmett hadn't ruled out the possibility that the murderer might have collaborated with somebody to disarm teenagers as large and powerful as Hammond and the rest, however he continually gravitated toward the notion of a lone assailant.

Thieves operating in pairs or groups were splashier about their heists and often trashed the places they robbed. There was security in numbers, a freedom to flaunt their crimes. Sophisticated burglars who worked alone were careful. Were it not for the missing items, most homeowners would never realize someone had been in their house. These murders had a meticulous quality that bespoke a cautious, plotting, self-reliant person, similar to a rogue thief. While a rogue usually had a signature method for breaking in, popping the locks or removing windowpanes, a consistent distinguishing pattern, this killer was continually changing.

The physical similarities of the victims suggested they were hand-picked, yet the method of death varied, as did the location of the body dumps. To stab somebody to death, the assailant had to get close to his victims, a choice that struck Emmett as calculated, however the victims' builds implied that they would be able to fend off any attacker. Incapacitating a kid that young and that size would take a sly, inventive mind. Everything about the murders screamed how smart the perpetrator was, only when it came to the killer's identity, the cases went mute.

Emmett skimmed through Hammond's file a final time. In the crime scene photographs, Evander's body was splayed across an alley adjacent to a construction site. Stalks of rebar sprouting from newly poured concrete were visible in the background, a veritable metal jungle. The blood from Evander's chest wound had seeped out onto the dirt alley in a practically perfect circle. Emmett closed the case. He couldn't look at it anymore.

The three-story tenement on Bruce Street where Evander Hammond had lived was painted a muddy taupe, the nondescript hue that resulted from mixing together different colors of remnant paint. The steps had been coated too, and the wash was worn to the wood down the middle of each stair, indicating the path most traveled. Emmett was on the path least traveled, a path that was quickly approaching a dead end.

When he got no answer at the Hammonds' door, he knocked on the apartment a floor below hoping someone would point him in the right direction, as the girl with the baby had.

"Who is it?" a male voice demanded gruffly.

"This is Detective Emmett of the Newark Police Department," he shouted through the door. It was painted the same shade as everything else and peeling as well. The landlord had probably gotten a discount and blended indoor paint with outdoor paint. That was why it wouldn't stick to anything. "I'm trying to contact the relatives of Evander Hammond."

"What fo'?"

"That's police business, sir. If you open the door, I'll gladly show you my badge."

"Don't got to. I can tell you a cop by how ya talk."

Having a conversation through a closed door wasn't that different from having one with a person who didn't speak the language. Emmett talked louder and kept his sentences simple. "Then can you tell me how I can get in touch with someone in the Hammond family?"

"Boy's father is the janitor at Peddie First Baptist. You could find him there."

"Thanks," Emmett said to the closed door.

He was about to walk away when the man asked, "You after who murdered Evander?"

"Yes, sir, I am."

"When you find 'im, do us all a favor. Lock him up an' throw away the key. Hear?"

"I hear you, sir," Emmett replied. "I hear you."

The Oldsmobile didn't reappear in his rearview mirror the entire trip over to the church. Emmett had lost the guy, at least for the time being. If Kenny mouthed off to him the way he had Emmett, the kid probably wound up with a black eye to rival Edward's, but once the driver figured out that Kenny wasn't Freddie, he would return to Emmett's house or give up altogether. As Emmett arrived at the church, he prayed he would never see another Delta 88 as long as he lived.

Peddie First Baptist was a worthy place to say a prayer. From the outside, the church gave the impression of a medieval citadel, built of dark granite with a barreled body, domed roof, and hexagonal spires. A moat wouldn't have seemed out of character. Its stalwart exterior was contradicted by the vast tabernacle inside, which resembled the amber inner chambers of a spiraled seashell. The pews were rounded into arcs, theater-style, the shape echoed in the curved balcony, the lustrous convex pink marble seats for the clergy, and the arcade of arched windows made of Tiffany glass. The ribs of the gargantuan pipe organ added to the sense of immensity and that all earthly things were dwarfed by faith.

Emmett hadn't been to church for years. The majesty of this one humbled him. He had the feeling he was trespassing into a private club from which he had been denied membership.

A sign in the entry said that the afternoon's services were canceled. Anxiety over the riot had invaded every corner of the city. When Newark needed the prayers most, the ministers were too fear-stricken to open their doors.

Hammering resounded through the nave. Beneath the colonnade, a black man with talc white hair was standing on a step stool securing sheets of plywood to the stained glass windows, blocking the sunlight piece by piece. He was almost finished with a window depicting Jesus crowned by a golden halo. A dove soared in the sky above. The plywood had reached Jesus' neck.

"Excuse me, sir?" Emmett said.

The supply of nails held between the man's teeth prevented him from replying. He finished pounding and spit the nails into his palm. "No services today on account of the troubles."

"I'm not here for the service. I'm looking for Mr. Hammond, Evander Hammond's father."

"That's me." He got down off the stool. In spite of his hair color, Hammond had the sturdy frame of a youthful man who worked with his body for a living. Evander had clearly gotten his height and strength from his father.

"Do you have a minute to talk?" Emmett presented his shield.

Hammond sat heavily on a pew. "Sorry," he said, scooting in to make room for Emmett, who joined him out of courtesy. He would have preferred to stand.

Pews, in Emmett's estimation, were a form of discipline. While smooth, the hard, molded seats discouraged slouching or talking to the person beside you. If you didn't sit up and face forward, you were bound to be uncomfortable. If that wasn't discipline, Emmett wasn't sure what was.

He and his brother had sat side by side in church from the age when their feet didn't touch the floor until they were both so tall their knees pressed into the hymnal racks. Like prisoners, they contrived secret codes and games to pass the tedious hours of Sunday mass. They had thumb wars under winter coats and whispered jokes during choir songs that muffled their laughter. That was when Emmett had felt closest to his brother, when they were forbidden to play and talk and had found the means anyhow. Now they didn't speak unless it was necessary.

Hammond's legs were as cramped in the pew as Emmett's. He was too distracted to care. They sat apart, affording each other extra personal space. Four people could have fit in between them, five if they were packed together for a holiday service. From years of attending mass, Emmett could eyeball a pew and say how many could squeeze in, a skill as valueless as remembering the words to a TV jingle.

"The news bad or good?" Hammond asked.

"Neither I'm afraid."

"This kinda news can't be good no matter what, can it?"

"I'm only trying to get some information, sir."

"But nothing's changed. What's there to tell? I'd be repeatin' the same stuff."

"Repeating it can't hurt."

"Hurts anyway."

Resigned, Hammond looked up at the pulpit on the upper level. The elaborate rostrum was carved of wood with iron railings. Mounted on the podium was the image of a bird with its wings spread as wide as an angel's. "Ask what you came to ask, Detective," he said.

"Tell me about the day Evander went missing."

"I was home. Wouldn't have been 'cept I hurt my hip. Fell off that very stepladder." He indicated the stool he had been balancing on minutes ago. "I was laid up in bed. Evander came home from school. Asked me how I was feeling. Then said he had to go to the library."

"The school library?"

"No, the big one on Washington. Not much else to tell. He didn't come home." That put an end to Hammond's story.

"Did he go to the library often? Was he doing his homework."

"Evander didn't have much to do with books. Didn't need 'em. He was street-smart. He lived for music. He'd buy records and sell 'em to kids for a couple cents over what the stores charged so he could buy more. Made decent money too. I didn't tell that to the police right off the bat. Thought they'd peg him for a punk. He wasn't. Boys his age can't get no jobs. No record store would hire him. So Evander was his own record store."

To make a profit, Evander had to have been stealing some of the records and buying others legitimately, a common scam. Emmett had arrested a clerk at Bamberger's department store for turning a blind eye to her friends' shoplifting, friends who were cutting her in on the money they took in from reselling the stolen clothes at a discount. There was no reason to tarnish the boy's image and tell Mr. Hammond that his son's side business wasn't on the up-and-up.

"Did you suspect anybody? Any of his friends?"

"No, sir. Everybody loved Evander. Yeah, he was a smooth talker, always diggin' for an angle, bucking the system. It was just that he dreamed bigger than most."

Hammond's gaze drifted upward again toward the pulpit. It was flanked by a pair of gilded griffins, mythical beasts with the bodies of lions and the heads and wings of eagles. Legend claimed their instincts led them to buried treasures and that they built their nests of gold, making them tempting targets for hunters and plunderers. Emmett wouldn't have noticed them were it not for Hammond's description of his son.

"Evander didn't look his age. Didn't act it either. He was proper. Always said 'Sir' and 'Ma'am' and 'Please.' Before my hair went white, people'd mistake us for brothers."

Being mistaken as his son's brother was a compliment Hammond cherished, as much as Evander's memory.

"Why you interested in him after all this time?"

"Somebody killed your son. I want to know who. Don't you, Mr. Hammond?"

"Far as I've seen, what a person wants and what they get have a funny way of not being the same."

It was a suitable moral for church, for life, and for Emmett's whole case. He had started out seeing Ambrose Webster as an excuse to get out of the Records Room so he could reopen Vernon Young's murder. What he had wound up with was a series of crimes that refused to produce any leads. Emmett may as well have been plugging an electrical cord into a keyhole. The pieces didn't fit.

"Minister's got me puttin' up these plywood boards to save the windows from getting broke," Hammond said, seemingly changing the subject. "Have to do the outside's too. Afraid people'll throw stones and ruin 'em. What are they gonna do if the windows do get broke, I wonder? Used to be a statue 'a Saint Peter on the roof of this church. Got struck by lightning and smashed to the ground. Nobody ever replaced it. Too much trouble. Months go by and folks forget. Figured that's what happened with Evander. Too much trouble. With the rioting, I'd 'a thought the police had more important things to do."

"This is important."

"To the police or to you?"

"To me," Emmett admitted, to Hammond and himself. "Look, if you remember anything else, you can phone me." He gave Hammond his home number.

"All I do is remember, Detective. Hard to do anything else."

Remembering was its own kind of agony, separate from grief. Emmett could sympathize. He slid out of the pew and left Evander's father to continue covering the stained glass window of Jesus to keep it safe.

THIRTY-THREE

So many things to do, so little time. During his lunch break, Meers drove to his favorite Italian butcher's shop in the North Ward. He held the door for a woman exiting the shop, who was juggling a bundle of parcels.

"Thanks," she murmured, averting her eyes from his lame arm.

"You're quite welcome," he chirped politely.

Meers reveled in the discomfort of strangers. His pitiable appearance put them off, which was fine with him. Let them think he was weak and crippled. He wasn't. And he could prove it.

Two small oscillating fans labored to generate a cross breeze inside the butcher's shop. A mother and her young son were at the counter, ordering. Bored, the boy was mashing his cheeks into the display case, blowing on the glass to steam it, and licking the condensation. It disgusted Meers. Had he ever behaved that badly in public, his father would have throttled him right there in the butcher's shop. He cleared his throat, a hint to the woman to curb her child.

"We don't do that, dear," she scolded, tugging the boy away from the display case by his sleeve.

"Eww. What's wrong with that man, Mom? Look at his arm. It's all messed up."

The woman's face reddened. "Nothing, sweetie. Nothing. Help

Mommy carry these, won't you?" She thrust her purchases at the boy, then hustled him out of the store.

"Kids," the butcher commiserated. "Whadaya gonna do?"

Meers had a few ideas.

"You want the usual, sir?"

"Please."

"Three pounds of prime rib, comin' up. How are those dogs 'a yours?"

"Excellent, thank you. They're remarkable animals."

To keep the butcher from becoming curious about his large and frequent orders, Meers had told him that he raised hunting dogs and asked for a quantity sufficient to feed three, full-grown bloodhounds. Meers had never actually owned a dog. His father didn't like them. Be it a pure breed or a feist, the mongrels employed by some to locate small prey and keep them bayed, dogs diluted the purity of hunting. "A man who gets a dog to do his work for him is wasting his time and the dog's. If you're gonna cheat, why bother?" was his father's maxim. Meers didn't condone cheating either. The only edge he had in his hunting was foreknowledge of the sewer tunnels, but he believed the inability to use both of his arms tipped the scales back into balance.

"These are some nice ribs. Cut 'em myself this morning." The butcher presented a tray of marbled slabs from the display case.

"Perfect. Would you kindly trim them for me?"

The butcher obliged, slicing white ribbons of fat from the meat until each slab was pristine. "You must really love them dogs," he said. "Hell, I'd sleep in the doghouse myself to get this much prime rib."

"You'd have to do more than that," Meers told him.

Uneasy, the butcher laughed off the comment, wrapped the meat in paper, and calculated the tab. "That'll be seventeen bucks."

The meat for Meers's imaginary dogs cost a small fortune. He didn't hesitate to spend the money. He would soon reap the returns.

"May I have a bag? I have difficulty carrying things." He played up his infirmity to embarrass the butcher, who fumbled to load the parcels into a paper sack.

"Oh. Right. Sorry."

Meers luxuriated in the butcher's guilt as a beautiful woman would the stares of men on the street.

"Those dogs'll be happy tonight," the butcher said, still blushing.

Happy wasn't the word Meers would have selected, but it would do.

His lunch break was almost over and he had to get the prime rib on ice. He went straight home. On the way, Meers got stopped at a road-block. A National Guardsman in fatigues was going from car to car, inspecting the drivers. If they were white, he let them through. If they were black, he directed them to pull to the curb and wait to be inter-viewed. Meers zipped through the blockade unquestioned.

A three-floor walk-up off Passaic Avenue was where Meers called home. It was the same apartment where he had lived since he and his father relocated to Newark. The building canted to one side when they moved in and had been slanting farther from vertical each year. The two-room apartment was at the rear of the building and got direct sun-light for just a few short hours a day. Even with the lights on, the rooms remained gloomy. There were more shadows in the apartment than pos-sessions.

Meers put his three pounds of prime rib into the refrigerator, which was all but empty. He didn't eat much, an egg and a piece of toast for breakfast, broth and crackers for dinner. A small amount of food could satiate him. For lunch, he would have a plain ham sandwich. That would be plenty.

He fixed the sandwich and ate it standing at the kitchen sink, star-ing out the window at the back of another apartment building. Pots of withered plants teemed on the sills, strangled by the heat. Meers ate without tasting, chewing automatically to get the meal down. He had lost his taste for all things. Food, like the rest of ordinary existence, had become bland. Only one endeavor could coax him to hunger, and that was hunting.

He rinsed the plate in the sink, dried it, and replaced it in the cup-board. With minutes to spare before he had to leave for work, Meers went into the bedroom. He reached under his bed, removed a set of loos-ened floorboards, and pulled a mahogany jewelry box out from his special hiding place between the joists.

Inside the jewelry box, on the top tier, four human fingers lay on the red felt lining. They were his jewels, rarer than diamonds or rubies. Meers admired each of them, their differences and eccentricities. Some had deep wrinkles around the knuckles or torn cuticles or filth beneath the nails, all unique. Though each was from a different boy, the fingers ascended as they would on a single hand, from the pinkie to the ring to the middle, sloping downward at the pointer. Meers was almost finished with his first set. There was space for one more finger on that tier and room for more on the tiers below. He rubbed the empty spot, giddy with anticipation. He would soon fill it with Calvin Timmon's thumb.

THIRTY-FOUR

Life had come to a standstill at Emmett's house. When he got home, his arms full of grocery bags, Mrs. Poole and Edward were in the exact positions he had left them. She was sitting on a kitchen chair and he was acting as sentinel at the bank of windows in the living room. It was entirely possible that they hadn't moved the whole time he was gone. The television was tuned to a soap opera. Neither was paying attention.

"I'm glad you're such a talented cook, Mrs. Poole, because it was slim pickings at the market. They were all out of everything on your list."

At each of the three different grocery stores Emmett had gone to the entire stock of milk, juice, meat, and eggs was already bought out. Coolers for frozen foods sat bare, and the dry goods had been whittled to a limited selection of spices, condiments, and muffin mixes. The empty markets were somehow eerier than the destruction done by the looters and fires. Raided stores spoke of what had passed. Stripped grocery shelves portended what was to come.

"I'm starving," Edward moaned. "Better be something worth eating in those bags or I'll eat the bags."

"In a minute, you might wish you hadn't said that."

Emmett unpacked the bleak assortment of provisions onto the

coffee table: a jar of peanut butter and one of apricot jam, biscuit mix, cans of lima beans, wax beans, and beets as well as a lone pack of hot dogs and a loaf of pumpernickel bread.

"You weren't kidding about slim pickings, Mr. Emmett."

"This stuff makes army rations look like Easter dinner."

"It's the best I could do under the circumstances. There's always the bags."

"Don't tempt me." Edward was examining the picture on the can of wax beans with distaste. "Are they supposed to be this color?"

Mrs. Poole gathered the medley of disparate foods. "Y'all might want to cross your fingers and say a prayer."

"I'd cross my legs too if I could." Edward handed her the wax beans as though passing off a dirty diaper.

"At least we have the hot dogs," Emmett said.

"Eating 'em on pumpernickel, that's sacrilege. There's probably something in the Geneva Conventions about how you can't even force prisoners of war to do that."

"Okay, I'll eat the hot dogs and you can have the box of baking soda from inside the refrigerator for dinner."

"I guess pumpernickel's not *that* bad."

"Any sign of our friend in the Oldsmobile?"

"Nope. Wasn't sure if I should keep looking."

"I can't be sure myself. If he hasn't come back by now, we could be in the clear."

"What about our houseguest? He comin' back?"

"Not for a while. Don't rush to dry those tears."

"I'm just glad I won't have to share my hot dogs with him."

"Anything on the news about the riots?"

"At noon they showed the same footage we saw this morning and gave some spiel about the mayor, how he was 'confident that everything would be resolved in a timely fashion' and blah, blah, blah."

"What else would the mayor say? That Newark was falling apart at the seams?"

"It's weird. I look out this window and everything seems normal. A mile away, who knows?"

"You wouldn't want to see it," Emmett told him somberly.

"I've seen a lot."

"This is different. Saigon wasn't your hometown."

Mrs. Poole brought out plates of peanut butter and jelly sandwiches with a measly helping of crackers. "Decided I'd save the hot dogs for dinner, considering it's all the meat we have." She put Edward's tray across his wheelchair and gave each of them glasses of tap water. "Usually, I'd make you boys eat at the table. Today hasn't exactly been usual, so I'll let that slide."

"Where's your plate?" Emmett asked.

"I'll have my lunch later. Seeing as you're home, I thought I'd wash up."

Unwilling to leave Edward alone, Mrs. Poole hadn't had a moment to herself or even a change of clothes since she arrived at the house two days ago. Emmett wished he could do something for her. His mother's clothes had been donated to their church for a rummage sale, as had her personal belongings and toiletries. There was nothing feminine left in the house. He hadn't noticed until then. The absence suddenly made the place feel barren.

"Go ahead. Take your time," Edward told her, hungrily munching a cracker. Once she was out of earshot, he said, "You know these are stale, right?"

"Try ancient. Ma bought them. They're over a year old."

"Think it's hazardous to eat 'em?"

"Do you care?"

"Naw. I like to live on the edge."

Hazardous or not, they inhaled the food, gobbling up the crackers and polishing off their sandwiches. Edward picked at the crumbs. "It really is a sin to make PB&J with apricot jelly. May as well use ketchup."

"Then I'll tell Mrs. Poole to put ketchup on yours and save the jelly for me. I wouldn't want you committing any sins."

Emmett took their plates into the kitchen. As soon as Mrs. Poole was finished freshening up, he planned on heading over to the public library. Though Hammond's case was four months old, Evander wasn't a frequent patron. Someone might remember seeing him. It was a long shot. Those were the only kind Emmett had to bet on.

He could hear the volume on the TV rise to compensate for the racket he was making washing the dishes. Prior to his brother's return home, the television had been collecting dust. Occasionally, Emmett would switch it on to catch the nightly news. Otherwise, he read, mainly from his mother's ample stash of novels and classics. She had been born into the Depression era, when a book was a commodity prized as highly as gold or pearls, so she could not discard a single one, even after she had read them a hundred times. They were too valuable to part with. Her will dictated that, upon her death, the collection be given to Saint Casimir's, a heartfelt donation considering her attachment, however Emmett did not comply with his mother's wishes. He couldn't part with the books either. They were his fondest reminders of her, memories too valuable to donate.

Her impressive collection filled four tall bookcases, which stood opposite the television, positioned as if the two were at odds. To Emmett, they were. He couldn't get into any of the programs on TV. They were too contrived. He only showed an interest because Edward enjoyed them. If they didn't watch television together, then they wouldn't do anything together. The hours he spent bathing his brother, cooking his meals, or helping him get dressed didn't count. Those were obligations. Watching TV with Edward was a choice.

"What's on?" he asked.

"*Gilligan's Island*. But I've seen this one. The Professor builds a car out of coconut shells and vines and Gilligan drives it into the lagoon."

"Doesn't that happen on every episode?"

"Pretty much."

"Should I switch the channel?"

Edward was capable of doing so on his own, as evidenced by the change in volume, yet Emmett continued to do it for him. That was his form of participation.

"Be my guest."

As Emmett clicked the dial, he caught a flash of movement outside the front window. He lifted the corner of the shade.

"What is it, Marty?"

"Two men. Coming toward the house."

"The guys from last night?"

"Doubt it. These two have on cheap suits. And one's got a tie clip. Nobody in the mob wears a tie clip. They're cops."

Edward relaxed a little. "For a second there, you had me nervous."

"You should be."

"Why? What're they after?"

"Same thing as the gangsters. They're after Freddie."

A firm knock sounded at the door. Emmett flipped off the safety on his service revolver.

"I still got the twenty-two under here." Edward patted the pillow that acted as a booster on the wheelchair so his long legs wouldn't hang over the footrests.

"Good. Go in the kitchen and cover me."

Emmett answered the door. There would be no need for introductions. He knew it was Ionello and Vass. The detectives were standing shoulder to shoulder at the top of the stoop. They made an unlikely duo. Ionello's hair was scruffy and his suit rarely saw the light of day. Tufts at the shoulders attested to where the ends of a hanger had dug into the fabric. Of the pair, he presumably did the undercover work when necessary, posing as a car thief or potential buyer. The tie clip was an effort to look the part of a detective. Vass, on the other hand, was nondescript: average height, average build, and bland features that were the archetype of average. He probably pretended to be an average friendly guy too, as he had with Freddie when he went to Luther Reed's body shop to shake them down. However something in Vass's eyes said that he had an above average temper.

"You wanna tell us why you sprung our suspect, Detective Emmett?"

Vass was trying to come off as casual, but anger was an anchor in his voice. He had his hand on his hip, pushing aside his jacket to brandish his badge and gun. In Emmett's experience, cops who kept them both on the same side sent the message that there was no difference between the two.

"Come on in, gentlemen, and I'll explain."

Ionello pushed into the house first, but it was Vass who took the lead in the conversation.

"So? Explain."

"Freddie Guthrie is a material witness in an ongoing murder investigation."

"Then he coulda stayed in jail," Ionello said, adding his two cents.

"The boy had a court date. I simply brought a scheduling error to the attention of the prison staff."

Vass exhaled loudly through his nose, venting the frustration boiling inside him. "You could have talked to him at Newark Street," he insisted.

The laugh track from a television show interrupted, as if mocking him.

"He's a minor. He shouldn't have been at Newark Street."

"This ain't none of your business," Ionello barked. "He's ours."

"'Ours?'" Emmett played dumb to prompt the detective into incriminating himself.

"Ours as in the Auto Squad's," Vass explained, a smoke screen for Ionello's outburst. "Where's the kid now?"

"Home would be my guess."

Footsteps creaked upstairs, and Ionello made a grab for his gun. Vass's hand went to his as well. Emmett got between them and the staircase.

"Home, huh?" Ionello said.

The detectives drew their revolvers as footfalls descended the stairs.

"Put down your guns. He's not here," Emmett shouted. "It's not him."

Mrs. Poole appeared on the staircase. Seeing pistols pointed at her, she gasped. "Lord in heaven."

"I told you he wasn't here."

Humiliated, Ionello and Vass lowered their weapons, only to discover that Edward had wheeled out of the kitchen, and he had a bead on them with the .22.

"I'm not the cop here, but the way I understand it, if a couple strangers come into my house and start waving guns around, that gives me every right to shoot them. Take my word for it guys, Uncle Sam didn't send me home from the war for havin' bad aim."

The detectives holstered their service revolvers. "Stay away from Freddie Guthrie," Vass warned as he and Ionello eased out the front door. "Got it?"

"Yeah, he's 'yours.' I got it." Emmett hurled the door shut behind them.

"Um, Marty," Edward said, motioning at Mrs. Poole, who was frozen on the stairs, ashen with fright. "I think that little incident might be grounds for quitting."

Emmett took her by the arm and guided her down the steps into her chair. "I've lost count of how many times I've had to apologize to you, Mrs. Poole."

"This'll be the fourth," she informed him, still shaky.

"Then I'm truly sorry. For the fourth time."

"You could at least have the decency to let the same goons in as yesterday. I liked these new ones even less."

Emmett had to laugh. So did Mrs. Poole. Then the telephone rang, startling her anew.

"Lord Almighty," she declared. "My heart feels like a cricket in a pickle jar."

"I don't know about that cricket stuff, but I could use a nice, stiff drink. Whadaya say, Marty? A little bourbon maybe, to calm me and Mrs. Poole's nerves?"

Emmett gave Edward an admonishing scowl as he picked up the phone.

"Mr. Emmett?" a voice said.

"Otis? Is that you?"

"Mr. Emmett. It's my fault. I fell asleep on account 'a that double shift. Couldn't keep my eyes open."

"What's your fault?"

"He's gone. When I woke up, Freddie was gone."

THIRTY-FIVE

Time was against him. Ionello and Vass had a ten-minute lead. The roadblocks might slow them some, though not much. Emmett pushed the speedometer to sixty on residential streets, passing and dodging other cars. He had committed the intersections with barricades to memory, circumnavigating all except two of them. At the first, he flashed his shield and flew through. At the second, on Washington and William, he was delayed by traffic.

Emmett anxiously tapped his thumb on the steering wheel. He was willing the line to move faster and he was willing Freddie not to go to his mother's house. The kid had been pining to go home. He shouldn't have been shocked that Freddie made a break for it. Emmett had just assumed that he got the picture: his apartment was the least safe place for him to be.

The line moved up by a single car. The pace was infuriating. With evening approaching, the troopers must have been making the interviews lengthier to dissuade people from entering the Central Ward. Emmett imagined them reciting the speech about the curfew to every driver. When it was finally his turn, a middle-aged National Guardsman in fatigues greeted him with a cheery smile. Emmett could picture the man as an insurance agent or store clerk in everyday life. His smile seemed incongruous with the fatigues.

"Sir, we're here to remind you that the mayor has imposed—"

Emmett thrust his badge in the man's face. "I'm in a hurry."

Flustered, the Guardsman stepped aside, as if he were the one who had been impolite. "Pardon me. Go right ahead, officer."

Reservists like him would be fish out of water in the Central Ward. If Emmett had a second to spare, he would have warned the man. But he didn't.

Given the military presence throughout the ward, he couldn't race through the streets and risk being stopped. The speed limit felt ridiculously slow. Emmett itched to floor the gas. Gliding along at twenty-five was as exasperating as being corralled at the roadblock.

Dusk had drifted down the skyline and shadows were blossoming from the crevices in between buildings. There was no breeze to dilute the smoke that permeated the air. The neighborhood was deserted, Rose Street included. Emmett swung into a parking space up the road from Freddie's building, hunkered low in his seat, and trained his eyes on the tenement's front door. He couldn't tell if Ionello and Vass had beaten him or not. He would give it five minutes, then go inside. Emmett didn't have to wait long. The detectives came out in half that time, alone.

An audible sigh of relief escaped Emmett's lips. Freddie wasn't home. Ionello and Vass had to be wondering where he was. Emmett was wondering that too. He watched the detectives get into a brown sedan and let them pull away before he left. Freddie could have been anyplace. City Hospital, where his mother was, topped the list. Fortunately for Freddie and for Emmett, Ionello and Vass wouldn't think to look there.

In order to find Freddie, Emmett would have to find Lossie, which meant he had to find Cyril. Since he never got Cyril's last name, Emmett skipped the hospital's main desk and went straight to the emergency room where Cyril had been admitted. The waiting area was a refugee camp of women with children huddled on their laps and men whose wounds were wrapped with rags or ripped T-shirts improvised into bandages. For all Emmett knew, it could have been the same people from last night.

The admitting desk was swamped, so he stopped a nurse in the hall.

"I'm looking for a patient who was brought in yesterday night. Can you help me?"

"I'm going on break. You can ask at the desk." The nurse was haggard from hours in the packed ER. Her once-neat bun was loose and lopsided.

"Please," Emmett said, showing his shield. "A cop cutting the line won't go over too well."

The nurse contemplated that for a second. "All right. What's the name?"

"I don't have a last name. His first is Cyril."

"Lotta good that'll do ya."

"He had a head wound. It was pretty serious."

"That's a start. Stay here."

Emmett stood in the corridor, apart from the mob, as the nurse begrudgingly went to the admitting desk and scrolled through a voluminous stack of papers. She returned with Cyril's last name and his room number.

"It's Denton. Cyril Denton. His skull was cracked, right above the eyebrow. He's on the third floor."

"His injury, is that life threatening?"

"No, but he'll probably have a headache for the rest of the year."

Shouting echoed through the hallway. "At this rate, I might too," the nurse said. "It's been like this all day."

"It wasn't me," a man protested loudly. "It wasn't me, my brothers."

The inebriated plea was issued by a black man strapped to a gurney. An orderly was pushing him toward the elevator with two patrolmen as chaperones.

"My brother. My brother," he repeated. "Tell 'em it wasn't me."

The man's left arm was handcuffed to the gurney while his right hung in a sling. He also had a cast on his leg, and his head and shoulders were completely covered in a fine, white powder, as though a bag of baking flour had exploded in his face. To the crowd at the admitting desk and those in the waiting room, the scene was a welcome diversion from their misery. They gawked at the strange spectacle of the man dusted in white. Emmett recognized what the powder was. When intoxicated prisoners became unruly, officers would sometimes douse them with a fire extinguisher. The carbon dioxide usually knocked them out. Apparently, the extinguisher hadn't done the trick.

"You with them?" the nurse asked him.

The entire fifth floor of City Hospital was sectioned off as a prison ward. Emmett presumed that was their final destination.

"Not today."

"I only get fifteen minutes for break. Will that be all, Officer?"

"Yeah, thanks." He tossed her a quarter, saying, "Have a cup of coffee and a doughnut on me."

The nurse gladly accepted the quarter and the gratitude. It seemed to be the first thank-you she had heard all day.

Compared to the emergency room, the third floor was unnaturally quiet. Emmett's every step thumped through the stark corridors. He peered through the window in the door to Cyril's room. Cyril was asleep in the bed. His forehead had been stitched, and he was wearing a foam neck brace for the whiplash caused by his forehead colliding with the sink. Lossie was napping in a chair beside his bed. Her cheek was black and blue and distended. It would ache once she awoke.

"She's okay."

Freddie had come up behind him, hands buried in his pockets sheepishly.

"Are you?" Emmett was careful not to let on how grateful he was to see him.

"Yeah. I'm okay."

"That was a dumb move."

"I couldn't stay there. Not when she was here. Figured you'd catch up with me."

"Ionello and Vass came to the house. They're trying to catch up with you too."

Freddie leaned into the wall, absorbing the bad news.

"This isn't some con you're running. These people mean business. From now on, you've got to listen to me and do what I say. You have to promise."

Taking orders was tough for Freddie to commit to. He fidgeted with the belt loops on his dungarees, then finally said, "All right already. I promise."

"Your fingers aren't crossed, are they?"

Insulted, Freddie showed him his hands.

"Okay then, let's go."

"Will they be safe here?" Freddie was too short to see in the window to the room where Cyril and his mother were. He just looked at the door dolefully.

"Yes, they'll be safe."

"Promise?"

"Yup." Emmett put out his hands. "See? My fingers aren't crossed either."

The lamps in the parking lot popped on in unison as they got to Emmett's car. It was seven o'clock on the dot, an hour into the citywide curfew. Emmett didn't hear any police sirens or gunfire. The night was starting off well.

"We gonna need this?" Freddie asked. The empty cardboard box sat atop the passenger seat.

"Not anymore."

Freddie gladly tossed it to the ground. The feather-light box flopped onto the pavement like a fallen pillow.

As Emmett was pulling out of the hospital's parking lot, he happened to check his rearview mirror. "Damn. I spoke too soon."

"What is it?"

"The guy in the Oldsmobile. He's back." The contour of his trademark Borsalino was outlined in the glow of Emmett's taillights.

"Aw, brother." Freddie sunk in his seat to hide.

"Don't bother. He's seen you."

"I thought you got rid 'a him."

"So did I." Emmett's ruse had worked, temporarily. "I didn't give the guy enough credit. I bet he picked up my trail at your house. He may be smarter than he seems."

"I sure hope not."

"Me neither."

"Now whadda we do?"

Emmett removed his jacket. "If he wants to follow us, he's going to have to keep up."

They took Market Street and were soon stopped at a checkpoint on Central Avenue.

"I'm taking this boy home from the hospital. He's a witness," Emmett explained to the Guardsman on duty, who took special note of his gun holster and police badge.

"Be careful, Detective. It's getting rough out there. Wouldn't wanna wind up right back at the hospital, would ya?"

That was precisely what Emmett was attempting to avoid. "We'll be careful," he said.

The Delta was briefly detained at the blockade, then hard on his tail again.

"Why didn't you make that army man slow him down like last time?"

"We need something more."

"Like what?"

"We need to get this guy arrested."

Emmett led the Olds onto Route 280, an interstate highway that cut through Newark and fed into the 95 Turnpike. The speed limit on the highway was fifty miles per hour. Emmett pushed it to seventy-five. Traffic was almost nonexistent because people were staying clear of the riot-stricken area altogether. The two westbound lanes were wide open.

"He's gaining." Freddie was facing backward, holding on to the headrest. "The Delta's got a five-liter V-8 engine. That's a fair match for your L-head Flat 6."

"I don't think a fair match is what he's after. Tell me if he comes around on my left."

"He's comin' around on your left."

The grille of the Olds crept into Emmett's side mirror. Soon they were neck and neck. He gunned the engine, nosing into the lead. A station wagon was puttering along in his lane and Emmett was closing in. The Delta's driver edged up, preventing him from changing lanes.

"You see that car, right?" Freddie asked nervously.

"Hold on to something."

Emmett jammed the brakes, letting the Oldsmobile speed ahead, then swung in behind him, leaving the station wagon in the dust. Freddie slid across the seat, gripping the armrest for dear life. To counter, the guy driving the Delta did the same, switching lanes and breaking to regain the advantage, that way he was chasing them.

Freddie glanced back. "He's so close, I can hear him breathin'."

"There's an off-ramp after the bridge. Highway patrol uses it as a speed trap. We keep him behind us, the patrol catches him first."

In the distance lay the Passaic River, its dark expanse creating a broad gap between the city lights. The needle on the speedometer tottered at ninety and the river was fast approaching. They hurtled over the bridge with the coupe glued to their bumper. Emmett listened for sirens and looked for flashing lights, expecting one of the Traffic Division's big-motored Chryslers to swoop in any second.

"Where are they?" Freddie cocked his head from side to side.

Emmett smacked the steering wheel. He realized his error too late. "The patrol cars must have been pulled off duty to help with the riot. We're on our own."

The white lines on the road were whisking by. The Oldsmobile filled Emmett's rearview mirror. A string of freight cars was lumbering along on the train tracks that ran parallel to the highway, visually distorting the speed they were traveling. The tracks veered off a quarter mile ahead and were replaced by an embankment. Beyond was a shallow basin.

"I'm about to do something dangerous."

"*About* to? Everything you done's been dangerous."

Freddie braced himself against the dashboard as Emmett mashed the accelerator into the floor, outpacing the Delta, then lurched into the lane closest to the median and dropped back until they were fender to fender. The embankment was fifty feet away. The Olds started breaking. Emmett matched him and jerked the wheel to the right. Metal screeching, he forced the coupe off the road, hoping it would blow a tire or fishtail to a stop, but the driver lost control and jumped the embankment just as the freight train passed. The car went airborne, the hood popped, and the Delta went careening into the basin.

"Gotcha sucker," Freddie cheered. "Guess you won't be followin' us no more. Wait. Why you slowin' down?"

Emmett pulled onto the shoulder, kicking up a cloud of dust. "Stay in the car."

Gun out, he ran over to the Oldsmobile. The windshield was cracked, and blood was oozing from a gash on the driver's forehead, the cut nearly identical to the one Cyril had received at his hands. On the floorboard lay the Borsalino hat. Emmett frisked the guy, found a Beretta in a holster, and threw it aside into the dirt.

"He dead?' Freddie was standing at the top of the embankment.

"Didn't I tell you to stay in the car?" Emmett felt for a pulse. "And no, he's not dead. He's out cold."

Air wheezed from the guy's nostrils. "I think he broke some ribs. He might have punctured a lung." Emmett put the guy's arm over his shoulder and lifted him from the car seat by pulling on his belt. "Come get on the other side of him."

"Uh-uh. That jive ass turkey was about to run us off the road."

"Please?"

"Man," Freddie groaned, taking the guy's other arm. "This sucker's fat too."

The driver was short but heavy, an onerous load. They struggled to carry him to Emmett's car and get him situated. On the off chance he regained consciousness, Emmett cuffed him.

"You'll have to squeeze in the middle, Freddie."

"This cracker best not get any blood on me." He clambered in from the driver's side. "I can't believe you takin' this gangster to the hospital after he tried to kill us. You white folks is too nice."

Emmett got in behind him, so the three of them were crammed into the front seat together. "Who said we were going to the hospital?"

THIRTY-SIX

Valentine's was an unassuming café on a corner of Mount Pleasant Avenue. It was the safest corner in the entire North Ward. Nobody littered or shouted or even jaywalked there. That was because the café was Ruggiero Caligrassi's unofficial office. A red-and-green wind-frayed awning veiled the windows in shadow from the streetlights, making it impossible to see inside.

"I don't know about this idea 'a yours."

"If you've got a better one, I'm all-ears. If not, let's see if our pal has a name. Reach in and grab his wallet, will you?"

"No way."

"What? You can pick the pockets of strangers but not his?"

"That's for money."

"And this is for your protection."

"Okay, okay." Freddie fished through the guy's pockets. "Here," he said, proffering a flimsy wallet.

The driver's license said the guy's name was Tomaso Amata, twenty-three, five foot five. The picture wasn't too flattering, though it was more presentable than he was at the moment. The bloody cut on his forehead had coagulated into an ugly mound, and a single stream of blood had dribbled down the bridge of his nose. At first glance, Amata looked as if he had been shot between the eyes.

Emmett went to the passenger side and unlocked the handcuffs. He slung Amata's arm across his neck, then hoisted him to his feet. "Now when I say stay put, I mean it this time."

"I ain't going nowhere," Freddie swore. "A brotha ain't safe in the North Ward. You even wear black in this neighborhood and you'll get beat up."

"You can drive, right?"

"Don't got no permit, but yeah, my dad showed me how."

"If you hear shots, don't stick around." Emmett threw Freddie the car keys, entrusting the kid with their lone means of escape. "Promise?"

"Promise." Freddie pulled the door closed and depressed the lock.

Amata's head lolled forward, and the tips of his shoes dragged as Emmett hauled him into Valentine's. A handful of men were seated in the café's licorice black leather booths, cigarette smoke coiling from ashtrays alongside demitasse cups of espresso. They all stared at him, then at Amata, and said nothing.

"I'm here to see Mr. Caligrassi," Emmett announced as a drop of Amata's blood splashed onto the octagonal tile floor.

Behind the bar, an old man in shirtsleeves and a waiter's bow tie was operating the espresso machine. He promptly put aside the coffee-pot and slipped behind a curtain into a back room, like a butler summoning the master of the house. A rotary fan plugged in by the bar ticked off the passing seconds.

Sal Lucaro came out a moment later. His eyes seized on Amata, whose body was getting heavier and heavier. Holding him also hampered Emmett's access to his gun.

"I said I wanted to see Mr. Caligrassi."

The men in the booths averted their eyes, registering Emmett's request as an insult. Lucaro gave him a caustic glare and darted behind the curtain. The man who emerged next wore a silk necktie and had hair the color of dirty snow, furrowed from the marks of a comb. He had the distinguished affect of someone so important that "hurry" didn't exist in his vocabulary.

Ruggiero Caligrassi didn't introduce himself. That wasn't necessary. Emmett knew who he was and he knew who Emmett was.

Caligrassi glanced at Amata and laced his hands behind his back as a general might when inspecting the troops. It was the same stance the manductor, head of the monastery at Saint Andrew's, adopted during his daily appraisal of the novitiate, his expression tinged with the indifference of authority, just like Caligrassi's. On the day Emmett was to have taken his vows, he had requested a private audience with the manductor, during which Emmett told him that he could not continue on his path to the priesthood. The two years as a novice were merely the first of thirteen required to ascend to the title of Jesuit. The lengthy commitment wasn't what deterred Emmett. He could not, in good conscience, take those vows. In his mind, it would have been more grievous than the sin he had already committed.

Upon learning of Emmett's desire to discontinue his studies, the manductor simply nodded. He was a slim man in his forties with the imperturbable countenance required of clergy, yet it was obvious he would have preferred for Emmett not to go. Admitting as much would have been out of character, an impropriety. The basis of the faith was that a Jesuit's life and labors would only be blessed while doing God's will rather than their own. Personal opinions were incidental. The manductor could not employ his to sway Emmett's choice or strong-arm him into staying. A Jesuit deferred such power to God.

"Have you prayed on your decision?" the Manductor asked. Emmett told him he had. "Then you must do what God puts in your heart."

What beat in Emmett's heart was guilt, but it wasn't God who instilled it there.

"This man is an . . . associate of yours, I believe." Emmett made sure his voice did not betray the strain of carrying Amata upright.

"Yes, he is," Caligrassi replied, his tone patient.

"He needs to go to a hospital."

"Looks that way."

"I could have left him where he was. By the time anybody found him, it would have been too late. I'm here because I'm hoping that counts for something with you."

"I see." Caligrassi gestured for Lucaro to help with Amata.

A tense instant arose during the transfer. Emmett was ready for him or the others to try something. Instead Lucaro, a man who thought nothing of shooting Vernon Young in the back, carefully laid Amata on a booth with a gentleness Emmett hadn't imagined him capable of.

"So?" Emmett said.

Caligrassi pursed his lips, contemplating. He went to the bar and took an empty demitasse cup off the counter. In his hands, it looked like a piece from a little girl's tea set.

"There's a crack in this cup, a hairline crack. That doesn't mean it'll break. Doesn't mean it won't."

At that, Caligrassi smashed the porcelain cup against the counter, shattering it to bits. The handle remained whole, clasped between the tips of his forefinger and thumb.

"I won't use a cup with a crack in it. You understand, Detective?"

Emmett finally did. He understood that Otis Fossum's name had never actually mattered. The ability to get the name, to bend and break the wills of others, was what was crucial to Caligrassi. That made him who he was. His performance with the cup had been for the sake of the men in the café, to put Emmett in his place for entering mob turf bearing a wounded foot soldier as a bartering chip. Caligrassi had to show him up to save face. Emmett played along. He hoped Caligrassi would too.

"The man you're looking for, the one from that night behind the dry cleaner's, he moved to South Carolina once he realized who it was he saw. He's gone. He's no threat to you or Mr. Lucaro anymore." The lie was stated with such conviction that Emmett almost persuaded himself it was true.

Acting unconvinced, Caligrassi shrugged vaguely. "If he's gone, then it can't hurt for you to give me his name."

"If I do, then we're done? With everything?"

"Then we're done."

Emmett let out a resigned breath. "His name is Horace Barnes."

Caligrassi blinked soulfully. He didn't believe him. Even if Emmett had given Caligrassi the real witness's name—Otis Fossum—he still wouldn't have believed him. The name had become irrelevant.

Horace Barnes was the manductor from Saint Andrew's. He had died of coronary arrest a year after Emmett left the monastery. For Barnes, power had rested in his piety. For Ruggiero Caligrassi, power was shattering a cup and pressuring a police officer in front of a room full of men in order to assert his authority. All Caligrassi cared about was getting Emmett to call "uncle." So that was what he did.

"Don't you have other things to do, Detective?" Caligrassi remarked. "We are having a riot, you know."

Emmett walked out of Valentine's into the unforgiving night heat, leaving Tomaso Amata with his breath hissing through his injured lungs, while Otis Fossum was at home, awake in the dark because that was his daytime, unaware that he was, at last, free.

Freddie unlocked the door for him and gave him back the keys. "Didn't hear any shots."

"Not in this part of town, at least." Emmett was too drained to think about what might be happening elsewhere.

"No more guys gonna be following us?"

"Nope."

"One down. Two to go."

Between the cops and Luther Reed, there was no lesser of those two evils.

"I'm hungry," Freddie said.

"Me too. You like hot dogs?"

"They all right."

"I'm not sure these will be."

"I'd eat 'em anyway."

"Me too. Let's get out of here."

As Emmett drove, a clacking noise emanated from the side of his car where it had impacted with Amata's. "That sounds bad."

Freddie rolled down the window for an evaluation. "Fender's dented. Paint's scratched. And the headlight's done for."

"You're the expert. How much do you think it'll cost to fix?"

"Couple hundred, easy."

"I guess I'll really be needing that money you owe me."

"Gotta keep me alive if you wanna collect." Freddie was half joking, half not. "Am I stayin' at your house again?"

"Of course. I have to protect my investment, don't I?"

"That your old bed I slept in? From when you was a kid?"

"Yup."

"It's nice. For a bed." That was Freddie's form of thank-you.

"Yeah," Emmett agreed. "It's a good bed."

They were stopped at an intersection, waiting for the light to change. Both of them stared out the windshield as if it were a movie screen and the film they had been watching together had ended. There was nothing left to do but go home.

THIRTY-SEVEN

Telling the difference between day and night was nearly impossible from inside the pen. Subtle changes in temperature were the only hint that the sun had risen or set. The room stayed cool, sodden with the stench of sulfur and the rancid breath of the sewers. Meers tried to make the cage as commodious as possible with the carpeting, mattress, and ample food, though he could do nothing about the smell. That was a separate torture, one he was inured to.

"It stinks in here. You know that? Huh? You hear me? I bet you do."

Calvin had been trying to taunt him into a response for the past hour. Meers intentionally alerted him to his presence by stomping heavily over the pen so dirt would rain down from the ceiling. What Calvin didn't realize was that Meers had been in the refinery for two hours, observing him through the peephole in the floor above the cage.

From that vantage, he had seen Calvin pacing. The kid hadn't cried, at least not yet. That or Meers had missed it while he was at work. However, he doubted it. Calvin wasn't the crying type. All the others readily wept, especially Ambrose Webster. He bawled from the start. Meers didn't take any joy in their tears. In fact, they perturbed him. Crying was a sign that his pet's composure was unspooling, a factor that would adversely affect the game. But Calvin was different. Although he was a fraction of the size of Ambrose Webster, he possessed the quality Meers desired most—ingenuity.

Like his other pets, Calvin had scrutinized the cage for a way out. He probed for weaknesses and attempted to squeeze through the bars. Meers had built the cage so the bars were deceptively wide-set. He checked anatomy books to ascertain the average size of an adult male human head, then spaced the bars a centimeter under those measurements, a tease on his part. Once Calvin was convinced he couldn't fit in between the bars, he foraged for things to form into weapons. The carpet was glued down, not nailed, and Meers had extracted the springs from the mattress because they were metal. What made Calvin special was that when his search didn't pan out, he practiced putting his arms through the cage bars to test the maximum distance of his reach, in case his captor should come close to the cage. That made Meers smile.

"You don't know who you dealin' with, man. People be lookin' fo' me. And when they find you, you gonna be sorry."

Meers loved listening to him. Calvin was cocky, self-assured, his voice devoid of fear despite the circumstances. Meers wished he had a tape recorder. He toyed with the idea of buying one. Perhaps after supper, he thought.

He was preparing Calvin's dinner in the room above the pen, purposefully making plenty of noise to remind Calvin he was there. Meers had installed a hot plate and carted in an ice chest for provisions. The evening's meal consisted of half the prime rib he bought from the butcher and another carton of whole milk as well as two potatoes wrapped in foil that Meers baked at home, dinner fit for an athlete in training. He warmed the potatoes beside the hot plate as he fried the steaks. The aroma of cooking meat wafted from the pan and was immediately overpowered by the sulfur.

Based on his trials, serving the prime rib rare made it easier for his pets to digest. Well-cooked meat had caused John to become sluggish, just slightly, though it was perceptible to Meers. Sweets had a similar effect. For those reasons, he prepared only nourishing food. Water was also a necessity. Meers provided a full bucket in addition to a bedpan to collect waste, both soft plastic, making them ineffectual weapons.

"I got me a black belt in karate," Calvin shouted. "I can kill a man with my bare hands."

"Too bad we didn't get that on tape, huh, John?" Meers lamented, flipping the steaks.

John's decapitated head sat on an old metal filing cabinet, ogling Meers as he cooked. He had recently replaced John's eyeballs with glass eyes to make them seem more realistic. The plastic irises had a dull sheen, and the whites were as vivid as a doll's, set off against the papery skin of the face. The glass eyes had come from a medical supplier. Meers had given the excuse that his father lost his eye in an industrial accident and claimed the extra was for him to wear when cleaning the other, so he would never be without. The clerk had commended him for being such a dutiful son. Because the glass eyes wouldn't sit flush in the sockets, they bulged with shock, as though John continued to be appalled by the acts Meers committed.

"I think I should get a tape recorder. What do you think, John? Then we'll be able to save him for posterity. Won't that be fun."

"I hear you up there," Calvin hollered. "You must be stupid if you think I don't. You a punk. Can't face me like a real man, can you?"

The steaks were sizzling in the pan, muffling the curses that accompanied Calvin's provocations.

"He certainly is working up an appetite with all of that yelling, isn't he?"

Initially, Meers had difficulty getting John to eat. He would repeatedly sniff the servings and sample a tiny bite, afraid the food was poisoned. Once assured each meal was harmless, John wolfed them down. Meers imagined that the man ate better as his prisoner than he did living on the streets. From him, Meers learned to estimate the portions. He had to give enough to stoke stamina, but too much would induce lethargy. It was a surprisingly precise science.

"These steaks look tasty, don't they, John?" When Meers stuck a fork into each slab, juice and blood flowed into the pan with a steamy hiss. The meat was almost done.

Julius Dekes had been cautious of the food too and had refused water as well. The entire first day, he wouldn't eat. He grew listless and thirsty. By late in the second day, Dekes's hunger won over. Through the peephole, Meers witnessed him devour an entire meal and lick the paper plate clean. He kept the boy an additional day longer than the rest to let him recover. As it turned out, Julius Dekes was worth the wait.

He was wily, fast on his feet, and took every side tunnel in the sewer line, attempting to throw Meers off his track. In the end, it didn't work. When Meers found him, Dekes fought violently, flailing and biting, before Meers managed to plunge the knife into his liver. Stunned, the boy sagged, aware that the blade had entered his body. Julius Dekes died with his eyes open, gazing at Meers with the same vacant stare of the glass eyes in John's head.

"Never leave an animal to suffer," Meers's father always lectured. "Killin' em is your right. Being cruel ain't."

That was the phrase that played in Lazlo's mind when, at the age of nineteen, his father suffered a stroke. He had been standing at the stove boiling soup, then suddenly fell to the floor, sending the hot liquid splashing around the apartment's cramped kitchen. He was paralyzed, his jaw clenched, unable to speak or protest when his son put a pillow over his face.

A knife would have created too much blood, and the neighbors would have heard a gunshot, so Lazlo smothered his father. The stroke would have caused him to be terminally bedridden, as Lazlo had been during his episode of polio. He could not let that fate befall his father because that would have been cruel. Lazlo called the police and told them that his father must have expired while he was away getting help. The police believed him, and there was no inquest. Eli Meers's death was ruled as "natural causes."

According to his father, killing was his right. Being cruel wasn't. That was why Meers took special care not to be. On birds and animals, the organs were in similar places, depending on the size of the prey. Eccentricities did exist among the species, the location of the heart or the amount of entrails, yet that was only significant when it came to cleaning them. With humans, the organs were virtually in identical positions. Meers always aimed for the areas that would ensure a speedy death. Stabbing Julius Dekes in the liver killed him in under a minute. That was merciful by Meers's standards.

Following the hunt came the arduous process of removing the body. Meers trekked back to the refinery to retrieve the sled and harnesses in order to clear Dekes's carcass from the tunnel. Though the remains would never have been found had he left them, the consequences of decay outweighed the effort required for eliminating them. The sewers were filthy and foul by nature, but they represented Meers's private world, and he would go to extremes to preserve their sanctity.

"It's feeding time," he proclaimed. Meers placed the piping hot food on a paper plate and retrieved the milk from the cooler. As with the cage's trapdoor, the lone light in the pen was controlled from the observation room. The instant he switched off the bulb, Calvin's voice erupted from below.

"Hey. Hey. What chu' doin'?"

Soundlessly, Meers slipped into the pen, and his eyes quickly acclimated to the darkness. His others pets had huddled at the rear of the cage whenever the lights went out. Calvin, on the contrary, was at the bars, fondling the air, ready to grab whatever came in contact with his hands. He groped at nothing as Meers slid the meal into the open slot at the bottom of the cage, the carpet dampening the noise. The smell of the steak piqued Calvin's reflexes. He was reaching out from between the bars toward Meers and raking the darkness with his fingers.

"You in here? Huh, sucker? You such a tough guy, come on over here by this cage. Come and get me."

Meers would give Calvin his shot. He would give him a head start. He would give him time to escape. After that, he would hunt him.

THIRTY-EIGHT

Sirens were caterwauling from somewhere in the distance, momentarily drowning out the chatter on the police band radio. The fervor over the previous night's spate of fires had been supplanted by a new mayhem. Reports of snipers on rooftops were flooding into dispatch. Emmett was keeping a running list of the locations getting the heaviest fire so he could plot a safe course home.

"Raise the volume," he said to Freddie.

"Newark police, hold your fire. State police, hold your fire," commanded the dispatcher. "You're shooting at each other. National Guardsmen, quit firing at the buildings. When the sparks fly, we think it's snipers. Be sure of your targets."

"They shootin' at each other?" Freddie was astounded.

"Apparently."

An ambulance driver came on next, responding to a request for assistance. "Request denied. We won't come anywhere on South Orange Avenue east of Norfolk. Been there twice. Been shot at twice. Repeat. Request denied.

"How about the shotguns? Can we use shotguns?" someone from a patrol car was asking.

"Knock that off," dispatch ordered. "Do not use any shotguns."

"But they have 'em. They're shooting at us and they have shotguns."

The various forces had finally gotten on the same radio frequency, but that hadn't lessened the number of misunderstandings. Listening to the confusion was nerve-racking. It made Emmett's head throb.

"Can I turn it down now?" Freddie asked.

"Please do."

Roadblocks were set up at short intervals along Broad Street. That forced the morass of traffic slowly onward like barges through locks in a canal. Few had heeded the curfew that prohibited driving. Newark rarely saw jams of that magnitude, except during the Christmas rush. The riot was the opposite of a holiday.

"Can't we go around?"

"We can try."

Emmett cut onto Raymond Boulevard. He planned to leapfrog the mesh of blockades at the center of the ward. A parade of old furniture was piled along the gutters. Ratty sofas were dumped beside broken chairs and stained mattresses, as if people were setting up house on the sidewalks.

"Lotta folks must be moving."

"Not moving. Renovating. They got new furniture from looting stores."

"See anything nice?"

"We don't have time to shop right now, Freddie."

"I was only askin'."

Up ahead on Mulberry, two patrol cars and a jeep were pulled to either side of the street. The thoroughfare was choked to a single, narrow lane. There were no officers, troopers, or Guardsmen to be seen.

"The cops just left their cars right in the middle 'a the road?"

"Maybe they were called into one of these buildings on an emergency."

"Can we fit through?"

"Yeah, we can fit. But I think we should back up, go another way." Emmett felt as if he was riding into a trap.

"What for? Mulberry goes straight to McCarter Highway. That's fastest."

Against his instincts, Emmett cruised onward. Suddenly, a gunshot rang out, loud as a firecracker. He smashed the breaks, coming to a bucking halt in between the police cars.

"Okay, back up. Back up," Freddie urged, diving under the dash.

Emmett was about to floor it when he noticed a mix of police officers and state troopers skittering around the cars parked at the curb. They hadn't abandoned their vehicles to attend to some emergency indoors. They were taking cover behind them.

"We can't stay here. We have to get out of this car."

"No way. I ain't movin'."

A patrolman poked his revolver over the hood of a sedan and took a shot at the three-story apartment building on the right side of the street. The sniper immediately returned fire. One of the bullets glanced off the sidewalk, ricocheting into the rear windshield of Emmett's car and shattering it.

"I'm outta here," Freddie said.

Emmett dragged him out the driver's-side door and forced him to the ground to take shelter by the rear tire.

The sniper let off another round. The muzzle flash flared in the darkness. Emmett tracked the shot and pinpointed the sniper's position at the top floor of the building on the opposite side of the road. He saw somebody leaning out of a window onto the fire escape and taking aim.

"It's so loud." Freddie's hands were clamped over his ears.

"That's because it's a rifle. You can go deaf from the noise." Emmett checked his pistol. The barrel was full. "At the academy firing range, we'd put spent shells in our ears to plug them."

"You got any 'a those shells on you?"

"I might in a minute."

More bullets whizzed down, splashing the asphalt.

"Why don't they shoot back at 'im?"

"I don't know what the state troopers are carrying, but a service revolver fires six rounds. Most cops have another six to twenty-four bullets on their belts. My guess, they ran out of ammo and they're waiting for backup."

That was why the cars were stopped in the middle of the street. This was an ambush that had turned into a standoff.

"You gonna back 'em up?"

"The sniper has the upper hand. I move and he'll pick me off. To him, we're fish in a barrel."

"Then that guy's a fish too." Freddie was pointing at a black man who was walking on their side of the street. The cigarette held in his fingers illuminated the swinging arc of his arm as he strolled along, unconcerned.

"Hey. Get down," Emmett whispered. The man ignored him. "Get down. There's a sniper."

"He ain't gonna shoot me. I'm a Negro. You-all the ones in trouble."

A gunshot clapped. The man dropped midstride.

"He shot him," Freddie said in awe.

Emmett ducked to look under the parked cars to see if the man's chest was rising and falling. It wasn't. Blood flowed from his torso. When Freddie tried to look too, Emmett wouldn't let him. "Don't. Trust me."

"Psst. Hey. You a cop?" A patrolman was signaling Emmett from behind a nearby fender. With his jacket off, Emmett's badge and gun were on display. "How many rounds you got left?"

"Six. I have more. Except I can't get to them." The extra box of shells was in the pocket of his jacket, which was in the car.

"I'll cover you."

Freddie was hunched against the hubcap. "Won't the sniper see you?"

"He might."

"Well? Weren't you sayin' something about fish in a barrel?"

"We need the ammo," the officer pressed.

Even if Emmett made it into the car without being hit, the rifle could pierce the car's roof. "What you need is to get into that apartment building."

"We been trying. He's got us pinned and dispatch won't answer our calls."

"How many are you?"

"Seven. Four cops. Three troopers."

"Seven to one," Freddie mumbled. "And he's winning."

"We've got to draw his fire somehow so your men can get inside."

"He just shot that guy. I ain't gonna stick my noggin out for target practice."

"You won't have to. Bring them behind those parked cars and go around the rear of mine. You can sneak in without being seen." Emmett's car bridged the gap between both sides of the street. "I'll fire into the air, make him think I'm a bad shot. That should buy you time to make it inside."

The patrolman slipped away to talk the idea over with the others, then reappeared. "Okay. We'll do it."

"Move fast. Remember, I only have six rounds."

"No," Freddie said. "That's not all you got."

From the waistband of his dungarees, he produced the Beretta Emmett had taken from Tomaso Amata when his car ran off the road. The kid had gone from packing a water pistol to carrying a real gun.

"Picked his pocket after all?"

"It was on the ground. Finders keepers." Freddie handed the Beretta to him. "You mad?"

"I should be. Except you're the only one with any bullets. Now, if he shoots in your direction, get under the car," Emmett instructed, a weapon in each hand.

"Under the car. Got it." Freddie tucked his knees to his chest, making himself compact, and put his fingers in his ears preemptively, anticipating the fire fight to come.

Single file, the patrolmen and troopers snaked along the gutter. The parked cars acted as a curtain, concealing them from sight. Emmett sneaked over to the jeep and crouched by the back tire. Firing directly at the building could cause another ricochet. He couldn't risk hitting any windows in case there were people inside. Aiming high above the roofline, he fired two shots from his revolver, then lunged toward the jeep's front wheel.

The sniper responded in kind with two bullets to the rear of the jeep. The first blew out the tire with a howl. The second lodged in the chassis. His aim was alarmingly accurate.

Emmett took two more potshots. The replies hit the jeep's hood as he was dashing for cover behind another car. He cranked off another pair of shots, emptying his .38, and the sniper tracked him to his next location. The bullets pinged against metal as Emmett knelt beside the door of a Buick. One of them broke through the car's window, showering him with glass. He holstered his revolver and switched to the Beretta, priming for another exchange. More shots erupted, rapid-fire. The sound said they weren't directed at Emmett or the street. He peeked over the Buick's trunk. Multiple muzzle flashes illuminated the interior of an apartment. The patrolmen and troopers had gotten to the sniper and were swapping fire.

"Freddie, are you okay?"

"Yeah. I'm deaf. But I'm okay."

Staying low, Emmett hurried over to him. "If you were deaf, you wouldn't have heard me ask if you were okay." He got Freddie to his feet. "Come on. Let's leave while we can."

The police band radio was still on, the yammering voices competing with gunshots. Right as Emmett started the ignition there came a crash of breaking glass. The police and troopers were forcibly pushing a shirt-less black man toward a three-story window. Then they shoved him out. Arms wheeling, the man dropped to the pavement like a sack of meal and landed with a sickening thud.

Freddie's mouth fell open. "Did they just . . . ."

Emmett shut off the radio. He couldn't stomach listening anymore. He couldn't stomach any of it anymore. "Yes. They did." He gunned the engine and sped away.

After a few minutes, the morose silence got to be too much for Freddie. "Your repair bill's gone up," he said, motioning the broken rear windshield.

"Another fifty?"

"Try double. Doubt you'll be able to collect off 'a the guy who did the damage."

"I doubt I will."

Emmett didn't care about the windshield. He didn't want to look back. The glass was fractured into thousands of tiny pieces, the fissures blurring the view, but the image of the shirtless man falling to his death would remain clear and unblurred in Emmett's mind forever.

THIRTY-NINE

Porch lights were lit all along Emmett's street. Such hot weather would normally have drawn neighbors out onto their stoops. Not that night. Residents were cloistering themselves inside, as if the madness of the riot was communicable, a plague they feared catching.

Edward opened the front door for Emmett and Freddie and spun aside to let them through. Tired as he was, Emmett couldn't help noticing that Edward's dexterity with the wheelchair was improving. It was the last thing he ever imagined his brother would be good at.

"We keepin' the wagons circled or what?"

"No," Emmett replied, too beleaguered to go into detail. "Not anymore."

"Glad to hear it." Edward didn't push for an explanation. Emmett's and Freddie's faces told the story for them.

"See any tanks?" Edward asked.

"No, no tanks," Freddie replied. What he had seen couldn't compare. "Can I watch TV for a little?"

"Yeah, go ahead," Emmett told him.

In a show of kindness, Edward ceded full reign over the television dial. "It's all yours."

That put renewed bounce in Freddie's step. He began flipping channels, his nose inches from the screen.

"Did Mrs. Poole go to sleep?"

Edward shook his head. "She's in the kitchen. She'd had her fill of TV. I gave her one of Ma's books."

"That was nice of you."

"What can I say? I'm a nice guy. This is the part where you say, 'Yeah, Ed, you are a heck of a nice guy.' And I answer, 'Well, gosh, Marty. You're swell for mentioning it.'" Edward wanted some credit for holding down the fort and rolling with the punches, literally.

"I'm getting a glass of water. You want one, Mr. Nice Guy?"

Thanks was a word Emmett and his brother reserved only for sarcasm. His offer stood in as gratitude and an affirmation of Edward's efforts.

"Sure. That'd be grand."

Mrs. Poole was sitting at the kitchen table, reading a paperback romance Emmett didn't recognize as his mother's.

"Oh, you're home. I didn't hear you come in."

She closed the book. On the cover was an illustration of a woman with windswept hair and a man in a dapper suit. A train station filled the background. Luggage was stacked at the woman's feet to foreshadow an imminent departure. The couple was passionately locking eyes, love thriving on drama and upheaval.

"Is that any more interesting than the programs on TV?"

"A little. Me, I'm partial to these kinds of stories. They're like fairy tales. Not too real."

Life had been all too real for the past few days. Emmett could understand why Mrs. Poole would seek an escape.

"Can I fix you something to eat?"

"I promised Freddie hot dogs."

"Did you tell him we don't have no regular buns?"

"No, I saved that surprise."

"I believe we've had enough surprises for today, don't you, Mr. Emmett?"

More than enough for an eternity, he thought.

Together, the four of them ate their hot dogs on pumpernickel in front of the television watching *Green Acres*. Freddie was too hungry to complain about not having a proper bun. He complained about the show instead.

"This 'posed to be funny?"

"It's grown-up humor," Edward said.

"Then remind me not to grow up."

The program ended with Eddie Albert and Eva Gabor gazing lovingly at each other the way the man and woman on the cover of the paperback romance did. No matter how much drama or upheaval came to pass, the endings on television were always tidy. Emmett had no illusions about the riot ending as neatly. He couldn't help hoping though.

"If y'all will excuse me," Mrs. Poole announced, "I'm going to sleep."

The clock hadn't struck eight, yet it felt like the wee hours of the morning. She said her good nights, then the three of them continued to watch TV until Freddie dozed off on the couch.

"You should take him upstairs," Edward said.

Emmett was himself half asleep in their father's lounge chair. He nudged Freddie's arm. "Come on. Time for bed."

Eyelids heavy, Freddie acquiesced. He let Emmett steer him up the stairs, crawled under the covers, and immediately drifted back to sleep. Freddie fit in his bed better than Emmett ever had. From the age of twelve on, his feet hung off the end of the mattress. Edward's did too. Growing up, they had shared the same bedroom and the same bedtime, and they both wound up with cold feet because the sheets could never cover them from head to toe. Edward always fell asleep first. As soon as his head hit the pillow, he was out. Sleep didn't come that easily to Emmett. For years, he wished that Edward would stay up and talk with him. He even tried keeping him awake, telling stories or knock-knock jokes. None of it worked. Eventually, Emmett gave up wishing and accepted that he and his brother were completely different, right down to how they slept.

"Why don't you hit the sack yourself," Edward said when Emmett came downstairs. "I'm gonna go sit on the porch. Give you some peace and quiet."

"If I go to sleep, how are you going to get into bed?"

"I'm getting so I can do it myself. I been practicing."

It was the sort of progress Emmett wasn't sure if he should praise or pretend to ignore.

"Go on. Go to sleep, Marty. You look like hell."

"Thanks." There was the word, withheld entirely except as a wisecrack.

"What are brothers for?"

The screen door screeched opened and closed, the final coda of their conversation. Emmett unbuttoned his shirt and collapsed onto the couch, but sleep eluded him. He lay there, remembering.

In the summers of their youth, he and Edward would sneak over to the river to cool off. The water was the color of a dusty mirror. It reflected the sky as ashy white even when it was blue. Swimming there was prohibited. The City Health Department posted signs about the danger of pollution. He and Edward paid them no mind. They would do cherry bombs off the docks by Brill Street or swim out to the tugs pulling barges to catch the waves that formed in the boat's wake and surf them back to shore. He and Edward had whiled away countless hours swimming and playing by the water, seeing who could skip stones the farthest and trying to catch the crabs rumored to have swum up from the bay, though they never did. The crabs may as well have been imaginary creatures from some boyish fantasy. The mere idea of them gave those hot days purpose, just as the Passaic gave them refuge from the heat. For Emmett, summer was synonymous with the river, and it was inextricably tangled with the memory of what happened one summer day when he was eleven and Edward was seven, a memory he kept hidden under the floorboards of his heart.

They had been following the river's edge on a jaunt through a make-believe jungle, whacking the reeds that grew near the shoals with sticks, and venturing farther from home than they had before. At a crook in the river, they came upon a giant drainage pipe that jutted out from a craggy outcropping of rock and dirt. The corrugated metal pipe was four feet in diameter, too small for an adult, but tailor-made for them.

"Let's pretend it's a secret cave."

"I don't wanna," Edward had whined, backing off from the pipe.

"Don't be chicken." Emmett climbed inside.

"What if something's in there? Like rats?"

Unafraid, Emmett stomped on the floor and banged the pipe's sides. "Nope. No rats."

"But it's dark."

"There's nothing to be scared of. I promise."

Edward gave in. He took Emmett's hand and crawled into the gullet of the pipe.

Sunlight glinted off the algae-slicked walls. Waterlogged leaves were piled thick as snowdrifts. Emmett took the lead, advancing into the pitch-black.

"Wait for me, Marty. I can't see."

"Hurry up. I found something."

"What? What is it?" Edward's plaintive voice quivered along the rippled metal.

A rusty mesh grate blocked one end of the pipe. The lower side of the grate was peeled aside. Trapped in the mesh tines was a black-and-white checkered soccer ball.

"It's a treasure. We've gotta get it."

"It's a ball, Marty. I don't care about a dumb ball."

"You're messing up the game. Just help me."

They tried to pry the ball from the grate, but the tines were embedded in the foam.

"Do you hear that, Marty?" A hushed rumble rose from the depths of the pipe, like the echo of the ocean in a seashell. "It's getting louder. Please. Let's leave. I wanna go," Edward begged.

"It's your imagination. It's nothing."

Those were the last words Emmett spoke before the rush of water hit them. The torrent knocked him down, forcing water up his nose and under his eyelids as it thrust him through the pipe and dumped him into the shallows, close to shore. He burst up from under the water and shouted his brother's name. Edward wasn't in the river with him. Water continued to spew from the pipe. Emmett realized that Edward must have been holding on to the mesh grate. He was still inside.

Emmett slogged to shore and screamed his brother's name over and over again. Because of the gushing water, it was impossible to get anywhere near the pipe's spout. Finally, Edward's body came pouring out with the deluge and splashed into the river. Emmett swam to him and dragged his body to the rocky beach. Edward's face was a milky blue. Wet leaves clung to his arms. Emmett flipped him on his stomach and wailed on his back. It was all he could think to do. But Edward wouldn't breathe. Emmett pleaded with him, and he pleaded with God to make his brother breathe.

"Don't leave me, Edziu. Please don't leave me." Crying, Emmett rocked him and prayed. His eyes, nose, and throat burned from the water. He thought it was from praying so hard. He promised he would be good for the rest of his life if God gave Edward back to him. That was when a man in a rowboat appeared on the river, the answer to his prayers. Emmett flagged him and he rowed over, took Edward from Emmett's arms, and carried him to the closest street where they stopped someone in a car who drove them to the hospital. The doctor's were able to revive Edward. Emmett had bruised his brother's rib cage beating on him, which forced the water from his lungs. Edward had been breathing shallowly since the beach. Emmett was too distraught to notice.

The trauma wiped the entire incident from Edward's memory. He couldn't recollect anything about the drainage pipe or almost drowning that day. All he recalled was swimming earlier that morning. Emmett had told his parents the truth about what happened. They chose not to tell Edward and made Emmett promise not to say anything either. Although part of him yearned to come clean, Emmett was afraid of what Edward would think, that he wouldn't want him as a brother anymore, so Emmett honored his parents' wishes. In spite of the pact, Emmett believed that Edward sensed there was something he wasn't privy to, some family bond he had been excluded from, and he spent his days resenting Emmett, not for nearly killing him, but for having a secret he wouldn't share.

Emmett had allowed his brother to hold on to his anger, to nurture it and indulge it until it twisted into what they had now. From the day of the accident forward, Emmett listened to Edward breathe in his sleep, grateful for each inhale and exhale. It was a nightly reminder of what he had almost done to him.

The hinges on the screen door creaked and the door bumped the frame, sending a shiver through the silent house. Edward rolled in from the porch. Emmett pretended to be asleep. He heard Edward wrestle himself into bed, struggling to position his legs and get comfortable. Emmett wanted to help. He knew not to. Edward had to learn to take care of himself. Emmett had to let him learn. Edward's breathing soon fell into a rhythm as steady as a metronome. Then, and only then, could Emmett sleep.

FORTY

Morning came on like a fever, a hot flush that awakened Emmett from a deep slumber. The bright light made his eyes pound. His shirt was drenched in sweat. When he sat up, his head spun.

"Just 'cause it's Saturday is no excuse for you to lay in bed all day," Edward said wryly, sipping coffee and eyeing him from across the living room.

"What time is it?"

"Seven. Here." Edward wheeled over and gave him his coffee cup. It tasted watery to Emmett, weaker than tea.

"That was all that was left of the coffee grounds," Mrs. Poole apologized, coming slowly down the stairs. "And I used the last two eggs to make that biscuit mix you brought home. They're ready, if you're hungry." She was holding on to the doorjamb for support. As she walked into the kitchen, her limp was more pronounced than usual.

"I told her we have aspirin in the medicine cabinet," Edward whispered. "She's being stubborn. Won't take it. Been driving me crazy."

"Who does that sound like?"

Edward took his coffee back as punishment for the remark. "Woke up on the wrong side of the couch, huh? Just get her the pills, will ya?"

Emmett got the aspirin from the bathroom, popped one himself, and went into the master bedroom to change into clean clothes. Mrs. Poole had made the bed, sheets tucked in to perfection. Her purse lay on the nightstand, propping up a timeworn photograph of a young black serviceman in uniform, her husband before his accident. Though he was gone, Mrs. Poole still slept beside him each night.

"I told him to wait for you to eat, Mr. Emmett. He wouldn't listen." She and Edward were seated at the kitchen dinette. She had set a place for him as well as Freddie.

"I'm not one to stand on ceremony. Even if I could." Edward was judiciously rationing the butter he spread on the warm biscuit.

"Go ahead. Start eating. Freddie probably won't be up for a while anyway." Emmett put the bottle of aspirin next to Mrs. Poole's plate. "Take these. You're going to need them. He might be a handful today."

"You mean Freddie, right?" Edward said. "Right?"

Mrs. Poole hid a smile behind her napkin. Because Emmett was suggesting that the pills were for something besides her back, she consented to taking them. "If you insist."

"I do."

The biscuits were a consolation for the tasteless coffee. They were delicious. Emmett could have finished his in a single bite.

Edward was stuffing himself and talking with his mouth full. "These are terrific. I mean really terrific."

Emmett was happy to see his brother's appetite returning. When Mrs. Poole put the rest of the biscuits aside for Freddie, Edward was actually disappointed.

"The kid's a midget. He couldn't eat that many."

"I have a feeling you wouldn't leave him *any* if it was up to you." She wrapped the remaining biscuits in foil.

"Fine. Save 'em for the pip-squeak." Edward gave up the fight and lit the last cigarette in his pack. "So, Marty, you off into the wild blue yonder again?"

That was where Emmett felt like he was headed, more of the infinite unknown. He had hit a wall with the murder cases. Emmett wasn't sure what to do, and he had nobody to go to for advice, nobody except Edward.

"Come outside with me for a minute," he said.

"What for?"

"I have to talk to you about that crabgrass."

Edward coasted out onto the porch. "Crabgrass. Very subtle. You want the gun back, is that it?"

"No, I have to ask you something. Say I told you there were four dead boys, all stabbed a month apart, one in the heart, one in the abdomen, one in the leg, and one in the neck."

"I'd say the crime rate's going up."

"What if I said they were all missing a single finger—the pinkie, ring, middle, and pointer."

"Is it a gang thing? Some kind of initiation?"

"I can't imagine anybody would want to join if it was."

Laundry hung on the line in the yard. Pillowcases and towels cast square shadows across the sallow lawn. Even the crabgrass was shriveling. The drought would be the death of the entire yard.

Edward tapped his cigarette into an ashtray on the porch railing meditatively. Then his expression changed. An idea had floated to the surface.

"What?" Emmett asked.

His brother took an earnest drag off the cigarette, working himself up as though preparing to pull off a Band-Aid. "One time, these guys came back from the cathouses in Da Nang telling secondhand stories they'd heard from the marines stationed there. Said one of them was showing off, talkin' big about how many gooks he'd killed. Some guy tried to call the marine's bluff. So this marine, he took out a string and put it over his head like a necklace. The guys said they thought it was dried flowers, maybe one of them Hawaii things, the whadaya call 'ems, leis. Turned out they were ears, ears cut off the Vietcong, and strung like beads. What you said about the fingers got me thinking of that."

A cascade of possibilities clicked into place. From the beginning, the severed fingers had seemed deliberate to Emmett, yet he hadn't been able to puzzle out the purpose for their removal. The notion that they were trophies, the killer's keepsakes, made a macabre sort of sense.

"Why did that marine kept those ears?"

"Sick as it is, I think he was proud. Wanted to remember what he'd done."

Somebody wanted to remember Evander Hammond, Julius Dekes, Tyrone Cambell, and Ambrose Webster. What Emmett couldn't get a fix on was why.

Edward finished his cigarette, having smoked it down to the filter. "No coffee, no food, and I'm outta smokes."

"I'll bring you some and more food if I can find it."

"Sure you don't want the twenty-two?"

"I won't need it."

"Will I?"

"You shouldn't." Emmett tried to sound certain, but he hadn't been certain about anything the last three days.

"Hey Marty."

"Yeah?"

"Where's the thumb?"

"What?"

"You said a pinkie, a ring, a middle, and a pointer. Where's the thumb?"

Emmett mulled that over on the ride to City Hospital. It was nearly eight and the streets were as desolate as if it were dawn. He wound up behind a patrol car at a stoplight. Protruding from each window was the barrel of an M-16, pointed straight up in the air, standing at attention. The department didn't have that kind of firepower. The riders had to be National Guardsmen. Emmett was stuck in the middle of Bergen Street with nowhere to turn off when the patrol car unexpectedly hit the breaks, compelling him to come to a halt too. Both of the M-16s on the right side lowered, aiming for a bar with handwritten signs in the windows that read SOUL BROTHER.

Without warning, the riders fired their M-16s. Bullets popped and glass cackled until the bar's windows were pulverized and the casings were splintered. When the Guardsmen were done, the signs were gone.

"Kennedy ain't with you now, you nigger bastards," one of them shouted, and the patrol car cruised onward.

The daily papers and television news were fraught with images of the Vietnam War. That was thousands of miles away. This was a block in front of him. A surge of mournful awe struck Emmett right down to the marrow. He let the patrol car get a solid lead, then cut onto another road the next opportunity he got.

Outside the hospital, a mass of people were jockeying for position behind an army green truck. A canvas cover arched over the flatbed. Guardsmen were distributing emergency food from the back, doling canned goods into the crop of upraised hands. Since the grocery stores were sold out and few in the projects had freezers, food was becoming scarce, as scarce as it was at Emmett's own home. Though his household was desperate for food too, Emmett wouldn't dare get in line.

A woman snatched a box of rice from somebody and a scuffle ensued. Two Guardsmen jumped off the truck to break up the fight. The others continued dispensing provisions. In their fatigues, the Guardsmen seemed identical to Emmett. Distinguishing them from the men who had just shot into a bar without cause would be like picking a single raised arm out of the crowd. There was no discernable difference. Their actions were what set them apart.

Emmett quickly made his way to the morgue. This time, the corridor was lined with gurneys. Sheets were draped across the bodies, stacked two deep. On some, the feet drooped over the sides, paper tags hanging from the big toe. Emmett wondered if the coolers had conked out on Dr. Ufland after all.

"I'm doing the best I can," the doctor was saying into the telephone. "Yes, sir. I understand, sir." He hung up with an irritated groan. "Stop calling me every five seconds and maybe I could do my job."

"Do you have a minute?"

Ufland pushed his glasses up the bridge of his nose and squinted. "Detective Emmett is it?"

"That's right. I was here on Thursday."

"I remember now. That was that slow day," he said with a rueful roll of his eyes. "You'll have to forgive me, Detective. I haven't slept in awhile. Twenty bodies in forty-eight hours tends to make a coroner cranky."

It wasn't the coolers that had broken. It was the riot. Three corpses on gurneys awaited autopsy, all males, all black. Buckshot was peppered into the flesh of the one closest to Emmett. The skin puckered around the pellets as though they were burrowing ticks. The second man had multiple holes blown through his upper torso. Dried blood was matted on the wounds. Large-caliber gunshots had ripped through the belly of the third victim, mutilating his body beyond recognition.

"High Velocity Double 0 ammunition. Not standard issue to the department. You see why, Detective? Every shell has nine or twelve slugs, each a third of an inch in diameter. Made mincemeat out of him. Anyhow, these three'll have to take a backseat to this guy." Doctor Ufland was referring to the body on the slab. He was young, white, with a single bullet hole puncturing his chest. "The police director's been hounding me to get him finished."

The face was familiar. It was Patrolman Nolan. Emmett crossed himself and softly said a prayer.

"You know him, Detective?"

"A little."

"The crew that brought him in said a sniper got him. It was a through and through. He died instantly," Ufland said, sympathetic.

Emmett regretted being harsh with Nolan the day before at the station. He recalled thinking that the kid wouldn't make it through the weekend. He hadn't.

"Is he who you're here about? Did Director Sloakes send you?" The doctor began to get antsy.

"No, Sloakes didn't send me. I had some questions for you."

"As long as you don't mind if I work while you talk."

Ufland didn't wait for an answer. He took a scalpel to Nolan's sternum and the flesh parted in a solid red stroke. Emmett had to turn away.

"I brought some reports for you to look at." He fanned out the autopsies from the first three murders. The papers partially blocked his view of Nolan's body. "I realize you didn't do these procedures, but I was curious if you saw anything in common with them?"

The doctor gave each a cursory gander, then flipped aside the skin on Nolan's chest. "All knife wounds. Different points of entry."

"Is there anything about the points of entry that's similar?"

"Similar? No. What they have in common is that they're precise. Here." He pointed with a bloodied knuckle. "The knife went right between the ribs into the heart. On the second, it hit the liver. The third's to the femoral artery in the leg. The victims bled out quickly, either internally or externally."

"Doc, do you remember Ambrose Webster, the kid with the severed leg and the missing finger?"

"You find the finger?"

"Um, not yet, but take a look at the diagrams, at the hands."

Ufland's patience was wearing thin. "I see more missing fingers. So?"

"Doesn't that strike you as peculiar?"

"What strikes me as peculiar is this many dead men in my morgue. I don't know what's going on up there. I do know what's ending up on this table." Overworked, Dr. Ufland was taking out his frustrations on Emmett. "I see what you're getting at, and it's a stretch, to say the least. This connection of a few missing fingers is tenuous. It's a fluke. People don't just go around killing Negroes."

"You've got twenty bodies right here in this morgue that say otherwise."

"Lightning doesn't strike twice, Detective. It strikes over and over and over in different spots every time. Take my word for it. Better yet, take theirs." Indignant, he motioned to the collection of corpses. "I'm too busy for fantasies. This is no place for them."

Nolan lay on the slab in front of Emmett. The young patrolman who had been so excited about being a cop was now a cadaver, a casualty of the riot. Dr. Ufland was right. Newark was no place for fantasies, not anymore.

FORTY-ONE

Emmett sat in his battered car in the hospital's parking lot, gripping the stack of autopsies as though the answer to what he should do next would somehow be transmitted from the pages to his hands. His hallowed logic had landed him right back where he began—with no leads. He debated whether he should pay Lieutenant Ahern a visit, but his dignity forbade it.

He stuffed the reports into the glove compartment. It was so full the lid wouldn't close. He had to take everything out to get the files to fit again. The source of the problem was the oversize manila envelope containing the photographs from Ambrose Webster's crime scene. Emmett had completely forgotten about them.

There were twelve eight-by-tens in total. Because they were taken in the dark subway tunnel with its sooty walls and metallic track, the color snapshots could have been mistaken for black-and-white. The only hues that stood out were those of Webster's clothes, his yellow T-shirt and faded blue dungarees, speckled with mud. Even the blood from his neck looked gray.

Rafshoon had varied his angles. Some were panoramic, others close-ups. The pictures had a magazine quality. They were crisper and more exacting than the average photo album fare, and the shots appeared hauntingly posed. Ambrose Webster could have been a prop. The location in the tunnel had struck Emmett as strangely staged and inaccessible. The photographs confirmed that. It was an odd place to dump a body, odd to the point that it didn't smack of being accidental.

Flipping through the stack of pictures, he was reminded of what Doctor Ufland had said about finding the lost digit for the family's sake. Emmett studied each print to see if, perhaps, the missing finger was caught on film. The camera's flash reflected as white on the rails and glimmered on the gravel along the railroad bed. He had to comb every inch of the photos to differentiate the flash from what might be the flesh of a finger. In the top left corner of one of the wide shots, Emmett noticed some sort of opening, a frame for a small door. He couldn't make it out clearly. If it was some sort of passage, that might have been how the killer disposed of Ambrose Webster's body. Emmett had to get a closer look, but he wasn't going back to the train tunnel, not if he didn't have to. Albert Rafshoon's studio address was written on a label affixed to the manila envelope.

The photography studio turned out to be Rafshoon's apartment on the lower floor of a two-family house. Nobody answered at the front door. Given the number of killings in the past two days, Rafshoon might have been away on call. To be certain, Emmett went to the rear and had to negotiate around the junk on the porch to get to the door. Through a window, he could see into Rafshoon's home. Dirty dishes were jumbled in the kitchen sink, and the table was a haven for a month's worth of newspapers and mail. Emmett rapped loudly on the glass, then saw motion inside. Albert Rafshoon threw open the door, winded and puffing.

"Sorry to bother you," Emmett said, badge at the ready.

"Not as sorry as I am. I was in the cellar working and you scared the hell outta me," Rafshoon panted. He wore a white undershirt, and were it not for his belt, his trousers would have dropped to his ankles. Foregone was the artistry he normally employed for covering his bald spot. His scalp lay bare and beaded with sweat. "Who are you? Whadaya want?"

"I'm Detective Emmett. You took pictures of a crime scene for me on Thursday."

"You're gonna have to be more specific than that, pal. Too many dead people this week. I lost count."

"It was at the Warren Street subway station. Ring a bell?"

"Yeah, sure. A spade with no leg. So much for his career as a ballerina."

Emmett shot Rafshoon a withering glare.

"What? It was a joke."

"Well, this isn't." Emmett presented the photo. "I need to see what that is," he said, indicating the corner section of the picture that showed the portal. "Can you blow it up for me?"

Rafshoon examined the image. "I'd have to play with it. Get it in focus. I could do it for you in a week."

"No. Now."

"Fat chance. I got six crime scenes ahead 'a you. My dance card's booked solid."

Emmett put his foot in the doorway. "It's important."

"And my paycheck isn't?"

"Do I look like I'm kidding?" Emmett pushed into the kitchen, imposing on the man's physical space. Rafshoon had to tilt his chin up to meet Emmett's gaze.

"No, you look like you wanna pound me into a pulp. Which is why I wasn't gonna let you in. You cops are always pushy," he muttered as he led Emmett through his rat's nest of an apartment, past miniature mountain ranges of boxes and hoards of books, and down to the cellar.

Red-tinted lightbulbs gave the basement an eerie glow. The walls and windows had been coated with black paint. Basins of soaking photos were arrayed on every available surface while drying pictures hung from string, similar to the laundry on the line in Emmett's backyard.

"Lemme dig out the shot." Rafshoon rooted through a tottering stack of four-by-five negatives encased in glassine envelopes. Numbers were scrawled on each with a grease pencil.

"That's some filing system you've got, Albert."

"Pushy and a smart-ass. A winning combination," he grumbled, thumbing through the pile. "Ah, here it is."

"So what's next?" Emmett wanted to spur the process along. The chemical fumes felt like a balloon being inflated inside his head. The smell could have given him a hangover.

"Hold your horses. Rome wasn't built in a day."

No city was ever built in a day, Emmett thought, but it had taken less than three to bring Newark to its knees.

"We gotta put the negative into a holder, then we put the holder in the enlarger, and then we get everything lined up just right." Rafshoon went step by step as though he was explaining how to bake a pie. He fed the negative into a machine that resembled a drill press, tinkered with some knobs and levers to position it, and switched on a timer. A bright light was projected through the image onto a sheet of paper.

"There she is. Snug as a bug in a rug." The timer ticked breathlessly. Rafshoon tried to fill the vacuum in the conversation. "You hear that the White Sox signed Aurelio Monteagudo?"

Emmett put a hand on his hip, uninterested.

"Not a baseball fan. Okay."

The timer halted and the enlarger light clicked off. Rafshoon transferred the blank page to a tray of liquid and swished it from side to side. Slowly, an image began to emerge. Emmett leaned in to get a peek, but Rafshoon snatched the paper with tongs and moved it to another tray.

"Have to put it in the fixing solution," he said.

Emmett elbowed him aside so he could see what was developing. Sloshing in the solution was the image of the gray tunnel wall. At the center, clear as day, was an access door. Emmett's elation was overrun by a wriggling sense of fear. He would have to reenter the subway tunnel. He broke for the stairs.

"What about the picture?" Rafshoon was rinsing the print under a stream of water.

"I saw what I needed to see."

Rafshoon dropped the photo into the water with a splash. "Typical cop."

Typical was exactly how these murders were meant to seem—another black teenager dead, one of many stabbed over drugs, gang territory, or less, nothing that would arouse concern, nothing out of the norm. The devious precision astonished Emmett.

An alley, an empty lot, and a dead-end street, those were public, neighborhood places that would foster the appearance that the killings were local and personal. But Ambrose Webster had been left deep in a train tunnel, a remote location on city property. It was a break in the pattern. The door in the photograph was the clue Emmett had been longing for, however, the prospect of going into the tunnel alone to investigate had him hyperventilating right up until he parked in front of the Warren Street subway station.

The riots had shut down the entire transit system, including the subway service, further derailing the city. A sign outside said the station was closed until further notice. The entry was locked. Emmett's stomach caved. To get in, he would have to go through the opening of the train tunnel that was one street over, off Wilsey. He got the flashlight from under the front seat of his car, grateful that he hadn't returned it to the station house, and started walking.

The New Jersey Institute of Technology dominated the blocks surrounding the subway station. Less a campus than a collection of brick monoliths, the school could have passed for some corporate headquarters. Emmett had always envisioned Edward attending college there, studying to be an engineer or some kind of scientist. He had the brain for it, the talent. Of the two of them, Edward had the most potential. What tripped him up were his own choices. He didn't have to take a job at Westinghouse just because their father had and he didn't have to enlist in the army. He could have applied for a scholarship as Emmett did or waited until the draft. Would that have changed the outcome, Emmett would never know. He was sure, however, that his prayers had been answered. That day by the river when Edward came close to drowning, Emmett had begged God to give him his brother back, and God had. Now Edward would be his responsibility for the rest of their lives, proof that prayer worked. It worked better than Emmett expected it to.

As he stood at the yawning mouth of the tunnel, he raked his memory for a prayer to ward off his apprehensions. Nothing came to mind. He took a big breath, as if he was about to dive into a pool, and stepped into the tunnel's chasm.

The flashlight carved a shallow channel into the gloom, and darkness closed in behind him. The musty odor of diesel fumes from the trains was as thick as incense. Emmett would have to make it to the station and continue on to get to the point where the access door appeared in the photograph. He was counting on the station lights being lit. They weren't. The flashlight's beam shined off of the pale tiles, the concrete platform, and the iron struts between the tracks. It was the halfway mark. Emmett had farther to go.

His pulse was outpacing his footsteps. He could have run—nobody was there to see him—except the restraint required not to run kept the anxiety corked in his ribs. He trained the flashlight on the left side of the tunnel where he had seen the door in the picture. The wall went on and on, uninterrupted, and Emmett began to doubt himself, questioning if the image had been inverted in the developing process. He visualized the actual crime scene, how Ambrose Webster's head was tipped to the side and how his torso was lumped across the tracks. Emmett realized he had passed the very spot where the body had lain. Then he saw it, a squat, industrial door, as wide as it was tall, inset into the cement. It was like something from a submarine. When he tried the handle, the door opened toward him, releasing a walloping stench. Gagging, Emmett had to step away. The smell confirmed that the door connected to the city's sewer system.

Once he caught his breath, he shined the flashlight inside. The beam illuminated a narrow corridor. It was an offshoot from a larger pipe some yards in, where water was burbling over mounds of sludge. A pair of grooves were rutted into the mud, running from the main pipe up the shaft to the door where Emmett stood, a clear trail.

Ambrose Webster weighed close to three hundred pounds. How anybody could have carried him anywhere, alive or dead, had been a riddle to Emmett. But Webster hadn't been carried. He had been dragged on some sort of cart. Lying prone, he would have fit through the scaled-down door, then he could have been rolled off whatever the apparatus was and left on the rails. That was how Webster's body had gotten on the subway tracks. How he had gotten into the sewers was a different matter.

The smell and the strain on his nerves were becoming too much for

Emmett. Light-headedness was setting in. He ran along the tracks until he burst from the tunnel's jaw into daylight, choking on the fresh air. Whoever killed Ambrose Webster had braved the vile, claustrophobic sewers. That made him a stronger man than Emmett, and that was as petrifying to him as the tunnel.

FORTY-TWO

City Hall was closed. Not because of the riots, but because it was Saturday. The building was one of Newark's crown jewels, a white, wedding-cake-style structure that was more regal than official. It was the last bastion of eminence in a city steadily degenerating into a slum. Emmett cupped his hand to the glass door and looked inside. A watchman was sitting at the front desk doing a crossword puzzle. Holding his badge to the pane, Emmett tapped on the door, prepared to plead his case so the watchman wouldn't make him wait until Monday to visit the Department of Public Works.

"You here for the meeting with the mayor?" the watchman asked. His hair was white, his hands gnarled and arthritic. He would have been of absolutely no benefit if ever there were an actual break-in at City Hall.

"Yes, yes I am." Emmett couldn't turn down the free pass.

"Third floor. Meeting's already started."

"Thanks."

The vaulted entrance hall was as palatial as a Greek temple. Cream-colored marble columns fretted the walls, and a dome with a circular window at the center let the sun pour through the ceiling. A sweeping twin spiral staircase shaped like the f-holes on a violin led to the second floor. Emmett climbed the steps, making a show of his departure, then had to hunt for a back stairway. The Department of Public Works was on the bottom floor.

Since it was Saturday, the corridors were empty and the door was unlocked. The city engineer's office occupied the first of two small rooms. The second was a storage area. Emmett would have preferred not having to sneak in. He could have used some help sorting through the racks of long, flat drawers containing city maps and blueprints. One set of racks was for the gas lines. Another was for electrical, a third for water, and an entire section was devoted to the lengthy history of Newark's sewer system.

The earliest sewer maps dated to the 1880s, and the paper they were hand-printed on had grown tan and silky with age. Skipping drawers allowed Emmett to jump forward in time to the 1920s, when the city's antiquated scheme of open gutters and runoff ditches was reconfigured into a complex network built to service twenty-two municipalities along the Passaic River, a span of eighty square miles. A few more drawers down and he had leapt forward to the present day. The current maps were so convoluted that he had difficulty deciphering them. From what Emmett could ascertain, household wastewater was funneled into the sewers through twelve-inch pipes, which fed into larger mains called trunk sewers that wove beneath the streets. The system culminated at a treatment facility, labeled PUMPING STATION, which was out by Newark Bay. Emmett recognized the place, a forgotten fragment of his childhood emblazoned on the map.

Growing up, kids had referred to it as "the stink house," and for good reason. The pumping station was where Newark's raw sewage was treated. A perpetual funk permeated the marshes surrounding the treatment plant, an area that came to be known as "the dumps." Undeterred by the smell, each spring many a citizen would make the pilgrimage there to collect mushrooms from the meadows or fish for eels in the bay. Come fall, bird hunters claimed the land as a prized shooting spot. They would retrieve fallen geese from among the vestiges of broken boats that would wash into the shallows after storms. In winter, children went ice-skating on the frozen ponds. Regardless of the season, the breeze off the marshes was tainted with the haze of waste, though it didn't keep people away. During the summers, Emmett and his brother would head for the dumps and wade into the water, grabbing in vain at fish that were far too fast for them to catch, enjoying themselves too much to be bothered by the smell. Unbeknownst to Emmett, south of the pump station was what the map termed "the Newark shaft," a cast concrete, pressure tunnel that plunged some three hundred feet down into the bay, like an expressway to hell. Even the diagram was intimidating. All those years, he never knew it was there. He was glad he didn't.

Emmett scoured the map until his vision blurred. Finally, he found the portal hatch into the subway. It had been added in the 1930s when the rail system was being constructed. Judging by the map's key, the hatch connected to a submain that was sizable enough for a man to stand erect in. Unfortunately, the submain connected to several other lines in the sixty-eight-mile circuit of sewers that was linked to virtually every structure in the city, making it impossible for Emmett to identify where Ambrose Webster might have gotten in. According to the map, rainwater from the streets ran through a variety of pipes, some minuscule, some huge, but he couldn't detect any freestanding entries and was hard-pressed to believe that Webster would climb into a manhole of his own volition. Emmett's latest revelation was becoming another impediment. He was right back at the beginning yet again.

Although he knew it was wrong, Emmett took the map. He rolled it tightly to fit under his jacket. Unlike the flashlight on loan from the patrolman that wouldn't be missed, this was a government document. How he would replace it, Emmett had no clue, however, he needed to study the map more closely without the possibility of being caught. In order not to stir suspicion, he went upstairs to come down.

"Is the meeting done?" the watchman asked, taking a breather from his crossword.

"Not quite."

"Mayor gonna get us outta this?"

"He's trying."

"These niggers are screwing everything up. City's in the crapper. What can you do, huh?"

"What can you do?" Emmett repeated. The map was slipping from under his arm. A second longer and it would drop.

"You have a nice afternoon, Officer," the watchman told him, then he resumed his puzzle.

A riot was raging through Newark. Having a nice afternoon was not in the cards.

Emmett stored the map in his trunk and put on the police band to catch the latest. The dispatcher was assigning patrols to certain blocks to clear rooftops of debris so nothing could be dropped over the sides as artillery. Some were even requested to hold their positions to deny snipers from occupying them. The force's best offense would be a strong defense. As soon as dispatch was finished issuing details, a distress call came in for an officer assist.

"We got twenty Guardsmen and troopers directing fire at Hayes Homes. Somebody threw a toaster out a window and it hit a state trooper. A freakin' toaster. Damn near took his ear off. We're at Hunterdon and Eighteenth. Send somebody ASAP."

Strafing fire was chattering against brick, audible over the radio. Emmett had to get to a phone. The building closest to Hunterdon and Eighteenth was where Ambrose Webster's grandmother lived.

He double-parked at a pay phone, but the phone directory was gone, torn out. He dialed Otis Fossum's number because he remembered it. The line rang once and Fossum answered with an apprehensive, "Hello?"

"Good. You're awake."

"Even I can't sleep through gunfire, Mr. Emmett."

"Otis, I need to reach that woman who lives by you in Hayes, the lady whose apartment you visited with me. Do you have a telephone directory?"

"Nope. Got stoled."

Emmett wasn't surprised. That was the projects. Everything from the priceless to the inconsequential was subject to theft.

"When things calm down, could you go and see if she's okay?"

"I dunno. Of all the favors I done fo' you, this'n is the only one that could get me killed." There was a pause on the line. "I ain't sayin' no, Mr. Emmett. All I'm sayin' is it's dangerous. A guy couple floors below me got shot in the arm just standing at his window."

"That's why I want you to check on her. Whenever, Otis. Whenever you can."

"I'll do it, Mr. Emmett. I owe you for losin' that boy 'a yours anyways. You ever find him?"

"Yeah, I did. So how about we call it even?"

"It's a deal."

"Oh, and Otis, I took care of your problem. Once and for all. You don't have to worry about them anymore."

The phone line went quiet again. "Thank you, Mr. Emmett. You're a . . . a real nice man." That was high praise from Fossum. "I'll call your house. Let you know how the lady is."

"I'd appreciate that."

As Emmett hung up, gunshots blasted nearby on Hill Street. They were .38s. Emmett could tell. The first time he heard one fired was at the academy, though it wasn't on the range. His class had been issued their weapons and a cadet was admiring his under his desk when it accidentally discharged, blowing a hole through the desktop and into the ceiling. Emmett never forgot that sound.

Using the edge of a building as a blind, he stole a glance around the corner. Two jeeps were stopped in the road. A posse of patrolmen and troopers were scrambling into a barbershop, weapons raised.

"Help," someone yelled. "Help me."

Emmett shucked off his jacket to expose his gun holster and shield, ensuring nobody would mistake him for a civilian. That didn't guarantee they wouldn't shoot him. But it might make them think twice.

"I'm a police officer," he announced, approaching the barbershop with his service revolver drawn.

The front window was in pieces. A row of red vinyl barber's chairs faced cracked mirrors. Broken shards of glass glittered on the linoleum. Emmett couldn't tell if the place had been looted or if the troopers and patrolmen had wrecked it. They didn't notice him. They were circled around a black kid about Freddie's age. He was spread out on the floor with a bullet hole through his cheek. Blood wreathed his head.

"I'm a police officer," Emmett repeated.

Some of them turned, looked him up and down. "It's all right. We got him," an officer said, as if Emmett was horning in on a bust.

A trooper rifled through the kid's pockets and pulled out a crinkled wad of cash. He counted it. "Seven bucks."

The trooper went to put the bills in his own wallet. A patrolman stopped him. "Hey. What's wrong with you? There are five of us. Not including this guy." He jabbed a thumb at Emmett. "Sorry, buddy. We got here first," he said as they divvied up the money over the corpse.

Emmett looked at the kid's face. The bullet hole was the size of a dime. Were it not for the blood, it could have been a birthmark. He realized that it was the kid who had been calling for help.

"What did he do?" Emmett asked in a daze, shock making his mind gluey.

"He ran. We told him to stop or we'd shoot, and the nigger ran," a trooper explained, justifying their actions. He was chewing gum and holding his gun so casually it may as well have been his car keys.

"Hey, how 'bout this?" A patrolman pulled a pair of scissors from a jar of blue Barbicide, shook them dry, and arranged them in the kid's palm. "Pretty convincing, huh?" The rest agreed.

"Who's gonna call it in?"

The men responded with round of "not me's."

"I did it last time," was the other patrolman's excuse. He had a seat in one of the barber's chairs. "Ay. Take a little off the sides, will ya?" he kidded to a trooper.

Another trooper was punching the buttons on the shop's register and shaking it, attempting to jimmy the cash drawer. When it wouldn't budge, he banged on the sides. "Stupid thing won't open."

"You could shoot it," somebody suggested.

"Waste 'a ammo."

"Not if it's full 'a money."

The trooper took aim and Emmett backed out the door.

"You leavin'?" a patrolman asked, as though he was bowing out of a party early.

"He's a detective," the other officer said. "He can do whatever he damn well pleases."

"Hey, you in a radio car? Maybe you could call this in for us."

Their behavior had rendered Emmett speechless. They stared at him, waiting, until he could formulate a response. "No, I'm not in a radio car. Sorry."

Except Emmett wasn't sorry, not for them. He was sorry for the kid with the bullet in his face lying on the floor of the barbershop. He was sorry for Newark.

FORTY-THREE

The noon sun was leering down on the city. Its heat felt like contempt to Emmett. He walked to his car, totally unaware that he was still holding his gun until a black woman sitting at a second-story window hid inside at the sight of him.

Rubbed raw by anger and regret, he was ready to go home. He had been running a debt on his body from lack of sleep, and the tab was coming due. He craved a shower, a decent meal, and his own bed. Most of all, he wanted the riot to end.

Come Monday, Emmett would have to concede failure on Ambrose Webster's murder. It was a dry well. His track record in Homicide was starting in the red. He had been assigned two cases, neither of which he was able to close. The disgrace was as pitiless as the weather. Lieutenant Ahern wasn't aware of the other killings, and Emmett wasn't beholden to inform him. Revealing his theories would only have made him seem naive and inept. The files regarding the deaths of Evander Hammond, Tyrone Cambell, and Julius Dekes would go back on the shelves of the Records Room, unsolved, destined to be forgotten. That was if the Fourth Precinct remained standing through the weekend.

The dispatcher was prattling on the police band. Emmett shut off the radio and shut him up. He was swollen with the sense of defeat.

He had tread every avenue of the investigation to no end, with the exception of one: he never made it to the public library, the last place Evander Hammond went prior to his disappearance. Emmett reserved no hope that anybody would recall Hammond, but a quick visit would close the book on the quartet of cases altogether, absolving Emmett of any further responsibility. Guilt was something he would have to absolve himself of.

The library was in the opposite direction from his house, however it was a straight shot up Broad Street from where he was. Driving there would require Emmett to hurdle a slew of barricades. He didn't have the energy to bounce around like a pinball avoiding them. His shortcuts hadn't gotten him anywhere, literally or figuratively.

"What happened to your car, Detective?" The patrolman overseeing the first checkpoint ogled at the hole in his rear windshield.

The truth wasn't worth rehashing. Emmett thought of his classmate from the academy who had put the hole in the ceiling. "Accidental weapons discharge."

"Boy oh boy. The guy who did it get in hot water?"

"You could say that."

A yellow school bus was parked across the street. Cops, troopers, and Guardsmen were traipsing in and out. The bus was a hive of activity.

"What's the school bus for?" Emmett asked.

"Orders were that when we made an arrest, we had to hold the coloreds until another unit could come and transport 'em to headquarters for booking. Couple 'a hours go by and we got too many arrests for the patrol cars to carry. So they sent the kiddie bus."

"Why? How many arrests have you made?"

"'Bout sixty."

"Sixty?" The number was astronomical for that early in the day. "What were the charges?"

"Different stuff. Mainly disorderlies or resisting." The patrolman lit a cigarette and leaned into Emmett's window to brag. He had missed his morning shave, and his stubble came in gray. "Get this. We had one 'a those old-type milk trucks pass through. The colored guy driving says he's going to see his grandma. Going to see his grandma? You believe that? He didn't even try to make up a decent lie. We check in the back 'a this milk truck and guess what was inside? A frickin' stockpile of hand-guns, rifles, air pistols, knives, plus a bag of brass knuckles and a ma-chete. A goddamn machete," the patrolman exclaimed. "This old milk truck was an arsenal on wheels."

Emmett got the feeling the officer had been retelling that same story all morning to whoever would listen. Swapping gossip was a favored pas-time of cops. The city was in a state of emergency and that hadn't changed.

"What happened to the driver?"

"Whadaya think?"

"Is he on the school bus?"

"Naw, this was before the bus got here, before they told us to wait on transports. You know the rule: you beat 'em up, you lock 'em up. Guys in charge of that shift took the milkman to booking."

"What about the weapons in the truck?"

"You're looking at 'em." The three National Guardsmen on duty at the barricade were outfitted to the teeth with additional weapons. They had two rifles apiece and extra pistols on their belts. "We gave the rest to the fellas at the other checkpoints. None of 'em was interested in the brass knuckles. Or the machete. Those went to headquarters. Too bad, really. Picture it: some colored guy's giving you lip and you whip out that machete." He pretended to wield an invisible blade, slicing at the air. "Hell, that'd be hilarious. Scare the bejeezus outta 'em." The patrol-man chuckled and flicked ash from his cigarette, concluding his tale. That reminded Emmett of Edward's request.

"Is anyplace open around here where I can buy a pack of those?"

"I wish. Everything that ain't burned to the ground is closed. Had to bring my own coffee in a canteen. Crazy, huh? We might as well be on the moon."

The moon would have felt less alien, Emmett thought.

"Have a good one, Detective," the patrolman said, as though it was an average Saturday, then he directed the next car forward.

Emmett breezed through the subsequent blockades, his badge greasing the path. He was beginning to believe this trip to the library was pointless. By the time he decided to turn back, he was already there.

Various branches of the public library were located throughout Newark. Evander Hammond had visited the one on Washington Street, which was the flagship, the original. It was a noble building with a foreign air. The rounded windows and chiseled limestone lunettes made the place appear as if it had been uprooted from the streets of Rome and plunked in the middle of the Central Ward, a stranded stranger that stuck out from the run-down storefronts on the block.

"We're closing, sir," the woman at the front desk informed Emmett when he entered. Reading glasses dangled from her neck, and the bridge of her nose bore indentations from their constant wear. The name plaque on the desk said MRS. DORSEY. The sign below it stated that library hours were from eight until five on Saturdays.

Emmett checked his watch. "It's eleven-thirty."

"Well, because of the . . . recent events we thought it best." She refrained from using the term "riot." The term had become a profanity.

"Maybe you can help me, ma'am. I'm a police detective," he told her to curry favor, "and I just have a couple of questions."

Mrs. Dorsey blushed. "I'm sorry, Detective. I didn't mean to be rude."

"No offense taken." After the last three days, Emmett was too numb to be offended by anything because everything he had seen was offensive. "Can you tell me if you recognize this boy."

He gave her the photograph included in Evander Hammond's murder file, a snapshot from a birthday past. In it, Evander was proudly modeling a new pair of sneakers. Glee beamed from the picture. He had the confident smirk of someone who thought they were entitled to the pot of gold at the end of the rainbow, his new pair of sneakers a taste of what was to come. But Evander's rainbow had ended in an alley with a knife wound to his heart.

"This would have been a few months ago," Emmett said. "He was a big kid, strongly built. Very friendly. A lot of personality. Definitely not a regular."

She studied the photo. "We get so many people through here. I can't say that I recall him."

"Is there anybody else I could ask?"

"The head librarian. He's in every day. He's upstairs, shelving. Just follow the squeaking."

"Follow the squeaking?"

"The wheels on the book cart, they're noisy. That's how you'll find him."

The high ceilings of the second floor's main gallery made the eight-foot-tall bookshelves appear diminutive by comparison. Wood paneling refracted Emmett's footfalls while the books muffled them. The effect was similar to having cotton stuffed in one ear. Emmett stopped to listen. He heard steady squeaking and trailed it, glancing down each row of shelves. The noise was difficult to track. It came from everywhere and nowhere.

"Hello?" he said. No one replied. Emmett bobbed his head back and forth, weaving between the aisles as the bookshelves hurtled by. The deeper into the stacks he delved, the farther away the squeaking sounded. Finally, he spotted the wooden book cart standing unattended between two rows. Emmett called out again. "Hello?"

A man rounded the end of the aisle wearing earphones and carrying a cassette player under his right arm. His left arm was lame and hung at his side, swinging of its own volition. He was slender and boyish with a man's angular face, his pale hair thin at the crown. He gazed at Emmett inquisitively, like a deer in the woods, removed the earphones and clicked off the tape.

"I'm Detective Martin Emmett. The woman at the front desk suggested I speak with you."

"I apologize, Detective," the man said, his voice deep and liquid smooth, not at all what Emmett would have predicted. "Were you calling to me?"

"Actually, I was."

"I'm trying to learn French. Hearing the language spoken is said to improve retention."

"Is it working?"

"Un peu." He made the sign for a little bit with his fingers and placed the cassette player on the book cart. The tape he was listening to was of Calvin Timmons shouting threats and degrading insults from the cage. The threats were as titillating on tape as they were in person.

"I'm Lazlo Meers. How can I be of service?"

Emmett showed him the picture. "This is Evander Hammond. Do you remember seeing him sometime in April?"

Meers examined the photograph intently. He had noticed Hammond during a school field trip. The kid was a class clown. He goofed off during the library tour and was constantly whispering while Meers's gave a speech about the Dewey decimal system. Hammond was as strapping as a full-grown man, and he had the strut of somebody who savored the spotlight. Meers salivated at the idea of taking him down a notch and making him squirm. He had already dispatched his pet John and was seeking a replacement. He thought Evander Hammond would make splendid prey. As the class was leaving the library to return to school, Meers pulled the boy aside on the pretense of earning a little money. He offered Hammond cash to help him move boxes of books up from the basement after hours. Hammond jumped at the chance.

"I'm afraid I don't recognize him, Detective. Is he in some kind of trouble?"

"No, sir. He was killed."

"How awful." The fact that someone had traced Evander Hammond to the library and to him was a feather of concern tickling Meers's conscience. He attempted to get a read on the detective's level of interest. "This was in April you say?"

"Yes, it was back in April."

"And you haven't apprehended his attacker?"

"No, sir. Not yet."

Although Emmett was new to Homicide, the one question he knew to expect was: *how did it happen.* It was the first thing he would have asked. Curiosity came a close second to shock. The librarian wasn't shocked or curious. Emmett might as well have been asking him for directions.

"Are you sure you don't recognize him, Mr. Meers? Here, take another look at the—"

When Emmett tried to hand him the picture, Meers began breathing heavily. He leaned against the bookshelves for support.

"Are you all right?"

Meers was tugging at his tie like it was suffocating him and he couldn't get any air.

"What is it? What's wrong?"

"Asthma." Between gasps, Meers said, "My inhaler is on the cart."

Emmett had more he wanted to ask, but if he wanted answers he would have to help the man. He rifled through the book cart for the inhaler. That gave Meers time to reach under his pant leg and retrieve the cattle prod from the sock garter strapped to his leg.

"I don't see it. Let me call for an ambulance."

"That won't be necessary, Detective Emmett."

Meers jabbed him with the electric prod. Stunned, Emmett's legs gave out. Meers shocked him again, immobilizing him.

"Forgive me, Detective. I don't normally behave this crudely. There really was no other way." Meers took the tiny flask of ether from his pocket along with a handkerchief and sprinkled drops of the sedative onto the cloth. He clasped the kerchief to Emmett's mouth, muzzling him as he drifted into unconsciousness.

"That's right. That's a good boy. Breathe it in and off to sleep you go."

Meers inspected his new pet. He was tall, muscular, and clever enough to have found him. That made him a desirable adversary.

"This is a lucky day indeed."

He went downstairs to the front desk. The library was dark, the windows and doors shut tight. Mrs. Dorsey had her purse over her shoulder and her glasses on, ready to lock up.

"You go home," he said sweetly. "I'll take care of things."

"Very well, Mr. Meers. Where's the policeman? I didn't see him leave."

"That's odd. He left five minutes ago." Meers was taking a chance that Mrs. Dorsey had been away from her desk at some point in preparation for closing.

She hesitated, perplexed. "Oh, I must have been turning off the lights in the other room and missed him. Okay, then, I'll see you Monday. Be careful getting home, Mr. Meers. With all of the terrible things that have been going on, the later it gets, the more dangerous it'll be."

"I'll be careful, Mrs. Dorsey. I'll be just dandy."

FORTY-FOUR

Fortune was fickle. It could undermine the best-laid plans in the blink of an eye or deliver an unpredictable surprise to one's doorstep. That day, just when it appeared his plans were about to unravel, fate smiled on Lazlo Meers. He had considered Calvin Timmons a windfall—strong, shrewd, an ideal candidate. Then came Detective Emmett, a gift fallen from the heavens. It was almost too perfect to be believed. As he fitted Emmett into the harness, Meers had a flush of delight. He hadn't been that excited since his father first took him into the mine shafts as a boy.

Mine Hill, where Eli Meers was in charge of the day labor, was an open-pit mine west of the Wallkill River. The soft ores on the surface had been shaved clear, and shafts were dug into the main crater, rail laid for cars to cart the ore up from below. The earth looked ruined, raped, and the air was smoggy with grit. Stripped of grass and trees, the stone gorges and mounds of rock created a forbidding landscape, but it didn't frighten Lazlo. Like his first hunting trip, their visit to the mine shaft was another tutorial on manhood. This time, instead of handing Lazlo a rifle, his father gave him a lantern and led him into the darkness.

The rumble of the ore cars on the tracks made the ground tremble underfoot. It was as though the earth was shifting with them inside.

Underground, the sun ceased to exist. To Lazlo's amazement, the cavern walls twinkled when the lamplight hit them, turning the mine shaft into a hidden galaxy.

"We got geologists from fancy universities coming here and poking around every other week," his father had grumbled, affecting annoyance. Lazlo sensed his inner satisfaction. "They say there are more mineral species here than anywhere else in the world. They say this place is special."

For Lazlo, it was special. The mines were a realm all his own. He was hundreds of feet beneath the ground, yet it felt as if he was aloft in the sky with the stars.

He envisioned those sparkling stars while he dragged Detective Emmett through the library using his harnesses. The man's body glided across the slick floors. Meers slid him onto the elevator and pulled him through a back corridor to the Cadillac, parked at the rear entrance.

Getting Emmett into the trunk would have been impossible. Meers didn't have the strength for it. His only alternative was a risky gambit: putting the detective in the front seat. Meers used all his might to hoist the heavy man into the car. Once inside, he removed the harness as well as Emmett's gun and badge, which he tucked in his pockets. As he hopped in behind the steering wheel beside his new companion, Meers daubed perspiration from his face with the handkerchief he had used to sedate Emmett.

"Pardon me, Detective. That was impolite. Alas, this is the only handkerchief I have. You understand."

Shortly after leaving the library, a state trooper stopped him at a roadblock. Meers was ready. He had been practicing his speech in his head.

"Officer, can you help me? My business associate, he's sick. I need to take him to the hospital right away. Which is the quickest route?"

The trooper gave Emmett the once-over. "What's wrong with him?"

"He's a salesmen from out of town. One minute he was making a joke about balance sheets, the next he was on the floor. I don't know. Maybe it was the heat. I pray it wasn't a heart attack." Meers bunched his brow with feigned worry. He wished he hadn't blotted his face. His sweat would have embellished his performance.

"I'd radio in for you, except all of the ambulances are busy." The trooper was genuinely concerned. "Don't take Central Ave. It's got five checkpoints. Take James to Sussex. I'll call ahead and tell the others to watch out for you, let you through fast."

"Thank you, Officer. I'd appreciate that."

"Hope your friend's gonna be all right."

"Me too."

Meers sped off, wondering how groggy Emmett would be from the ether. He would also have burns from the cattle prod. That could compromise his fitness. Meers would minister to him that night and dress his wounds. With the riot rocking the city, a missing detective might go unnoticed for days. It gave Meers time.

The officers at the following barricades ushered him through as though clearing the way for a visiting dignitary. "Isn't that nice," he commented to the slumbering Emmett. "You policemen are quite gentlemanly."

He arrived at the zinc works, parked the Eldorado indoors, and tumbled Emmett out of the passenger seat onto the sled. "Much better," Meers cooed as soon as he harnessed up again and could tug Emmett's body smoothly across the concrete floor.

The unforeseen pleasure of having two pets to hunt did create a logistical problem. He couldn't put Emmett in the cage with Calvin. They would gang up on him, and Meers couldn't have that.

"Where to put you, where to put you. . . ." He tapped his lip, debating.

Meers settled on chaining Emmett to one of the warehouse's steel pylons and taping his mouth shut.

"Not to be ungrateful, but you are tiring me out, Detective."

Normally in the hours leading up to a hunt, Meers would have a light meal, take a nap, then go to the refinery to prepare the final dinner. Once his pet had eaten, he would give him three hours to digest the food. Detective Emmett put a kink in Meers's plans. He would do without his ritual. The anticipation was too tantalizing.

From the peephole, he could see Calvin in the cage, sleeping on the mattress. He was amazed the boy had slept through the commotion he made securing the detective. The lunch Meers cooked for him was gone. The bedpan was full. To rouse him, Meers stomped around the storeroom floor and banged the pan he fried the steaks in against the hot plate. When he returned to the peephole, Calvin hadn't stirred.

"This is vexing. Very vexing indeed, John. What if he's sick? What then?" Meers sought counsel from the mounted head. "He can't be sick. Not this one. He can't. This should wake him."

Meers took a leftover iron rod from his early construction attempts, cut the light in the pen, and crept down to the cage. He threaded the rod between the bars, inching it inward until he gently poked Calvin's thigh. The rod abruptly jerked from Meers's grip. Calvin had grabbed it and was pulling Meers toward him, scrambling to his feet for leverage.

"Come 'ere, you damn gimp. Come here where I can reach you." Calvin's fingertips grazed Meers's arm. "You 'a chicken. I seen you. You ain't nothing. You a cripple. I'm gonna get you. And when I do, I'm gonna hurt you."

Startled, Meers stumbled backward, then fled.

"Run away, chicken," Calvin squawked. "Run away or I'll get you."

Fury pumped through Meers's entire being. He clenched his teeth and stalked around the storeroom. Calvin had tricked him. Caged, the boy's sole weapon was his intellect, and he had deceived Meers handily.

"How could I be so stupid, John? How?"

Meers's wrath simmered into rapture. A grin brimmed on his lips. This would be an unparalleled hunt.

"Do you think it's time?"

The wizened head stared at him, apathetic as always.

"I do."

He changed from his work shoes into hunting boots and removed his dress shirt. The white cotton undershirt below barely veiled the concavity of Meers's chest and scrawny ribs.

"No flashlight for this one," he said. As punishment, Calvin would be deprived of the benefit of light in the sewer tunnels. Meers switched the bulb in the pen back on, not out of compassion but because the total darkness would stop the hunt before it started.

"You comin' down for a real fight?" Calvin jeered.

"Did you know, John, that a stab to the lower intestine is said to be the most painful death imaginable? Well, it is. Consider the samurai committing hara-kiri. It would take them hours to die of their self-inflicted wounds. The feces would leak into the gut cavity and leach into the bloodstream, a slow poisoning. Too cruel?"

The head's glass eyes stared past Meers.

"No? I don't think so either."

Meers grasped the rope that raised the cage's trapdoor and cranked the winch. Iron clanged as the door lifted open. He would allot Calvin five minutes. After that, the game would begin.

"Soon, John. Soon," he assured the head.

To pass the time, Meers swept his bowie over a pale pink Arkansas sharpening stone, polishing the edge to a mirror shine. Once the five minutes were up, he put his Case XX knife in his pocket, strapped on the miner's helmet, and sheathed the bowie knife.

"After I'm done, we'll eat his dinner. We'll celebrate. Would you enjoy that, John? I thought you would."

When he went into the pen, the cage was empty. Calvin was gone. The iron rod was too. Meers cursed himself for leaving it. He had been fooled once. He wouldn't be fooled again. Calvin could have been standing just inside the access door, prepared to clobber him with the rod. Meers hurried back up to the storeroom and shut off the pen's light to prevent it from radiating into the tunnels. He could see well in the dark. Calvin couldn't. An iron rod was harmless if the boy didn't know where to swing it.

Meers unlocked the cage door and stepped inside. He peered through the access hatch: no Calvin. Switching on his carbine lamp, light burst into the tunnel. The brown brick walls stretched endlessly in both directions. The drought had dried the dirt accumulated on the tunnel floor, creating a canvas for Calvin's footprints. They led to the left. Meers listened to see if he could hear anything. The sewer was silent.

In spite of his limp, he was limber in the tunnels. He loped along at a fast clip, scanning the ground for tracks. The sewers were ideal for his hunting because the prints of his previous kills were usually washed clean in time for the next. Even so, Meers could distinguish the old from the new. Those he saw were widely spaced, indicating that Calvin was walking briskly and had tripped often. At every tunnel intersection, Meers took caution. Calvin might have been perched behind any corner. Meers took out his knife. He would be ready for the boy when they finally met up.

Dry dirt gave way to mud as he moved into a larger tunnel in pursuit of the footprints. The lamplight swelled, filling the space. Beams danced over the brick walls, reflected off the gurgling sewer water. There was no sign of Calvin. Meers studied the tracks. They were closer, deeper, the edges messy. Eventually, they stopped altogether, as though Calvin had dematerialized.

"I'm impressed."

This was another hoax. Calvin had forged into the tunnel, then backtracked, approximating his own footsteps in the dark.

"But I'm not dumb."

As Meers turned to recommence with the real trail, the iron bar came swooshing by his ear.

"Yes you is," Calvin said. He had sneaked up on him.

Meers dodged the blow and swung at Calvin with his knife. Calvin ran, using the lamplight to see by. Since Meers couldn't keep pace with him, he let Calvin get the lead, driving him into the darkness. But Calvin got wise and stopped sprinting. Meers saw him fifty yards in the distance. He had one arm outstretched, feeling the wall, and he was tapping the rod to and fro like a blind person with a cane.

Calvin spun to face him, squinting and holding the rod as a baseball bat. "Come and get me, asshole."

The invitation was another trap. Hand to hand, Calvin would have the advantage, so Meers stood still. Calvin couldn't see him because of the scorching lamplight.

"Come on," Calvin challenged. "Come and get me."

Meers snuffed the lamp on his helmet, and the tunnel went black.

He could hear Calvin's heavy breathing over the trickling sewer water. His pupils took a second to focus. Once they did, he saw Calvin swaying the rod in front of him as an antenna. Meers tapped the helmet, pretending it was a mechanical failure. Calvin fell for the ruse and rushed at him, a lion charging a wounded animal.

Iron rod flailing, Calvin closed in. Meers got low and started toward him, shortening the gap between them. When they collided, Meers rammed the bowie knife into Calvin's stomach. The blade dug in to the hilt. Calvin cried out and the rod crash down on Meers's left shoulder, dropping him to the ground beside Calvin.

"Damn you," Meers spat. Injured, he scuttled away, sloshing through the mud. He put the lamp back on. He wanted to see every nuance of Calvin's pain.

The boy was crumpled on the tunnel floor, his clothes sopped in blood and muck. The rod lay at his side, a relinquished sword. He was holding his abdomen and contorting his face in agony.

"See what you made me do?" Meers yelled, tears in his eyes. His voice echoed through the sewers. It hurt for him to stand. His clavicle was shattered. He could tell. The skin was broken too. Blood seeped onto his undershirt. "See?"

Calvin's wound was so excruciating he couldn't speak. His mouth formed words, yet they wouldn't come out. His body had gone limp.

Pain triggered Meers's impatience. He resented having to wait for Calvin to expire, but rage prevented Meers from sparing him. He sheathed his knife, collecting himself.

"Good-bye, Calvin," he said. "It's been a pleasure."

With those final words, Meers abandoned the boy to die alone in the tunnel in the dark.

FORTY-FIVE

Rain marched on the corrugated roof of the zinc refinery, awakening Emmett. The drought had broken with a sudden deluge. He felt like he was inside a huge drum someone was beating on. Woozy, he struggled to keep his eyes open, then the pain in his wrists and the pungent odor of sulfur roused him into full consciousness. To his horror, he realized there was tape across his lips.

Emmett didn't know where he was, only that he had been bound to a steel girder. Bolts nudged into his spine. He bucked to see if he could loosen the chains wrapped around his chest. They were too tight. The padlock securing them brushed against his palm.

The last thing he could remember was being at the library. Gradually, the hazy bits and pieces gelled together. The librarian had faked an asthma attack and hit him in the thigh with something that burned. His badge and gun were gone. Their absence stung him as badly as the burns.

As far as Emmett could tell, he was in some sort of defunct factory. Rivet holes dotted the floor where machinery had formerly been affixed. Broken windows along the roofline let in the remaining daylight. The sun was setting. He had to get his bearings before he lost the light entirely.

Waning rays shimmered off a cherry red Cadillac parked inside the cavernous factory. The car had come in through a rolling garage door, which was closed. Other than the Cadillac, the place was empty. On either side of him, concrete spanned for yards, smudging into darkness. Emmett couldn't move or call for help, and the windows were too high to see any landmarks. All he could do was concentrate and commit what he could see of the layout to memory.

Pins and needles were fizzing in his forearms, the result of having them strapped tightly behind him for too long. He wiggled his fingers to get the blood moving. Once he regained feeling, he would attempt to stand. If he could shimmy to his feet, the chains might loosen and fall, then he could step right out of them.

Flexing his muscles gave him a head rush. Whatever Meers doped him with hadn't fully worn off, and it induced waves of nausea. Emmett took deep breaths through his nose, willing himself not to throw up. With the tape covering his mouth, he could suffocate if he did. As soon as the queasiness had abated, he began rocking his shoulders back and forth, gaining momentum by pushing his feet against the ground. Slowly, he inched up the girder, muscles quaking as he held a low, leg-searing squat. He had risen a foot off the floor when a lightbulb popped on in a room at the opposite end of the factory. Sacrificing his progress, Emmett slid down to the concrete and lowered his eyelids so it would appear, from a distance, that he was still knocked out.

Meers staggered into the light and collapsed into a chair, shouting, "Goddamn him, John. Do you see what he did to me?"

Nobody else was in the room from what Emmett could see, leaving him to wonder who John was and whether or not Meers was alone.

"He's sorry now," Meers claimed, trying to convince himself of triumph. "He's the one who's sorry."

Blood stained Meers's undershirt, but not rain. That told Emmett he hadn't come in from outside.

"This is bad, John. It's serious. I need to go to the hospital. Give me a lie, a lie to tell the doctors."

Meers was hurt, an edge for Emmett. If he left for the hospital, that would give Emmett the opportunity to get free of the chains.

"I'll say I fell. They'll believe that, won't they, John? Won't they?" he whimpered. "That's what I'll do. I'll put the detective in the cage, then I'll go and tell the doctors at the hospital that I fell."

The cage, Emmett thought as he closed his eyes. Rain was pounding on the roof like an oncoming locomotive. He could hear Meers limping toward him.

"Are you awake, Detective?" He lifted Emmett's chin from his chest and ripped the tape from his mouth. "Are you? Don't play opossum with me. I'm in no mood for that."

Meers pinched Emmett's ear, digging his nail into the soft cartilage and twisting hard. Compared to wearing a chain around his leg for three hours a day at the monastery, the wire tines boring into his flesh, this pain was insignificant and momentary. Emmett didn't flinch.

"I apologize for that, Detective. I had to be sure." Meers was contrite.

The timber of his footsteps told Emmett that Meers had gone in the direction of the Cadillac. The car's trunk creaked, and after some indistinguishable clatter, something was being drawn toward Emmett. Wheels were rolling over the concrete floor. Not being able to open his eyes was more agonizing than Meers wrenching his ear.

Exertion from ascending the girder had warmed Emmett's muscles, though he couldn't account for his reflexes. Eyes closed, it was impossible to tell if Meers had a weapon. Emmett wasn't certain his body would cooperate for a fight. His plan was to lull Meers into complacency, then he might become careless.

Meers undid the padlock and began the meandrous process of untying the chains. Emmett's nerves were jangling. He couldn't allow himself to get too worked up or else he would start to sweat, and a sleeping person wouldn't perspire. Loosed from his bonds, he slumped forward, pretending to be passed out.

"Here we go. One arm. Then the next," Meers said, as if dressing a baby. "Upsy daisy."

Some kind of vest was saddled over Emmett's shoulders and fastened tight at the waist, then he felt himself being wrangled onto a rolling dolly and heard a clamp snap onto the vest. He sensed the tautness of being connected to Meers and the tug of being conveyed across the concrete. Every fiber of his being yearned to jump up and throttle Meers, except now they were conjoined. If Emmett tried to run, he wouldn't get far.

The direction they were headed was toward the room with the light on. Soon Emmett was coasting down a ramp, going below ground level. The sulfurous smell was consumed by the rankness of sewage, the same stink Emmett had encountered in the subway tunnel. When they stopped moving, Meers hissed in pain from his injury. Emmett opened his eyes for an instant. The room was ten by ten with exposed stone and dirt walls, and at one end was a life-size cage that Meers was dragging him into. Heart pounding, Emmett shut his eyes and waited.

The dolly wouldn't fit into the cage door, so Meers had to finish the last few feet using his own brawn. Because of his lame arm and wounded shoulder, his whole left side useless. He was pulling the rope that bound them together with his right arm, grunting and braying from effort. When at last Emmett's heels cleared the cage door, Meers exhaled in relief.

"I've had bigger, Detective, though none quite as cumbersome as you."

Meers bent over him to remove the vest. His hot breath gusted on Emmett's cheeks. He unhitched the clamp and the rope went slack.

"I promise you'll be right as rain by tomorrow." He petted Emmett's head, consoling him.

Emmett leapt up and rammed Meers against the bars. "You won't."

The cage door swung closed, trapping them inside. Emmett got his hands on Meers throat and choked him. Meers's face went red. He was worming as Emmett raised him off his feet. In desperation, Meers kicked Emmett in the thigh where he had shocked him with the cattle prod. The intensity of the pain caused Emmett to let go.

Meers unsheathed his bowie knife and squared off with him. He swiped at Emmett, herding him toward a door that opened into darkness, a portal identical to the one Emmett had seen in the subway tunnel, only much larger. Emmett lunged at Meers, who maneuvered like a cornered animal, and he slashed at Emmett's chest. The blade was so sharp that Emmett didn't feel the cut until he saw a red arc well through his shirt.

Just beyond the cage lay a plastic flashlight. Emmett thought it must have been by the door and Meers had knocked it over while transporting him. The flashlight had rolled within reach of the bars. Emmett dove for it, anticipating Meers would pounce. When he did, Emmett hammered a fist into his bloody shoulder. Meers momentarily withered, giving Emmett a window to escape through the access door into the dark.

"Thank you, Detective," Meers shouted.

His gratitude made Emmett go cold. Faltering through the pitch-black, he switched on the flashlight. Terror seized him. He was in a tapered brick tunnel so constricting that he had to crouch or the top of his head would hit the ceiling. The stench was revolting.

"Here I come," Meers proclaimed.

Emmett broke into a full sprint and cut into a different tunnel, fear pulsating through him like a live current. Mud sucked at his ankles, hampering his progress. Having to hunch did too. The water flow was getting heavier. Rain washing into street gutters had been funneling into the sewers. Narrow as they were, there was a distinct possibility the tunnels could fill.

Elbows grating across the brick, Emmett glanced back to see if Meers was close, then tripped. He pointed the flashlight to see what he had stumbled over. On the tunnel floor lay a rotting corpse. The body had been decapitated. The skin was bloated and shedding, the hands devoured down to the bones by rats. Emmett fought not to wretch. That was when he heard squeaking, getting louder and louder. He shined the beam behind him. A gray tide of rats was cascading toward him, trying to outrun a tumult of water. Emmett sprang to his feet.

At a fork in the tunnel, he made the snap decision to go right. The tunnel split again, then again. The maze was endless, more intricate in reality than on the sewer maps he had read. He veered into a tunnel that was larger and he could run upright. Sewer water splashed with his every step. As he ran, the flashlight's beam caught on something metal, steal footholds driven into the wall. It was a maintenance ladder. Overhead, light flickered through the slots in a manhole cover. Emmett scaled the rungs into a vertical shaft and attempted to raise the cover. It wouldn't budge. He forced his shoulder into it. Still nothing. Manhole covers weighed about fifty pounds, which Emmett could have handled. Something had to be on top of the manhole, a parked car or a truck. He would have to locate another ladder.

When he climbed down, Meers rushed at him, his knife glinting like a flare. Emmett pivoted on the rung and kicked Meers aside. But the metal rung was slick and he fell, dropping the flashlight. It got carried along with the current. Emmett chased after it, following the submerged glow. He had to get to it before the batteries gave out.

Emmett plunged into the water, scooped up the flashlight, and rode the current to flee from Meers. The churning flood had swept him from his feet as well and he was flailing for solid ground. Emmett dodged into another tunnel where the water level was lower, panning the flashlight wildly for another manhole. He was bounding through the tunnel, eyes focused upward, when something caught his pant leg.

"Help me."

Calvin Timmons was sprawled on the tunnel floor. His clothes were soaked black with blood. He had pushed himself up the wall so he wouldn't drown. Emmett took his hand. It was cold. The kid was fading. Blood continued to seep from the cut to his lower abdomen.

"I'm here," Emmett told him. "I'll help you. What's your name?"

"Calvin. Calvin Timmons."

"Calvin, my name's Martin. I've got to find us a way out. To do that, I have to leave you alone for a minute."

Calvin gripped Emmett's hand and wouldn't let go.

"Promise you'll come back?"

Emmett had broken promises to his brother, to himself, to God. He was the last person to be promising anything to anyone. But he did.

"I promise, Calvin. I'll come back."

He was scouring the walls for ladder rungs when Calvin began wheezing, a warning to him. It was too late. Meers tackled Emmett, sending the flashlight skittering away. The beam wound up facing the opposite direction, making it difficult for Emmett to see. Meers got on top of him and raised the knife. Emmett caught his arm, fighting him.

The shadowy light carved Meers's features into gargoylish relief. Wet hair was plastered to his forehead. Thrill burned in his eyes.

"Let me do it," he whined, like a child who had never gotten his way.

Emmett bashed Meers's arm against the bricks, loosening the knife from his grasp. It landed in the muddy stream as Emmett threw Meers off of him. Crawling and splashing, Meers rooted around for the blade. Emmett yanked him up and pressed him to the tunnel wall. Meers gouged his fingers into the cut on Emmett's chest. Emmett howled in pain. Countering, he kneed Meers in the stomach and felt something metal in his pocket. Emmett thought of Freddie and his pickpocketing trick. He struck Meers again, this time in the shoulder, dipping into his pants pocket as Meers reeled in pain. Inside was a pocketknife.

He let Meers get free and scrabble for his bowie. That gave Emmett a chance to open the three-inch folding blade. Meers unearthed the knife from the slippery sewage and charged at him, rearing it back. Before Meers could bring down the bowie, Emmett thrust the pocket-knife between his ribs. Meers gazed at his beloved Case XX with the red bone handle protruding from his chest. He lurched and fell to the floor into the muck, spitting up blood, then he went still.

"Martin?" Calvin called out weakly. "You still here?"

"I'm still here, Calvin. I'm coming."

The water level in the tunnel was rising. It was up to Emmett's shins. As he turned, Meers grabbed him by the ankle and clung on with his last ounce of strength. Emmett forced his head underwater. Meers writhed, unable to hold his breath, and Emmett put all his weight on Meers's body. Soon Meers ceased to fight. He stared at Emmett from under the water until the awareness drained from his eyes and they went dull.

"Martin." Calvin was sputtering on the rising swell.

Emmett retrieved the flashlight, went to Calvin, and lifted him to his feet. The kid groaned. His breathing was shallow.

"Don't you leave me, Calvin." It was what Emmett had said to his brother the day Edward almost died. "Don't you leave me."

Bleeding profusely from the chest, he carried Calvin on his back, searching for a ladder, praying for a ladder. The flashlight began to flutter.

Water had reached the batteries. The light would soon give out and they would be trapped in the dark. Emmett prayed harder.

Farther down the tunnel, a row of metal rungs caught the beam's light. "I see something, Calvin," Emmett said, but Calvin had lost consciousness.

Emmett leaned him against the wall and quickly climbed the shaft. Rain was dripping through the manhole cover. When he pushed, the cover quivered. Straining, Emmett exerted everything he had left in him and lifted the cover clear of the hole.

Heavy rain pelted his face. He blinked hard to see. The red and white lights of a patrol car were flashing up the road, a beacon of rescue. The manhole had let out a half a block from a police barricade. Cops in rain slickers were interviewing the drivers of window-fogged cars as water sluiced off every surface toward the gutters. Emmett imagined the body of Lazlo Meers washing through the bowels of the city, carried by rainwater on a course for the Newark shaft, the three-hundred-foot pipeline into the abyss of the bay, never to be seen again.

The patrol car's lights shimmered on the water-glazed street and refracted off every raindrop. The rain would quench the drought. The drought would end. The riot would end, and as with all endings, it would happen not when it was wanted, not when it was needed, but when it was through.

FORTY-SIX

Pale light was coming through Emmett's bedroom window. Drizzle pattered on the glass. It could have been early morning or near dark. He couldn't tell. Mrs. Poole was sitting at the foot of his bed in a chair brought upstairs from the kitchen. She was reading the newspaper. Emmett wasn't sure how long he had been asleep. He was still weak and tired. When he tried to sit up, the stitches in his chest ached.

"Lay back, Mr. Emmett. You're supposed to be resting." Mrs. Poole got up to prop his pillows and gave him a sip from a mug of coffee. "Should taste better than yesterday's, I expect. The markets are open again. Freddie went and bought us fresh groceries."

"You gave him money, let him loose, and he came home?"

"He was worried after you, Mr. Emmett. We all were." She put her hand on his. "Now I'll let you be."

"No, stay. I'm awake. What's the paper saying about the riot?"

Emmett knew there would be no mention of Calvin Timmons or himself in the news. They didn't rank amid the chaos.

"How 'bout I read to you for a bit?"

"Are you trying to get me to fall back to sleep?"

"You're too smart for your own good, Mr. Emmett."

"There aren't many who'd agree with you on that. Myself included."

Mrs. Poole settled into her seat and read the newspaper to him from cover to cover. On the front page, Police Director Wallace Sloakes was quoted as saying he was immensely proud of the conduct displayed by Newark's police force, the state troopers, and the National Guard during the city's strife. Buried on page five was a piece in which Mose Odett condemned the department for its flagrant abuse of power. His article was a fraction of the length of Director Sloakes's. Somewhere in between was a blurb about Inspector Plout and his brave struggle to hold the Fourth Precinct together. Plout was portrayed as the valiant captain of a marauded ship, when in actuality, Emmett hadn't seen the man emerge from his office since the conflict began. The reality of the riot was already being distorted. Like a bad rumor, that week's events would be modified and remolded every time the stories were told and retold until innuendo grew into truth and fiction solidified to fact.

"Oh gracious, listen to this," Mrs. Poole said glumly. "'Flames ripped through the entire block of Boyden Street razing countless tenements and leveling an abandoned warehouse. Area residents claimed they smelled a strange odor during the blaze. The fire department has yet to comment.' Lord knows I always feel bad for folks who lose their homes in fires. It's so sad, so final."

The warehouse where Luther Reed cut and processed his drugs was on Boyden Street. Reed's boobytraps would have been futile against the inferno.

"What're you grinnin' about, Mr. Emmett?"

"Nothing. I was just wondering what the smell must have been."

Mrs. Poole read on. "'Another suspicious fire broke out at a residence on Gold Street. Assumed to be the result of arson, police are investigating.'"

Emmett would have wagered that the house that was torched was the discreet gentlemen's club frequented by off-duty brass. The arson was somebody's rendition of revenge. It would hit ranking officers harder than the riot did.

According to the newspaper, twenty-six people had been killed during the course of four days. Over fifteen hundred were arrested. An estimated ten million dollars in public and private property was damaged or lost. The devastation was incalculable despite the calculations. The paper's op-ed section closed by saying: "Newark will rise from the ashes, better and stronger than before." Even the ever-optimistic Mrs. Poole didn't sound convinced reciting those words.

Emmett wasn't certain either. To be better and stronger, things would have to change. The newspaper was proof that, so far, nothing had.

"Mind if I ask you something, Mr. Emmett?"

It was the very same question he had posed to her the first day she starting working for him. He answered with the same reply. "Depends on the something."

"Is it true what Edward said? That you were going to be a priest?"

Emmett owned up to it. "Yes, that's true."

"Why didn't you?"

The guilt he harbored about his brother's accident had led him to the priesthood, then led him away from it and toward the police force. Years of punishing himself had gotten Emmett nowhere but alone. Now he had a chance. He had Edward back.

"I guess I wasn't the right man for the job."

"I think you would've made a darn fine priest, Mr. Emmett. Maybe the Lord just meant for you to be a detective instead." Mrs. Poole smiled.

"Maybe."

A knock came at the bedroom door. Freddie peeped through the crack. "Can I come in?"

"You boys talk. I have to get supper started," Mrs. Poole said, an excuse to give them some privacy.

Seeing Emmett laid up and bandaged turned Freddie shy. "How ya feelin'?"

"I'm okay. I hear you were running errands."

"Figured maybe I could do odd jobs for you to pay back that hundred I owe."

"I have a screen door that needs oiling. A garage door too."

"No problem."

"Ever pull up crabgrass?"

"I can learn."

"You've got a deal. As long as you promise to go to your court date."

"Promise," Freddie vowed.

"Seems you may be off the hook with Luther Reed, at least for a while."

"No kidding? What about those detectives? They still gonna want the tape?"

"With the riot and Reed out of commission, they shouldn't give you any trouble."

"At least for a while," Freddie added knowingly. "I found a place to hide it like you told me to. A place nobody'd ever look."

"Is it under the mattress of my old bed?"

Freddie's jaw dropped. "Damn."

"Your secret's safe with me."

Emmett got up, too sore to move any speed other than slow. Freddie came to his side to lend a hand.

"Aren't you s'posta to stay in bed?"

"Yup."

"We goin' downstairs?"

"Yup."

"Thought so."

Freddie helped him put on a shirt and take the staircase a step at a time. Mrs. Poole put her hands on her hips when Emmett shuffled into the kitchen with Freddie in tow.

"Don't yell at me," Freddie said, preempting her. "It was his idea."

"Is Edward in his usual spot?"

"He's been keeping it warm all day," she replied. "Freddie, help me set this table. And don't forget the napkins."

"You heard the lady," Emmett told him, smirking.

"Yes, ma'am." Freddie sighed.

"I have to borrow this for a little." Emmett took one of the kitchen chairs out to the porch. Edward was indulging in his new hobby, watching people's windows across the yard, his substitute for television. Rain was dripping on the tin awning melodically.

"Should you be lifting heavy objects in your present condition?"

"I shouldn't be doing anything in my present condition."

Emmett winced as he sat down beside his brother. The welts on his legs smarted. The doctor at the hospital had identified them as electrical burns and informed Emmett he was lucky not to have any permanent damage. His physical injuries weren't permanent. Any lasting damage from his encounter with Lazlo Meers remained to be seen.

"Jesus, Marty, you're gettin' as crotchety as me."

"We make quite a pair."

Sitting there together, they would have been eye to eye if either would look at the other.

"You wanna tell me about it? You don't have to if you don't want to."

Emmett told his brother everything. He wanted to. He gave Edward his theory on the murders as well as the details about being held at the factory, the hunt through the sewer tunnels, all of it. The porch became his confessional. At the end, he told Edward what he had done to Lazlo Meers.

"I drowned him. I didn't try to arrest him or take him in. I just drowned him."

"He treated those boys like they weren't human. Like they were animals. Like they didn't matter."

"Did that give me the right?"

Edward grew quiet. A soft breeze blew past carrying the scent of a neighbor's garden. Somewhere, something had survived the drought to bloom.

"There are much worse things than killing somebody, Marty." He was talking about more than the case.

While Emmett's experience had been harrowing, he couldn't fathom what his brother had endured in Vietnam, what any solider faced in war. Torture of the mind could be a fate that surpassed pain or death. Emmett knew that was true from experience.

"The kid, Calvin, he gonna make it?"

"When I left the hospital, they told me he would be in intensive care for a couple weeks, but yeah, he'll live."

Unlike Evander Hammond, Julius Dekes, Tyrone Cambell, and

Ambrose Webster, Calvin Timmons would live. Yet the relatives of the murdered boys would never have the satisfaction of seeing their sons' killer brought to justice or having their cases closed. In the end, Emmett had no hard evidence to connect Meers to their deaths. He could give a statement and Calvin could testify about Meers's attempt on his life, but that wouldn't corroborate the other crimes. Lieutenant Ahern would demand evidence, evidence Emmett didn't have, that was if Ahern didn't laugh him right out of his office. Police Director Sloakes had little to feed to the press or pin on him. That wouldn't necessarily prevent Sloakes from trying to bury Emmett anyway. In the eyes of the Newark Police Department, he had yet to solve a single murder. He would, at last, get out of the basement, though he didn't see a point in returning to Homicide. Then Edward reached out and patted his shoulder, a fleeting gesture that was over before Emmett fully felt it.

"You're a hell of a cop, Marty. Don't tell yourself different. You'll go back to the job and everything'll be okay."

That simple statement was what Emmett had waited his whole life for. His brother's confidence in him was all the assurance he needed or would ever need.

It was getting dark out. Lights in the houses across the yard were coming on. The smell of supper wafted out from the kitchen. Dinner would be ready soon. They would all sit around the table, he and Edward and Freddie and Mrs. Poole, and they would say grace together. Emmett had a lot for which to be grateful.

"If this rain lets up, should be a clear night," Edward said.

"Should be cooler too."

"Thank God for that."

"Thank God for that," Emmett seconded.

They had resorted to discussing the weather. For them, it was a good sign, a beginning.

The rain was absolution for that week's heat wave, a temporary reprieve, like the sweet breeze from the neighbor's garden. Summer promised to be long and hot and harsh, a season of penance that would stretch on and on. That night they had a few hours of forgiveness from the heat. A little forgiveness was all anyone could ask for. Eventually, fall would arrive, then winter, though the city would not see the rebirth of spring for some time to come. No matter what the weather held, Newark was Emmett's home and there were no seasons in the heart.